T0245608

ANOTHER Dance

ANOTHER Dance

ANGELA YOUNGERS

BookPress®
publishing

This is a work of fiction. Names, characters, businesses, places, events, locales, and incidents are either the products of the author's imagination or used in a fictitious manner. Any resemblance to actual persons, living or dead, or actual events is purely coincidental.

Published in Des Moines, Iowa, by:

Bookpress Publishing
P.O. Box 71532
Des Moines, IA 50325
www.BookpressPublishing.com

Publisher's Cataloging-in-Publication Data

Names: Youngers, Angela, author.
Title: Another Dance / Angela Youngers.
Description: Des Moines, IA: Bookpress Publishing, 2024.
Identifiers: LCCN: 2024912685 | ISBN: 978-1-960259-03-5
Subjects: LCSH Widows--Fiction. | Ballroom dancing--Fiction. | Grief--Fiction. | Man-woman relationships--Fiction. | Romance--Fiction. | BISAC FICTION / Family Life / Marriage & Divorce | FICTION / Romance / Contemporary | FICTION / Women
Classification: LCC PS3626 .O86 A66 2024 | DDC 813.6--dc23

First Edition
Printed in the United States of America
10 9 8 7 6 5 4 3 2 1

For the two loves of my life,
Toby and Aubry.
You will always be my greatest purpose.

Another Dance is a work of fiction that deals with mental health, suicide, drug abuse, and substance misuse.

PROLOGUE

Pitch

An inclination of the body either forward or backward resulting from a directional swing

The screams of my children used to elicit in me the natural parental reaction: concern whether someone is hurt, frustration over the same dumb sibling fight they're always having, annoyance at the high shrieked peals of my daughter and even higher yips of my son. But now, when I hear their screams, I fall into an even darker place. I think about my husband's last night with us. Is this the sound that sent him over the edge? Were the kids and I too much to handle? Did he not love us enough to stay?

When I hear my children scream—no matter if it is from laughter, anger, fear, or hurt—all I can think about is Jason and how he will never hear those screams again. And how maybe…he didn't want to.

1

Hesitation

*A step taken in which progression is temporarily stopped
and weight remains on the same spot for more than one beat*

"Anything new this week you'd like to talk about, Annie?" Dr. Collins asks as he peers at me from behind his black-framed glasses, his dark brown eyes watching closely for any nonverbal cues of avoidance or discomfort. His search is bound to be a short one, as I have already ventured into the land of avoidance, choosing to focus on his clothes rather than the state of my mental health.

I really wish he would consider a less stereotypical fashion choice. His tan blazer pulled over a green and gold argyle sweater vest practically screams for a pair of tweed elbow pads to complete the ensemble. I've been going through this silent judgment of his wardrobe ever since I started making the weekly journey to the brownstone where he welcomes patients into his first floor office. My internal snideness is probably due to some sort of attempt at projection or self-preservation, or at least, that's what Dr. Collins has suggested in our many debriefings. Really, my physical judgment is isolated to his fashion choice; he's a handsome man, probably in his fifties, with smooth brown skin, a stubbled square jaw, salt-and-pepper hair shorn close to the scalp, and prominent thick brows that seem to communicate endless combinations of expressions while listening to endless combinations of clients' issues. Honestly, I enjoy his reactions and often keep a mental tally of how many I can draw out of him in our one-hour sessions, probably in a weak and misguided attempt to avoid actually opening up and getting anything productive out of them.

My gaze drifts to his hands. He clutches a brown leather journal in one and a heavy gold pen in the other, waiting to record any breakthroughs or revelations. I wonder if he has made predictions about my future well-being within those pages.

"Annie?" He softly cajoles me out of my silence. All too aware of my resistant nature, he turns the conversation to a topic I am more willing to speak about. "How about the children? How are they doing?"

This I can talk about easily. They're the reason I'm here, the reason I do anything anymore. I answer readily, happy to redirect attention. "Well, they're a lot more resilient than me, of course. I mean, they're kids. Kids bounce back, right? The first few months it was 'I miss Daddy' and 'When's Daddy coming home?' But now, they only mention him once in a while, and it seems to be out of the blue."

"How so?" He leans forward, as if preparing himself for some insightful observation that will get me my money's worth.

"Well, Thatch was watching some Lego movie he and Jason used to watch, and he just turned to me and said with a big smile on his face, 'This was Daddy's favorite part.' Then he went right back to watching the movie and picking his nose." I try to keep my face impassive, but the memory squeezes my heart in a vice grip.

"That should be encouraging. Your son is able to talk about his father with positive associations. I think that's a great sign of

Thatcher's acceptance and progression," he explains, his voice a celebration of the natural process of grief. His face sobers when he sees my glum composure. "What's the problem then, Annie?"

I won't say it, but I know the answer immediately: I'm the problem. My two children seem to be moving forward easily these days, and I'm still stuck. Even worse, I sort of wish they were still stuck, too. Then I wouldn't be alone in my misery. But that's wrong, not something a good parent would feel; so instead of telling Dr. Collins and officially claiming my throne as Worst Mother of the Year, I just shrug, saving the reveal of my ineptitude for another day.

"What are your feelings about Thatcher's and Penelope's acceptance of their father's death?"

I shrug again.

"Now, Annie, I thought we talked about this. If you want to actually recover from the trauma of Jason's death, you need to share your feelings, let me in. Otherwise, why are you even bothering to come here every week?"

I examine the swirls of wood grain on the floor, my eyes refusing to meet his. Dr. Collins exhales audibly as he waits out my stubbornness. Sometimes he wins, sometimes I do, but when I do, I'm at least self-aware enough to realize that I'm still losing.

"Annie, please talk to me."

His sincerity finally lands home, finding an unguarded point of entry, and I try to give him the answer he's wanting. "I guess it makes me sad. Sad that he's talking about Jason in the past tense like it's nothing. It also makes me a little jealous. That he can smile when talking about Jason and I just can't. And being jealous of my child is so…wrong. It's just wrong, and I feel horrible…" My throat closes up and I purse my lips, hoping that was enough to appease the doc.

Dr. Collins leans forward and catches me within an admonishing gaze. "Annie, please don't use negative labels when discussing your responses. You are feeling your feelings. They seem like all valid reactions, considering the situation."

Ah, the "situation." The situation that has left me visiting the psychologist's office every Tuesday afternoon for the past ten months and taking a hefty daily dose of Paxil so I can continue to provide and care for my six-year-old son and four-year-old daughter. The situation where my husband of nearly ten years left me. Left us, his family. Well, left everyone, actually. That's what happens when someone is no longer of this plane, dimension, reality, or whatever else it's called. They leave and they don't come back.

"Annie, you're doing it again."

"Doing what?" I ask nonchalantly.

"Getting lost in your thoughts and shutting me out. Every time we start to make a little headway, you just mentally check out. We've talked about this. You can't do that. You can't keep avoiding the truth. You have young children. They need you."

This pisses me off because I *am* trying. Coming here every week is me trying. It's not my fault that my brain shuts down every time I get close to sharing something authentic. And none of this impacts my ability to take care of my kids. At least, I don't think it does. I tell him this exact thing, unable to hide my strained tone edging toward rudeness.

"You can't be at your best if you aren't taking care of yourself. And you can't always take care of yourself by yourself." The dad-like chastisement is not my favorite and I squirm, checking the clock to see how much time I have left.

Dr. Collins is normally on the verge of being saintly in terms of his patience level, but I can sense he's losing that patience quickly. He goes on to say something about my not taking full advantage of the resources provided to me, and how I may be robbing my children of the mental health of their only surviving parent. That is the jab that usually gets me, and I lash out.

"What do you expect me to do?" I'm annoyed with how angst-ridden I sound. I'm a thirty-five-year-old widow, not a hormonal teenager, but sometimes it's hard to tell the difference, even in my head.

"I know you aren't keen on the idea of support groups, but I really think this would be a great opportunity for you to connect with others who have gone through similar situations…" There he goes with the "situation" thing again. He always refers to my current plight as my situation, not the flaming bag of dog shit that is my life.

"No. I'm not keen. Plus, when am I supposed to have time to do this?" We've had this exact discussion multiple times, increasing in intensity over the past month. Ever since I commemorated the one-year anniversary of Jason's death with two bottles of wine and a midnight call to Dr. Collins's private line. I launch into my prepared defense: "I have a job, two kids, and a house to keep up. Yeah, Nick is there to help out, but I can't have him watching the kids every night. He already watches the kids while I'm here every Tuesday."

"It's not every night, Annie; it's once a week. Your pick: Mondays or Thursdays. Just a group of people getting together to talk about their situations and share some stories and strategies."

I bite the inside of my lip at his use of the word "situation" yet again, as well as the unnecessary alliteration, and make a last ploy to get him off my back with motherly rationalization. "I can't. I can't just abandon Thatch and Penny. That's two evenings away. I have to be home, make them dinner, put them to bed. That is my life. I don't get to go to sad circles, hold hands, and drink weak coffee. I have a life to live." I sigh, ready to claim victory with my sad reality.

"But are you *really* living your life, Annie?" I hate how he always says my name to make me accountable. Dammit. Instead of answering him, I glare, nostrils flaring. He must see this as a

welcoming sign, proceeding with, "Annie, you need time for yourself. To heal, to grow, to learn who you are without Jason."

"But you want me to go talk to a group of people who have lost
their loved ones to suicide. We don't even know if that really was
the case with Jason. It could have been an accident." It could have
been, but Dr. Collins wouldn't know because I haven't been able to
tell him the whole story, not even a year later. Because this is the real
issue. The actual situation. The reason I have to come to therapy and
make sure I'm not a danger to myself or my children.

I just can't accept that my husband might have killed himself on
purpose.

2

Axis

The center of rotation

~ Thirteen Months Prior: March 22 ~

"Thatcher, pick up your coat! Don't just leave it on the floor! And Penny, please stop whining. I'll get you some apple juice in just a second. Just let Mommy wash her hands," I plead as I transfer defrosted chicken from the microwave to the pan by the sink and attempt to catch any falling chicken juices before they seep through the cracks of my fingers. I don't know why I try so hard with dinner; it's not like the kids will eat anything other than frozen chicken nuggets and boxed macaroni and cheese, but with Jason promising to be home for dinner, I wanted to have an adult meal, even if it is just baked chicken and rice.

"Mommy! Mommy! Penny just hit me with her cup!" Thatcher hollers even though he is standing a mere one foot away from me. Penny, my deceptively angelic-looking daughter, sticks her tongue out at her big brother and runs off cackling. Well, joke's on her. I still

haven't given her any apple juice. I'm sure she'll figure it out soon enough and return to wreak more havoc. But for now, she is long gone, and Thatcher turns his eyes indignantly from me to the Penny-sized outline in the air highlighting her getaway.

"Sorry, honey. You know how she gets when she doesn't nap." I turn my attention back to the meal. I let a curse slip when I realize I still haven't preheated the oven.

"I fucking hate Penny!" The adult language spewing out of my kindergartner's mouth should be shocking, but he's been riding the bus to school for the past seven months and has picked up a few colorful additions to his vocabulary; I may have contributed just a bit myself.

"Please don't talk like that, Thatcher," I lazily chastise him while still focusing on the raw meat in front of me.

"But you just said it!" Again, he yells at me with such passion that I have to silently commend him for his enthusiasm. Oh, the days I used to have such passion. Now, I just want to throw this chicken in the oven and use the bathroom before I pee myself. How life changes.

"Thatcher, can you please just go watch your tablet or something? Daddy is going to be home soon. He doesn't need all this screaming and fighting." On cue, Penny shrieks in pain from the other room as I hear claws skitter across the hardwood floors. She's tangling with Marshmallow again, the cat I thought would be an effective incentive to finally get her potty trained: "You stop peeing in a diaper, and we can get a cat." That was the deal, and it worked great. But, in addition to refereeing two kids, I now have a spirited cat that doesn't back down from a fight, which is usually with my youngest child's face.

"Penny! Leave the cat alone. She's going to scratch you if you keep pulling her tail!" It isn't lost on me that everything said in the past few minutes has been yelled, as if we are standing on the ground

floor of a rock concert rather than a suburban kitchen. It can be headache-inducing, for sure, but this is my life. I chose it, and I love it…most of the time. I repeat this mantra as I toss dinner in the oven and set the timer for forty minutes.

Thatcher is still standing in the middle of the kitchen, staring at me with his big blue eyes, exact replicas of mine, as his pale freckled face reddens with the injustice of his sister getting away with murder, or in this case, getting the best of him for once. His mouth opens and closes as if he is trying to find the words, and his fists are balled up next to his hips. I look at my blond mini-me and try to swallow any signs of amusement, experienced enough to know that I must tread cautiously or a full-blown tantrum could erupt.

I try a diversion tactic and ask, "Thatch, can you help me clear the table? I'll count it as a chore towards your allowance—"

"I DON'T WANT TO CLEAR THE TABLE!" he interrupts, actually stomping his foot and storming out of the kitchen. I hear his tablet pop on in the living room. Well, I guess I did ask him to watch his tablet. I'll take that as a win and chock up the rudeness to his state of hunger. That's what I try to tell myself to justify my children's poor behavior. They're hungry. They're tired. It's not that they're assholes; my kids are just going through something…something developmental…every day…for years now. I sigh and move on to boiling the macaroni and tossing nuggets in the air fryer.

With the kids being less than two years apart, sibling rivalry is a very real thing in our household. It astounds me how they can be the best of friends and the worst of enemies, all in the span of ten minutes. While the fighting, whining, screaming, and destruction can get exhausting, I still wouldn't give up being a mom for anything in the world. I love hearing their creative stories and ideas, and I enjoy seeing new experiences through their eyes.

I can spend hours just looking at their adorable faces, itemizing the traits they inherited from me, Jason, or some distant relative. While Thatcher looks more like my Scandinavian side of the family, Penny has inherited her father's tan skin and golden-brown hair. However, she inherited my smaller frame and heart-shaped face, while Thatcher is going to be tall and lean like Jason. In public, they are well-behaved, curious, and common recipients of compliments from strangers. However, I get the whole picture, the whole realistic, sometimes-kids-are-little-harbingers-of-pain-and-destruction pic-ture. But despite that, I love them with my entire being, for which I blame biology.

I soak in the silence for a good five minutes and busy my mind by weighing the costs and benefits of parenting, not even caring that I don't know where my daughter is until I hear her scamper up the stairs and make a beeline for her brother. Immediately, they start bickering.

"Penny, let go! This is my tablet! Get your own! Pennnnnnyyyy!" I hear a smack against flesh followed by two sets of wails.

"What is going on?" I holler as I turn the corner to see both my children sobbing on the couch.

"Thatcher hit me!" Penny's squeal overlaps with Thatcher's cry of, "Penny pinched me!"

Then comes the sound of sweet relief: the garage door. I hear Jason's Jeep roll into our connected garage just before the door opens and he timidly enters the chaos of our life.

"I heard them the moment I turned the engine off. Getting hun-gry, I suppose?" My husband of ten years makes his way into the kitchen, filling the doorway with his broad six-foot frame. A retired combat medic specialist in the U.S. Army, he now works in the emer-gency room at Lakeview United Hospital in downtown Chicago. Four or more days a week he drives to the Naperville Metra Station, catches the Amtrak, and makes the forty-five minute trip to the hospital

where he takes care of victims of gun shots, sexual assault, construction accidents, and other random mishaps. Meanwhile, I cart the kids around and work part-time from our home office, validating or denying insurance claims. We met in college while attending Loyola, and while we were both trained as nurses, I discovered that my severe inability to handle blood and gore impeded my medical future. Now, after fifteen years and multiple other changes to life, I still adore that first glimpse of him after his return home, especially when he's just saved me from having to intercept another sibling fight.

He catches me in my mental nostalgia and brings me back to the present with a cocked eyebrow and conspiratorial grin. I take a deep breath, the tension in my shoulders instantly releasing. Now that he's home, I have my partner in crime. Sure, I usually play bad cop and he gets to be the fun, handsome cop that the kids always choose over me, but just by being home, he makes everything seem more bearable.

He shrugs out of his coat and heads over to me, planting a quick kiss on my lips.

"Hello, beautiful," he whispers in my ear before turning to the kids, who have stopped crying and are now smiling up at him with glassy eyes. "Children! What is all the ruckus? We aren't fighting again, are we?"

They both launch their little bodies onto his, clinging to his torso, shoulders, and neck. A twelve-hour shift at the hospital and he still has the energy to hold both of them up while they bounce literally and figuratively from topic to topic. "Daddy, Penny did this." "Daddy, Thatcher did that." "Daddy, guess what I got to do today?" "Daddy, look at my owie!" "Daddy, Daddy, Daddy!" For some reason the repetition of his moniker isn't as annoying as my own, and my heart swells with the sounds of their ecstatic greetings.

Sometimes I think we would all drift away without him to keep us grounded, steady, and whole. But for now, I smile and focus on finishing dinner, knowing that all is well in the world now that Jason, our center of gravity, is home.

3

Check

A step with distinct stopping action,
generally for the purpose of changing direction

It's dark when I pull into the connected garage of my nondescript suburban house on the corner of Baybrook and Shoreline Drive. After my appointment with Dr. Collins downtown, I drove back, picked up my prescription from the pharmacy, stopped for groceries at Whole Foods, and, because my children don't like healthy food, then at Jewel-Osco for the old standbys: hot dogs, chicken nuggets, macaroni and cheese, and fruit snacks.

I sit for a moment in my Subaru Forester to pause before the onslaught of information and interrogation begins. My moment of silence is brought to an end as I see the door to the garage open and two small heads, one blond and one brunette, pop out. They've found me. I press the button to open the trunk and make my way to the back of the car, their little bodies bouncing up and down lightly as I am weighed down by groceries.

"Mommy! You're home!"

"Uncle Nick let us have candy!"

"I didn't take a bath."

"I have to go poop," my daughter announces before marching off to the first-floor bathroom.

"You know that you can have Uncle Nick wipe you, right?" I half-heartedly holler in her direction, knowing it's a lost cause.

"She doesn't want me to wipe her. I told her I would, but she yelled 'No!' and ran away. Kinda hurt my feelings." My younger brother, Nick, is sitting on the couch watching the Cubs play. On the floor by his feet are the remnants of a frozen pizza dinner. I put down the grocery bags, pausing in my retrieval of the rest, and purposefully place myself in between him and the television screen as I pick up the paper plates, juice cups, and neglected crusts.

"Hey, you're blocking the game!"

"Seriously? It's spring training. It doesn't even count."

"That's blasphemy. The baseball gods will smite you for that." He wags his pointed finger at me, a teasing warning for my daring to question the validity of sports. As siblings go, we don't look much alike. My fair features are more of the Swedish persuasion while his dark hair, green eyes, and pale skin hail from our Scottish ancestry. He always tries to claim Penny's green eyes as his genetic contribution, but everyone else comments on how they are the same color as her father's. I know the latter to be true because those eyes still haunt my dreams.

"How were they?" I ask the question I always ask when I leave Nick with the kids. He moved in around ten months ago; at the time, we figured it would be just for a couple of months to help me with the kids and give me time to attend sessions with Dr. Collins. As a single thirty-year-old man financing his own carpentry business and about to come up on the end of a lease, it had seemed like a mutually beneficial solution. Plus, the kids absolutely adore him, and they need a positive male figure in their life. So I'll keep him around as long as he's willing to stay.

Before Nick can jump into the specifics of the evening, Penny shouts through the door that she's done, and I go complete my motherly duty of wiping her butt.

My hands washed and the groceries inside and put away, I lean against the counter, scarfing down the last piece of frozen pizza as Nick reports on his evening with the kids: minimal arguments, one scratched cheek (from Penny, not the cat), one bit leg (by the cat, not Thatcher), and two pieces of pizza each with a cup of mandarin oranges. Not Nanny-of-the-Year accolades, but my brother does a good job of keeping my children alive and entertained when I have to tend to my mental health needs.

"So, how's it going with Dr. Collins? Anything new or just the same 'tell me what's bothering you this week' talk?" he asks, doing his job of keeping me accountable. If someone had told eighteen-year-old me that my then thirteen-year-old-brother would become my source of domestic stability, I would have laughed. But it's true. And I cherish that because he's all I have. Our mother died during his senior year of high school, and we haven't spoken to our dad since we were both in elementary school. Now he's grown into being the man of the house, able to fix the many wears and tears in our home and hearts.

"A bit of both. Talked about the kids: about how they seem to be accepting Jason's death in a healthy way, able to talk about him randomly and positively."

"Yeah, Penny was playing with my face scruff tonight. Said that her daddy didn't have a beard."

"Oh, well that's nice. At least she remembers what he looked like."

"Annie…" He senses that I'm going to my dark place again, and his tone pulls me back.

"I know, it's not worth getting into. I'm just irritated Dr. Collins keeps pushing that damn support group."

"Why don't you want to do it?"

Ah, the big question. I don't know if I even understand why I'm so resistant. It's not that I am against therapy of any kind: couples, group, physical. I'm pro-therapy. But going to a support group of people who have lost loved ones to suicide; it feels so...sad. And final. I just don't know if I can be around others telling me that it will all be okay and that Jason's demise isn't a reflection on me and the kids. That would be a lie because it is a reflection. We were his whole life, and if he didn't want to have a life anymore, then he didn't want to be with us. Of course, I think this but can in no way verbalize these thoughts to my brother. So instead, I shrug and turn to take care of the dishes in the sink.

"It just seems like if you haven't noticed any great progress since starting therapy, maybe you should change it up, try something new."

I spin to confront him. "Who says I haven't made progress?"

Instead of answering, he gestures toward me, a look I have seen too many times when he thinks I am being completely bull-headed and antagonistic. I can't really argue with his assessment, so I silently return to the dishes.

Nick doesn't push, instead moving to head downstairs for the night. For the most part, the basement is his, with a guest bedroom and bath, but the kids do like to run around the large living space down there. Nick brought his television, couch, and chair when he moved in, but other than that, it's fairly sparse. Jason and I never finished furnishing that room. We moved in when Thatcher was two months old. Then we had Penny. And then time just got away from us. Now, it's an open space where the kids run off their winter energy and Nick retreats when he's had enough of the family-man gig for one night. And I never go down there. I can't. I won't. It's just still too much.

I hear small feet landing heavily on the second floor. "You two better be getting your pj's on and not jumping!" I don't know why I even bother; they won't listen, yet the part of me that wants to be considered a good mother feels like I should put in the effort.

Before he disappears down the stairs to his blissful privacy, of which I am extremely jealous, Nick turns and says, "Annie, I'm here if you need me, but I'm also here for the kids. We always have a good time together. I think you should do something. Maybe not the support group, but something that gets you out of the house, something completely for yourself." He pauses, a catch in his throat as a heaviness falls between us. "Something that might help bring you back. Because you're still not you. You know it and I know it. And I'm sure the kids know it, too."

I open my mouth to argue at the sheer audacity of his insinuation, but I find myself speechless, shocked at the sting of his words and my own numbness when hearing them. Sure, ever since becoming a mother, I've always found it difficult to carve out time for myself, something Jason would help me remedy. But with his death, so too went my own sense of self-preservation.

Nick stares at me sadly, knowing I can't offer a good comeback, then says, "Just think about it." He says good night and leaves me there wondering why everyone seems to know what I need while I still have absolutely no idea.

~ ~ ~

"Annie, Thatcher will be fine. It's good for kids to be away from their parents. It creates a healthy attachment."

"Not at three months old, Jason!" I'm currently trying on different outfits, frantically striving to find something that fits my postpartum body. Jason is lounging on the bed, back against the headboard,

his long legs stretched out and crossed at the ankles. He watches me with amusement, and a mischievous gleam shines in his eyes every time I lift a shirt or dress over my head. We are going out on our first overnight date since having Thatcher. Jason's mom, Maggie, is staying over while we head downtown for dinner and drinks, ending with a hotel stay. My mother-in-law isn't one to visit often, but Jason asked for her help, realizing we needed a night away. He's looking forward to being alone; I'm more excited about not having to wake up and attach an infant to my nipples three to four times in a night. I pull a cotton sundress over my head, throw it on the large pile of discarded clothes, and growl in frustration. "Nothing looks good! I don't even want to go out!"

I flop face down on the bed next to Jason, groaning into the mattress. I feel his weight shift next to me, and then strong, gentle hands are rubbing my shoulder blades. I quickly start to forget about clothes, losing myself in the sensation of Jason's touch.

He leans down and speaks quietly in my ear. "You are beautiful. I love you and your body, and I want to have sex with you on hotel sheets uninterrupted by our infant son. Can we do that, please?"

I roll over to meet his gaze as he hovers over me. "I'm sorry. I really do want to be alone with you tonight. I'm excited, I am. But I'm nervous about leaving Thatcher. What if your mom doesn't feed him enough? What if she lets him cry too much, or she doesn't let him cry enough?" I'm beginning to spiral, and Jason reaches up to stroke my hair. The calming effect is instant and I nuzzle into his touch.

"She kept me alive, right? She actually has more experience than either of us. She's going to be just fine. Thatcher is going to be fine. We need this time together, Annie. I miss you. I want you. If we want to be good parents, we have to be a connected couple." He grins as his eyes scan my body. "And I am so ready to connect tonight."

I play at being annoyed by his raging libido, but in reality, it's exciting that I can still affect him like this. "Fine. You're right. But what am I going to wear?"

"Honestly, I don't care what you wear. Only that you aren't wearing it later tonight," he says huskily, his lips hovering over mine.

I smile and close my eyes as our lips meet and his body presses into mine. As my arms wrap around his back, I feel a sharp tingle followed by a warm release from my breasts.

"Uh-oh. You're going to need to find a new bra." The bed starts shaking with our laughter as we both look down at the milk-soaked cups of the only non-nursing bra I own. I disentangle from his arms and make a scene of going to the bathroom to clean up, making sure to flash him before I playfully slam the door in his face.

~ ~ ~

I sit in bed, a glass of white wine perched on the nightstand, and stare at the blank TV screen. I find myself doing this many evenings after I put the kids to bed, seeking refuge by watching a comforting rerun or staring at nothing while I travel through memories of my life before.

Jason was always insisting how important it was to have alone time, to keep some semblance of who we were before we had kids. And for a while, we did. The last year before he passed away is when we drifted away from that, and eventually, from each other. He picked up extra shifts, took on more responsibility, and spent less time at home. It became common for him to only help put the kids to bed twice a week. Even when he wasn't working, he found excuses to leave the house, run errands, and disappear to the basement. I should have been more vocal about my concerns, but I was in survival mode, dealing with the growing personalities of busy toddlers and trying to be a great mom and a good employee, all while turning into a mediocre wife. At least, that's how I see it in hindsight. However, I'm still in survival mode, and, as Nick pointed out, I'm still not me. Unless this is the new me, which I'm not ready to accept.

What I can accept is that something needs to change. Dr. Collins wants me to learn who I am without Jason? To spend some time with myself? I'll give it a try, but I'm worried that I may not like who I find.

4

Wind Up

A rotation starting from the ankles

"I fold," I announce as I take my place across from Dr. Collins. I spent the whole week considering how I would propose my compromise. But once I'm settled in his stark home office, feeling the pressure to speak, it seems like the forward first liner won in the end.

"Hello to you, too, Annie." Really? Almost one year together and he still expects niceties? Another clue to his never being married. Okay, so I don't know that. I don't know anything about his personal life, but based on the lack of family photos and absolutely zero mention of a family, I have deemed Dr. Collins a perpetual bachelor. I roll my eyes, but soften the gesture with a strained smile and terse greeting. This apparently pleases him, as he asks, "So what exactly do you mean you fold? About the support group?"

"No. I'm not going to the support group, but I am open to other options." A thinly veiled downturn of the mouth illogically causes an upturn in mine. I shouldn't want to disappoint or trick my therapist...which is maybe why I'm in therapy in the first place. "I want to do something for myself, but I don't want to attend your…that group. Sorry, but it's not for me." Dr. Collins sighs, settling back into his worn, brown leather chair. His blue jacket bunches up around his shoulders, making him look like an academic turtle.

"Why are you so resistant to this, Annie?"

"Why are you so pushy about this, *Dr. Collins*?" I stress his name, a knee-jerk reaction to my irritation. "The point is to get me to learn how to be by myself, right? Jason's dead. There's nothing I can do about that. But I'm not, even though I sometimes feel like it."

"And what makes you say that?" He straightens up in his chair, clasping his hands in his lap and cocking his head to the side in prime listening position.

I sigh and look toward a corner of the ceiling. It's better not to see his satisfaction at my long-awaited acquiescence. "I do the same thing every day. It's like I'm in purgatory, just going through the motions, my body set on an assembly line: get the kids ready, drop them off at school, work at my computer, do laundry, pick the kids up, fix dinner, put the kids to bed. That's it. Then all I do is sit in my room, zoning out or missing Jason. And then I wake up and it all resets." I look down at my hands. "I feel like a ghost, a shadow of myself. I feel like I'm fading away."

My therapist knows this is a pivotal moment, and he gives this admission the space and time it deserves, letting it hang in the room, living its truth. Then he offers, "But your brother is there, right? Can't he help you break up the monotony?"

"Yeah, Nick's there, but he has his own life. And whenever I'm with him, I just feel like such a buzzkill that I'd rather cut him loose than force him to spend time with me." It's true, Nick has offered to hang out with me and the kids, but I usually decline. We sometimes eat dinner together and have our evening chats when cleaning up or going over the week's schedule, but that's the extent of our "hanging out." I look up at Dr. Collins. "I don't want to ruin his life just because mine is ruined." In an attempt to lighten the mood, I add, "Plus, baseball season started."

He leans back a bit, crossing his legs. He likes that I am finally starting to open up, but it's still not enough. Softly, he says, "You need companionship from adults, Annie. You need to confide in someone: your brother, me, the support group. There are so many options."

"The support group is not an option. Please, don't ask me anymore." Ice floods my voice, and a heaviness hangs in the air as he assesses me silently.

"I only want to help you and your family. That's my job. You just admitted some pretty large feelings of loss and despair. I think the group could really—"

"No." I cut him off, not wanting to hear this spiel for the umpteenth time.

"Annie, can you please just tell me why?"

I take a moment, trying to put into words a feeling I've had ever since he first introduced me to the idea. "I don't want to listen to people talk about the deaths of their loved ones. I have Netflix and YouTube for that."

"Well, I don't think that is a quantifiable substitute…" he tries to interject, but I find myself suddenly flooded with explanations, a rush of water finding the crack in the dam, threatening to tear the whole thing down unless the pressure is released.

"I can't sit there and listen. I just can't. I already spend most of my nights sitting and listening to my own thoughts. I don't want pity. I just want to change it up, do something, get out of my head. I want to escape the constant memories of Jason. I need to move forward, but I think I need an activity, not another therapy session." I end with a deep breath in and out, the waters having leveled enough to stave off any more leaks. I wait, staring hopefully at my therapist.

"Okay, what were you thinking?"

"I don't know exactly. Do you have any ideas?" His face instantly brightens. I know I've been resistant, but seeing him light up at the notion of actually being able to help me makes me realize how immovable I've been.

"Well, let's see. There are pottery classes, cooking workshops, fitness camps—"

I jump in quickly. "Yeah, I want to do something active, something where I'm up and moving. Maybe yoga or a Zumba class? And since Nick is already watching the kids on Tuesdays, I was hoping to limit my coming into the city and find something after my meetings with you. I know that's a lot to ask, but it would definitely make me feel better." I am probably putting too many stipulations on this, and I grimace as I wait for the admonishment I know is to come.

Dr. Collins thinks for a minute, mimicking my own previous assessment of the ceiling and floor, before zeroing in on my face. "How about this, Annie? Let's use the rest of your session to talk about what you hope to gain from a new pastime, and we'll try and get you set up for something as soon as possible." I nod, excitement building at the thought of something new to look forward to. "But if you still refuse to talk about Jason's death with myself and others, then I at least ask that you be completely honest and open with me about everything else during our sessions. We both know that you are holding back, and I'm hoping that today is the start of a new pattern."

I nod and lose myself in the planning, excited about the possibilities. But I also feel Jason's memory tugging my hand, wondering why I am so eager to move forward and away from him.

~ ~ ~

Jason is waiting for me as I exit the green room. It's the last night

showing of a student-written and produced play, Saturday at the
Speakeasy, *of which I have been a part for the past two months here
at Loyola. I always loved singing, dancing, and performing in high
school, but when Mom was first diagnosed with breast cancer my
junior year, I knew I needed a more practical career path. But that
didn't mean I couldn't dabble in the arts for fun. Mom and Nick
weren't able to make it to this production; the chemo has been rough
on Mom lately and Nick didn't want to leave her, but Jason was able
to make it for the last show. He was at boot camp the past three
months, another reason I needed something to occupy my time. But
now, here he is, holding a bouquet of red roses, looking freshly
shaved, showered, and devastatingly handsome in a white polo and
khaki carpenter pants.*

*"Annie!" He hollers, a wide smile stretching across his face as
he opens his long arms. I run and jump, my legs wrapping around
him and refusing to let him ever leave me again. I don't even care that
other people are staring. All I want is to kiss this man, inhale his scent,
and rediscover every detail about his body I may have forgotten while
we were separated. He talks through our kisses, conveying endearments about my performance, my voice, and my body. His hands
clench my butt as he continues to hold me up, and I can feel the evidence of what will be a heated reunion once we get back to my dorm
room. Thank goodness my roommate is gone for the weekend.*

*I finally pull my face off of his and look him up and down while
still wrapping myself around his body like a cherished scarf. I run
my hands over his shorn hair, the blunt newness tingling across my
palms. "I missed you so much. Please don't leave me again. Please?"*

*He purses his lips and clouds settle in his previously bright eyes
as he gently sets me down. "Annie, you know I can't promise that."
Along with nursing school, his plan is to be an Army medic. Not only
will it cover the cost of most of his college loans, but he wants to*

follow in his father's footsteps, helping soldiers during battle. Unfortunately, his dad died in Iraq six years ago, but Jason still has the dream of honoring his father's legacy. I don't want Jason to go overseas, but I love his passion and sacrifice. Plus, he looks damn fine in a uniform.

"Hey, let's not ruin our reunion. I just got back. Can't we just enjoy this moment before worrying about the next time I leave?"

My heart sinks at his wording, but he's right. I want to enjoy this moment, enjoy him before worrying about the future. I nod and he smiles in return, catching my chin in his hand.

"Are you ready to go?" I nod more vigorously this time, and he gives me a peck on the lips, our expressions collapsing into giddiness about finally being alone.

An hour later, I am stretched across Jason's bare broad chest as he strokes my hair. OneRepublic's "Stop and Stare" is softly playing on the radio. Both of us sweaty and satisfied, the beating of his heart is a lullaby, making my eyes heavy as I start to drift off. Jason gently shifts beneath me and lifts me off of him, turning me so that we are lying on our sides, looking at each other. His fingers trail down my ribcage softly and my skin shivers.

"Hey Annie, you know I love you, right?"

An alarm signals inside my head causing my body to tense and my eyes to shoot open. "Yes. Why? Is something wrong?"

"Shhh," he calms my worries by stroking my hair and temple. "Just listen. I love you so much, and I know how much you hate it when I'm gone. But what if you had assurance I would come back to you?" I look into his emerald eyes, wondering where this is all headed. We've talked numerous times about my abandonment issues spurred by my dad's absence, but I was fairly certain we were rock solid. I hadn't been questioning that until this moment.

My concern further intensifies as he sits up, grabs his boxers from the floor, and, in one quick move, hops out of bed while pulling them over his muscled glutes. He walks over to his duffel bag, which he'd dropped next to my dorm room door, forgotten, as we ripped each other's clothes off. He grabs a small parcel from inside. As he walks the short distance back to the bed, I start to realize what is happening. Any remaining air escapes my chest as he bends down on one knee and holds out what I now recognize to be a dark velvet ring box and reveals a perfect tiny round diamond perched on a small band of white gold.

"Annie Brennan, will you do me the honor of becoming my wife?" Anticipation tenses his body, his face tight with restraint as he awaits my answer. I try to swallow gulps of air, my head becoming dizzy, and I rise out of bed, letting the sheets fall. I turn to him, not even thinking of how I'm answering one of the most important questions of my life without a stitch of clothing on. "Yes! Yes! Of course!"

I jump into his arms, wrapping every part of my body around his, and we laugh and cry, bare flesh warm in contrast to the cold metal of my new ring. We lose ourselves in each other once again, and I go to sleep knowing that this is the start of the next chapter. This is what I have been waiting for my whole life, to find my other half. To find who I am with this person and move forward together for the rest of our days.

5

Change Step

A three-step sequence used to change
weight from one foot to the other

Who am I? I often wake up, groggy and hesitant, wondering this very question. I know who I used to be: Annie Obless, happily married mom of two working an average job in order to enjoy her average American life. Annie, slightly calloused daughter and sister who learned to be a bit wary of others and keep her circle small. Annie, suburban mom with a loving nature and a rebellious past that resurfaces at times through snark and mischief.

But what form of Annie am I now? A year after the previous Annie was shattered, the various pieces displaced, lost, and forgotten? Am I Annie Obless, working mother of two who never gets enough sleep or eats enough vegetables? Am I Annie, sister to an eternal bachelor, secretly hoping he will stay single so he can continue to unplug my toilets and mow my lawn? Or am I Annie, widow who was so blind to her husband's pain that she couldn't even fathom how he could ever leave her?

Which Annie am I and can I even stand to be her anymore?

I wake up the following Tuesday, asking this question and glancing over at Jason's empty side of the bed as I always do.

Who am I without Jason? Well, today is the day I start my journey of finding out. Dr. Collins and I agreed on an activity: I am going to a ballroom dance class. I said I needed to start moving. What better way than dancing?

After going over my past interests, Dr. Collins helped me pick something convenient and well-reputed in his own neighborhood. It's a small dance studio called Truitt Two-Step Studio on Halstead and Weber, a mere five blocks from his office on Fremont Street. I'm nervous about many things: having to talk to new people, looking clumsy while dusting off my dancing skills, but mostly about not knowing what one wears to a ballroom dance class. Surely not a gown, right? That would be absurd…I think.

One of my human alarm clocks interrupts my superficial worries and scampers from the doorway to jump on the bed, knocking the wind out of me for a good beat. An entire king bed to myself and my daughter still manages to hit the bullseye of my gut.

"Hey sweetheart. How'd you sleep?" I hug her close and start combing my hands through her mane of tangles.

She answers with a simple "Good." I'm still working on conversation skills with this one.

She cranes her head to the doorway as Thatcher staggers in, rubbing the sleep from his eyes.

"Mommy, I had a dream," Thatcher whines as he comes over to my side.

"Oh, honey. That's okay, we all have dreams. What was your dream about?" I pull him under the covers so that I am surrounded by my babies. Morning snuggles and reassurances: these are what make up for all the tough times.

My son curls up into a tight ball, his head tucked into my side. His sister sits up, awaiting his big story reveal, showing that she can in fact listen when she wants to. He begins slowly, knowing he has the full attention of the room and relishing it. "I had a dream that there was tapping on my window. It kept going tap, tap, tap, like that." He pokes the soft of my stomach to illustrate his point. "And then, when I looked out the window, Daddy was in the yard waving at me."

"Daddy's in the yard?!" Penny squeals with excitement and launches herself out of bed and out of the room.

"Okay. Well, that's nice, right? Daddy was checking on you." I start stroking his hair, trying to calm myself down at the same time though my heart is pounding.

"Yeah, but I wish he would come back. In real life. Not just my dreams."

"Oh, honey. I know."

Penny's screams for Daddy cause us both to startle. I run in the direction of her voice and end up in Thatcher's room scattered with Lego bricks, Marvel action figures, and Pokémon cards. Penny is standing on his short bookcase, looking out the window and scream-ing for Jason. I grab her, and she starts to thrash at me, hollering, "I want to see Daddy! I want to see Daddy!" I hug her little body tight, trying to avoid her flailing limbs, but she throws her head back and catches me square in the nose, causing my eyes to instantly water and my stomach to plummet with nausea.

"Goddammit, Penny!" I yell in reflex and I drop her roughly to the floor, leaving her crying even more violently. Thatcher looks on pensively, soaking in another moment where Mommy has lost her cool.

Every day I tell myself I am going to be calm and collected, and every day I fail. It just gets to be so much with the fighting, whining, and crying. I'm not a perfect mother, clearly, but at least I am a good enough mother that whenever I do lash out, I am flooded with a torrent of guilt that leaves me exhausted and depressed the rest of the day. I was really hoping this would be a good day, one without a guilt monsoon.

Penny floods me with hurtful lashings of "I don't like Mommy!" "I want Daddy!" and "Mommy's mean!" I take a deep breath and kneel next to her, my knee stinging with the bite of a sharp Lego. I grab my girl and drag her onto my lap, apologizing and rubbing her back. She eventually relaxes into my embrace and clings to me tightly. I look over to Thatcher, beckoning him to join in on this floor hug. He obliges, and we sit there rocking in the middle of Thatcher's room, a mass of grief, disappointment, and remorse.

"I'm sorry, guys. I'll try to do better. I will."

Thatcher lifts his head, his pooling eyes drilling into my own. "I miss Daddy."

"Me too, baby. Me too. But it's okay. We're all going to be okay." I kiss both of their heads, hug them tighter, and try to calm them with soft soothing, wishing someone would do the same for me.

Eventually, the three of us rise from the floor and make our way to the kitchen. I usually instruct them to get dressed before coming downstairs, but after this morning's little trauma, I figure we can change it up. Nick is pouring himself a cup of coffee, already dressed in his self-directed work uniform of a Carhartt button-up shirt and jeans.

"Good morning, kiddos!" Nick announces brightly, revealing that this is not his first cup of coffee. He's usually not an early-morning person, but he's been working on an important project, helping with the renovation of the public library. He has had the opportunity to work with different tradespeople in the area, so the networking has definitely lifted his spirits while promising to fill his wallet.

Thatcher and Penny attack his legs with gleeful squeals, freeing me up to get my own coffee and use the bathroom. When I return, I ask, "Hey, Nick, are you still good to get the kids ready for bed tonight? I have that class, so I'll be later than normal."

"Oh yeah! The dance class! How you feeling? Are you nervous? Excited? Nervous and excited?" His cheesy enthusiasm is annoying in my noncaffeinated state, and I just glare at him from across the kitchen island. He directs the kids to go watch television while we get their breakfast, and he sidles up next to me. "So, really, how are you doing? What's with the crazy eyes this morning?" So I wasn't successful in hiding the remnants of our freakout.

I sigh and launch into it, capping it with, "You know, just another weekday morning in the Obless household." Nick snorts, causing me to evil-eye him into silence. "I don't know, is that a sign? Am I not supposed to be doing this?"

"Ah, sis. You can't look at it that way. The kids are dealing with the loss of Jason, too."

"I know, but I'm really starting to worry about Thatcher. He seems fine, but he has these moments where he just seems so distant." I try to capture my thoughts, having collected moments where I will catch my little man in somber speculation.

"Well, I wonder where he would be getting that from." The heavy sarcasm draws me out of my trance to find Nick staring at me, catching me doing the exact same thing.

I sigh and hang my head. "I just keep messing up, Nick. I'm worried that I'm ruining them somehow with all my issues."

He shifts uncomfortably. "Annie, you're doing just fine. It's been a lot, but the kids are okay. And every parent loses their temper. Remember our childhood?" He nudges me, and we share a collective laugh over memories of being scolded from our own childhood. Even though we don't remember much of our dad, we do remember his temper. And Mom was just as spirited until she didn't have enough energy to get after us because of her sickness, which caused me to act in ways where I should have been chastised on a daily basis. Mom-guilt begins to morph into daughter-guilt until Nick squeezes my shoulder, bringing me back.

"Hey, I'm here, remember? You've got to use me more; that's what I'm here for! To help you and the kids. Anyway, I have to make sure I earn my keep." He jostles my shoulder playfully.

"Well, if you want to start making dinner, I'd be down for that."

He breaks away and starts clearing off the counter. "Let's not get too extreme. Remember where my strengths lie. In the kitchen, not exactly." I toss a dish towel at his face, and he successfully ducks.

"Fine. You want some pancakes?" I start maneuvering through cabinets, collecting my ingredients. The kids' favorite breakfast item is definitely needed this morning. Plus, it'll make me feel less guilty about being gone this evening.

Nick collects his wallet and lifts his travel mug in answer. "Nah, I have to get going. But really, we're all set. I'll pick the kids up and then I have their whole evening planned: go to McDonald's, let them wear themselves out in the PlayPlace, then come home and watch the Cubs' spring training while they rub Uncle Nick's feet."

"Babysitter of the Century, right here," I scoff, rationalizing that he is pulling my leg—I hope. He snickers at my annoyed look and waves before he heads out the garage door. "Have fun tonight. Remember, you deserve some time to yourself. It's going to be great!"

6

Action

A weight change

This is going to be bad. So, so bad. I look around the dance studio, a long room with buffed lightwood floors, white walls, a large mirror spanning the length of the studio, and blinds covering the windowed front entrance, probably to save students from the embarrassment of being seen by gawking passersby. Right next to the entrance is a counter with an iPad for signing in. I already paid and entered all my information online, so the reassurance of seeing my name pop up on the registration tab alleviates at least some of my anxiety. I guess I'm where I'm supposed to be.

I step away from the counter to let an older couple, a man and woman most likely in their sixties, sign in, and I awkwardly stand by myself waiting for the start of class. My body is buzzing with anticipation, nervous for the hour-long class. But I soothe myself, knowing that once it is over, I can decide if I'm coming back next week or forgetting all about this rediscovery of Annie Obless venture.

Dr. Collins had offered me quite a bit to mull over in the hour between our session and the studio check-in time. When I brought up Thatcher's dream, he tried to reassure me it was normal for little kids to dream of deceased family members. He explained the young child's mind is more receptive to memories of loved ones through their subconscious minds, so I should take it as a good sign that Thatcher still remembers his father and feels his presence. He didn't tell me my constant dreams and nightmares about Jason are normal, but I haven't told him that I dream about Jason every night. I also didn't tell him I'm feeling guilty about trying to put Jason in the past by moving forward. And thus, the reason I need therapy is further exacerbated by my refusal to share this type of information in therapy. What a cyclical conundrum.

Now that I'm here, my insecurity and general sense of foreboding about the class is further increased by the fact I seem to be the only singleton. Dr. Collins assured me this was a class open to couples and individuals; we even checked online during registration. But that doesn't make me feel any better as I discreetly survey the room. Currently there are seven couples and me. Five of the couples resemble the one that followed me in, probably married since their twenties and ready to spice up their retirement with some new moves. There's an attractive gay couple, their color-coordinated outfits of slacks, argyle sweaters, and bowties putting everyone else to fashion shame. The last couple is young, giddy, and handsy. My guess: newly engaged and preparing for their wedding reception. My gaze lingers on them longer than socially acceptable as my thoughts carry me to my past and another dance meant for the future.

~ ~ ~

"Jason, you have to lead! I'm waiting for you!" We clunk around, tripping over feet and shoulder-checking one another. In the

bedroom, Jason and I have always been compatible, but this waltz is starting to make me question everything I thought I knew about our physical chemistry. He grunts in frustration, squeezes my right hand, and purposefully slides his foot aggressively forward, shoving my shin back. "Ow!" I yelp out in shock and pain, earning curious glances from around the room.

The dance instructor, a silver-bunned lady with a thick accent and constant clipped tone of judgment, scurries over to us. "You two are fighting for control. You need to give into one other. Become one instead of two. Annie, let him lead you. Jason, hold her secure and be confident so she knows you have her." She adjusts our shoulder-holds and postures, then dashes off to another couple.

I look up at Jason, and I can barely stifle my laughter at his strained concentration. His brow creases as he looks down at our feet, counting the steps. He's breaking the first rule of ballroom dancing: don't look down. He peers up to catch me grinning at him, and his face breaks into a sheepish smile.

"I'm usually so good at picking up new things. I don't know why I can't get this," he admits. I send him a reassuring smile and squeeze his hand.

"Well, music and rhythm are different from shooting a basketball. You can't be perfect at everything," I tease as I remove my hand from his shoulder to tug at his ear. He responds with a slip of his hand from my waist to my butt for a quick squeeze, earning us a critical sneer from one of the older female patrons. That's okay. I'm about to marry this man, and nothing can bring me down. Not even a botched waltz. I make sure he knows that. "It's fine, babe. I don't care if we have a choreographed dance. I'm just having fun trying something new with you." We exchange a peck on the lips, then continue on, trying to match each other but stepping on a few toes along the way.

~ ~ ~

I jerk my gaze away from the couple, caught off guard by the vivid memory. I'd forgotten the details of those six weeks of dance classes before our nuptials, which were all for naught anyway. Once the first dance rolled around, we were too relieved and smitten to do anything but hold each other and sway.

I thought this night was supposed to help me move forward, and all this is doing is sending me back. I can't do this. This just isn't going to work.

I start to back up before turning and bumping right into the solid chest of a tall man. He steadies me with both hands on my shoulders and bows slightly to meet my eyes. "You okay? You're here for class, right? Ballroom Basics?"

I mentally rush to navigate all of my possible options: tell him the truth and be obligated to stay, lie and look like a wandering weirdo off the street, or just remain silent and come off as a socially-inept freak. The truth tumbles out amidst my ego-preservation. "Uh, yes, I'm supposed to be in the class. Annie Obless." I frantically look from side to side, trying to plan my exit. He must notice my unease, and he releases my shoulders to hold out his right hand. I eye it suspiciously before shaking it. I might be trying to ditch class, but it doesn't mean I have to be rude.

"Nice to meet you, Annie. I'm Milo. I'll be your instructor for the next eight weeks." A crooked smile curls upward to his shining dark brown eyes. He may have a boyish grin, but his looks are far from boyish. I take in his squared jawline, mussed hair a shade lighter than his eyes, and sloped nose large enough to add character to his otherwise symmetrical features. His eyes twinkle with knowing as he asks, "So where were you going? It looked like you were trying to escape." He's totally surmised my intentions, and my fight-or-flight reaction is raised further on high alert. I could make a run for it, but then I'd never return. And then I would have to explain to Dr.

Collins how I couldn't even make it five minutes in the class without shutting down. I could respond to Milo with a quick retort and impress or intimidate him with my sardonic cleverness. Unfortunately, my brain has been wiped clean of any witty banter, so instead I try to save face with a sprinkle of the truth.

"No, I wasn't sure if this was going to work. You see, I don't have a partner…"

His face brightens, and he opens his long arms wide as if officially welcoming me. "Oh, that's fine! We usually have a few singles in class, but if not, you can just partner with me. It works better if I have someone to model the moves with anyway."

Shit. This is the worst-case scenario. Now my moves will be on display for all to see and scorn. "Oh. Well, I don't think I'm dressed appropriately, either." A weak excuse, but it hadn't escaped me that while I opted for exercise apparel including black leggings and an oversized gray sweatshirt, everyone else is dressed for date night: short sleeve dress shirts and slacks for the older gentlemen, while most of the women are in skirts or dresses. The younger woman is even donning a figure-hugging black cocktail dress that showcases her red hair and her generous cleavage. I'm definitely being outshone tonight. Not that I don't have my own physical blessings; I've always been fit and curvy in the right places, but I've also had two children and am nearing the age of forty. Not to mention that I've essentially covered my figure in a cloth trash bag of a sweatshirt. I'm starting to wonder if there was something stated about the dress code in the fine print of the registration. If so, Dr. Collins did me dirty, possibly setting me up for some social experiment about fashion failure. Could it be karma for all my mental lashings of his own fashion choices? Milo himself is wearing fitted black jeans and a long-sleeved cream Henley. And he looks good. Very good. It's not lost on me I am not the only woman, nor man, currently ogling our handsome host. Many students are raising eyebrows and looking him up and down. And there's a lot of him to look up and down. He's tall. Jason was six feet; Milo is a few inches taller with long, muscular legs. He's broad and lean, and I'm having a hard time breathing while talking to him. How am I ever going to dance with this Apollo?

"I think you look great." His compliment brings an instant blush to my cheeks. "Stay. Please? Give it a chance. I want you to stay."

What the hell is it with this guy? That's my first instinct—to not trust someone to be so warm and inviting. But his gaze is so sincere and his stance so solid that I struggle to object. I'm surprised to hear my own response when I say, "Yes, of course…I mean, I came here to learn to dance. Let's get to it." I even top off my declaration with a little pirate-elbow swing. Completely unnecessary, but his ensuing smile is enough to make me forget my awkwardness and settle into my decision to stay.

"Cool. Okay, well hang out to the side while I explain, and then I'll grab you whenever I need to show a position. Sound good?"

All I can do is nod as he jogs over to the middle of the mirrored wall and introduces himself to the class. As he gives his opening spiel about what we will cover over the eight weeks and how he usually runs the hour-long class, I sneak glances at all my classmates, paying more attention to them than Milo's instructions, which probably isn't wise. Eventually, he asks for introductions. As we begin, I can't help noticing how each couple interacts. The engaged couple, Lorraine and Dave, are eloping to Rio de Janeiro this summer and wanted a head start on dance basics. Dave never stops touching her, his hand always on her back or arm. George and Wanda are a retired couple who just moved to the city to be closer to their grandkids. They needed a reason to come into the city, and they loved dancing when they were courting as high school seniors. Wanda listens intently as George tells their story, intimately picking a piece of lint from his shoulder. Ted and Nathan have been together for four years and thought it a shame they've never learned proper dance moves. The other four couples state their names and a bit of their backstory. They vary from holding hands, to hovering close, and one couple even stands far apart; Mary and Leo clearly need to reconnect. After everyone else introduces themselves, I stand there dumbly wondering why no one is talking.

Milo gestures my way. "How about you? Annie, right? What brings you here?"

Oh no. I was so busy gawking I didn't even think about how I was going to answer this. I'm already the sad singleton; I don't want to give them too much ammunition with which to pity me. So which opening line do I go with?

A: "My therapist suggested I try this in order to move on from my husband's death." *Uh, no.*

B: "I'm trying to reconnect to a past version of myself as I try to ascertain who I am as a thirty-five-year-old widow." *Probably not.*

How about C: "I thought I'd try out a new hobby while taking a break from my kids for a couple of hours."

Sure, C's the winner, I think. I deliver the line as I grin through my teeth. The classmates who have undoubtedly had children of their own smile and nod knowingly. Lorraine and Dave just stare at me like I'm a monster for suggesting I don't want to spend every moment with my kids. Ted and Nathan nod their heads as if listening to a ghost story while gathered around a campfire, and the others all smile politely, if not a bit tersely. Maybe "break from my kids" wasn't the best first impression, but it's too late now. Milo seems to pick up on my nervous energy and generously chuckles before redirecting the class with some posture and footing basics. I continue to overanalyze my words while trying to follow along.

It's not so much that I need a break from my kids; it's more I need a break from who I am when I'm with my kids. I'm always nagging, yelling, pleading, or rolling my eyes when I'm with them. They've probably been longing for a break from me, as well. But even though I've been looking forward to having some time to myself, I still find I miss them and can't wait to see them when I get home. Instead of enjoying my time away, I'm riddled with social anxiety and self-consciousness, causing any chance of an ideal care-free, unburdened persona to hide behind the flippant fortress that is Annie Obless.

I stand off to the far side, near the volatile coupling of Mary and Leo, and try to listen over their under-the-breath chidings. While my dancing experience is limited, I learned choreography for a few high school musicals, and I was a pretty big deal at some Greek parties my first few years at Loyola, at least until I met Jason. Then we opted for spending time alone rather than partying at drunk ragers. Anyway, I have enough rhythm and ability to pick up most of Milo's teachings. I even notice Lorraine's side eye as she critiques my form. I want to tell the soon-to-be blushing bride her newly-engaged bliss has an expiration date; it could all be taken away from her when she least expects it. But that wouldn't bode too well for my social future within this class, so I ignore her and focus on practicing my foot positions.

I startle slightly when I feel movement behind me and look up to catch Milo meeting my reflected gaze in the mirror. "You're a natural! See, aren't you glad you stayed?"

His sunny disposition taunts my own jadedness, and I respond with a scoff, "I suppose, except for the stink-eye I keep getting from that hoity-toity bitch over there and the doomsday sideshow of Mary and Leo's impending divorce." I bite my tongue too late and look away, hoping I didn't just create the worst first—actually second—impression ever.

"Whoa, there she is!"

I wince and instantly apologize.

"No, it's fine. It's just…that's the first authentic thing you've said tonight."

"Oh." Shame floods my cheeks, turning them a blazing red, and I try to look away, but he turns to move in front of me, forcing me to look him in the eyes. When he speaks, it's as if he is sharing a secret with an old friend, a feeling that makes me both uncomfortable and flattered.

"Hey, don't ever apologize for being honest. Truth be told, I agree with you on both fronts. I just can't say anything 'cause I'm the teacher."

"Oh," I mutter again, this time out of confusion rather than shame.

"But I'm also going to wager you're one of those people who hides behind snarky comments but is probably really sweet and vulnerable when you get to know them, right?" He waits for my reaction, but I just mull the comment over and look at him blankly.

"I don't know if I've ever been called sweet," I finally snap, which causes him to throw his head back and laugh out loud, breaking our conspiratorial exchange.

"Well, good to know. Let's go ahead and start focusing on holds. Come up here with me."

I bare my teeth in a pained grimace, looking longingly at my position to the side of the action. I'm not ready to be in the front, and I'm a little irritated with Milo, but he waves me up and addresses the class, forcing me to comply. "Okay everyone, let's go ahead and face your partner. Annie is going to help me show some basic building blocks of partner steps. Let's all give Annie a hand." The most awkward forced applause follows his lead, and all I can do is squeeze my face into a weird wince-grin that probably looks like I smell something rotten while also suffering from extreme menstrual cramps. My dancing partner is apparently amused by my discomfort and chuckles deeply as he grabs my hands and positions me in front of him. Our bodies are in profile to the class, allowing him to look out while he instinctively places my right hand in his left, maneuvers my left hand to rest on his shoulder, and holds my back right beneath my shoulder blade. Whenever I slack in position, he corrects me with a solid shift of his posture. He lets go of me to check how everyone is faring while I stand there in a daze.

It's been so long since I've even held another person's hands. Sure, I hold my kids' hands, but I also wipe their butts, clean their noses, and do whatever else needs to be done to make sure they are clean and unharmed. And Nick will give me the brotherly side squeeze once in a while, but there's something very different about holding the warm hand of an unrelated, attractive male. I'm still in my daze when Milo returns and brings us back into our hold so he can start going over some basic steps. I play the dutiful partner and let him lead, finding the moves come back to me a lot easier than I imagined.

We go over basics such as walking steps, rock steps, and triple steps. Milo creates a pattern of showing the positioning with me, which I thankfully pick up rather fast, slowing down to explain more in depth, circulating through the other pupils as I tread water and try to find my breath, then returning to his place as my partner. After he's satisfied with our general execution of the basic moves, he announces that we are going to just put on some music and experiment with what we've learned today. He goes to his phone and Bruno Mars's "Just the Way You Are" starts playing, the perfect background to playful dance blunders.

He appears back in front of me and asks, "Ready?" Without waiting for an answer, he takes my hands, knocks my elbow and shoulders into proper position, and starts leading me in a variety of steps. I'm pretty certain he is incorporating advanced steps he did not teach the class, but I try my best to keep up, only dragging my feet a few times before starting to glide more easily.

In the closed position, his chest presses against mine, and his chin rests close to my forehead. He angles so he can talk to me while we dance. "You did a great job of keeping up with what I was throwing at you tonight. Did you say you've danced before?"

I squeeze his shoulder, a reaction to questions whose answers might reveal too much. I wanted to move, not talk, during this class. Who knew I was going to be paired with the only male in the room who could possibly carry on a conversation while dancing? "Yeah, I took a ballroom dancing class over ten years ago. And I was in a few musicals during high school and college," I say, leaving out the bit that it was almost twenty years ago.

"Very cool. That's actually my goal: to be in musicals, and hopefully on Broadway one day."

"So how do you plan to do that? Just audition?" *Dig deeper, Annie.* Listen and avoid, that's my main priority.

"Audition constantly. I'd say that's my main job. Professional auditioner." He chuckles at his own pain, no stranger to being humble. "It helps that I have my BFA in musical theater performance from Roosevelt. And I try to do whatever I can: act, sing, dance. Anything to hone my craft."

I've moved from attempted deflection to actual interest. He's pulled me in like a spider in his web, dazzling me with his casual dialogue. "Are you in anything right now?"

He moves us around the room, watching the other students dance and offering helpful sentiments. After he reminds Dave to stand like he's pinching a quarter with his shoulder blades, he returns to our discussion. "I am. We're getting ready to open *Rent* in a few weeks at the Auditorium Theatre."

"What's your role?" I manage to ask, scuffing my foot as he

drags me along, breezily answering that he plays Roger.

"Kind of a rockstar then, right?"

"I guess you could say that." He angles his head, and I catch a confident wink.

"So, if you want to be on Broadway, why aren't you in New York?"

"Oh, you know. All the normal excuses: money, responsibility, family. Oh, and money. Did I mention money?" I laugh, eased by his continued self-deprecation. I almost lose my breath when he suddenly raises my hand and twirls me, pulling me in close on the return. My breasts press against his body, and I can feel his voice rumble inside his chest as he says, "Plus, if I was in New York, I wouldn't get to be dancing with you right now, would I?"

Was that flirtatious? Is this flirting? It seems like a foreign language; it's been so long. But why would he be flirting with me? It's got to be a move he uses on all the singletons. I jerk away from the easy exchange we've experienced so far and push back with cynicism.

"So, I have to ask. How old are you? You don't really seem old enough to be leading a class."

"Ouch." He plays at being insulted, but amusement pushes through any feigned hurt, relaxing my previously terse demeanor.

"Well, I was expecting someone ancient and mean to be leading this class. Not someone so young and...spry."

"Spry?"

"Yes. Spry. I stand by it." I look over to see some of the couples trying to mimic Milo's artistic additions to no avail. Some laugh. Nathan and Ted seem to be arguing about who is leading, and Leo and Mary continue to look more and more pissed off. I consider asking Milo if we should place bets on whether or not they return, but he answers me before I can proposition him.

"I'm twenty-seven. Not ancient, but just give me some time and maybe my mean side will sneak out." *Oh, thank goodness,* I think. While he looks youthful, or at least more youthful than me, at least he's old enough to rent a car. And old enough for me not to feel too guilty for getting a little winded from our close contact.

"I doubt that. You seem very capable of getting along with any-one. Even me."

I try to look down at our feet, but he quietly reminds me "eyes up" before saying, "Thank you. I try my best to do just that. It's nice you noticed." I look up and can't help but return his smile. He adds, "And I don't know how anyone couldn't get along with you."

His words cause my stomach to flutter, and I look to the side as if observing the other dancers. We continue dancing in silence, our feet floating across the floor as Milo leads us effortlessly.

The songs have been shuffling, and I've been pretty preoccupied with our conversation, but my ears perk up as a familiar initial drum beat introduces OneRepublic's song "Good Life." I stumble, and Milo stops moving in time to help me stabilize.

"You okay?" He creases his brow with concern, and I force myself to respond.

"Uh, yes. I'm great. But my legs are just getting tired. It's been so long since I've been this active. Maybe I didn't stretch enough." Or at all, but he doesn't know that.

Milo doesn't look like he buys my lie, but he checks his watch. Realization dawns on his face. "Well, I need to make some announce-ments and end class anyway. Why don't you take a seat?" He's being so nice, but I just need to get out of here.

"You know what, I actually need to get going and relieve the babysitter. But this was great. Thank you." I'm starting to walk away as I say this, my sweet escape a mere fifteen feet away, but Milo advances toward me.

"You're coming back next week, right?" He looks at me pointedly, as if he expects me to say no, turn, and run for the hills. I want to run. I want to disappear into the night and never return. I want to be suspicious of this man who is too nice and too eager to learn about me, but he's been so genuine, intriguing, and exhilarating to dance with I blurt out my answer before I can think.

"Yes. I'll be back. See you then." I shoot him an apologetic smile, turn, and almost burst through the glass door. I don't slow down, even though I'm having trouble breathing, until I am sitting in my car, safe from curious eyes. Only then do I drop my head on the steering wheel and let the gasping sobs free from the caged prison of my ribs.

OneRepublic was Jason's and my band. We saw them live together three times, danced to their music at our wedding, and made love to their albums several times. Ryan Tedder was an integral part of our entire relationship, even though he didn't know it, and I haven't been able to listen to his music since Jason's death. I was completely blindsided by it tonight. Which is dumb because, of course, I'm going to hear lots of music at this class. What was I thinking?

I'm wanting to move forward, but there've been reminders of Jason more than ever since I decided to do just that. I have to wonder if he's trying to tell me something. I turn my head quickly, thinking he is there, watching me, judging me for my abandonment of him and the kids. But it's just one of the couples leaving the studio…this time.

Am I completely off base here and trying to see signs where there are just coincidences? I can't help thinking if only I had been better at noticing the signs, I wouldn't be in this position in the first place.

I sob myself hoarse and huddle in the driver's seat as I watch the other dance class students file out of the studio. I sit long enough to watch Milo leave the studio, lock up, and scan the small parking lot. His gaze stops on my vehicle, and I scoot down lower, trying to make myself invisible. I've embarrassed myself enough this evening; I do not need him to find me soaked in a pool of my own tears and snot. Luck comes through for me, and I watch him amble down the block, probably toward the nearest 'L'-train station.

I did it. I made it through the first class and managed to stay undetected despite having a panic attack in the parking lot. And I'll go back. Because even though it hurts, being able to feel this pain and continue on is just what I needed. I think I just might be on the right path to finding myself again.

7

Pressure

Applied body weight, providing stability

~ Thirteen Months Prior: March 22 ~

"Honey, please just eat your chicken nuggets. Mommy is tired of wasting food." Penny is going through a stage where she doesn't eat anything. Seriously, she's subsisted on apple juice and the occasional saltine cracker for the past month. And it's not like I get any joy from feeding my daughter a worse-than-prisoner's diet. I would love for her to eat the food I make. In fact, it dominates most of our dinner conversations, as it is at this exact moment.

Jason occupied the kids while I finished dinner and I was even able to heat up a can of corn, so I can revel in the fact that I do sometimes give my children vegetables, even though it's the starchiest and most buttery vegetable I could choose. Seated around the table, Thatcher is happily sitting next to Jason, telling him about playing football during recess while I negotiate with our terrorist-of-a-daughter. We've learned long ago it is impossible to have an adult conversation at the dinner table, so we just smile at each other across our plates and wait until cleanup, which is the only time the kids seem to vanish.

I end up tossing away the majority of the food on Penny's plate as I clear the table, and Jason shakes his head with disapproval. "She really needs to start eating what we give her."

"I can't force it down her throat. Believe me, I've tried." I dump the plates in the sink and start filling it up with soapy water.

"Maybe we should just stop fixing her a plate. Give her three crackers on a paper towel. Dinner, done. Dishes, done." He punctuates his statement by throwing a handful of utensils in the soapy water, sending soap suds to freckle the front of my shirt.

"Hey babe, we need to talk about this upcoming week."

Jason groans in response while picking up the various art and school debris on the kitchen counter. "Why is all this shit just scattered all over?"

"I haven't had a chance to pick it up yet. And they wanted to show you." My husband grunts and continues to toss papers in the trash. "Honey, about next week?"

"What about next week, Annie?" he grumbles, a large handful of junk mail and artwork landing in the bin.

"Remember, my brother needs me to go to the bank with him on Tuesday, so I need you to pick up Penny from daycare and be home before Thatcher's bus. Then we have Thatcher's conference Wednesday night. And then your mom is arriving on Friday afternoon—"

"I don't have time for all of this! I just picked up a double on Tuesday—"

"Why did you do that?" I quickly interrupt. I'm irritated—I specifically told him we had a lot going on this upcoming week and mentioned my brother's appointment.

"Geez, Annie, why do you think? These kids are expensive! This

house is expensive! Our life is expensive!" I recognize this finance tunnel vision. As the main provider, Jason sometimes stresses over our funds, even though we are always fine. I try to stop this tirade early.

"We don't do anything expensive—"

He blows right past my input, pacing around the kitchen. "You know what I mean! Doctor appointments, daycare, clothes. I'm trying my best to keep us afloat here, and it seems like there is always something else. Now your brother is slapping us with another burden..."

"It's not a burden. This is a big deal for him. He just needs the signature for the loan. He's not borrowing any money from us—"

"And I have to deal with my mother coming to visit and shoving her new boyfriend down my throat." He slams his hands down on the counter and braces himself there, chest heaving and cheeks red. So that's what is really bothering him: his mom's visit.

Maggie Obless lives in Kalamazoo, Michigan, which is only a few hours away, but we maybe see her twice a year. She and Jason have always butted heads, and, according to him, ever since his dad died, it's been even tougher to connect. Jason idolized his dad and wanted to emulate him in every way, and Maggie wanted anything but for Jason to go into the armed forces after Robert's death. When Jason defied her wishes and still enlisted, that solidified their rocky relationship.

I get along fine with Maggie, but I do wish she would be more open to spending time with her grandchildren. She was a bit more apt to babysit when we only had Thatcher, but with two young children, the offers have been few and far between. She's now coming next week with plans to introduce us to her new boyfriend, Friedrich, and Jason's been touchy about it ever since she announced her travel plans.

I walk up behind Jason, place my hand on his back, and start rubbing circles across his shoulder blades. I feel him start to melt into the touch, but he still won't look me in the eye. "Hon, it's going to be fine. I'm sure this new guy will be more than cordial, and if not, he's probably not going to be around long anyway." He remains silent, so I continue. "And even if he does stick around, it's been nearly twenty years. It's about time she found someone again, right?" Maggie has by no means stayed celibate since losing her husband, but she's never purposefully introduced us to any of her paramours, either.

He relaxes his posture and finally speaks. "You're right. It's just…you know how I get around my mom. I hate that I'm still that dumb teenager around her. I just wish she could have picked another week. There's already so much going on at work, and now there's all these appointments. I'm just anticipating all the stress the week ahead is going to bring."

I reach his neck and continue massaging the base of his skull. "Don't stress. We'll get through it. We always do. Just one day at a time, right?"

Jason straightens up and turns to pull me into a tight embrace. He kisses the top of my head and responds into my hair, "I'm sorry I was so short with you."

"It's okay. I understand. It gets to be a lot sometimes," I say while buried in his neck.

He holds me for another moment, then asks, "Would you and the kids be okay if something happened to me?" I stiffen and jerk backwards so I can look up at him.

"Excuse me. Where did that come from?"

"I don't know. I've just seen a lot in the ER lately. Makes a person think, you know? And then hearing about my mom with this new guy. I mean, we've never talked about it, but what would you do if I died?"

I search his face, waiting for the punchline. When I don't get one, I offer it. "Well, I'd be sad, that's for sure."

"Yeah, yeah."

"I'd probably wear black for a year and cry every night in our

bed." Jason rolls his eyes at my attempt to bring levity to a serious question. "No really, I'm sure there'd be talk about me. Every time I'd go to the store or to the kids' school, they'd say, 'There's the saddest woman that ever lived. Her husband asked what she'd do without him and she promised to mourn him forever.'" My melodramatic depiction causes him to untangle himself from my grasp, but I pull him back into a hold. "Jason, why even talk like that? The kids and I would be devastated, of course. But I'd survive. I'd have to. For the kids."

He looks at me solemnly, then kisses the tip of my nose. "I know you would. You're such a good mother."

"Hey. I love you." I hold him prisoner with my gaze, not allowing him to escape until he puts an end to this ridiculous discussion. I see the moment he relents and his eyes soften, his body relaxing under my palms.

"I love you, too," he whispers. The kids choose this exact instant to scream from the other room, interrupting our tender moment. I hear Penny fall to the floor, probably throwing a fit or playing the victim after driving Thatcher to retaliate physically. Jason closes his eyes, sighs, then offers to check what's going on. As he's walking away toward the sound of the crime, he stops and asks, "But you would be fine? You know, without me?"

I look at my husband, curiosity turning to concern. "I don't know, babe. I really can't imagine my life without you, and I really don't want to try." He nods and smiles before turning away, and, for a long time, I wonder if I said the right thing, if I should have said more, and if it would have changed anything.

8

Footwork

Foot position and action

The next week goes by as normal. There are tough mornings trying to get the kids up and ready for school followed by lonely work days at home sitting in front of my computer. These are punctuated by hectic evenings where my overtired kids discover a second wind and spend the majority of the night fighting and roughhousing, only to balk about going to bed before passing out from pure childhood exhaustion. I barely see Nick the rest of the week because he's so busy with the library job, but we manage to connect over dinner that Saturday night: pizza, wings, and beer purchased by me out of guilt and bribery.

"Hey, Nick. You've got something in your beard." I eye the streak of bleu cheese dressing dripping from his thick facial hair. He dabs at his chin lightly, barely touching the white residue, and I do my best to stifle any laughter, letting him enjoy the rest of his meal. "So are we all set for this week's schedule?"

He launches into dutiful uncle mode, even dropping a fresh piece of cheese pizza on each of the kids' plates. "Yep. You need me Tuesday, right? Therapy and dancing?"

"I want to go dancing with Mommy!" Penny hollers mid-chew, cheese and sauce debris spraying the table top in front of her.

Thatcher is quick to scold her. "You can't go dancing, Penny. It's just for Mommy. She needs her adult time. Right, Mommy? That's what Uncle Nick told me." Oh, Thatcher. For now, it is fine how he explains to his sister the ways of the world, but eventually I will have to put a stop to the mansplaining.

"Kid, nothing is sacred with you, is it? You don't deserve this." Nick makes a play to steal Thatcher's plate away, and Thatcher giggles with delight.

"Mommy, what's therapy?" Penny asks, and I struggle with how to make this applicable for a four-year-old.

"So therapy is a time for Mommy to go and talk about her feelings with a doctor."

"But do you, though?" Nick mumbles under his breath. I stare daggers at him across the table, causing him to take a long pull from his beer bottle.

"Feelings about what?" Penny asks, oblivious to the sibling battle that is currently brewing.

I shoot another wide-eyed warning at Nick to keep his mouth shut before I turn to Penny. "Well, feelings about anything, honey. But mostly, feelings about what it's like now that Daddy isn't here with us."

Penny casts her eyes down to her lap and mumbles, "Daddy died."

My heart clenches. "Yes, sweetie, yes he did. And we miss him very much, don't we?"

Thatcher chimes in, "Should I go to therapy, Mommy?"

"Why, honey?"

"Well, I miss Daddy a lot, and I think about him a lot. So should I go to therapy?"

I've wondered the same thing, but I've been so focused on keeping life as normal as possible for him and Penny that I never got around to it. I start to doubt my actions as I broach the topic carefully and with curiosity, as Dr. Collins would say. "Do you think you're having difficulty accepting that Daddy is gone, Thatcher?"

His big, soulful eyes pan from me to Nick before going back to his pizza. "No. I know Daddy is gone. I just miss him."

His words destroy me, but I trudge through the sinking sand of my emotional terrain and make sure to validate his feelings. *Thank you, therapy.* "Well, honey, we can talk about Daddy. Anytime you want."

"But it always makes you sad. And sometimes mad." Thatcher's words land with sharpened tips. Has he been avoiding the topic of Jason because he doesn't want to upset me? The thought that I have put this immense burden on my first-grader causes my brain to freeze, and Nick thankfully jumps in.

"Hey, buddy. Just because someone is sad doesn't mean they don't want to or need to talk about something. Your mom and I will always listen to you when you want to talk, you know that? And actually, it's good to be sad at times. That's how we know we're human."

"And not robots!" Penny jumps in, ignoring the heavy weight that has settled over the dinner table.

Nick doesn't miss a beat. "That's right! We don't need no evil robots in here! Or zombies!"

Both Thatcher and Penny shout out, "Zombies!" Nick and the kids start to exchange crazy ideas of what they could be instead of humans until I find a moment to interject.

"Hey, kids." I reach across to hold each of their little hands. "I want you to know that I do miss Daddy, and I do get sad sometimes.

But I will never be mad at you about wanting to talk about him."

"But you'll yell at us to go in the other room or you'll look mean—"

"Yeah, Mommy, you get a mean face like this!" Penny piggy-backs on Thatcher's explanation, wrinkling her nose, crossing her eyes, and holding her hands out like claws. *Read the room, kid,* I think.

Instead of responding tersely and giving credence to their hyperbolic perspectives, I keep my voice calm and try to explain adult emotions. "Well, guys, when I do get mad after you mention Daddy, it's usually about me more than it is about you. And I don't think I look like that at all, Penny." She giggles and drops her monstrous caricature. "I do get mad when you two don't listen, but from now on I will make sure to always listen when you want to talk about Daddy, okay?" They nod their heads, hints of smiles emerging at being the center of attention during such an adult conversation.

"And that goes for me, too, okay guys?" Nick takes a big bite of a bleu cheese-smothered chicken wing, and his beard is a mess of dressing and hot sauce. The kids start giggling and pointing. "What?" he asks, playing clueless.

"Your face is icky!" Penny points and cackles.

"My face is icky? That's not nice!" Nick continues on with his act.

"Yeah, your face looks like a trashcan!" Thatcher's always had a way with words.

"A trashcan! Well, your face looks like a toilet!" I look on with a small smile as Nick and the kids continue their battle of insults, watching him as he finally starts trying to clean his beard, but missing the spot and making it even worse. The kids are in stitches with laughter, and all I can think about is how much work I have yet to do. On my footwork, my feelings, and my parenting.

At the end of dinner, Nick and I start clearing the table. He nudges me with his shoulder, both hands holding dirty plates. "So, therapy and dancing on Tuesday, right?"

I nod, swinging my own load of dishes over his bent frame as we move through our familiar cleanup choreography. "Yes. Therapy and dancing. I think that's a good place to start."

I'm continually working on being okay with being alone, though it just makes me long even more for the days when I was part of a team.

~ ~ ~

"Oh, God," I exhale with satisfaction as I sink into my pillow, my body weightless but unable to move, the pure dichotomy of a truly good love-making session. I lay there, letting the sensation tingle through my extremities. With a four-year-old and a two-year-old, it's rare that we ever have the bed to ourselves, but somehow Jason and I found ourselves giddily alone after getting the kids to bed by seven. A few glasses of wine, a couple flirtatious looks, and I was naked and flat on my back in no time.

Jason spreads out next to me, placing feather-light kisses down my shoulder, to my neck, and across my breasts. I close my eyes and whimper with pleasure. He speaks into my skin, "You are so beautiful. Beautiful. And so fucking sexy." He shifts suddenly so he's on top of me, his naked length against mine once again. Our lips connect in a long, languid kiss, both of us drunk on the unexpected alone time. I reach up and stroke his back, whispering into his mouth, "I think we should have another baby." Jason's body instantly stiffens, and not in the delicious way it did mere minutes ago. My eyes open wide to reveal him staring at my face with a look I can only describe as shocked horror.

"What the hell, Annie?" He lifts himself from on top of me, scoots off of the bed, finds his boxers tossed in the corner, and pulls

them up, effectively putting an end to our adult play date. He stands at the foot of the bed, raking his hands down his face.

"What?" I play dumb. Sure, maybe bringing up the idea of another baby during sexy time wasn't the best move, but he didn't have to jump off me with such gusto.

He stares at me, piercing me with his indignation. "Seriously? You really think we need another baby? We already have our hands full with two." He starts pacing, a caged animal hoping to flee a life-time of entrapment. "You're not off your birth control, are you?"

"Really? You think I would do that?" He sends me a side glance mid-pace then averts his gaze quickly. "Of course not, Jason! I wouldn't do that to you. I wouldn't do that to us! I just thought we could talk about it. I didn't think it was going to turn into…" I gesture up and down in his direction as if trying to quantify this adult man meltdown, "whatever this is."

He stops and turns fully toward me. "Now? You thought we could talk about this now? While I'm conveniently turned on and you're conveniently naked?"

Okay, the way he puts it makes it sound like I planned this, which is not at all what happened. Sure, I've been quietly contemplating the thought of another baby for a while now. Ever since Penny started walking, I have been holding private debates with myself over whether or not I'm ready to be done with baby milestones. I decide to concede a little but try to steer us back into Logic-ville. "Okay, I see how you might think I set this up, but I didn't. And as for talking about it now, well…yeah. It's not like we get a lot of time alone to talk about this sort of stuff."

He rushes to the bed and sits next to me. His voice is softer, calmer, but still laced with bridled panic. "Exactly, Annie. We already don't have a lot of time. Having another baby would only take even more time. We're just about to get rid of diapers. We're actually starting to sleep through the night." Uh-oh, he's trying to take a detour to Logic-ville, and now I'm not too sure who is in the driver's seat.

I attempt to counter with another point. "I know, but the kids would love to have a baby sibling—"

"Then let's get them a dog, or a cat, or maybe just a big doll they can pretend is a baby sibling. Annie, I just can't. I love our kids, but I'm done with babies. And it's not just the time; it's money, childcare, your work schedule—"

"I could quit until all the kids are in school," I desperately suggest. I'm losing him, and we both know who is going to exit this conversation the winner, but I can't help making a few last hollow attempts.

Jason looks at me, and the pity I see there pierces me deeper than I thought possible. He proceeds cautiously, almost consoling me as he says, "I don't think we could do it. And if you really think about it, take the emotion out of it, you know we can't. Annie, where is this really coming from?"

I blink my eyes furiously and make a move to turn away, but I'm still trapped in the blanket. He places his hands on my shoulders and starts gently kneading, and I search my psyche, answering as I discover the reason myself. "I guess I've just been thinking about my parents a lot: how my dad left, my mom got sick. Sure, I have Nick, but I sometimes wish I had more. I don't even have any close girl-friends what with having the kids and working from home—"

"You have me," he offers, still behind me, rubbing the knots from my shoulder blade.

I sigh and continue. "I know, but what if something happened? What would I do? Who would I have? I'd be all on my own...just like my mom was." I pause, thinking of the trauma from my past and how having a younger brother to divert my attention saved me many times over. I twist out of Jason's grasp and turn to look at him. "I just don't want our kids to ever feel like they're on their own. I want them to have someone to go through life with. Especially the tough parts."

He shifts on the bed to catch my gaze with his, holding my upper arms, giving me stability in more ways than one. "I get your fear, Annie, I do. When my dad died, the loss seemed unbearable and unending, but I got through. You got through it, too—twice. We're tough, and our kids are tough. Now, I'm not planning on going anywhere. I want us to get through the tough parts together, and we'll make sure to teach them how to do just that, okay?"

"Okay," I give in. My baby outburst was obviously a symptom of something deeper, but I'm not ready to admit that out loud yet.

Jason reaches up and holds my chin between his thumb and index finger. His thumb strokes an arc on my upper neck as he asks, "Are you okay?"

I slowly nod my head.

"Are we okay?"

Again, I give him the slow nod, but add in a half-smile.

"I love my life with you and the kids. And I love you," he says, looking deeply into my eyes.

I can no longer resist. I melt into his touch, displaying my white flag of surrender. "I love you, too."

His forehead presses into mine, and he leans in for a demanding kiss. When we break apart, he makes a promise he could never possibly keep. "You don't have to worry about being alone, okay? We're in this together." He kisses my forehead, and we snuggle back onto the bed, his arms wrapped around me as I breathe in his scent, a small tear escaping the corner of my eye and falling into the sheets, one of many to be absorbed by this marriage bed.

9

Frame

*A dancer's body position with
regard to proper dance hold*

Dr. Collins is all abuzz and ready to hear about my first night at the ballroom dancing class. He sits down in his leather chair, fingers interlaced and settled on his stomach, ready for a full report. I could play hard to get as I normally do and try to change topics, but I find I actually want to talk about last week, so I dig in with the details.

"The actual dancing was fine. Fun even. There weren't any other singletons there, so I danced with the instructor. He's a nice guy. Talented. Enthusiastic. Way too positive. And I picked up on the moves fairly quickly."

"That's great, Annie. I'm glad to hear you found some success during the first class."

"Well, let's not get ahead of ourselves," I say as I proceed to tell him about the tragic ending to my evening of dance.

"Well, first of all, thank you for telling me. It's nice to hear something from you without having to coerce or trick you." My brain tumbles on his verbs of choice, but he continues quickly. "So, what was the impetus for the panic attack?"

Still mulling over his previous sentence, my answer becomes a more automatic response than if I had my full wits about me. "I heard a song by OneRepublic. It was one of Jason's and my favorite bands."

"Are you telling me you cry every time you hear music that reminds you of Jason?" He is really going for it tonight, ready to finally figure me out as he jots down notes in his journal.

"Well, no. But…well, to be honest, I don't really listen to music much anymore. I used to before Jason passed away, but now I usually just sit or work in silence." I always thought I just needed quiet after being inundated with the loud sounds of my kids, but maybe I've been purposefully avoiding music.

"But don't you love music?" It's not accusatory, but his factual assessment stings me with the realization of a loss I didn't even know I'd been experiencing.

I do love music. I really do. Dancing lifted my spirits more than I thought possible. It was only when I heard that song that I hurtled back to reality where I'm one half of a couple that used to attend OneRepublic concerts, danced in the kitchen, and spent entire nights in bed listening to the radio and indulging in one another's bodies before we had kids.

I nod stiffly, and Dr. Collins proceeds.

"Just because Jason is gone doesn't mean you have to stop enjoying yourself. It certainly doesn't mean you should isolate yourself from meeting new people and trying new things. That's what I was trying to show you. This year has left you more of an island than Jason would have ever wanted, and deep down, you agree. How do you think Jason would react to finding out about your panic attack the other night?"

"I guess he would tell me I need to pull myself together. But he was always the cool one under pressure…Well, at least I thought he was… but I guess I didn't really know how it was affecting him." We sit there in silence, realizing what I've just admitted.

Jason was always the one to have around in a crisis. Between his medical and military training, no emergency was too much. He could calm everyone down with his stern yet sturdy directions. He was fast-thinking, decisive, and collected. And he often was the one to take control when the kids were injured. I miss that in my life. But maybe I was putting too much on him. Maybe he needed me to take control once in a while. Maybe he needed me to save him. My vision begins to blur as I choke down a sob.

Dr. Collins cuts through my quickly descending thoughts. "Annie, you cannot blame yourself for not seeing the signs. Jason could have talked to you; he could have made an effort to tell you what was going on."

"But I did see the track marks," I gasp out. This detail was, of course, in the police report, but I've never admitted this to Dr. Collins. He knows, but he's never pushed. However, he sees his opening and cautiously proceeds through the door I've let creak open into my otherwise protected fortress.

"And he told you it was from work, right? He lied, Annie. He had the chance to come clean, to get help, and in the end, it was his mistake, not yours." His assuredness is stabilizing, but the doubt within me is still scratching at my conscience.

"Unless it wasn't a mistake." A single tear escapes and slides down my cheek. I don't know what it is, but since the first dance class, I feel like something within me has been dismantled, allowing me to start seeing the reality of Jason's actions and the effects of those actions more clearly. I'm sad, but I'm also angry.

Dr. Collins leans forward, his journal long forgotten as he tends to my open wounds. "We're never going to know, Annie. As you said, Jason's dead. And I do want you to work on yourself, but you must start with accepting how you ended up in this situation and being okay with whatever reason that is. Talking about this is important. It's a great step in your healing, Annie. I'm really proud of you." He grabs a box of tissue from his desk, leans over to hand it to me, and waits for me to collect myself.

As I blot my tears and attempt a delicate swipe at my snot-ridden nose, I have to admit it feels good to start confiding in my therapist, but I'm in need of more than just the one emotional breakthrough to become truly better. However, I can keep working at it. And I want to. I want to laugh with my kids, I want to handle the emergencies, I want to listen to music, I want to dance. And more than anything, I want to forgive both myself and Jason, but I'm not quite there yet.

An hour later, I walk into the dance studio, face scrubbed clean (from a stop in a McDonald's bathroom) and free of teary mascara runs. I'm also showing up with a bit more ensemble eloquence tonight after last week's fashion faux pas. I'm wearing patterned leggings and a white T-shirt dress cinched at the waist with a braided belt. I also dug out some old character shoes I still had from college, the soles scratched in order to reduce slipping on slick floors. I've pulled my blonde hair up into a hair claw, letting my natural waves cascade out the top. I even put on eyeshadow and mascara, some of it still salvageable after my McDonald's spa date. I'm not looking to impress anyone, but I am aiming to be somewhat put together and non-pathetic in my lonesomeness.

I teeter a bit in my heels and look around the studio. My stomach drops with the realization many went with the workout clothing approach this week. While the older couples are still slacked up with collared shirts and blouses, Ted and Nathan are adorned with Lululemon joggers and hoodies, while the ever-handsy coupling of Lorraine and Dave look ready to rumba with yoga pants, spandex shorts, and matching Under Armor shirts. I secretly curse Lorraine for stealing my yoga pants, but it's fine because I'm here and ready to dance. Dr. Collins and I discussed how the music, movement, and adult interaction must have reawakened some dormant part of me, and I'm excited to learn a new dance tonight, and maybe even make it through the class without another sobfest.

Milo enters from a door in the back I'm assuming leads to an office or storeroom. His long strides quickly carry him up to the front of the class and I sigh with relief. At least he is still dressed presentably, opting for dark-washed jeans and a white button-up. The jeans hug his sculpted rear, and his open top buttons reveal a sliver of smooth chest. Since Jason, I haven't really had the instinct to pay attention to attractiveness, but Milo looks positively scrumptious all around, thanks to the mirrored wall at his back. Again, I'm not alone in my appreciation as I see the other women, Nathan, and Ted instantly twist their bodies to give him their full attention.

"Happy Tuesday, everyone! I hope you all had a good week practicing your footwork and holds, right?" He points at a few laughing couples, and then his gaze turns to me. His face instantly breaks open into a beaming smile, and I blush at the attention. "My partner! Annie, come on up and help me out." He beckons me over and grabs my hand when I reach his side. Still addressing the class, he says, "We're going to work on two dances this evening. First, my lovely partner and I are going to show you the waltz, then we'll spend some time workshopping it, and then we'll move to the foxtrot for the second half of class. We'll revisit these dances each class session as review, and we'll be learning one to two new dances each week." Heads nod in recognition, and Milo expertly angles me so he can start explaining the basics of the waltz.

I pick up on the steps easily again, which isn't too difficult when being led by an expert, but eventually I feel myself relax into the movement, focusing more on my body's responses to Milo's direction than any counting or foot placement. Once everyone is comfortable with the basic steps, Milo turns on some music, and we are left to freestyle. Frank Sinatra's "Come Waltz with Me" provides a classic beat, and I breathe a sigh of relief at my low emotional connection to the music which allows me to keep functioning.

After attending to the other dancers, Milo directs his full attention to me while we weave around the others. "It's really great having you as a partner. I usually have to steal a dance partner from one of the leaders, then try and help them once they're reunited. It's nice having you to help model."

I blush, not used to being the subject of gratitude. With little kids, that rarely happens, and since they are the ones I mostly interact with other than insurance companies and disgruntled patients, I'm not used to breezy niceties. "Uh, thanks. I'm glad my singleness has helped you out. I was just worried I was going to look pathetic coming here alone."

"Of course not! You don't look pathetic. You look beautiful." I stiffen at this compliment, trip on his left foot, my eyes widening in shock and surprise, and I avert my gaze, trying not to burst into adolescent giggles. He clears his throat while steadying our footing and getting us back on beat. "Sorry. Well… I mean…not really." His verbal stumbling eases me a bit, and I look back up to see him smiling sheepishly. "Okay, I'm being awkward. What I mean is I'm not sorry to say you look beautiful. You do. But I'm sorry if it made you uncomfortable." He scrunches his nose, waiting for my response.

"Uh, no. I'm fine. It's just…it's been a long time since I've been called that." My left hand digs into his shoulder and I try to release my grip by spreading my fingers, but instead, my hand slips and slides down his arm.

Milo breaks his hold to grab my hand and replace it, never breaking eye contact with me. "Well, that's a shame. Then I'm definitely
not sorry I said it." I can't stand the intensity of his gaze anymore,
and I look down, biting my lip. Something about his brown eyes is
so sincere, so honest, it hurts to look at. I don't know what to say, so
he eventually picks up the conversation again. "The point is, anyone
should be able to dance, even if they don't have a partner." We continue floating around the room in content silence, and I can sense he
wants to say something more.

"What? What are you thinking?"

"Well, it's really none of my business. I was just wondering what
brings you here, you know, alone. I remember you said you have
kids." He's cautious with his approach, slowly dipping into the suggested question about the whereabouts of a father, which I appreciate,
but it still doesn't make it any easier to discuss.

I've had to answer this a few times this past year: at parent-
teacher conferences, the one PTO meeting I attended, and at the grocery store when someone mistook Nick as my husband (*yuck*). I can't
really blame people for their curiosity, but it still brings up complicated feelings and sometimes initiates an immediate retreat. Since
Milo has graciously allowed me to dance with him and has just called
me beautiful, I figure I can provide him with an honest explanation.

I let us sink into the rhythm of a new song, a classical ditty I
know I've heard from Disney's *Fantasia*. It seems Milo went with
the traditional tonight. From the reaction of the other pupils, it seems
like a winning choice. They're all lit up, smiling and bouncing to the
music, even Mary and Leo. Seeing their joy gives me the courage to
jump into my dirty secrets.

"I'm widowed. My husband passed away a little over a year ago.
So…yeah, that's why I'm here alone." I gulp, expecting the usual
pity which always tears me down more than the actual admission.

Surprisingly, Milo doesn't offer me pity. He just has more questions. "Oh, I'm sorry. How old are your kids?"

"Um…well, they're four and six. Actually, my son is going to turn seven here in a few weeks, and my daughter is going to be five the first of July."

"Fun ages?"

"Uh, sometimes. They can be tough. They fight a lot, and of course, it's hard without their father…but they're good kids. And I have my brother helping out. He lives with me currently. In fact, he's the one watching them so I can be here."

"Well, thank your brother for me."

I blush again.

"Tell me more about your kids," he urges, and I do. We dance a few more songs while I prattle on about Thatcher and Penny. Milo smiles and leads us smoothly around the room as I describe their personalities and regale him with stories of chaos and unhindered emotion until it's time to move on to the foxtrot.

The rest of the class goes by quickly with a variety of strategies. Milo dances with one of the retired wives to show proper holding and footing while I step to the side. He then pulls the five-star-rated instructor move of working with each individual student, grabbing their hands, moving them into position, and even showing some of the men how to properly lead. I mimic the holds with an imaginary partner, catching my reflection in the mirror. I expect to see a tired and pathetic shell, but instead, I look strong, agile, and happy. I smile to myself, giving my reflection a last conspiratorial side glance just as Milo slides up in front of me.

"Looking good! Ready for a real partner?"

We take off, practicing the slow, slow, quick, quick pattern, and I find myself laughing and relaxing instantly.

At the end of the class, I linger, waiting for Milo to answer individual questions. I don't know what I want to say, but I know I want to talk to him once more before the evening ends. As the last couple heads out, he watches them exit then cocks his head toward me. He blows out a breath and starts rolling up his sleeves. "Geez. I. Am. Cooking!" He pulls at his shirt collar, waving it in order to get a breeze going. "I might need to prop the door open next time..." My eyes catch hold of a flash of scarring as he rolls up his left sleeve. His forearm is muscular, tanned, and covered in dark hair; but my gaze lingers on the inside of his arm where a slice of raised scar tissue slashes through the thin skin of his wrist, branding him with evidence of past injury. My world sinks into a black tunnel as the ground crumbles beneath my feet.

"Annie, you okay?" Milo's repeated question finally frees me from the enlarging pit threatening to pull me under.

I take a breath and try to blame my sudden idiocy on the heat. "Uh, yeah... it is super hot. I just wanted to say how much I'm enjoying this class. You do a really great job of teaching. And you're being so nice to me. Thank you."

I make myself look him straight on, refusing to return my gaze to the screaming mark of former life grievances on his arm, even though I feel like my lungs are collapsing.

"You're welcome. I really like having you in class, so thank you." We stand in silence, each waiting for the other to speak. When we do, it's at the same time.

"Hey, would you want to..."

"So, I'd better get going..."

"Oh, okay." He straightens up and makes a move to start cleaning up the music and locking down the studio. "Well, I'll see you next week, right?"

I nod and start walking backward to the door. "Yes. Yes, you will. Have a good week." Once I'm outside, I speed walk to my car.

I'm not sobbing this time, but my mind is racing. Mr. Positive, constantly smiling, can't-bring-him-down Milo has the markings of
someone who tried to kill himself. My brain cannot fathom this
development, and I spend the whole car ride home wondering how
someone as seemingly happy as Milo could have wanted to end it all
and how I could possibly be such a poor judge of character.

10

Brush

The action of closing the moving foot
to the standing foot and then out again

I'm woken by the rumble of the garage door cranking open directly beneath our room, clanking shut, followed by a turn of the knob, careful feet, and the door clicking locked. All of these sounds carry effortlessly up the stairs as the rest of the house has been silent for hours. While still frozen under the weight of sleep, I listen to soft-soled shoes squeak across the kitchen floor until they're kicked off into the corner shoe pile. Then my ears strain to hear sock-covered feet shuffling around the kitchen, the opening and closing of the refrigerator, the setting of something on the counter, followed by the creaking opening of a cupboard door. This midnight dance has been the music to my late night waking more and more as Jason has been picking up longer hours and multiple shifts in the ER.

And it's been taking a toll. On him, me, the kids. I don't know why he's so adamant about working extra hours. I know he takes his job seriously. Of course he does; he works in the emergency room *where life and death aren't just an overused cliché. It's reality. But my reality is I miss my husband. I miss falling asleep with him in the bed. I miss looking across the dinner table at him. I miss him smiling at our children's stories from the day. I miss knowing everything is okay.*

I wait a good five minutes, listening for more signs of movement, but Jason must be stationed at the kitchen island, eating leftovers I saved from a dinner made for four, only consumed by one. Eventually, my brain convinces the rest of my body I am not falling back asleep until I talk to Jason, and I throw the covers back and pad across the room and down the carpeted stairs.

Jason's back is toward me as I descend the stairway. I'm sure he heard the pressure of my steps as I rose from bed, but he makes no move to turn around. He's so still, I almost wonder if he has fallen asleep sitting up. It wouldn't be the first time, but I go ahead and call out his name softly and reach out for his shoulder.

He's awake, his eyes glassy, red, and frozen on some scene only he can see in front of him. I reach out and caress his face and tuck into his side. "Jason." He blinks, eyes darting over to me, then back forward where he squeezes them shut and proceeds to reach up and run clawing hands across his face.

I frame his face with my hands and turn him to look toward me. I duck in close and whisper, "Honey, what happened?"

Instead of an answer, he folds into himself, head in his hands as sobs start to wrack his body, overcome by something I cannot wipe away from his memory. All I can do is hold him. When he is finally breathing evenly, he raises his head to look me in the eyes.

"I love you so much, Annie. I'm sorry you have to put up with me. I'm so sorry." A dark edge to his tone causes a chill to tiptoe across my skin, sneaking into the pit of my stomach.

I don't know what to say in response except I love him, too. I try to reassure him that I'm not putting up with anything, that I love my life with him. I want to know what he is sorry for, to know what happened, but when I ask about work, it's as if a curtain has dropped heavily. He straightens and tells me it doesn't matter, gives me a brief hug, and then starts to move around the kitchen, closing the house down for the night. The moment is gone, and he is back playing the role of dutiful husband and father.

I sit at the counter and watch him as he rinses orange juice from a glass. Water soaks the hem of his thermal, and he pushes the sleeve up to hug his elbow. My eyes glance at the needle marks of a medical instructor, one in charge of letting nursing students practice basic skills on him while also doling out life-saving or attempting-to-save decisions.

He carries so much burden, and I try my best to swallow my own desire to share my concerns with him. My worries can't spill onto him when he has no space left to catch them.

"You ready for bed?" He speaks to the room at large, his eyes still downcast. His avoidance of eye contact with me hurts, but I respect his need to push forward, so I keep quiet and follow him up to our bedroom, hoping the kids let him sleep in rather than allowing their own excitement to dictate his rest.

I should be grateful I actually get to go to bed with Jason next to me, but for the longest time, I can't fall asleep, afraid his nightmares will somehow leak into my own dreams. And if we are both haunted, then what will we do?

~ ~ ~

The day after my second dance class I feel like I would rather be stuck with forlorn dreams and nightmares when all hell breaks loose in my home—and by all hell, I mean the flu. It starts with

Penny, or as I like to call her, Patient Zero. It's only a matter of time before the rest of the household will get sick. And it's never conveniently at the same time; no, the illness prefers to cascade through the family like a waterfall, bouncing from rock to rock, trickling on a flat stone for a break, a moment of ignorant bliss before crashing down even stronger, drowning anything in its wake before finally plunging into the deep end and coming out in calmer waters after it's been carried away with the current.

After two days of Penny having high temps and throwing up, Thatcher crawls into my bed early Friday morning, his little body heated enough for me to instantly know the second wave has settled in. Saturday morning, I'm doubled over, my guts twisted with the piercing stabs of sharp cramps. Though I manage to take moderate care of the kids, my feverish state leaves me delusional and shaky at times. At one point, I hide in the bathroom and curl up beneath the toilet to cry. I'm overwhelmed, exhausted, and scared this will never end. And more than anything, I miss Jason. This is the first major family sickness I have experienced since his death. Sure, he was never a great patient when sick himself (like most men), but he was always great at sharing the burden, the night shifts of cleaning sheets and children, and the camaraderie of fighting the battle together. He was a great caregiver, and his absence is an even bigger ache than the chills rippling through my body.

As usually happens when the epitome of sickness or suffering is reached, it eventually gets better. Both kids finally sleep through the night, at least until 4 AM Sunday morning, at which time they both manage to crawl into my bed, each snuggling into my side, my body bookended by their moppy heads and sprawling limbs. Even my symptoms lessen by Sunday afternoon, and all three of us are ready to reenter the world of school and work come Monday. Of course, that's when the final victim is claimed.

"Annie, I feel like my intestines just escaped my body through both ends," Nick groans as he lays draped across the living room couch Monday evening. Marshmallow sits curled at his feet, cleaning herself, happy to have a sedentary body nearby that won't constantly pull her tail.

I lean down, jab a thermometer in his ear, roll my eyes at his pained protests, and wait for the concluding beep. "One hundred and two. Yep, you have what the kids and I had. Sorry, bro, but get ready for at least twenty-four hours of physical torture." He slaps his hand over his eyes and groans dramatically. Normally, I would rib him about this, but the poor guy really is in for it, so I'll let this slide. Instead, I opt to be the doting sister. "Can I get you anything? Water, crackers, a blanket?"

He peeks at me through his fingers. "Nah. I'll just crawl down to the basement and do my best to hibernate through this."

I shake my head in a playful *tsk tsk*. "Just like a mother bear birthing her babies in her sleep. Seems like the easy way out if you ask me." With the same symptoms, I was changing bedding, doing multiple loads of laundry, and feeding the kids even though the sight of food made me gag. The burden of mothers…who aren't hibernating bears.

Nick groans again as he sits up, then looks at me with sudden realization. "Oh shit, sis. I don't know if I'll be able to watch the kids tomorrow night."

"Oh. I'll just message Dr. Collins and reschedule. Or cancel. It's not a big deal."

"Yeah, but what about dance class?" Nick's words strike me dumb.

"Oh, yeah." With all the craziness of the last week, I had sort of forgotten about dance class on Tuesday. Sure, during lucid moments when I wasn't running around tending to sick children or trying to find a moment of solitude, I did have passing thoughts about the markings on Milo's arms. I wasn't by any means scared off, but I was curious. If anything, I found myself daydreaming how I would ask him about it without offending him. Sure, it was none of my business, but I was technically his dance partner. Heck, that practically made me an assistant instructor, right? Shouldn't that give me a bit of privilege in terms of intel about his past?

No, no it should not. My erroneous rationalizations had to be due to my malnourished mind, but that didn't mean my curiosity was quelled. Well, I guess I'll have another full week to consider my approach since there is no way Nick will be capable of taking care of himself, let alone two active and needy children tomorrow night. Just then, said children come running up from the basement, panting as if out of breath.

"Mommy! Mommy! Marshmallow pooped on the carpet downstairs!" Penny, always the tattletale, proudly announces this to me.

I instantly glance over at the white ball of fur currently flattening her ears as if she knows we are talking about her. "What?"

Thatcher and Penny dutifully repeat their rendition of Marshmallow's unmentionable act.

"I know what you said. I just…what, is the cat sick, too?" I raise my hands in defeat, cursing the cat's name, giving up any pretense that I have even an ounce of control over my life at the moment. To punctuate the scene, Nick suddenly shoots up, surprising all of us and sending the cat running to the basement (hopefully, not to poop on my carpet any more). The kids jump to my side, afraid of whatever has possessed Nick to jerk up from his previously catatonic state. He proceeds to rush into the nearest bathroom, close the door, and aggressively heave whatever is left in his body into my overworked toilet.

"Is Uncle Nick okay?" Thatcher asks while staring at the bathroom door. His concern warms my heart and I rub the top of his head in assurance.

"He's fine, buddy. Just sick like we were."

"Why does he sound so gross?" I swallow a laugh at my daughter's observation.

"Well, honey, that's just how Uncle Nick is when he's sick. Gross. Hey, let's get baths going. Uncle Nick can take care of the cat poop when he's feeling better."

"Aren't you going to clean it up?" asks Thatcher as I corral him toward the stairs. The kids don't understand my aversion to the basement, so instead of answering, I ignore the question and holler to Nick through the closed door as I pass. "Nick, you need anything?" Instead of answering, he just dry heaves. "Okay, don't worry about tomorrow. I can take a week off."

A conflicting sense of relief and disappointment settles within my chest, but I tell myself it'll be fine. I'll just pick up where I left off in a week. But for now, I have to avoid the basement, take care of my children, and nurse my thirty-year-old brother back to health.

11

Count

A method of breaking down and keeping track of moves

It's Tuesday evening and the kids have just finished a meal of macaroni and cheese with a fruit cup on the side. A culinary master-piece in their world. Since they can't go to the basement—their favorite stuffed animals having been threatened if they bother Nick—they have turned the front den into a "classroom" in which Thatcher is taking Penny through centers. Pretty much, he's just bossing his sister around, but they are getting along and there's some math and reading getting snuck in there, so I'm all for it. Sure, I'll need to yell at them to clean up their mess, but for now, I'm letting the kids run rampant as I stand at the kitchen counter, eating the remnants of their macaroni and cheese straight from the saucepan. The wooden spoon is a bit clunky, but I don't want to dirty any more dishes; we don't have any clean spoons anyway (I blame a week of eating mostly soup), so it suits me just fine to nibble off the wide brim, lost in a peaceful moment of not having children or a sick brother calling out my name every minute.

"Mommy! Someone's at the door!" Thatcher hollers, disturbing my calm. Penny starts running around, squealing and giggling, as if she's never seen humans approach our house before. (To be fair, we don't get many visitors.)

"Do not open that door!" I say as I jog to the front door, saucepan and wooden spoon still in hand, shooing away my children as they push up against the storm door. A quick check of the wall clock reveals it's after eight. I sigh, just now realizing how far behind schedule I am in getting the kids to bed. Now, the kids are all riled up, making bedtime an even further away destination. As I flip on the porch light and crack open the door, my eyes widen in disbelief.

"Hey, Annie." Milo stands just below the two steps to our stoop, hands in his pockets. In the yellow illumination of the porch light, I can see he's still dressed from class, a combination of active and relaxed with gray sweatpants and an olive green long-sleeve T-shirt, his hair sticking up in various directions. His version of relaxed looks very different from mine as I am currently wearing baggy sweatpants and an oversized sweatshirt, my unwashed hair pulled into a ponytail. I also realize I have no makeup on, and even worse, no bra. I subtly cover my chest with my pot of macaroni.

I finally manage to squeak out a greeting. Thatcher and Penny cling to my legs, looking out from behind me.

Words form after a moment of silence and a shy smile from my unexpected guest. "Oh, um, what are you doing here? I didn't know dance instructors made house calls."

He chuckles and shifts nervously. "I, uh, had your address from your registration. It, uh, it worried me when you didn't show up, especially after last time."

I tilt my head to the side, unsure of his meaning.

He steps up to the top of our porch, clears his throat, and shrugs his arms, bringing attention to the distant slashes on his wrists. "You noticed my scars. I thought they might have scared you away."

"Oh, uh. I'm sorry, I didn't think you saw me—"

"Didn't see you staring? You weren't very discreet." He says this with a laugh, but my cheeks still blaze red.

I sputter out an apology and he shakes his head. "No need to apologize. Actually, I just wanted to make sure that wasn't the reason you didn't show up tonight."

"He's really tall," whispers Thatcher. I had almost forgotten they were there, witnessing this awkward encounter.

"Like Daddy!" shouts Penny, effectively breaking the stillness and bringing me to action.

"Well, thanks for stopping by. You certainly didn't need to, but—"

"Actually, I was hoping we could talk."

"Oh." My heart flutters and plummets at the same time, a weird pattern of palpitation brought on by flattery and suspicion. "Um… sure. Hey kids, why don't you go get your pajamas on." Amidst their protests, I add, "Then you can get a snack and watch something."

"*Zombies!*" I wince at the mention of the Disney musical they've watched over and over, but I need them to lose interest in our visitor, so I agree with a sigh, and they shout in celebration as they run upstairs.

I turn back to Milo, still patiently standing outside, watching with amusement. "They're absolute maniacs, and they're obsessed with that movie. Don't be surprised if you hear them belting out the lyrics." I open the door wider, gesturing toward my infected living area. "I would invite you in, but we've been sick this last week, and I haven't had time to fumigate everything. Mind if we sit out here? I should be able to hear the kids if a crisis occurs."

"Of course."

"Okay, just give me a minute to make sure they're doing what I asked." *And put on a bra,* I think.

When my kids are successfully occupied in front of the television,

Milo and I sit on the top step of my front stoop, listening to the occasional moth ping against the light sconce. His long legs look almost comical bent at such a sharp angle, but everything else about him is at ease. In contrast, my body is tightened with worry at what would draw Milo all the way to the suburbs on a Tuesday evening.

We both rest our arms on our knees, backs curved, Milo turned toward me. I focus my attention on surveying the shadowed sidewalks of the neighborhood for intruders, troublemakers, or, more likely, dog walkers.

"So, you didn't just bail on dance class because of me?" Milo finally asks, my body almost convulsing with the sudden jolt of surprised humor.

"No, of course not. I love dancing. And I love your class…and your teaching…and dancing with you." *Okay, Annie; shut up now.* "As I said earlier, we've just been cursed with a plague on our house." I don't know what comes over me but I raise my fist and dramatically recite, "A plague on both your houses!"

Milo tips his head to the side, his lips pursed in a closed smirk, brows raised in surprised delight. Uh, yeah, definitely escalating on the scale of weird tonight.

"Sorry, I've had very limited interaction with adults."

He drops his head and chuckles, a sigh of relief escaping at the same time, and I'm surprised to realize Milo must have been just as nervous as me to have this conversation.

"Okay…So, no. I didn't want to miss class. Actually, I would have been healthy enough to attend, but my brother, also known as my kids' babysitter, is sick; so I didn't feel it would be acceptable to leave my kids with him while he's holed up in the basement."

"Wow. Okay, well good. About the not wanting to miss class. I feel bad for your brother, though."

"Ah, he'll be fine. I stepped on his head as a baby and he recovered, so a little stomach bug isn't going to do him in." We share a small laugh and settle into comfortable silence for a minute, both enjoying the slight breeze and watching the insects flutter in the beam of porch light. As he looks off into the distance, I turn and observe his profile. His eyes are darting everywhere but toward me, so I can surmise he's thinking of how to bring up the next topic. He made the first move of coming out all this way, so I figure I should make the next move of mercy. I don't necessarily want to ask this question, but I know I need to, for the both of us.

"So… should I ask about your scars?"

He turns his head first, then shifts his whole body, angling toward me. "You can. I mean, that's why I came here, so yeah."

I do a quick audio check to listen for any sign of child distress, but a negative finding allows me to turn and give him my full attention. I take a deep breath and say, "Okay…so tell me about your scars."

He takes a breath, preparing to dive into his past. "The thing is, I talk about this a lot. It's been a long time, and I'm a different person, but it still is pretty heavy. You're okay hearing this, right? I mean, with losing your husband and everything?"

I flinch at the insinuation, but try to hide it through a wincing smile. "For sure. I'm fine. Completely different scenarios."

His eyes glance over me, up and down, before settling into his story. "I did try to kill myself when I was sixteen."

"Oh, Milo." I blanch at the thought of such a young kid thinking his life was done.

"I know. It seems crazy to me now, how I thought I knew who I was, what I wanted, and what the world was like. Shit, at twenty-seven I still don't always know, but at least I know a little bit more every day."

I smile, choosing not to vocalize how even with eight years on him, I'm still clueless most of the time, and I let him ease back into his narration.

"So yeah, I was a bit of a bastard as a little kid. My dad left my mom when I was five, and even though she tried her best, I still ran wild, threw fits, was just an overall jerk. Maybe it was because I didn't have my dad around, but all in all, I was a butthead, and I knew it."

I interrupt for clarification. "Did you see your dad at all then?"

He looks sideways at me, clenched teeth evident in the tense workings of his jaw. "Not at all. He was gone. Still is. It's been twenty-two years. Nothing. Not even after I sliced my wrists open."

His blunt wording draws me up, but I can't act shocked or insulted. This is his story, not mine. "Okay, so you were a bad kid. There are lots of bad kids. How do you wind up with these?" I gesture toward his arms, still safely hidden behind cotton sleeves.

"I, uh, I got into some pretty bad stuff. My mom and I lived in Albany Park, and it wasn't uncommon for me to sneak over to Navy Pier at twelve years old. My mom was always working between two jobs, so I just did what I wanted. I made friends. Met girls. Drank. Smoked. Dabbled with a few drugs. Luckily none of those stuck, but my drug of choice happened to be the girls. What can I say? I've always been a lover, not a fighter." He smirks sheepishly, and my stomach flips. "So, I grew up pretty fast. Then, when I was fifteen, I met this one girl. Reagan. She was from Lake View, which was a completely different world from mine. But we had a similar backstory. Her mom died when she was four. Lots of time alone due to working single parents. Sneaking out young and running around Chicago. Well, I fell fast and hard. Anything Reagan wanted, I would do, even if I had to break the law to do it. Let's just say, I got really good at running from cops." A mischievous twitch of the lips gives me the impression he's not entirely ashamed of this talent.

"We were together for a year, and most of the time it was great, but she would get these bouts of depression where she wouldn't want to see or talk to me. I would confront her, and she would get angry, hit and scream until I had to walk away. A few days later, she would wonder where I was, begging me to come out with her, be with her, as if nothing had happened. It was tumultuous at best. She was always accusing me of cheating on her. Sure, I was a flirt, but I loved *her*. And I had seen my dad be a shit to my mom and even if I was a shit, I was not going to be a cheater like him. And I wasn't going to leave her like he left my mom and me. But it was tough to escape her moods. Eventually, her sadness became my sadness. It was hard to separate, and it became more like an obligation than a want, you know? Like I had to stay with her even if I wasn't happy. We just existed together, mutually unsettled and miserable." He turns his attention to the concrete between his feet, apparently finding it easier to look away as he dives into his backstory and past failings. I continue watching silently, afraid if I interject, it'll break his concentration and end his retelling. And for reasons I don't quite understand, I need to hear this story.

"Well, Reagan tells me she just can't do this anymore. That she's tired and doesn't want to live, but she doesn't want to leave me. She claims she won't go through with it because she doesn't want to hurt me. Well, all I can think about is how I am making her suffer by making her stay alive, so I agree to do it with her. Remember the whole 'I'd do anything for her'? Well, we make this plan to do it on New Year's Eve. She's stolen some pills from her dad; and we are supposed to take them at midnight, fall asleep in her bed in each other's arms, and never wake up. We really romanticized the whole thing, which makes me cringe now, but we were sixteen, probably thinking we were unique, the only teenagers to ever feel lost and untethered."

I think back to my own teenage years and have visions of arguing with my mom, placing the blame on everyone else in my life, wanting to escape the confines of a caring mother and tolerable brother. I was such a brat. I try to think of a young Milo and Reagan without instantly judging their idea, but it is hard, especially as a mother. I can't even entertain the idea of one of my kids being in that much pain.

He continues, shifting his weight and trying to alleviate the discomfort of sitting on pavement for a prolonged amount of time. His voice is steady, but the pain of talking about the past is evident behind the wall of forced control.

"Well, we weren't supposed to leave any notes or clues, but I couldn't do that to my mom. Sure, I wasn't always the greatest kid, but I loved her and knew she loved me. I had to say goodbye. So, I wrote a note. Only thing is, I wrote the note the morning of New Year's Eve and placed it in her bedroom thinking she would be working all night. Well, she came home between jobs…she was supposed to be catering…and she found the note. She found me out on the streets hanging with my friends for what I thought was the last time. The woman was livid. I swear she pulled me by my ear the entire way home and locked me in my room. She called in to work and refused to let me leave the house, call anyone, do anything. I was going nuts thinking of Reagan. I couldn't let her believe I just abandoned our idea, abandoned her; but my mom was incapable of being swayed. So finally, when she let me use the bathroom; I nabbed a steak knife on my way and locked myself in our only bathroom, sat in the empty bathtub, and tried to rip through my wrists at midnight. I got through both, but not deep enough to cut through any artery, just enough to lose some blood and black out. My mom was suspicious after ten minutes, broke through the door, and called 911. She saved me. I woke up on New Year's Day in the hospital with my wrists bandaged and my mom asleep in the chair beside me."

"And what about Reagan?" I have a pit of dread in my stomach as I ask. Milo hangs his head lower and focuses on rubbing his right hand along the rugged pattern of the porch step as he answers.

"She went through with it. Her dad was at a party with co-workers, so she took my dose as well as hers and was found around the same time I was waking up in the ER."

"Oh my gosh. I am so sorry, Milo." I reach over and touch his shoulder, surprising myself at my boldness in wanting to comfort the man forever haunted by a first love. He turns to look at me, and I have the urge to pull him to me. I'm shocked by my body's response, but I ignore this strange and poorly mistimed desire and focus back on him.

"That was probably the toughest time for me. Before, I didn't really want to die, I was only doing it for her, but once I lost her, then my own depression set in. I had only been borrowing hers, taking on her sadness, but when she went through with it and I wasn't there, I felt like I had abandoned her. I myself had been abandoned, and I had been so sure I would never be like my dad. But there I was, breaking promises and leaving her on her own."

I have to stop him. "Okay, but please tell me you realized you weren't in the wrong, right? Like, how did you get here, being the person you are now?"

He holds his hands up, trying to tamp down my indignation. "Now, now. I'm getting there. Be patient."

Patience has never been my strong suit, but the kids seem to be doing fine, caught in a zoned-out musical stupor, so I inhale through my nose and nod for him to continue.

"For months, I tried to ignore everyone, everything that used to make me happy. Really, I didn't know how to be happy anymore. Eventually I learned my brain had rewired itself, almost mimicking the disease I didn't know Reagan had."

"Bipolar, right?"

He nods.

"So how did you find out?"

"Her dad. He met with me after my mom reached out. She didn't know what to do. I was carrying so much guilt I thought I should be punished, that such a miserable existence was my penance for failing Reagan. Then her dad started visiting me. At first, I wouldn't talk to him, but then he started sharing stories about Reagan, about her mom. Even with so much grief, he was able to make some sort of sense, to figure out a way to keep moving forward while not forgetting what he loved about those he had loved and lost. Eventually, I was able to come to terms with what had happened, as well as realize the road I was on before I had met Reagan was bound to lead me to tragedy. So I started fresh. We moved to Lincoln Park, I enrolled in a new school, started helping my mom more, actually hung out with my mom and forged a friendship with her, kept a relationship with Reagan's dad. And then, I tried out for the school play. And that was it. I found my joy. That turned into the school musical, which turned into dance classes, singing in choir. And what I loved most, what brought me joy also brought others joy. And that's what I want to do. Help bring others joy…and sometimes help them find a release from pain, just as I did."

Our eyes hold on to each other's gaze and I'm lost, but in a non-scary way that seems foreign. My attention falls to my cuticles, picking at them to hide the emotion swelling within my chest.

I want to find joy again. I want to make it through a whole day and not feel the immense stab of heartache, the guilty notion of not being enough for my kids, the fear I am somehow to blame. While dancing, I was able to overcome some of the negativity. Was that joy? And was it from the dancing or from this man sitting next to me? I shift away, my internal voice scolding me that this wasn't supposed to be about finding and connecting to another person; this was supposed to be about finding and connecting to myself. So why do I feel like I need to be around Milo more and more?

I'm about to talk, not sure exactly what is trying to spill from my mouth, but we both jump as a small body slams against the storm door. Penny claws at the door, growling and roaring in her best zombie impression.

After I regain my breath, I tell her not to smear the window and I'll be right in.

"But Uncle Nick needs help!" she whines through the glass before retreating back into the house, probably hearing the start of one of her favorite musical numbers. I see a stiff-legged remnant of my younger brother standing in the entryway, cradling his hands in his head.

I stand and crack the door open. "What do you need, Nick?"

His voice is low and staccato, his thoughts obviously jumbled. "Sorry, I ran out of Motrin. Do you have anything up in your room? I can get it." He makes a motion to take a step, and he nearly crashes into the wall.

"Nick, don't. I'll get it. Just give me a second." I close the door and turn toward Milo, who is now standing and smoothing out his shirt. "Hey, I'm sorry. I have to get back in. My brother needs me… and probably my kids."

"You've got a lot of people relying on you, huh?"

"Well, not usually Nick. He's pretty self-sufficient, but he's a baby when he's sick—"

"I can hear you!" A pained grumble travels through the door, and we both bite back a laugh.

"Well, I'd better let you get inside." He seems disappointed as he prepares to say goodbye.

"Thank you so much…For coming out here to check on me… for sharing your story… Thank you."

"You're welcome." He goes to turn toward his car but stops abruptly and turns. "So you'll be back next week, right?" His face lights up, almost as if he's hoping I'll say yes. It makes the back of my neck tingle, and I swallow a smile.

"Unless another sickness claims us all, but yes, I should be back."

An unhindered smile breaks across his face. "Good, because I missed my partner. It's you and me, Annie. I'll see ya." He tosses me a wave and strides over to his car, a polished silver Acura sedan. A bit spendy for a dance instructor and stage actor, but who am I to judge another's budgeting? I watch him open the door, slide in, start the ignition, and back out of the driveway and onto the road. I wave absently, going over everything that just happened: his surprise visit, his shared story, the closeness I felt while listening to him. It makes me wonder, should I be letting more people in? Am I allowing myself to feel my own emotions, or am I just borrowing from others, alive and deceased? And if that's the case, how will I ever find joy again, let alone bring others joy?

12

Stride

A separation/transfer of weight

    Jason hollers out in his sleep, sending me rolling out of the way just in time before his palm slams down on my side of the mattress. His fingers clutch the sheets, the muscles of his forearm tensed in the invisible altercation racing through his sleeping mind. I kneel next to the bed and try saying his name, calmly but forcefully. I need to wake him. I always need to wake him up when he does this, which has started happening more frequently.

    "Jason! Jason, it's just a dream. You're fine."

    He flips over and buries his face in my pillow, pulling the sides in as he burrows desperately for cover. His moans of distress increase in volume, and I worry the kids are going to wake up. I reach out carefully to touch his bare back, rigid and knotted in battle.

    "Jason. I need you to wake up. Come back to me. Just wake up and come back." As my hand lands more firmly on his shoulder blade, his body freezes. His thrashing stills, and he slowly lifts his head, surveying his surroundings with bleary eyes.

"There you go. You're fine. It was just a dream," I breathe out, only then noticing the tightness in my own body as it starts to relax. My heart continues to pound in my ears with the rush of adrenaline, but I focus on Jason's pupils, watching them slowly constrict back to normal as his body moves up and down with his heaving breaths.

He reaches out to trail his fingers down my cheek, and he lifts himself up so he is propped on his elbow and angled toward me where I crouch on the floor. "Annie. Are you okay?"

I sigh with relief, a nervous laugh escaping my lungs as I press my face into his caress. "Am I okay? I'm fine. The question is are you okay?" It shouldn't be a surprise he would ask me this. He always asks after he wakes from one of his nightmares. And I always give the same response. Even if I'm not fine.

Because I'm not. I'm scared one of these nights, I won't wake up in time. I'm scared I won't be able to wake him up. And I'm scared it's getting worse and happening more.

"Come here." He leans over and pulls me up and over to him, cradling me into his chest. I curl my arms around his shoulders, my hand resting at the back of his neck. Our breathing begins to sync, our mouths so close we are inhaling and exhaling the same air.

"You know I would never hurt you," he whispers, his mouth moving to the sensitive skin of my neck.

"I know," I say, closing my eyes and leaning into the tender touches now dipping beneath my sleep shirt and across my lower back. "I just worry…" I let myself admit, a confession in the dark between lovers. "I worry I'm losing you."

He tips my face up to his with his free hand, while the arm across my back pulls me tighter against the hardness of his body. "Hey, you're not losing me. I'm right here." As if to prove it, he crushes his mouth to mine. Shaken by the possibility of losing him, I choose to now lose myself in him, and I match his intensity with every touch, kiss, and sound. Our kisses deepen, and he flips my body flush beneath his as I bring my knees up, holding him to me as he fits his hips between my legs. This is how I can keep him, make sure he doesn't slip too far away, and anchor him to his real life with me and the kids.

My fingers dig into the flesh of his back as his mouth moves across my skin, eventually pushing my shirt up to land on my bare breast where he takes my nipple into his mouth, my body arching in response. His hand finds its way between our pressed bodies, where he slides beneath the hem of my underwear and touches me in the way that always sends my body trembling with shocks of pleasure.

He growls against my mouth and increases his pace, my own hips moving against his hold as I beg for release. He sighs as my body quavers while riding the waves of climax, releases himself from the bind of his underwear, and fits himself firmly against me, both of us groaning with relief as he slides into me, pressure building with each thrust.

I cling to him, his body actively retreating from the nightmares as my body desperately seeks refuge within the shelter of his. Our eyes lock as he reaches his peak, the dark and stormy swirls in his eyes finally clearing into an unclouded sea of green, and we lay there, our bodies flushed and misted with sweat, neither one of us wanting to move nor break the spell of our own private world.

"I love you," he whispers in my ear before he pulls himself from me and heads for the bathroom.

"I love you, too," I say, my voice chasing after him as his naked silhouette disappears in the shadow of night.

I shouldn't feel so empty, his body having just joined with mine. I shouldn't feel so alone, having been as physically close as two people can be. But as I lay there in the dark, a coldness sweeps across my skin along with a fear that next time I might not be enough to pull him out of his tortured past. And I'll be left empty. And alone.

~ ~ ~

It's another Saturday night alone with nothing but wine and Net-flix to keep me company. After the week's sickness and a tumultuous day filled with tired whining, fighting, and crying, I am ready to hide away from everyone and everything else.

I am cocooned under the covers of my bed and gearing up the streamer's logo when a text chimes on my phone. Everyone who would contact me and not charge a call fee is under this very roof, so I flip my phone over quickly, wondering what spam text has decided to grace me with its delivery on a Saturday evening.

As I read, a smile twitches the corners of my mouth. There's no name, just an unsaved number, but from the context, I can pinpoint the source immediately.

Checking to make sure you had a better rest of the week and are still planning on dancing with me on Tuesday. I hope it's okay I texted this number. Please don't tell on me, but I continue to abuse my access to the registration spreadsheet.

I laugh out loud at Milo's candor. If it were anyone else, I would probably ignore the message, explaining I fell asleep, or my kids deleted it, but Milo's persistence and honesty surprisingly continues to win me over; my desire to clam up and run away is getting smaller with each new interaction.

The already-consumed half of my first glass of wine gives me a modicum of liquid courage, and I decide on a friendly spar. I quickly type, *Who dis?* and wait for the three dots. Not even ten seconds later, I receive a brief and factual *This is Milo*. Oh no. The poor guy really thinks I have this many people texting me that I would have no idea who he is? Or maybe he doesn't appreciate snark. I quickly tap out a reply, still playful, but making sure he can comprehend my sarcasm.

Yeah, sorry, I have so many dance instructors that I get them confused.

This earns the response of a laughing emoji, and I take another gulp of wine and settle into show surfing while focusing most of my attention on the text conversation.

Kidding, of course. Yes, the week was better. Much less vomiting and crying. My kids were even better, too. I wonder if he will understand the reference to my brother and realize too late I may have just handed the image of myself vomiting and crying on a silver platter, forever soiling his idea of me. *Nah, it's fine.* As I tell my kids, everyone poops, pees, pukes, you know, all the gross stuff in life. Nothing to be embarrassed about. I attempt to use this bravado in my next message, which could also work as a distraction just in case my last text didn't land successfully. *And on an unrelated note, who would I tell on you to?*

Ha ha. You're in a sassy mood tonight. I don't know how I feel about Milo calling me sassy, but my cheeks burn and I bite my lip.

I'm drinking wine. Might as well be honest.

I see. Are you out with friends?

I type faster than I think through my answer. *What friends? That's it, Annie, make him pity you.*

A frowny face emoji pops up on my phone screen. Instead of waiting for some awkward response, I try to amend my wrongdoing. *No. Very much in. Kids are asleep and I'm in bed, drinking wine and watching TV like the badass I am.* I'm curious as to what is keeping him talking to me. If he's just at home, lazing around like me, maybe it's just a way to pass the time. I go ahead and bite the bullet. *What are you up to?*

Out with friends.

Oh, so he's not at home. He's actually socializing and having a life. Then why the hell is he wasting his time texting me? Another short response pops up as I am questioning his sanity.

Karaoke.

Sounds fun. I used to love karaoke, but it was never Jason's favorite, so it was on the rare occasion we would stumble into a karaoke bar. However, once we had kids, spontaneous stumbling wasn't even an option.

You should come out sometime.

It's my turn to send a laughing emoji. Seriously, is he for real? I can't believe an attractive, talented man almost ten years my junior would actually want to hang out with me. I jot out a fiery response. If he's just playing with me, I need to shut it down.

I'm a 35-year-old widow with two kids. What fun would I be? My fingers tap on the comforter as I wait nervously for his response.

I think you are LOADS of fun. Stop selling yourself short. I stare at his message, stunned by his brashness. Another bubble pops up.

See you Tuesday?

I respond with a thumbs up, a bit unsure how to reply to his insinuating he wants to hang out with me beyond class. Is this normal instructor-pupil confidence building, or is this flirting? I haven't been single for over fifteen years. I'm so unsure of everything. I see the dots showing he's writing or reading, but I decide to ask a pretty important question, in case this is flirting.

What is your last name, elusive dance instructor?

Why? Are you going to report me?

No. Just hoping to return the favor with a bit of my own stalking.

First a smiley face, then a simple, *Warner.*

OK, Milo Warner. I will see you Tuesday.

Can't wait.

I can't help smiling as I create the contact information for Milo Warner and settle in, pretending to watch *The Vampire Diaries* while re-reading our text conversation over and over for the next hour.

13

Tap

*To touch the inside edge of the ball of
the free foot to the floor without weight*

I'm sitting in Dr. Collins's office, listening to the tick of the clock, the soundtrack to our silence. A large white face, inky black Roman numerals, and a thin ring of dark brown wood stare back at me as I try to answer his question about why I was so quick to lose my temper.

It was because of an incident at home that arose as I was trying to leave for my appointment. Inspired by a recent viewing of *Edward Scissorhands*, Thatcher gave all of Penny's Barbies jagged, geometric haircuts. Her ensuing meltdown threatened to make me late, which caused me to lash out, screaming at both kids, and resulting in all of us crying.

"I was going to be late, and I didn't want to insult you." This is true. I hate being late, which unfortunately is an occupational hazard of being a parent, especially a single parent.

"I would have understood, plus, I still get paid." He smiles at his own confession. I frown at him, but actually, I'm pleasantly surprised by his hint of playfulness. Most of the time it is business and bore with Dr. Collins, which is definitely the professional and non-law-suit-inducing route for a shrink, but I like seeing more of the human within. It makes me want to invest more of myself, which is also a shocking revelation unto itself.

"Well, yeah, but I want to be here."

"Do you *want* to be here, or do you *have* to be here?"

"Both?" Pursed lips and squinted eyes tell me to try again. "I *want* to be here. I do."

"Do you?" he asks without a beat.

"Of course, I'm paying for it, aren't I?"

"Yes, but can you explain to me why you want to be here, but not take other opportunities to talk about what happened and how you are doing with others in similar situations?" Okay, way to forge past the passive-aggressiveness and just jump right into blatant confrontation. He's always been so damn adamant about the support group. I have no idea why he seems to take it so personally. It's not like he gets paid extra if I go, but the guy acts like it would redeem my soul or something. To match his blatant attack, I go on the defensive.

"To be fair, we don't know if it's similar. We're only making assumptions."

He takes his glasses off and examines the lenses. "Annie, at some point you have to come to terms—"

"I *have* come to terms," I say flatly, hoping to put an end to this probing. The moment of silence as he replaces his glasses allows me to think of a valid response. "Anyway, I *am* talking to someone. My dance instructor came over and talked to me about his past experience."

A pause filled with blank staring precedes his reply. "Your dance instructor? From ballroom class?"

"Yeah."

"He showed up at your house?"

"Uhhh, yeah."

"When?"

"Last Tuesday when I missed class." I didn't realize I was going to be interrogated for my adult interactions beyond dance class. I thought this was what Dr. Collins wanted. I wait, confused, as he looks off into the far corner of the room, as if working out some complex theory.

Finally, he takes a breath, his shoulders rising, and says, "So what did you two talk about?" Interest piques in his voice. I adjust my position in the chair, hoping this is a new, better direction and give him a watered-down version of Milo's story. He listens attentively, his face void of reaction. When I'm done, he asks, "So how is that different from group therapy?"

"Well, it's not a group. And I'm not being forced to share. I was just listening to a…to a friend…and getting to know him more." I look down to inspect my cuticles, my cheeks heating with the thought of our casual texting.

Dr. Collins looks at me through narrowed eyes. "Annie, are you starting to have feelings for this man?"

"What? No! Huh?" I blurt out dumbly.

Again, he removes his glasses to fiddle with them. I'm starting to get suspicious the glasses tic is a cue of bad news. "Do you think it is wise to get involved with anyone while you are still grieving, especially in your situation—"

"My situation! Please stop saying my situation. It makes it sound like I'm trapped!"

"Do you feel trapped?"

I make a move to refute but find myself speechless, gaping at him open-mouthed. He repeats the question as I search the walls for answers. As my gaze lands back on him, I sigh and answer.

"Yes."

I do feel trapped. It's no secret that having children is a lifelong commitment and one not to be tread into lightly. I knew what I was signing up for. Heck, there was a time I thought I wanted another, but I never thought I'd be doing it alone. I planned on having a part-ner to share the burden, the joy, and the years. With Jason gone, it's all on me, and when I make a mistake, there's no one else to blame or help fix the problem. There's no way out; it's just how life ended up, but it doesn't mean I don't get angry about it.

Dr. Collins takes my admittance and expands, almost reading my mind. "Is that why you get angry? Because you feel trapped?" I nod and he takes the cue to continue. "So you keep it together as much as possible, but sometimes, especially when you are being kept from something meant especially for you, you can't help but explode, right?"

"Is that messed up?" I plead silently for him to give me a straight answer. Tell me I'm a bad mom and I'll just accept it, or tell me it will get better.

"It's normal for any parent, Annie, and given your sit–what you have gone through, it's perfectly understandable." He smiles like he truly understands, and I feel my chest expand with the emotion I've been trying to tamp down with distraction and sarcasm. He asks another question, a bit quieter. "What makes you feel less trapped?"

I sit back and cross my arms over my chest, thinking of the answer I want to give versus the truth. I want to be able to say seeing my children laugh, learn, and get along makes me feel less trapped; but in all honesty, any thought of them feels tethered to an invisible anchor keeping me rooted in place. I wish I could say that talking to Dr. Collins or even my brother makes me feel better, but it actually makes me feel worse, realizing all that I'm doing wrong, which just sends me into a thought spiral of shame. And work, well shit, who in the history of the world has ever claimed working from their home office, chained to a computer screen and a set of cheap headphones, has made them feel anything but trapped?

So what makes me feel less trapped?

"Dancing. Dancing makes me feel less trapped," I blurt out. Dr. Collins nods with raised eyebrows, encouraging me to continue. "Enjoying music again, doing something for myself, meeting new people beyond those who live in my house or only know me as Jason's widow– that makes me feel…alive. And yeah, maybe even flirting with my cute dance instructor, but it's harmless. I just…I just want to feel like my own person again. I still want to be the best mother I can be, but I need to know I can be a good person who can stand on my own because…well, because I have to…because Jason left me alone, whether on purpose or not." I breathe in deeply through my nose and exhale through my mouth, trying to calm the squeezing in my chest.

Dr. Collins looks up at the clock and stands. "Well, it's time. Go feel a bit freer, and I'll talk to you next week. Call me if you need anything."

I glance between him and the clock, almost in a daze brought on by my deep, dark revelations. My eyes feel blurry and my stomach feels as if it is caving in on itself, but it's time to dance, and if I'm going to talk it up that much, I better show some enthusiasm.

When I get into my car and turn the ignition, the stereo clock blinks in bright green, and I bite back a smile at the fact there are only fifty more minutes before I get to see Milo again. And even though I just told my therapist it was harmless flirting, I'm worried I might have been lying. And lying in therapy always has a way of being revealed in the end.

When I walk into the dance studio ten minutes before class, Milo beams at me, his spotlight of attention almost paralyzing. I decide to walk straight into the gleam of his focus and meet the evening head-on. "Hello, Milo Warner."

His smile widens as he responds, "Why, hello, Annie Obless. Ready to dance tonight?" He holds out his hand, a Regency noble-man requesting my partnership. There's no hesitation in me tonight. I place my palm in his.

One hour later, we watch the last couple exit the studio before we lose ourselves in a fit of laughter. I am doubled over, unable to catch my breath, as I revisit the images of everyone trying to learn the two dances of the night: the quickstep and the swing. It was mad-ness. Like a Pentecostal church on a Saturday night, complete with jerky moves and speaking in tongues. Bodies were everywhere, wig-gling to the beat, bumping into other couples, and even sprawling across the floor a few times. Poor Lorraine—Dave tried to incorpo-rate a fancy lift into the swing before they were ready. She'll be icing her ass tonight, for sure. The surprising stars of the night were actu-ally Mary and Leo, whom I was happy to see were intense in their focus and refrained from any arguing. No one can deny the power of dance after seeing the evolution in those two. I share my observations with Milo through broken laughter.

He points at me with playful accusation. "Hey, don't go throwing stones. I don't think I've had my foot stepped on so much in my life. Be honest, was I just not in my teaching element tonight?"

I point back, glaring with amusement. "I'm rusty. I missed a week. And you just threw me into it!"

He raises his hands in surrender. "Okay, okay. I admit, it wasn't my best class. Maybe I shouldn't put those two dances together."

"I think the steps got a bit confusing." I wince with blunt honesty.

"Even with a break between?"

"Well, yeah. It's a lot of code switching. Plus, we don't know it as well as you. All these moves are just being filed in our brains and tumbling out on the floor as we try to keep up." I shrug. "But it's still fun. Don't be too hard on yourself."

"Well, I have to admit, I was a bit distracted tonight." As we've been talking, we've drifted back toward each other, our bodies recognizing the nearness we've experienced the last hour. As always when we're so close, I have to look up to meet his downward gaze, and as I do, I gulp at the way his eyes are skimming over my bare shoulders and down to my spandex-clad hips and butt. I opted for workout gear again, wearing an athletic tank and skin-tight yoga pants. They're no Lululemon, which has apparently sponsored Ted and Nathan for the duration of class, but it allowed me to move and sweat freely while still feeling and looking good. And guessing from Milo's attention, I think he shares the same opinion.

"Oh really? Whatever by?" I ask about the source of his distraction, trying to keep it blithe and lighthearted, but I have played this game before and I can read the signs. Granted, I haven't played in a while, but still. It's like a bike, as the saying goes. However, I can't focus on the exact wording of that platitude because he raises his hand and catches a stray tendril of my hair, letting it slide through his fingers. I stop my attempt at laughing, my breathing quickening.

"I was excited to see you. And maybe a bit nervous you wouldn't show after…you know, after I shared all that heavy stuff with you." His voice is deep and husky, his eyes still wandering over my face and body.

"Yeah…I…I was excited to see you. Excited to dance tonight. And…I appreciate you sharing your story with me. It was…helpful." Not the way to lean into the mood, but I'm just trying not to burst out in girlish giggles.

"Helpful?" His eyebrows raise, and he slips a bit back into business voice.

"Just to get a new perspective, I guess."

We hold each other's gaze until he looks down and grabs my left hand in both of his. He strokes my forearm with his left as his right fingers weave together with mine. The intimacy of his touch causes my breath to catch, but I don't retreat. It feels nice, even thrilling. We both stare, captivated by his exploration of my palm. "You know, you could share your story with me sometime…if you want."

"Uh, maybe. But, not tonight. I was already at therapy. This is supposed to be my escape from all that." Maybe a bit too harsh, but I'm wading into new territory here, territory I wasn't even sure existed. Yeah, I may have dabbled with the idea Milo was flirting with me and had fun entertaining the idea I could flirt back, but this is now slipping into undeniable interest, and I'm not quite sure if I'm mentally prepared for this tonight.

"Okay. In that case, I was wondering if you wanted to stay a bit longer? I could teach you the dances you missed from last week." He looks hopeful and, dare I say, desirous.

"I do have to get back, but I probably have time to learn one. Maybe I can learn the other one another time?" I really do want to learn the dance, but I don't want to push myself too far. Not yet.

"Yeah, we can do that." He releases my hand and takes a step back. Apparently, he has picked up on my deer-in-headlights reaction and is giving me space. He smiles, and he's back to just your friendly neighborhood dance instructor. "So, as you know from the review at the start of class, we did the Viennese waltz and the cha-cha. What are you feeling?"

I hate myself for being so gutless, but I pick the dance I know will require the least amount of contact. I've had a bit of experience with Latin dancing, and even though there's suggestive hip action, there's a lot of solo movement.

"How about the cha-cha?"

"Great. Just give me a second to take this off." My body stiffens with shock at the words, but relax momentarily as I realize he's talking about his crewneck. However, when he lifts his shirt, the hem of his white T-shirt underneath reveals a sliver of sculpted abdominal muscle below the navel, and one glimpse is enough to make my thighs melt.

He notices me staring and looks down at his forearms. He grimaces as he asks, "Is this okay? I make sure to keep them covered up for class, but it's so hot in here and I thought since you already knew…"

I rush to answer and try to save face at the same time. "Uh, yes. Of course. It doesn't bother me, really. Please. I want you to be comfortable."

"Cool. Thanks." His adorable half-grin sends me floating. He beckons to me. "Okay, now come stand next to me, and we'll practice in front of the mirror. How familiar are you with Latin dances?"

I answer half-heartedly, "A little bit" and let him go into his spiel about the Cuban origin and importance of the dance. As we go through the side steps, walking movement, and rocking steps, I try to pay attention, though my gaze sometimes lingers on the reflection of his lean torso, long legs, or toned arms. After we've gone through the steps, I make a break for it, telling him I forgot to text Nick who'll be worrying about me, what with the traffic and all. We holler an abrupt goodbye. Once I've closed the door, I drop my head to the steering wheel and let the self-flagellation begin.

I feel a mix of excitement, embarrassment, and guilt. Milo was definitely sending me signals, and the fact a younger man as talented and handsome as Milo would show any interest is a bit intoxicating. However, I acted like a complete idiot. He either thinks I am disinterested, or he thinks I am just ignorant of basic cues any middle schooler could notice. And finally, I can't believe I am reacting to another man the same way I once did with my husband. Sure, it's not like I'm dead; I'm obviously going to find other men attractive. Heck, I certainly did throughout my marriage. But my husband is dead, and that adds a whole other layer to the guilt spiral. Am I really ready to jump back into the dating pool, and if I am, does that mean I'm a bad wife, a bad mother, and an overall bad person?

Dancing was supposed to make me feel less trapped, but as I drive home to the prison of motherhood, I feel more trapped than ever, stuck between the reality of my life and the possibility of what I might want but don't know if I deserve.

14

Collect

*Bringing the knee and foot underneath
so blocks of weight are lined up*

~ Fourteen Months Prior: March 22 ~

The kids are asleep, and I'm finally able to climb under the covers of our cushy bed and put an end to another hectic day. I hear sounds of Jason piddling around in the bathroom: the water from the faucet as he brushes his teeth, the soft thud of a hand towel as he sets it down after washing and drying his face, and the general scuffle of items moving on the counter and his feet shifting across the tile floor. I sink into bed, listening to the comforting noise of my husband's presence after so many nights without it.

He moves into the doorway, leaning against the doorframe as he brushes his teeth. The lean bulk of his body blocks the bathroom light and sends a long shadow stretching across our comforter and my extended legs. I watch him in silence, both of us lost in thought and relishing the quiet until I break it with supposed pleasantry.

"So did you have a good day?" Work has been a tough topic of

conversation lately. Many items of discussion have been red-flagged, a minefield of anger and annoyance, but I desperately want to bring him back, to be with him, to connect. So I tread lightly, watching my steps but still edging forward.

He shrugs, gestures toward his suds-filled mouth, and makes his way back into the bathroom to spit and rinse. When done, he maneuvers around the foot of the bed and comes to perch on the edge next to me. I wait in respectful silence, but I prompt him with a pointed stare.

"It is what it is." This usual maxim annoys me because it gives zero information except a sense of reluctant acceptance, a trait I fear has been coloring our interactions for quite some time.

"Jason, you can talk to me, you know." He looks down and starts picking at the blanket. I reach up and cradle his face in my hand, his cheek rough on my palm with two-day scruff. He lets his head fall into my hold, resting his worries for a brief moment before rising up and away. "I've just noticed your night terrors have been worse, when you even make it to bed—"

"It's just a lot, Annie. At work, I have to make all these decisions, I'm in charge of all these people, and no matter how in control I am, there will still be mistakes and death. And then when I get home, the kids are loud and combative. I love being with them, but I just need time to wind down." I nod as I listen and reach out to hold his hand as he continues. "I'm sorry that I haven't been around as much."

"I miss you, honey."

"I know. I miss you, too." He adjusts his seat and leans down to rest his head in my lap. I run my hand through his hair, slightly damp from his quick facial rinse.

"We need to make time for each other. I feel like we haven't been connecting very much lately."

"I'm trying, Annie. I want to be there for you and the kids. But I need to be there for everyone at work, too."

"I know, honey. I know." We sit in content silence as I massage his scalp. His eyes close, relishing the moment of calm. When he leans up and away, I'm disappointed at the break in contact.

"I need to do a few things down in the office. A bit of paperwork I didn't have time to finish up today. Is that okay?" He laces his fingers with mine, grazing the length of them with his fingertips while waiting for my response.

"Yeah, of course. Do you want me to wait up for you?"

"No, you don't have to."

"Well, I'm going to read for a bit anyway. I'd like some time alone with you, at some point. Tomorrow, maybe we can wake up before the kids and..." I waggle my eyebrows suggestively and his face brightens.

"Morning sex? Oh, we haven't done that..." his hands move to my thigh and start squeezing, moving upward until he cups the soft cotton covering my right breast.

"I know." I coyly shoo his hand away, causing him to chuckle low in his throat.

"Well, in that case, set an alarm." He leans down and kisses me, his lips soft in contrast to the roughness of his incoming beard. "I love you."

"Love you."

"Good night, beautiful." He rises from the bed and heads out of the room. He stops and smiles back at me before disappearing into the hall, and I smile to myself as I pick up my book. Eventually, I doze off, my mind drifting between the story in my hands and the anticipation of the following morning.

15

Follow Through

*The passing of the moving leg and foot
underneath the body between steps*

That Saturday morning I wake up to the sound of heavy mouth breathing and find myself drowning in a tangle of tiny limbs. I was aware Penny had crept in around four, but Thatcher must have snuck in sometime after. Since I have a child tucked into each side of me, I lift my head carefully to check the digital clock on the bedside table. It's 7:08 AM on May 20—Thatcher's seventh birthday.

I look up at the ceiling and sigh. I've made a load of grand promises today, trying to make up for the dumpster fire that was last year's birthday. It was two months after Jason's death, and I was not thriving as a single parent. Nick hadn't moved in yet, and I was struggling with the balance of returning to a full-time work schedule, getting the kids ready for daycare and school, while also dealing with the financial fallout of a spousal death. At that time, I still wasn't able to sleep in my own bedroom—that would take another two months—and I was honestly unaware of the day, let alone the week. I committed one of the worst parental transgressions: I forgot Thatcher's birthday. When Nick showed up at the front door in the afternoon with an over-sized present, a dinosaur balloon, and an eager grin, I nearly screamed. Luckily, Thatcher was still at school, so Nick worked on decorating the kitchen, and I stopped by Walgreens and grabbed what I could find from the toy aisle. I vaguely remember Pokémon cards, a model car, and some sort of squishy ball that lasted less than a month.

When Thatcher arrived home, he was all abuzz about wearing the birthday hat as his class sang to him. When he asked why I hadn't sent him with treats, I made up some lie about not wanting to give him too many sweets in one day. I let him choose where we went to dinner and what we watched on television, sending treats on Monday. It worked out in the end, but part of me thinks Thatcher knew I had forgotten and was just trying to help me out. A kid shouldn't have to do that for his mother.

Here's hoping I can redeem myself this year.

Thatcher suddenly mewls and rolls over, his stale morning breath assaulting my face. I watch him blink his eyes open, and I can't help but smile at the slow realization dawning across his face as he remembers what day it is.

"Good morning, buddy! Happy birthday!" I whisper, not wanting to wake Penny. My sweet boy smiles at me and leans in for a hug. I direct us to scoot out of his side of the bed, and we tiptoe downstairs, opting for some Mommy-Thatcher alone time.

"What does my seven-year-old son want for breakfast this morning?" I deliver the question in a singsong voice which makes him squirm giddily as he shouts for chocolate chip waffles. His head looks too big for his skinny body in his tight Spiderman pajamas, and it reminds me we've been without Jason for over a year, Thatcher being a whole year smaller the last time Jason saw him. My eyes mist up, and I start digging in the cupboards for the waffle maker and my ingredients.

Heavy steps alert me to Nick's appearance from the basement. His voice is still croaky with sleep as he squats, holds his arms open, and hollers out a birthday greeting. Thatcher jumps off his chair and runs into his uncle's arms. Nick swings him up onto his hip and carries him over to my side where I'm starting to measure out dry ingredients.

"Oooh, waffles. My favorite! Thanks, sis!" Nick makes a move as if to steal the bowl of breakfast pre-op.

"They're for me! It's *my* birthday breakfast!" Thatcher states through breathless giggles, slapping at Nick's arms.

"What? Well, are you at least going to share?" he pleads, which causes Thatcher to laugh even more raucously. This turns into a tickle fight in which Nick is always the winner. After Thatcher's on the floor —safely away from any more tickles and regaining his breathing— he asks loudly, "Uncle Nick, are you going to spend the whole day with us?"

"Oh, sorry, buddy, but I have to work today." He shifts his attention to me to add details, watching as I separate the egg yolks from the egg whites. "We're starting in on designing the shelving for the library, and we don't want to get behind." He swivels back to Thatcher. "But I'll be here for dinner."

"Noooo! Now what am I going to do?" Thatcher cries dramatically.

I freeze in my breakfast preparation to confront him with a shocked retort. "Hey, I'm going to be with you all day!"

"I know, but Uncle Nick is funner." He sets his head in his hands, pouting on the kitchen floor.

"More fun," I correct him as I turn and try not to reveal how hurt I am by that comment. I get it. As the mom, I spend most of my time nagging them about cleaning up their messes, eating their vegetables, and leaving the cat and each other alone; but it'd be nice to be considered the fun parent once in a while, especially when I'm the only parent left.

"Hey, that's not true. Your mom is super fun. Did she ever tell you about the time she took me to a petting zoo and let me get in the pen with the donkey—" My eyes widen with urgency, and I interrupt this inappropriate story.

"Nope, haven't told him and not going to."

"Aww, why not, sis? It's how I learned about the birds and the bees. Maybe it's time—"

"Stop!" I put up my hand to halt any further discussion. I point at Thatcher. "You, go wash your hands if you want to help me with waffles. You," I point at Nick, "stop talking or else no waffles for you." He mock-groans and disappears with Thatcher. So far, the birthday is off to a much better start, but it's still hard not to imagine Jason being the one opening his arms wide and catching Thatcher in a big birthday bear hug. I feel my eyes well up, and I prepare to whip the yolks, letting a sob sneak out, hidden by the whirring of the beater.

It's now three o'clock, and we have run through Thatcher's wish list for the day and are now trying to figure out what to do for the two hours before dinner with Uncle Nick. After chocolate chip waffles, we played superheroes, went for a bike ride around the block, painted with watercolors, went to a matinee showing of the latest Pixar movie, ate our weight in popcorn and candy, and just recently pulled his chocolate cake out of the oven. I'm trying to convince my impatient children we cannot frost a warm cake and should instead walk to the playground when the doorbell rings.

Thatcher and Penny stampede ahead of me, shoving each other in a contest over who gets to look out the window first. I sigh with frustration and follow, sorry for the poor individual who has dared set foot on our property.

"Mommy! It's the tall man again!" Thatcher bellows as he rips open the door, Penny on top of him, both confident their recognition of someone I've spoken to before gives them permission to open the door.

Through the child-sized opening of the front entrance, I hear a familiar voice say jovially, "Hi, kids! Is your mom around?" I look over my children's heads and see Milo Warner, apparent house-call dance instructor extraordinaire, in the flesh…again. He's dressed for an evening out in dark jeans and a black T-shirt underneath an opened vintage turquoise-and-black bowling shirt with the name Danny inscribed in cursive above the left breast pocket. His forearms are bare, but I don't even waste time bothering to glance at the scars I know live there as there is so much else to take in. His dark hair is slicked back in a greaser style from the 1950s, and I swear his brown eyes twinkle as they take in my shock at his appearance. Me, I'm wearing worn jeans and a *Star Wars* shirt, for the benefit of Thatcher, and the greater good of the galaxy, of course. Thatcher and Penny complete the family-bonding look with their paint-and-food-stained Mandalorian and Baby Yoda shirts. But no matter my reasoning, I am vastly aware my own appearance is a stark contrast from the tall drink of water standing in front of me.

Penny, always the last one to get the hint, points up at me and shouts, "Here she is! Here's Mommy!"

"Hey!" he says enthusiastically, and all I can croak out is a questioning hello.

"Sorry to just drop by, but I wanted to talk to you about something. If you aren't too busy, that is." He waits, hopeful, on the top step, the four of us wedged within a small area of square footage as my kids have slinked out to stand on the step, propping the door open with their bodies, requiring me to hold it open and lean forward.

"I, uh…oh, wow. I'm just surprised to see you here," I blurt out, not sure how to proceed before I completely squander any sense of cool.

"It's my birthday!" shouts Thatcher.

"It is?! That's awesome! Happy birthday!" Milo cheers as he squats to meet my son at eye level and asks, "How old are you, little man?"

Thatcher chooses now to play shy, twisting his hips and barely uttering out, "Seven."

"Seven is the best age." Milo holds up his hand for a high five, and Thatcher giggles as he slaps his small hand to Milo's.

"We're going to the park!" Penny announces. Here I was doing my best to persuade the kids to go to the park just moments ago, and all I was met with was reluctance. Now that she is telling a handsome visitor, it's the best idea ever.

"That sounds so fun!" My kids slurp up his attention like ice cream, squirming and laughing; meanwhile, I'm trying to get my bearings while watching him instantly win over my children. Any mother will admit "good with kids" is an instant turn-on.

I'm lost in watching the adorable interaction when Thatcher asks, "Do you want to come with us?"

"Oh, sweetie, I don't think Milo wants to go to the park—"

"I'd love to!" he interrupts, grinning as he meets my look of confusion. Then, just to add fuel to fire, he winks, and my heart actually skips a beat. What is this man's end game, here? Surely, he did not show up to hang around a single mom and her two loud and goofy kids?

Thatcher and Penny throw their arms up and whoop in celebration. I corral them back inside and direct them to put on shoes and bring a light jacket in case they get cold, even though summer heat is already starting to settle in the Illinois suburbs. I slip on a pair of shoes and step outside with Milo as we wait for the kids, the sounds of their hectic preparations traveling through the glass of the storm door.

Finally alone, I take the chance to talk to Milo without prying little ears. "You really don't have to come, you know."

"I know, but I want to. I love kids. They're always so happy."

A condescending laugh escapes me, and I quickly apologize. "I'm sorry, but that's not entirely accurate. Do you know how many times they tell me they hate me in a day? That I'm the meanest mommy ever?" I'd like to think it's a universal truth that kids can be having the best day of their lives one moment, especially around other people, but when they are alone with their parents, the melt-downs and verbal abuse tend to balance out the exuberance.

Milo responds casually, "Yeah, I suppose I did that to my mom, too, but it's always because I knew she would still be there after the nasty words were exchanged. I guess I took it for granted at times. Don't worry, someday they'll realize how lucky they are to have you."

The simple recognition of what I go through every day makes something within my chest bloom. I actually feel seen when I talk to Milo, and I haven't felt that way in such a long time. Nick sees his big sister, someone he needs to help out. Dr. Collins sees a patient, a project he must improve. Thatcher and Penny see their mom, the person who does everything for them. But when Milo looks at me, I don't sense any slapped-on labels. I feel like he just sees and responds to who I am at the time. And for a woman who isn't sure who that is, it's reassuring there's still hope that person will be worthy of acknowledgement.

I'm about to comment, to thank him for trying to ease my pain, but the quiet quickly explodes into two kids tumbling out of the front door, arguing about who gets to carry what. Their arms are full, and I demand some explanations.

"We want to bring these to the park!" Thatcher cries, holding out his arms, laden with a myriad of toys: Hot Wheels cars, a couple of action figures, two balls, and a stuffed Pikachu. Penny has her own treasure trove complete with a My Little Pony, her own stash of Hot Wheels cars, a drawing pad, and a baby doll. I step away from Milo and toward the kids, my hands on my hips.

"Absolutely not. Put it back."

"Why?" and "No!" are the answers from my ever-obedient children.

"Because, I'll end up being the one that has to carry everything. How about this, you can each bring one toy. One. That's it."

If alone, I'm sure they would continue to battle against my compromise, but since Milo is observing silently, they acquiesce in record time.

Penny chooses the baby doll and Thatcher decides on a squishy Chicago Cubs novelty baseball. I'm not familiar with the ball, and I ask Thatcher where he got it.

"Oh, Daddy bought it when he took me to the baseball game." That's right, two summers ago Jason and Thatcher had a father-son day in the city. The memory of my two boys, returning with new baseball caps and sunburnt ears and necks, knocks the wind out of me. No one seems to notice as Thatcher continues, pointing at Milo as he says, "I was hoping he could play with me since Daddy can't."

I go to open my mouth in protest, but Milo steps forward and holds out his hand. "Great idea, Thatcher. Say, will you show me the way to the park?" Thatcher places his hand in Milo's, and Penny begins squealing about wanting to hold his hand, too. Eventually, Milo is sandwiched between the two, throwing back the occasional smile as the kids prattle on about anything that crosses their mind, and I trail behind, having a hard time distinguishing between the image in front of me and memories of Jason doing this exact thing.

Grievances after One Hour at Playground:

- Thatcher plummeting from the monkey bars and getting the wind knocked out of him
- Penny welcoming a ball to the eye when Thatcher is hurling it at her a bit too forcefully (Thank goodness it's soft)

- Penny getting mulch in her eyes when Thatcher is throwing handfuls in the air
- Penny gaining too much speed on the slide, falling, and dirtying up her leggings from a hard landing on mulch
- Both kids complaining of being too hungry and thirsty to walk home on their own

Unexpected Pleasant Moments after One Hour at Playground:

- Thatcher running and hollering with excitement while playing an altered version of football with Milo while using the Chicago Cubs squishy ball (which eventually hit Penny in the eye)
- Penny showing off her courageousness when asking Milo to push her higher on the swing
- Milo talking to my kids like they are actual people (some adults forget kids are, you know, actual people)
- Milo showing off his robot dance moves to Penny and Thatcher who painstakingly try to copy his moves with little success, but much laughter
- Milo offering to give turns to each kid and carry them on his shoulders as we walk back to the house
- Walking back home, making small talk as the kids point out neighborhood landmarks

We arrive back at the house just as Nick is pulling into the driveway. Milo lifts Thatcher off of his shoulders, groaning dramatically as he places him on the sidewalk. The kids run over to Nick's truck hollering "Uncle Nick!" and shouting out versions of the day. Milo and I watch the scene of reunion in comfortable silence, his hands in his pockets and my arms crossed over my chest. Nick picks a kid up in each arm, balances them on his hips, and walks over.

"Hey, man. I'm Nick. I'd shake your hand, but—" he jostles the kids and they burst into staccato giggles.

"I'll shake his hand!" Penny announces, and she and Thatcher go back and forth grabbing Milo's hand. He plays along, and I have no idea where his patience comes from. It reminds me of Jason, usually more capable of keeping his cool when I was about to blast off with anger. Seeing Milo with my children is grounding while also leaving me feeling as if I am floating in the stars.

I'm brought back to earth by the kids' laughter and I catch Milo introducing himself to Nick. "Actually, I didn't get the chance to formally meet you, but I was here a couple weeks back when your house was stricken with the plague." His eyes dart to the side and an upward quirk of his lips makes me smile at the memory of my embarrassing outburst.

"Oh, yeah, that was horrible. But it only made me stronger." The kids giggle and interject with musings of a superhero or elephant. Nick continues over their silly outbursts. "I wish I could say I've heard lots about you, but Annie's kept it top secret. You must be her guilty pleasure or something—"

"Enough, Nick," I say through gritted teeth, chiding my annoying little brother.

The annoyance continues when he asks, "So what are you doing here? Is Annie getting private dance lessons or something?" He looks over at me and smiles conspiratorially. I meet his suggestive grin with a pointed glare.

Milo just breezes off any awkwardness with a lighthearted chuckle. "No, not here on business today. Purely pleasure." He turns to me and winks, and my face instantly heats up. It reaches volcanic temperatures when I notice my brother gawking.

He manages to bring his jaw up for casual conversation. "Well, we were going to have this big guy's birthday dinner. Would you want to join us?" This was probably something I should have said, but I'm still hiding under my scarlet cloak of embarrassment, so luckily Nick has assumed man-of-the-house responsibilities. Thatcher and Penny start shouting about cake and pleading with Milo to stay. In response, he pulls his phone out, the first time I've seen it this entire afternoon, and winces. "Actually, I do have plans, but I appreciate the invite. Thanks." The kids express their disappointment with exaggerated cries of dissent, and he steps closer and locks eyes with the birthday boy himself. "Maybe another time, huh, Thatch?" He holds his hand out for knuckles, and Thatcher reluctantly bumps Milo's fist with his own, whining with disappointment, but the kid is floating on cloud nine from all the special attention he has received today, and he can't help but grin.

"Annie, I'll go ahead and take these two hooligans inside. You want me to order the pizza?"

"No, I already put in an online order. It should be delivered here within twenty minutes."

"Perfect. I need a shower. And so do you two stinky butts!" He starts walking backward, shaking the kids with exaggeration. "Milo, nice to meet you. Thanks for all your help going above and beyond with my sister." He turns to me. "Sis, I expect to see a full-out program at the end of your dance class matriculation."

If I had something to throw at him, I would, but I'm empty-handed, and I don't want Milo seeing how volatile I can be, so I just glare and give the fakest smile possible. Nick and the kids shout out a few more goodbyes before disappearing into the house.

"Wow, they are overflowing with energy," Milo says fondly as he stares at the calm space once filled with fervent energy. I'm lost in the moment as I stare at this profile of a man who has been so gentle, so earnest, and so enthusiastic with my children. A pang of longing shoots through my chest as I once again am reminded of Jason and his paternal presence.

I pull myself out of memory with a forced apology. "Sorry, I didn't mean for you to get sucked into a playground playdate."

He shakes his head. "No, really, I loved it. I haven't been to a playground in ages. I think I've mastered the monkey bars finally." He smiles and lifts his eyebrows triumphantly.

I swipe playfully at his arm. "I don't think it counts if you're tall enough to walk under it." We share in the amusement of remembering how much the kids got a kick out of him doing just that. Something dawns on me. "Hey, what brought you out here in the first place? Surely it wasn't merely to crash a seven-year-old's birthday?"

Realization widens his eyes, sending them to focus on a distant corner before coming back to my face. "No, but it ended up being a happy coincidence. Yeah, I completely forgot I came here to ask if you would maybe want to come watch my show next weekend. Remember, I'm in *Rent*, and it's opening night on Thursday. There are two more evening shows on Friday and Saturday, and a matinee on Sunday. It runs for three weeks." He's rambling as he runs a hand through his hair, a clue to his trepidation at asking me. His vulnerability is endearing as he assesses my reaction. "So, would you maybe consider coming to watch?"

I haven't been away from the kids on a weekend night in such a long time. When Jason's mom, Maggie, came and stayed for a few weeks after the funeral, Nick and I went for a drink at Applebee's. I ended up getting sloppy drunk and having to be carried up to my bedroom. Maggie was witness to my intoxicated breakdown, and that was just the start to her doubting my ability to take care of the kids, which led to a whole other slew of issues that still vex me. While it may have all worked out for the best, Maggie's and my relationship remains less than cordial. And that's why I don't go to Applebee's anymore. Okay, so that's not true, but it sure would be nice to have an adult night out that didn't end up with me wrapped around a toilet and commiserating about all of my life choices.

"Uh, yeah. I can't do Thursday or Friday night. I know Nick has work Thursday and a thing Friday. A date, maybe? Oh man, does he have a date?" I get sidetracked by this forgotten detail, and Milo politely clears his throat, bringing me back to the topic of our conversation. "But I'll check and see if he can watch the kids Saturday."

"Really?" The shield of indifference he's been holding instantly disappears with the happy inflection in his voice once I agree. "Great. Maybe we can get a drink or something after?"

"Um, sure, I might be able to." *As long as it's not Applebee's*, I think.

"Great!" he repeats. We stare for a minute before I break the tension.

"Well, I need to get in there," I say as I point a thumb towards the house. "I'm sure Thatcher is currently trying to persuade Nick to let him open his presents."

"He wouldn't be a seven-year-old boy if he didn't. He's a great kid. Both of them are. Thanks for letting me join in the celebrations today."

"Are you kidding me? Thank *you* for coming. You made their day, really. You helped me redeem myself after his sixth birthday." He raises an eyebrow in questioning. "Eh, first birthday after his dad's passing. Let's just say, I wasn't on my A game."

"Well, I'm glad I could help. And really, I had a lot of fun. With them and with you." He looks back down at his phone, curses under his breath, taps out a response, and puts his phone back in his pocket. "I really need to go. My friends are getting after me."

"Are you late?"

"A little, but it was worth it." His sincerity disarms me so much I step forward and wrap my arms around him in a hug. I can't help thinking about how much he gave today, and as I pull away, I automatically kiss his cheek, freezing the minute my lips make contact with the freshly-shaven skin at the corner of his mouth. We both hold our breath until I pull away and look up at him. "Thanks…again. For the invite and for…everything today."

"So next Saturday? You'll tell me if you can make it?"

"Of course."

"But I'll see you on Tuesday?"

"Definitely. Can't wait."

He makes a move, as if to hug me again but then jerks back. He grins and heads to his car. I watch as he drives down the street, wondering how someone I've known for a month has made me feel more whole than I've felt in over a year.

16

Hover

*A step with the feeling of elevated suspension,
used to change direction or rotation*

"My son is officially seven, and we all successfully survived his second birthday without Jason," I declare proudly to Dr. Collins.

"I'm glad to hear that, Annie. What do you think made it go so well?"

I look down at my hands folded on my lap. I'll tell him, but I'm going to be nonchalant about it. "Well, I didn't have any plans or errands, so I could be entirely present for the day. I let Thatcher pick what he wanted to do, within reason. We had a simple evening planned, just dinner with Nick. And the kids really enjoyed the surprise visit from my dance instructor."

"Your dance instructor?" He coughs lightly into his fist and directs me to elaborate with a pointed look and roll of his hand.

"Yeah, Milo. He stopped by to invite me to his show this weekend, and he got caught up in our playground outing. He's so good with the kids. Really patient, not afraid to be silly, and way more attentive than most parents are with their own kids." My voice softens into a dreamy rhythm while listing his attributes, a fact not lost on Dr. Anthony Collins, PhD, listening marvel.

"Annie, I thought we discussed how a romantic entanglement may not be the best for someone such as yourself." I pause and stare, shocked by this uncharacteristic chiding, which causes me to snap abruptly.

"We didn't discuss anything. You briefly mentioned it, and we moved on. That doesn't mean I agree with you."

"Do you think you can fully invest in a relationship right now?"

"'Relationship' is a very strong word," I stammer, but Dr. Collins proceeds with his quickfire questioning.

"If it isn't a relationship you are seeking, then what exactly do you expect to arise from these interactions?"

"I...I don't know!"

"Do you think the kids are ready for you to be involved with another man?" He holds my gaze, his eyes owlish, observing my reaction to his use of the kid-card. I narrow my own eyes and hold up my hand to halt any more unsolicited statements.

"Stop! I'm done trying to justify my feelings and actions to you. Sure, maybe I am enjoying the company of another man. And yes, he has met my kids, but only as a friend. I'm not a complete dirtbag of a mother; I know not to confuse them. I would think you would have more belief in me. And it definitely doesn't sound like you are on my side."

"Annie, I'm always on your side–"

"Then please trust me. I can handle this."

We remain in a silent stare, seeing who will fold first. Luckily for me, Dr. Collins is the one in my employ, so he eventually concedes. "I'm not here to pass judgment on you, but rather guide you to better mental health after all you have been through. It's never bad

to feel a connection with another human being, but in your situa—
um, state, I just want you to be aware of all the variables." He sighs
as if he's just lost an argument with an insolent child, which only
causes my defiance to flare even higher.

"I'm aware of all the variables, Dr. Collins. I am a grown
woman, thank you."

My outward confidence hides the fact I have been struggling
with many of the same thoughts ever since Milo sort of asked me
out, but it doesn't mean I want to hear them from someone else, especially someone else who doesn't even know the party involved. On
one hand, it feels good to have fun with someone, to flirt, and to lose
track of time while hanging out. On the other hand, I feel as if I'm
betraying Jason, and even worse, abandoning my children after
they've lost their father. I could have voiced this to Dr. Collins from
the beginning, which is what I pay him for, but now I refuse to do so
out of spite. I raise an eyebrow in stand-off, placing the burden of
furthering the conversation on him yet again.

"What do you think you're getting out of your interactions with
this man?" I shrug, and Dr. Collins frowns in disappointment. Since
I am trying to prove I am a capable grown woman, throwing a fit
isn't going to help my case. So I give in, rolling my eyes and honoring him with a sighed answer.

"I don't know, maybe confidence?"

"Okay. Anything else?"

"I guess it's nice to have someone who has experienced loss
before. Who can talk about it and show how he's changed and grown.
The person he talks about being before and the person he is now seem
so dissimilar. It's inspiring to hear his evolution of identity." I see a
hungry look in Dr. Collins's eyes, but I try to tamp it down. "And I like
the one-on-one aspect of our discussions. I feel almost…privileged…
to be hearing his story." I stop and pause, blowing out a huge breath.

"What?"

"Nothing."

"Annie, please, tell me what just came to mind."

"Well, I just wonder what he could possibly see in me. Part of me is suspicious, like it could be a ruse, a prank. I have so much baggage between the kids, Jason, weekly meetings with you," I say, gesturing. "I think I'm just waiting for the twist to be revealed. To have the story end badly, like it did with Jason."

Dr. Collins stares at me while thinking, his thumbs rolling over one another in a rhythmic meditation. His gaze is intent, calculating, as he stares through me. Finally, he locks eyes with me, raises his index finger, primed to make a point and potentially solve my life's problems. "Let me start by saying no person is without baggage. We've all loved and lost, Annie. It's not about being baggage-free; it's about knowing how to best package it so it fits into our lives." I nod silently, wanting to look like the dutiful patient but also calling *bullshit* in my mind. Thankfully, he's not psychic, so he goes on. "But the bigger issue is how you just phrased yours and Jason's story. Do you really think it ended badly?"

My jaw drops open, and I crease my brow with questioning. "Do I think our relationship ended badly with his possibly self-inflicted death? Uh, yeah. Of course, I do."

"Instead of putting a qualifier on it, what if you just accept that it ended? None of this 'bad' or 'good' delineation. Relationships just end. Lives just end. And afterward, you have the lessons and the memories. And luckily for you, you have your children. Do you call that a bad ending?" He stares me down, unblinking, waiting for my reaction.

I inhale sharply: I just disregarded the greatest gift in my life— my children. I would never say I wish I never had them, but I do wish I wasn't in this all by my lonesome. I guess wishes don't always coordinate politely.

"As you leave tonight, I want you to stop thinking negatively about yourself and your situation…sorry…and instead, I want you to think of what you're proud of, why others would see you as worthy, and what you're grateful for due to your past with Jason. Can you do that for me?" He waits for my agreement, a teacher checking the understanding of his pupil after assigning homework.

I nod my head, hoping I'm up to the task.

"And next time, I'll ignore any inclination to give relationship advice. I'm sorry. That was out of line."

"Thank you for saying so." His apology releases my creeping doubt. I'd been so excited to see Milo this evening, and Dr. Collins's concern sort of left me deflated, but now, it's like I've been given permission to enjoy again, and I hope to do just that.

"Well, our time's up. If I'm not mistaken, you have another appointment to attend. Have fun, Annie."

He waves me out and I walk to my car, my body poised to move and my heart buoyed with anticipation, both just waiting for direction.

I haven't been practicing at home, and it shows. We start tonight's class with a review of all we've learned. The waltz first, followed by the Viennese waltz, which I never learned, so Milo dances with one of the other students. She's flushed and giddy when he returns her to her husband, who has been standing off to the side with me. Then it's the foxtrot, to varying degrees of success, and then a half-hearted attempt at the quickstep with Milo shouting out directions. After the disastrous start to learning this dance, it seems most have given up and are just moving however they want to the music, which is fine, but not for me who is trying to keep pace with the only proficient person in the room. The cha-cha is next, and we finish off the review with the swing, thankfully without the acrobatic flourishes that were attempted last week.

For most of the dances, I'm merely doing my best to keep up, letting Milo's hands, hips, and feet push me in whatever direction is needed. I feel more like a dummy than a living, breathing partner. Other students have obviously practiced, but I guess it's easier when they live with their dancing companion. Thatcher is too short and doesn't take direction well. Penny could stand on my feet but would just get distracted. Sure, I could pressure Nick into practicing with me, but the poor guy already does so much. I don't want to force him into dancing with his big sister. So, I'd better use my time with Truitt Two-Step Studio's finest. (I don't know any of the other instructors, but I stand by this assessment.)

After practicing, we move into a new dance, the samba, and Milo takes the helm at the front of the room as he goes through the basic steps. We all execute them individually before breaking into lead and follow. This dance is more complex with ten basic steps, and we spend most of our time trying to master the beat and hip movement. Milo moves through the lines, fixing holds and modeling proper footing. I try not to show my disappointment at our lack of contact this evening, but my eyes continually drift to where he is, watching his intense focus, his gentle instruction, and his sharp movements. Maybe it's the hip rolls, but my head is getting a bit swirly; I stop to stabilize myself, checking my reflection in the mirror-covered wall.

It's easy to spot my flaws: dark circles under my eyes, the slowly deepening wrinkles next to my eyes and mouth, and the stomach pooch that never completely disappeared after giving birth to Penny. As I stand there, posture straight, gaze focused, I try to shift the narrative and follow Dr. Collins's directive of finding what I'm proud of. I may look tired, but it's because I take care of two kids. And that makes me strong. I may have wrinkles, but it's because I've smiled and laughed with those I love. And I may have the pooch, but I also have my babies. I'm putting myself out there, I'm starting to feel like a whole person again, and my leg muscles are super toned from the dancing. This is what I need to see when I look in the mirror. Not the poor abandoned widow trying to survive each day but the strong, capable woman who's already survived countless days.

"You doing alright?" I'm interrupted from my internal affirmation by the illustrious instructor himself. He stands behind me, meeting my gaze in the mirror.

"Yeah, I'm actually pretty great."

"Awesome. Can you show me?" *Oh, shit, he means the samba.* I was still thinking of my self-esteem breakthrough, but I already announced my competence, so I guess I better bring it.

"Oh, yeah. Sure." I start with the basics of walk, close, close, then move to the next whisk step, saying the steps under my breath as I follow the side-ball-replace movement.

Milo steps forward to intervene. "Your hip movement is too jerky. You need to smooth it out, let it flow naturally with your foot placement. Here." He moves flush behind my body and places his hands on my hips. "Okay, start with the basic again." As I go through the steps, he holds my hips and directs their movement. "If you feel like you're doing too much, you probably are, and you can end up losing your balance. Just try for natural."

I try my best to focus on my steps, but his proximity is distracting and when I look into the mirror, I stumble beneath his searing gaze. His eyes burn like molten chocolate as they catch mine in the mirror, testing and teasing. He presses even closer behind me, our foot placement almost interwoven, and he whispers into my left ear. "See, you just have to feel it. Stop overthinking and be aware of how your body moves and feels." His breath tickles my neck, and his palm stretches out even further, hands flattening against my skin as they creep lower. A throbbing from deep within floods my brain, and my breathing comes quicker and shallower.

The current music stops, and Milo swings his head toward the speaker system, back to classroom monitoring mode. He leans close to my ear one more time to excuse himself and breaks away. The emptiness at my back feels cold, and I turn to see most of the women in class staring at me. I force a smile and look down at my shoes, pretending to examine their clasps. Lorraine, who has been dancing with Dave nearby, sidles up next to me. She speaks quietly as the rest of the class makes small talk while Milo sifts through song options.

"God, I love Latin dancing. That's the main reason we're going to Rio. It's so sexy, romantic, intimate." She catches me in a sideways glance and winks. "I bet Milo would give you private lessons. Lord knows if I were in your shoes, I would jump on that opportunity in a second, if you catch my drift." I nearly choke on my own spit as she strolls back over to Dave, Milo giving the announcement for open dance time.

I had no idea anyone even noticed me in class, but if Lorraine could break her attention away from her fiancé, then I'm sure others have noticed how I keep track of Milo, hold eye contact a little too long, lean into him a bit too much. I see Ted and Nathan off to the side, looking from Milo to me, bringing their heads together to snicker and gossip, probably making light of the thirsty cougar. Maybe I'm embarrassing myself, playing too easy to get, soaking in his attention too eagerly. Here I was, just recently settling into a rekindled self-confidence, and now I'm back to self-doubt. My body is supposed to be what sways, not my entire mental persona.

Since everyone is free to focus on whatever dance they choose, Milo spends his time rotating around giving tips and corrections. I keep my spot in front of the mirror and focus on the steps I can do by myself, holding onto an imaginary partner's shoulders while I watch all the real couples create swirling lines of movement and color behind me. I try to get back to the moment before I sunk so easily into Milo's hold, but now I'm dancing with my own uncertainties and fears.

"Goodbye!" Milo waves to the last couple as they exit the studio, then turns to me. "That was fun, right? A good class? I had thought about adding in a new dance, but I think everyone enjoyed the review time, right?" He's buzzing with adrenaline, talking fast as he comes to stand in front of me.

"Yeah, it was great," I say half-heartedly.

He cocks his head and purses his lips. "Okay, that didn't sound convincing."

"No, it was fun. I needed the review, for sure. I don't really get to practice much on my own. Hard to without a partner," I scoff.

"I can practice with you right now. If you want." He holds out his right hand and signals for me to grab it. I oblige and we instantly start gliding across the floor in a waltz. I throw my head back and laugh. "What's so funny?"

I look around the empty studio, pointing out the obvious. "There isn't any music! Someone could come in and just think we are a couple of weirdos dancing in silence."

"You don't need music to dance," he scolds me playfully as he raises his hand to turn me. After I spin, he pulls me back into a sharp hold. "Just desire."

"What?" I almost laugh at the absurdity. Is this man messing with me right now? His curled lips hide a bigger smile, and I'm fairly certain he is. "Desire, eh?"

"Yep. The desire to move, to connect, to feel something."

He eases us to a standstill, his eyes capturing my own. His hand releases mine and floats up to my jawline where he traces it lightly with the back of his fingers and knuckles. I close my eyes, and I can sense him leaning closer, his fingers now trailing down my neck. I've imagined this, prepared for this, hovered over the possibility, but as I feel his warm breath tickle my lips, I turn my head away. He instantly retreats. "I'm sorry. I thought…I was pretty certain you were feeling this, too…I shouldn't have assumed."

I put my hands up, in surrender, in apology, in uncertainty. "No, I'm sorry, Milo…You're right, I am feeling whatever this is, but…I just don't understand it." I drop my hands to my sides, my shoulders sagging in defeat. I'm ready to be honest, no matter how vulnerable it makes me at this moment, and I hate being vulnerable (a big reason I'm going to therapy).

Milo stares at me and asks, "What don't you understand?"

"Why you would even be interested in me!" I quickly swallow, shocked by my outburst, and I make sure to lower my voice when I add to my blurted declaration. "I'm a mess, Milo. I started coming to this class in order to get my therapist off my back. He kept pushing this support group, and I just couldn't…couldn't be around people thinking my husband…so we compromised on this. And then you get forced to partner up with me, and you start showing up at my house, telling me about your past, playing with my kids. I mean, it makes sense for me to feel something. You're young, talented, attractive, and so nice. But there's no reason for you to be interested in me, in this. I'm older than you, I'm not very interesting, and I'm saddled with baggage. I mean, shit, I wasn't even enough to keep Jason from…" I stop, having blurted out way more than anticipated. My eyes are fogging, the corners unable to halt the building tears.

I'm arming myself, ready to deflect whatever rebuttal Milo has in store for me, or even ready to accept if he walks away. But he does neither. Instead, he steps forward, opens his arms, and encloses me in a hug. At first, I freeze, stunned by his response, but then I melt into him, resting my face against his sternum, relishing his scent, his warmth, and his silence. I start to sob, my body wracked with the strength of my gasps, and he just holds me tighter, keeping me steady. Eventually, my cries wind down and my body stills, slumped in his arms. He starts to rub my back, his arms stroking up and down, and when he pulls back, still holding my shoulders, he reaches up and brushes tears from my cheek with a thumb.

"I'm sorry. That was a lot. I shouldn't have…" I attempt to explain myself, but my mind and words are still jumbled.

"Stop," he interrupts, saving me from a futile attempt at linguistic expression, and I straighten at the sternness in his voice. "Stop apologizing. You always have a right to feel how you feel, and you deserve to be heard. I hear you, Annie. And I see you. I see how amazing you are, and I wish you saw it, too." His hands have moved from my shoulders to my face, and I feel myself leaning in closer—

My phone rings. The upbeat, old-timey ringtone identities the caller as Nick. My body tenses, ripped away from the moment, and I apologize. "I have to get that." I grab my phone from my bag as Milo starts gathering up his speaker, phone, and towels. As I talk, I still feel his eyes on me, an awareness so palpable it scorches my skin.

I hang up and our gazes reunite with a magnetic pull. "I have to get going. Nick promised the kids ice cream if they cleaned the basement, but we don't have any, and they're about to stage a coup." I shrug and pick up my bag, standing at a safe distance. "Thank you, for what you said. You've been really kind to me."

He nods, understanding the possibility of the previous moment has passed. "You're welcome."

I angle my gaze and smile. "Hey, I'll be there Saturday night." His face splits into a wide grin and I back away. "Break a leg, Milo."

"Bye, Annie."

I don't know exactly what happened, but I'm glad I'm stopping for ice cream. Not only will it placate my children, but it might help cool me down. If that doesn't work, I'll just take a cold shower accompanied by my daily dose of Paxil, because right now, my mind and body are both slipping into murky waters. And a large part of me wants to jump in, fully clothed, and see what lies beneath the surface.

17

Point

An extension of the free leg in a clean straight line

There's always one moment in a young woman's life when she must face her fears in order to step into the next chapter. Today is that day. If I want to continue on with my degree, I must scrounge up the courage, the focus, and the stomach in order to succeed. I must, no, I will dissect this cat.

Poor Fluffy lies on her side, her spine curled upward and her head slightly tilted forward as if she is asking a question from beyond her pet cemetery grave. Her gray and white hair is matted, stiff, and splotchy; symptoms of spending half a year or more in a commercial-grade freezer. I stand stiffly in my yellow smock, my hands held as rigidly as my rigor mortis-stricken feline friend. The scalpel shakes in my right hand, and I start to see in tunnel vision, my peripheral beginning to blur and blacken.

"Hey, partner. You must be Annie Brennan." I swivel my whole body in the direction of the voice, and I end up pointing the scalpel at a ruggedly handsome man. He's tall, broad, and muscular—at

least based on what I can tell while he is wearing the full body muumuu designated as our protective gear during this pagan ritual. He stands with impeccable posture. His face is angular with chiseled cheekbones, a strong jaw, and a slightly crooked nose. Vivid green eyes create a dizzying effect, appearing even greener against his tan skin and buzzed dark brown hair. I go to open my mouth in greeting, and my scalpel drops to the floor, clattering against the white tile.

"Oops. I'll get that. Good thing the patient's already dead, or we would have to sterilize this." I watch him as he bends over, the muscles in his neck flexing deliciously. When he stands up, he holds the scalpel out to me, handle-first like any gentleman would, and quirks his lips into a small smile. "I'm Jason Obless, your partner."

Ah, yes, we have been assigned partners for our cat dissection, so I will be working with Jason for the next three weeks as we dig through Fluffy's innards in order to learn the ways of medicine and physiology. I still haven't spoken since his arrival, and I finally find my voice, croaking out an awkward and slightly accented, "Hel-loooo." Smooth, Annie, real smooth.

"So, are you as excited as I am?" His lips twitch in a small smile again, and I find myself staring at them. They aren't thin, but by no means are they lush. Manly, that's what they are. Nice and manly… but still moisturized, which is important.

I realize I'm going to need to make conversation if I'm going to successfully partner up with this man for the next few weeks; instead, my attempt at charm comes out more as blunt honesty. "Actually, no. I've been dreading this day ever since I registered for this class. I'm sorry, but you definitely lost the lottery when partners were assigned."

"Well, hey, don't talk yourself up too much. You might set unrealistic expectations." His green eyes sparkle playfully, and he turns to examine our specimen. "So, this is it, huh?"

"Her name's Fluffy." I look down at the tiny, stiff creature with somber respect.

"Oh, did you read that somewhere?" He starts sifting through the instruction binder placed on our station.

"No. I just thought she deserved a name if we were going to be carving her body up into pieces in the name of science."

"Ooookay." He looks around the room at the other partners getting started on the initial cut, probably wishing he was with anyone else.

"Don't get me wrong, I love science—obviously. I want to be a nurse. But I'm still not looking forward to slicing through skin and seeing what's inside. That seems to be a pretty barbaric method, am I right?" I wait for his response as we continue assessing each other for potential partner chemistry.

He finally offers a terse response. "So probably not going the surgical route, huh?"

I frown, knowing he is making a pretty accurate observation. He locates the initial-day directions in the binder and starts to read them out loud.

"'With gloves on, maneuver your cat so it is ventral surface up on the dissecting tray.'" I frown with disgust as he completes the first step. "'Identify the gender...'"

"It's a girl," I interrupt.

"A female? How do you know? You've barely looked at the thing since I moved it." I'm not liking the accusatory tone, but I did tell the guy he drew the short straw in terms of partnering up, so I'll stand down.

"She's calico. It's extremely rare for a calico to be a male. If it was, it would have been a prize-winning stud. Male calico sperm is highly coveted in the cat breeding industry." He just stares at me, his face devoid of reaction. I try to save face and explain my nerdy

retrieval of information. "I watched a documentary. I'm not a crazy cat lady or anything. I mean, I like cats, but not more than the usual healthy amount..."

"Oookay," he repeats and turns his attention toward the cat corpse. "'Next step: 'To remove the skin, pinch the skin on the ventral surface of the neck...'"

I squeeze my eyes shut and turn away. "Can you do this part, please?" I plead, and he agrees succinctly. I would guess three minutes go by before he tells me it's safe to open my eyes. I heard some of the sickening sounds of the skin separating from the muscle, but I still wasn't prepared to see the cat peeled like an orange, free of epidermis. My stomach is turning, and my vision is blurring.

"Okay, now we need to open the body cavities. It says 'just above the pubic bone, make a longitudinal incision through the abdominal muscles.' You want to take the lead on this step?" He turns to me, and I shake my head vigorously. His shoulders sag in disappointment. "Annie, you have to participate in this project. Otherwise, you're not going to get anything out of it."

I wince and apologize. "I know, I'm sorry. I'm just feeling kind of woozy."

His gaze softens, and his voice takes on a more compassionate tone. "Well, I'm your partner, and I'm going to help you through this. Here, lift your scalpel and place it here..."

He directs me as I slide open Fluffy's torso. Unfortunately, I slice too deep and end up opening Fluffy's uterus, which reveals three tiny kitty embryos. One look at the fetal spillage sends my guts for a final loop, and I bend over and throw up the contents of my stomach directly onto Jason's sneakers. I remain bent over, covering my mouth in a rather useless gesture, afraid to see his reaction. The rest of the room has gone quiet, and I know everyone is looking at us.

Instead of angrily shouting, he utters, "Here, let's go get cleaned *up." He grabs hold of my upper arm and directs me to the closest door, delicately shaking his shoes at our station so as to keep his vomit-tracking to a minimum. We head to the women's restroom where he proceeds to clean us both up.*

It will be another three months before I tell him I love him, but in this moment, I know I have met my person.

~ ~ ~

My focus is spotlighted on Milo as I clap enthusiastically through his curtain call. He was extraordinary. He can dance (duh), he can act, and he can sing. I was nervous when I first sat down by myself twenty minutes before the show started. What would I do if he wasn't that good, if it was a mediocre production? Could I convincingly feign being impressed, and would I even want to lie to him? Luckily, I knew that wouldn't be an issue the moment he appeared on stage tuning a guitar. He was enigmatic, magnetizing, and undeniably hot in a black leather jacket and moussed hair. When he started singing his first song, "One Song, Glory," I knew I was going to be a mascara-streaked mess by the end of the show. I was not wrong.

The actors give their final wave to the crowd and exit the stage, signaling a mass exodus of audience members. I shuffle slowly behind a stream of talkative theatergoers, many of us headed out to the lobby to see our favorite thespians make an appearance. Butterflies assault my stomach as I prepare to congratulate Milo on a show-stopping performance. I figure he will have other friends and fans to talk to, so I keep in mind that our potential plans for a drink may go bust. Nick was all too supportive of my staying out late tonight. He made some stupid joke about seeing me in my walk of shame tomorrow morning, and I responded with an upward-pointed middle finger.

Ah, the love between siblings is a beautiful thing.

People are packed in the lobby, swarming the actors who pant with tired smiles, their thick stage makeup starting to smear with beaded sweat. The glamorous stage isn't always so glamorous up close, but all the performers seem to be high on adrenaline and bliss. I can't help it; a curl of envy slithers through my ribcage as I wish I could feel that level of happiness. It seems no matter how good I am feeling, there's always some shadow looming in the wings.

My dark thoughts evaporate when I spot Milo standing to the left of the green room entrance. A group of patrons are speaking to him as he leans down, nods and smiles politely, and shakes offered hands. The moment he sees me, a wide grin spreads across his face, and he stands tall, raising his eyebrows and looking over heads in order to indicate his need to get through. The audience members let him move between them, and he rushes toward me, bending down and scooping me up in a hug that lifts me off the floor. The back of his shirt is damp and his costume could use a spray down with Febreze, but I let it slide, pleasantly surprised by his enthusiastic greeting.

He sets me back down on the ground and takes a step back, holding my hands and assessing my ensemble. "Wow," he says, and my heated cheeks, red from the warm auditorium, reach a new level of crimson.

I did put a lot of effort into looking nice, dare I say, possibly sexy. My first thought was to wear black: classic, understated, and appropriate for a night at the theater. But the only black dress I own was the one I wore to Jason's funeral, and I didn't feel like that was the intended vibe. Instead, I dug in the back of my closet and found a dress I wore to a wedding three years ago. It's a bold blue with an even bolder neckline requiring me to wear a special bra. The knee-length skirt gathers at one side of my waist, creating a ruching effect which hides the bulges I attribute to past pregnancies, a thirty-five-year-old metabolism, and my love of bread. I even broke out black velvet heels, which I'm starting to regret, and a light black shawl for propriety, because, you know, we're in a theater. Milo's stare is tiptoeing the line of predatory, so I work on changing his focus to his performance.

"I'm the one who should be saying 'Wow!' You were amazing, Milo! Just fantastic," I croon, squeezing his hands and leaning in.

"You really liked it?" His lips curl up in a sheepish smile, and I emphasize my response with a purposeful nod.

Some more audience members pass by and offer their congratulations as he asks, "So, have you been enjoying your night out?"

I look to the side as if considering all I've done. Was it enjoyable to sit on my own and not have to worry about snacks or bathroom breaks for little stomachs and bladders? For sure. But beyond sitting in traffic and sitting in my auditorium seat, I haven't done much. I share this information, and he looks down at our feet, shyly drawing his gaze up when he asks, "Did you think any more about coming out for a bit? Most of the cast and crew are heading to a bar here on the loop. You could come, be my plus-one, hang out for a bit?" He absentmindedly swings my hands, trying to lure me in with soft tones and gentle persuasion in case I get skittish and make a break for it.

But that's not even an option for me. "Yeah, I would like that," I say, assured in my answer. For a change, I don't feel like running.

18

Compression

A spring-like energy to initiate or accelerate forward

Insistent knocks rock the flimsy bathroom door as I pull up my pants, swaying a bit from foot to foot with the effort. "Someone's in here!" I holler at the door, annoyed that this is the third time I've had to justify a locked bathroom with an announcement that, yes, I am currently peeing.

The keg beer has been cold, flowing, and effective, and I am feeling the mental numbness along with the constant need to relieve my bladder. I rinse with water since frat boys don't tend to keep soap readily available, wipe my hands on my thighs, and leave the bathroom, ignoring several glares from those waiting in line down the narrow hallway.

The floor feels as if it is rippling beneath me as I make my way down a winding stairway. It delivers me to a sparsely populated windowless party room in the basement, furnished with mismatched couches, a ping pong table, and a folding table being commissioned as a makeshift bar. Bottles of cheap liquor dot the surface, and I go *to grab the plastic half-gallon container of bottom-shelf vodka. A hand grabs my wrist, intercepting my attempt to keep my blood alcohol level rising.*

"Hey, sweetheart. How about I get that for you?" A guy with moppy brown hair, a nose too large for his face, and beady brown eyes stands in front of me. I've never met him before and don't feel like making new friends tonight, so I tell him no thanks and try to jerk my wrist out of his hold. "There's no reason to be a bitch about it," he snarls.

I try to pull away from him again and end up losing my balance. He grabs my waist, pulls my back flush against the front of his body, and breathes into my ear, "You've been enjoying the party tonight, huh? How about we go enjoy the party in my room? Get to know one another?"

I'm clawing at his hands, trying to pry them off my waist where he curls them into the waistband of my jeans. "I don't want to go with you," I slur, trying to escape. I look around, but the room is suddenly empty. My brain starts to wake out of its alcohol-induced haze as my fight-or-flight kicks in.

The plan had been for me and my roommate to watch out for each other tonight. I had asked Jason if he wanted to come; we had been flirting over Fluffy's stiff corpse the past two weeks but had yet to hang out outside of class. I put myself out there, invited him, and was rejected. So of course, I decided to drown my woes in cheap beer and liquor. That would have been fine if Emily hadn't run into her current crush and left with him over an hour ago. Since then, I've just been floating around the frat house, trying to find someone I know or disappear into the woodwork. Getting groped and sexually harassed was not on my agenda.

"Get your hands off her," a stern but controlled voice carries from the stairwell landing. I throw my head in that direction, and

relief seeps through my body. The guy lets go of me and puts his hands up in retreat.

"Jason!" I stumble clumsily to his side and cling to his arm.

"Hey, man. I didn't know she was with anyone. She was all over me. You should keep a leash on her." I feel Jason rip away from my hold, and too quickly for me to register, he punches the guy right in his oversized nose, sending his flannel-clad body crumpling to the ground. Time slows back down as I watch Jason rub his right fist, angry welts rising on his knuckles after connecting with the asshat's lying face. I reach forward, grip his left hand, and pull him back toward me.

"He's lying. I didn't want to go with him. I didn't even want to talk to him," I say, the words tumbling out of my mouth, tripping on one another.

"I figured," Jason says plainly.

"Are you...are you mad at me?"

"Why would I be mad at you?"

"Because I put myself in this situation." Ashamed, I turn my gaze downward. "I drank too much because I was sad...and disappointed...I thought you didn't want to go out with me...and then Emily left with Marcus..."

"Annie, stop." Jason interrupts my word vomit, lifting my chin up to look me in the eye. "You don't need to explain yourself, and it's not your fault. Okay?"

I nod my head stiffly. "Okay."

"And I did want to go out with you. But I was busy. And once I wasn't busy anymore, I came to find you. Sorry it took me so long." His green eyes search my face as his hands rub my upper arms soothingly. I'm so caught up in the moment and still under the influence, I don't even realize I've kissed him until we break apart.

"Sorry, I shouldn't have..." I break out of his hold and turn away

in embarrassment. He places a reassuring hand on my shoulder and directs me around to face him.

"No, it's fine. But I'd rather you be sober next time." He squints and smiles.

"Next time?" I ask coyly. We exchange bashful looks, and both notice the frat boy lumbering up the staircase, his hands covering his possibly broken nose.

Once we're done watching his shameful retreat, Jason turns to me and asks, "What are you doing tomorrow night?"

"You want to hang out with me?"

"I do, but first, let's get you home safely tonight."

We go to exit this horrid dungeon of a room, and I pull up short with a lurch. Still holding my hand, he stops, looks back with a worried expression, and asks, "Are you okay?" right as I throw up on the sticky linoleum floor, splattering his shoes and pants.

I place my hand over my mouth and stare at him, my eyes wide in horror. He purses his lips together and comes closer, pulling a puke-soaked section of hair away from my face.

"So, this is going to be our thing, huh?"

I can't help giggling from behind my palmed shield, and he quickly follows suit, chuckling past the shock, putting his arm across my shoulders, and guiding me out of this hell hole. We leave the mess for someone else to clean up and escape into the fresh air of night, planning our first official date. Though, I'm not sure if it will live up to the night he saved me from the flannelled frat boy.

~ ~ ~

It's officially a party at Whiskey Whiskers, where the majority of the *Rent* ensemble is scattered throughout. It's a quaint, old-fashioned pub located in a historic hotel on Michigan Avenue where two of the bartenders don handlebar mustaches and the red and brown upholstery creates a sepia tone, as if we are all posed figures in an old-time photograph. Milo has blended 1930s style with contemporary charm, decked out in a classic black T-shirt, a patterned gray vest, matching trousers, and a gray newsboy cap. The whole image is novel, eye-catching, and tingle-inducing; but instead of complimenting him out right, I play coy when he asks me what I think of his outfit.

"It's very cute," I say, followed by a long slurp of my amaretto sour. He rotates his whiskey glass, leaving rings of moisture on the glossy bar, and glares at me, his eyes glittering with a challenge.

"Are you making fun of me? After I spent so much time and effort trying to look good for you?" The left side of his lip quirks up, and I burst out in flattered laughter.

"Of course I'm not making fun of you!" I shake my head as if to remove any false emotion, and I give him my most serious face as I say, "You look very handsome, Milo Warner, as always."

"Well, thank you. That's more like it." He lifts his drink up for cheers, and we both take a satisfying sip.

We've sequestered ourselves at the far corner of the bar. Milo's back is to the wall, and we spend the night mostly absorbed in our conversation, broken by jovial interruptions from *Rent* participants. At one point, the woman who plays Mimi comes over and chats for a good fifteen minutes. She tells me what a giving scene partner Milo is and how he helped her learn the choreography when she was stuck. She's luminous, her soft russet brown skin and dark black curls glowing in the dim pub lights. Her talent and beauty are enough to make any girl jealous; the fact her wife is here tonight, however, takes the sting out of having just seen her and Milo kissing passionately on stage a mere hour ago. Not that I have any claim to Milo's lips, but being here with him and enjoying the nightlife is definitely making me consider planting a flag in the territory.

As always, Milo is kind and courteous to everyone who stops by, even when we're in the middle of a conversation. By the end of our second drink, the drop-by visits have become fewer, and, armed with full glasses, he proposes a game.

"Truth or drink. I ask a question. You answer, or if you choose not to, take a drink. If you answer, I take the drink. Then you ask a question and same rules apply. Up for it?" He looks at me with heavy-lidded eyes, and though deep honesty sometimes scares me, drinking does not, so I nod and prime myself by lifting my glass in the air. "Okay. For good sportsmanship, I'll let you ask first," he states formally as he leans in, ready to attack whatever I toss at him.

I search my brain, clicking my tongue while thinking. By habit, I take a drink.

"You're not supposed to drink yet!" he laughs.

"Oh, shit," I wince. "I don't know if I'm going to win this game."

We laugh until I can figure out a question.

"Okay, it's a doozy: Milo Warner, what is your favorite color?"

He acts as if he's stricken with indecision, before answering, "Green. Now a question for you. Why didn't you want to go to the support group?"

I almost choke on my drink. Once I regain composure, I sputter out, "Throwing punches right out of the gate. I'll just take another drink."

"Really?" He searches my face. He looks so casual and cool, leaning against the bar, one forearm resting while twirling his glass.

"Yep. That's okay. I know my penance." He watches me drink, a look of mock disappointment contorting his face. I guess he didn't realize how many walls I have built up, nor how much I practice with the imbibing of wine in order to help me out in various social situations. Game on.

The Game of Truth or Drink

(Sponsored by Drinks #3 and #4)

Q: "What made you choose ballroom dancing?"
A: "I like the elegance, the fact a lanky guy like me can look smooth, that anyone can really. I like the fact that once you know a dance, you join a community in which you can bust out some choreography and make something really beautiful. Plus, it's great for the core."

I drink.

Q: "What's the hardest part about single-parenting?"
A: "Everything. Okay, I'm joking. Kind of. But I guess having to be all the things at once: disciplinarian, nurturer, fun parent, mean parent, planner, improvisational thinker…as a pair, the roles can be split up and varied. But it's just me, all the time. And the nights. When the kids keep me up or wake up with a fever, it's sometimes hard to know it is going to be okay without someone there to tell me."

He drinks.

Q: "What are your big career plans?
A: "Continue what I'm doing. Obviously teaching dance classes. I have a hip hop one coming up this summer. Keep auditioning for shows. It's not always a lot, but I'm getting paid for performing, so that's the dream. Getting to Broadway when the time's right. Oh, and I busk."

"What? What do you do, and where does this happen?"

I take two drinks.

"Believe it or not, I'm a shiny dancer…you know, like Elton John's 'Tiny Dancer' only I'm the Shiny Dancer. I'm completely covered in silver, and I dance. And as to where, I switch it up between Maxwell and Michigan whenever I have free mornings and afternoons."

I take another long drink because...yeah... I need to see this.

Q: "How long do you plan on having your brother live with you?"

A: "I suppose until he's ready to leave."

He drinks but continues.

"So, you're leaving it up to him?"

"Well, yeah. He's helping me out, so I'll take him as long as he is willing. He's easy to live with, not that I see him much. He has a pretty successful carpentry business, and he lives in the basement, which I don't go down to anymore—"

"Why don't you go down to the basement?"

I drink, draining the glass.

Winner of Truth or Drink: Milo Warner

He slaps a hand on the bar with dramatic exasperation and announces. "Okay, I fold. We're both done with our drinks, and I think you know everything about me while I still know very little about you." He reaches over to my right hand, which is resting on the bar, lifts it into his left, and interweaves our fingers together. I look over at our conjoined hands and throw him a demure glance.

Final Q: "Why do you want to know so much about me anyway?" I smile softly and watch as he scoots further on the edge of his barstool, bringing our hands in closer.

Final A: "Because I like you." He draws my hand to his lips and grazes my knuckles. "Because you are beautiful." He places a kiss on the back of my hand and lingers. "Because I think you are worth getting to know."

I internally update myself as the winner of our Truth or Drink game because who can feel like a loser when someone says all that? Winning vibes course through me even more as Milo releases our hold and reaches forward, caressing the side of my face and leaning his forehead against mine. I close my eyes and lean in, lightheaded from the smell of orange and bourbon floating on his breath. I know I want to kiss him; I've wanted to ever since I met him, but I've never felt it as urgently as I do now. Maybe it's the alcohol's influence, but if this man wants me so badly, why do I keep dodging his advances? I've been vacillating between hurting and feeling numb for more than a year; the possibility of feeling something good is more intoxicating than the four cocktails flooding my system.

I open my eyes and catch a glimpse of something, someone to the side behind Milo's head. Short dark hair, strong crossed arms, and piercing green eyes appear in my sight, and I jerk away. *Not again*, I think. *Please, not tonight.* I don't want to see Jason right now.

I teeter on my barstool, and Milo reaches forward to balance me. "Are you alright?" The concern in his voice makes my eyes sting with the guilt of pushing him away yet again. I take a gulp of breath and stand, gathering my shawl around my shoulders.

"Yeah, I'm okay. I just need to use the restroom." I rise from my stool, reassuring him with a small smile I will return. I feel his eyes as I turn and walk away, my own desire pooling against the wall of guilt and hesitance.

I push open a black door with a gold-framed embossed W, and I let myself collapse once safely hidden inside the empty bathroom. I rush to an open stall, sit on the closed lid, and try my best to breathe past the incoming panic attack. Images from the past year attack me as I fight for oxygen.

The slap of tossed dirt against smooth mahogany causes my stomach to plummet and my body to recoil. Having cried myself dry,

I watch Jason's casket descend beneath the earth, red-eyed as I cradle each of my children's heads, their own little bodies wracked with sobs. I move through the day as if floating from moment to moment, never really landing. Later, alone with my sorrow, I see him.

I tell myself to breathe, five counts in and five counts out. When the visions first started, I thought I was going crazy. Sometimes, I would fall ill or collapse from the shock. I tried running away, but there was nowhere I could hide.

I look to the side of any room and I see flashes of Jason's body, cold and rigid over his desk, just as he was that early morning. I shun the basement, afraid I will be trapped in the nightmare of a memory that refuses to fade.

I grip my bare knees, half-moon impressions left by the cut of my nails. The sharp bite of pain usually brings me back into the present, but I'm still flashing back in time, a phantasmal prison of my own mind. Unfortunately, this is not new.

I begin to see Jason on a regular basis, often as he was before: tall, fit, confident, alive. He appears behind me in the bathroom mirror, his eyes dancing with affection as I brush my teeth. I see him trudging up the stairs behind the kids, his hands reaching up to tousle their hair. When I try to sleep in our bed, I roll over and see him on his side. Sometimes his eyes are closed with slumber; other times they're open, observing me in my stagnant unrest.

I duck my head down between my knees and begin rocking my head side to side. If I live in this moment, give this time to Jason, maybe he will let me have my own. But I've already given him so much of my time, so much of my life since his own ended.

Months after his death, I no longer startle when he appears. But he can't talk to me, explain what happened, nor comfort me. I begin to feel empty, dissatisfied with my brief encounters, and angry at his abandonment. But the sightings don't end, and I'm left with nothing more than silent hauntings.

I don't want to do this anymore. I don't want to see this. I don't want to be this woman who runs from her husband's ghost when finally regaining some semblance of her own identity. I will not be that woman.

I lift my head, take one last deep breath, and force myself to stand.

I open the door, lean over the sink; and splash water on my cheeks, chest, and neck. I check myself over in the mirror and make a statement to my reflection: "I am alive. I. Am. Alive. I am still alive."

I've had to remind myself of this several times these past fourteen months, but I am putting a stop to it. I've felt only partially alive for so long. I'm done. "Let's go live," I say, holding my own gaze, daring my reflection and any remnant of Jason's spirit to try and stop me.

Lunge

A strong, wide step in any direction
with a bending of the standing leg

"Everything okay?" Milo asks as he rises from his seat at the bar and takes a step toward me as I charge from the bathroom.

I stop abruptly, our bodies almost touching but still apart, making sure this moment with Milo is free of guilt, free of doubt, and free of Jason. This moment is for me. And I'm ready to ask for what I want. I stretch up to meet his gaze. "Can we go back to your place?"

The corner of his mouth twitches, and I notice his Adam's apple bob up beneath the smooth lines of his neck. His eyes scan my body, pupils blown wide, and he reaches for his hat, nodding in agreement.

"Well, let's go then." I reach out and grab his arm just above the elbow and steer him toward the door. We walk wordlessly out of the bar and down the block before he pulls me to the side, away from passersby and blaring horns.

He grabs my shoulder with his other hand and holds me in front of him, searching my face. "You sure you're okay with this? Seriously, we could just hang out, talk about whatever you want. You know you can talk to me about anything, right?" His hands have crept up to the curve of my neck, and he moves his thumbs in calming circles beneath my jawline.

"I don't want to talk anymore tonight." I bite my lip and lift my eyes to meet his, silently daring him to act while internally praying he doesn't reject me.

His eyes widen, darting from my gaze to my lips, and his body sways toward mine. Everything in me seems to inflate and lift as he closes the distance between us, and our lips join together in soft, short brushes. I feel his arms wrap around my back as his hands press firmly across the span of my ribcage. Our bodies rock into each other with easy lulling waves building into a more powerful surge of pressure and connection. The kiss, at first light and gentle with timid exploration, grows more insistent as our lips and bodies seek touch, pressure, and friction. One of his hands slides down to rest on the rise of my rear while the other cradles the back of my neck, burying his fingers in the hair at my nape. As I tilt my head to the side, he catches my gasp with his mouth and lightly slides his tongue against the side of mine.

We've danced around the possibility of doing this for so long; now we are here, the choreography progressing naturally. He leaves my lips and begins kissing the corner of my mouth, trailing down my jawline to the sensitive skin along the tendon of my neck. With a moan, my eyes roll back and to the side, only then catching a glimpse of the passing people and car lights.

I stumble backward, but Milo is holding onto me tightly enough to steady me. My clumsiness signals our return to earth, and we straighten up, entangled and out of breath.

Between full belly laughs, I choke out the only thing that can touch the fuzzy outskirts of my mind: "There are so many people around!"

A guffaw bursts from his body, an exhale of pleasure and relief. When he leans down and kisses my forehead and wraps me into his chest, I melt into him and ignore our audience, the entire city of Chicago.

As Milo shelters me within his hold, he whispers in my ear, "I'll make out with you on the streets all night if you want, but what I'd really love is to take you home now. Please?"

My body trembles with his declaration of desire, and, in lieu of a verbal response, I stretch up on my tiptoes and bring my mouth to his.

"So make out on the streets, is it?" he asks, his laughter vibrating in his chest as my smile grows wider against his own.

"Lead the way," I say, and we walk hand in hand, leaving the busy street and the city-goers oblivious of our newfound closeness, my car safely stowed away in a nearby parking garage, and any scars of our pasts behind us in the dark corners of the hipster bar in which I defied my husband's ghost.

Milo holds my hand for our entire trip in the ordered Uber, his thumb massaging the tender web of skin beneath my index finger. The constant touch leaves me feeling safe, possessed, and eager for more. It's only a twenty-minute ride to his apartment in the Bucktown neighborhood. We don't talk, and I fill the space thinking about what I saw and experienced in the bathroom at Whiskey Whiskers. Am I sullying Jason's and my history by going home with Milo? Am I really ready to be with another man for the first time in over sixteen years? And what is he expecting? I'm not twenty-seven. My body has lived almost a decade longer than his, and while I'm not in horrible shape, I'm definitely still concerned he will regret what he's received once he opens the wrapping paper on this present.

My confidence appeared easily when we left the bar, intoxicated enough to lose sight of everything but him behind buzzed blinders, but this waiting has left me time to sober up enough to crack open the door for my doubts and fears. Am I attractive enough? Am I too old for him? Will he like the way my naked body looks? Lord knows no one has seen it in a long time, excluding my children, who usually just point and laugh. Is this attraction just surface level? What will happen once we act on it?

The car comes to a stop, and the driver announces our destination. Milo thanks him and helps me onto the sidewalk in front of a three-story tan brick building on the corner of Grace and Kenneth. I scan the street and see a myriad of residential homes of varied designs interspersed with Tetris-shaped brick apartment buildings. Milo leads me to one of these, punching in a four number code into the security keypad and leading us to a plain, yellowed entry hall and down the stairwell to a below-ground-level apartment.

"This is my place. Ground floor isn't the most glamorous, but it's definitely the cheapest for us starving actors." He flicks a smile at me as he unlocks the door and holds it open.

I walk into a one-room apartment that, despite its lack of square footage or windows above street level, is bright and inviting. Amber wood flooring leads into an open space complete with a small kitchen, a dining table, a full-sized bed, and an open garment rack. Various prints of show posters and playbills adorn the walls, and an egress window lets in a shock of moonlight. Milo's essence envelopes me with a warm welcome, a simple apartment telling of a tenant who spends the majority of his time out in the world living life.

I suddenly feel more than Milo's essence as he comes up behind me, his hands landing on my thighs, flirting with the hem of my dress as they sneak up. His head dips to my neck, and I stretch it to the side to give him free access. The gentleness of our first kiss is gone, and it seems as if his desire has been brewing the entire car ride, his hands roving up and around. My skin is on fire, having not been touched like this in so long, and a deep ache of want thrums through my core.

Dexterous hands spin me so I'm now facing him, our bodies flush against each other. I gasp as I feel his need for me beneath the thick cloth of his pants, and he covers my mouth greedily with his.

We kiss and explore, our hands roaming over the curves and lines of each other's forms. I'm so lost within the pressure and heat of our kissing that I don't even realize I'm quietly crying until I taste salty tears trailing down my cheeks. He stops and pulls back, a spark of concern slicing through the arousal in his eyes as he cradles my head and wipes my tears away with his thumbs.

His voice is soft, yet gravelly, as he asks, "What's wrong, Annie? Is this too much?"

My chest blooms at the thought that this man, even on the precipice of physical intimacy, can stop and take care of me, showing just how kind, considerate, and mature of a soul he is. He has that same protective instinct Jason had, and with my eyes closed, it was easy to imagine I was kissing my husband. However, my eyes are open now, and it is clearly not Jason. While part of me is mourning the love and future I once planned and lost, another part, ringing loud and insistent throughout every nerve ending in my body, is eager to see what is next, to be alive in this moment.

"Annie?" he asks again, his hands sliding down and squeezing my shoulders.

I take a breath and wipe the remaining tears from my eyes, then lift myself up to tease his nose with mine. "It just feels so good to be kissed. It's been so long," I admit, whispering against the fine stubble of his cheek.

He moves closer to speak against my ear, his breath causing the back of my neck to tingle, a spark of sensation flying all the way down my spine. "I want to do way more than kiss you. Is that okay?"

I nod, unable to speak, and lose my breath as he captures my mouth in his once more, lifting me off the ground with ease and wrapping my legs around him. I dip a hand under his shirt and brace myself with a flat palm against his taut abdomen, the muscles tightening beneath my fingertips. He staggers toward the bed, helping me to yank off my heels and throw them on the floor. I tug at his vest as he alternates which arm he holds me up with, and after pulling each through, I dramatically toss the vest to a far corner of the room.

He lays me down on the bed and holds himself above me, his look of pure appreciation making me feel cherished, desired, and seen. All my nagging thoughts from the ride over evaporate beneath his stare, and I allow my brain to push pause and let my body take control.

My body tells me I need him even closer, and I reach up to weave my hands behind his neck and pull him down to me. Feeling his weight brings back a feeling of coming home, the human version of a weighted blanket in the world of intimacy. His back is smooth and muscled as I explore with my palms, tugging up on the hem of his T-shirt, wanting less fabric with which to contend. My right hand trails around his hip to his waistband, teasing the sensitive skin as my fingers glide and tickle beneath the coarse fabric. The shivers in his body make me feel powerful, and I smile and raise my eyebrows, giving him the go-ahead. After a few awkward repositions, some leg maneuvers, and a few mumbled apologies amongst giggles he's mostly naked except for a pair of black boxer briefs. I can't help but chuckle nervously.

"What now?" he asks, mock hurt coloring his voice even though he's unable to wipe the grin off his face. "You make fun of me in my clothes earlier; now you make fun of me without my clothes. You're going to give me a complex."

I try to laugh, but the pressure of his chest on mine makes it come out a bit constricted. "I just didn't take you for a boxer brief guy.

Aren't younger men all about the boxers?"

He shifts his body in just the right place, sending a curl of liquid warmth down my lower half. "Maybe they are, but I'm a dancer. I have to make sure everything stays in place."

"Well, trust me, you have nothing to get a complex about. You are a very good-looking man." My words are interrupted by a sharp intake of air as he grinds against me again. "And it seems like everything is perfectly in place down there." He goes to kiss me again, but I turn away, resting my hands against his chest, a barrier before we go any further.

"What's wrong?" he asks breathily, a hint of disappointment coloring his question.

"It's just...I'm the one who should be worried." I bite my lip, treading carefully.

"What are you talking about? Worried about what?"

"About you...seeing me naked."

"Annie, you're gorgeous, vivacious, effervescent, yummy..." He punctuates each adjective with a kiss on a different location: forehead, nose, cheek, mouth. I interrupt his efforts of seduction with one last blurt of self-deprecation.

"You've only seen me with clothes on. Believe me, when the bra comes off, gravity takes over." I make a pained face, but when he matches my gaze, he still has a drugged look, as if getting high on our nearness.

"Mmm, I can't wait. But first—" He shuts down any further interjections with a last kiss on the mouth, which leads to a tongue trailing down my neck, a nibble along my cleavage, and other caresses down my body. He makes his way to my underwear, black and lacy (no large laundry day panties tonight) where he slowly peels them down my legs while he begins kissing between my thighs, gently nudging my legs apart before moving to my center, where another perfectly placed kiss causes me to moan with pleasure.

The grip of his hands, swipe of his tongue, and breeze of his breath awakens over a year's worth of grief, loneliness, and life-questioning through an orgasm that radiates from my core to my limbs and leaves my body sinking into the bed, numb and satiated. He pops back up to lay beside me, a cocky grin plastered across his face. I try to roll over, but my eyes are still starbound until I finally manage to turn my head to meet his gaze.

"Oh my God," is all I can utter, which makes his grin stretch even wider.

"And I haven't even gotten your dress off, yet."

I take that as a challenge and muster the strength to roll over, hooking my leg over his hip and straddling his waist. I grab the hem of my dress and pull it over my head in one moderately graceful swoop, tossing it in a corner along with Milo's apparel castoffs. I feel his fingers dig into the flesh of my hips as I undo the front-clasp of my special black lace bra, and I sit astride him, as if awaiting his assessment.

"Wow," he breathes, his pupils large and hungry. "It's even better without the dress. Thank you, gravity." We exchange a coy smile, but it starts getting serious when his hands begin their journey across my naked skin. My body burns with need, and I lean over him, give him a long, deep kiss, and ask if he has a condom.

After a quick dash to a kitchen cupboard, complete with disposal of his aforementioned boxer briefs, he is back above me, his waist nestled between my thighs and my legs wrapped around his hips. I cry out from pleasure as he pushes into me, a feeling of fullness dominating all senses, both physical and emotional. My body stretches open beneath him, and I lose myself to the rhythm of our lovemaking, the connection of the moment, and the severance of past expectations of who I was supposed to be at this point in my life.

20

Variation

A process in which known and defined elements
have been changed yet retain basic characteristics

I'm wrapped up in everything Jason: his strong arms, his woodsy scent, and his soft sleep sounds. I shift inside his hold, and his body twitches awake. He nuzzles further into my hair and I rotate, our faces pressed together. "Hey, beautiful," he murmurs, his voice croaky from first morning use. His breath is heady and thick, but not unpleasant—I don't mind. After a month of dating, we finally slept together last night. My roommate went back home for the weekend, so we have the entire day to ourselves. In fact, I don't plan on leaving this dorm room unless I absolutely have to. Of course, that's when the pang of a full bladder overwhelms my groggy morning senses.

"I have to pee." Not the most romantic morning-after line, but necessity overrides poetry. I try to pry myself out of his arms, but he squeezes tighter despite my squeals of dissent. Along with a vice grip, he begins tickling me, and I manically try to kick my way out of the torture. I finally manage to drop my legs off the side of the bed and

slide my head down, landing unceremoniously on the floor, naked and unkempt. Jason swings his head over the edge of my twin bed, clearly amused by my clumsy escape.

"You could have just asked nicely," he says between laughs. "Or paid the toll." His eyebrows waggle suggestively, and I can't help but be lured back by those green-irised orbs.

"What toll?"

"Just a kiss."

I kneel next to the bed and lightly brush his lips with mine, but he reaches down and scoops me back into bed, deepening the kiss and pressing his primed body against me.

"Seriously, we have to pause or I'm going to pee myself," I say through muffled kisses. He finally releases me, and I throw on some clothes, rush to the bathroom down the hall, and quickly return to nestle in the warmth of our blanketed cocoon. Soft skin, tender touches, and tangled limbs become the sanctuary of the day, creating our own isolated world which we never want to leave.

~ ~ ~

I expected to be with Jason until we were old and gray. I expected him to be the last person I ever kissed, ever slept with, ever fell asleep beside. I never expected to be a widow before forty, raising two children on my own, and living with my younger brother. I never expected to be so familiar with loneliness.

I was nineteen years old when I met Jason. Emotions, both good and bad, were heightened; and our love was a jostling ride of deployment, reunion, dread, and anticipation. But through the years, the feeling of loss, need, and happiness dulled a bit and became a muted landscape replacing the once saturated color of my youth.

But the punch of pigment returned when Jason died, a blanket of black, red, and blue coloring and controlling my life. I shut down, shied away from the light, and retreated into a dark cave of my own making. I barely made it out, and if it wasn't for certain motivating factors, I'm sure I would still be curled up in that same cave.

I sometimes think back to moments and imagine how a different choice could have rippled into a different effect. What if I had held off on college to take care of my mom? What if I hadn't puked on Jason the first time we met? What if he hadn't returned to Chicago after boot camp? What if he hadn't been employed in an urban emergency room? And what if I hadn't fallen asleep while reading that night last March?

It's not worth it to wonder what if, I know. Life isn't a game that can be restarted, a video that can be rewound. It's a string of events that create opportunities and consequences, and how one reacts to them further instigates other events through cause and effect. Not a very idealistic way to see the world, but it certainly helps me when I find myself in the "what if" spiral.

That same spiral is what's occupying me as I bide my time lying in bed before I will have to do the inevitable: get up and use the bathroom in an unknown apartment. I've been hoping Milo would wake up, so it wouldn't be like I was snooping around, but I can't wait any longer; my bladder is about to burst. I carefully pull my legs up, trying to free them from the tangled sheets, which still cover Milo. I spot my underwear plopped on the floor next to the foot of the bed, but even with a thorough scan of the small room, I can't seem to locate my dress. Having lost some of my nude confidence since last night, I search for something with which to cover up. I spot a gray zip-up hoodie on top of one of the laundry baskets, put it on, and wrap myself in Milo's scent. Comfort, safety, and sex assault my senses, and I glance back at his sleeping form to make sure I haven't disturbed him.

I dash to the bathroom, relieve myself, and stand in front of the small cabinet mirror after washing my hands and face, trying to clean up the smudged makeup so I look a bit less "morning after." It's a lost cause. My face and chest are red from Milo's romantic wanderings, my hair is a mess of tangles, and my eyes are heavily lined with coal. Nick sure is going to have a heyday making fun of me.

"Oh shit!" I curse out loud, realizing I haven't thought of Nick or the kids since entering Milo's apartment. I rush out of the bathroom and start searching the perimeters of the room for my purse. I find it dropped on the floor next to the front door, and I dig through for my phone. I see a string of text messages from Nick starting at midnight.

Am I to assume you won't be coming home tonight?

Annie, I hope you haven't been murdered.

Don't worry, I'll raise the kids right. Teach them the ways of our people.

Seriously, check in when you can.

I quickly tap out a response: **Sorry. Didn't check my phone. I'm good.**

It's 6:12 AM, so I doubt he will be up yet, but I'm surprised to see the response bubbles pop up. He sends a thumbs up, quickly followed by an applause emoji, a kissing lips mark, and an eggplant. *Such an ass.*

Ease up. I'll be home soon.

Take your time. Kids are still asleep.

Why are you awake then?

Just doing my duties as Best Uncle Ever.

He punctuates this with a winking emoji.

A raised eyebrow emoji precedes my response: **Really?**

No. Just couldn't sleep well.

Oh. Sorry.

No worries. I'm glad you are enjoying yourself. At least... I'm assuming you are. Another winking emoji.

Okay. Bye. See you soon.

He responds with a heart-eyed cat face, and I snort, amused by his unshakeable pestering nature.

A polite throat clearing grabs my attention, and I turn, Milo's dark brown eyes pinned on me as he lays on his side, head languidly propped up on his hand. I stand and pull the hoodie further down, attempting to hide my undercarriage.

"Oh man," Milo whistles out.

"Sorry. I didn't mean to wake you," I stammer, still whispering with my hoarse morning voice.

"Don't apologize. I wake up and the first thing I see is a beautiful, sexy woman in nothing but my shirt. Now that's a good start to the day."

I smile and I'm sure my entire body blushes. "Well, I am wearing underwear."

"We can fix that." He smiles coyly and winks. "Come here."

I pad over to the bed, ready to sit down next to him, but he grabs my hips and lifts me on top of him. His groin strains against the thin material of my panties as he interlaces my hands in each of his and just looks up at me, a warm smile lighting up his face, still lined with red markings from his pillow. "Hi."

"Hi." I grin back and squeeze his hands, my own aching to run through his mussed-up hair. He looks even sexier this morning, and my body yearns to move against him.

"Everything okay? I saw you texting."

"Yeah, I just forgot to message Nick. He wanted to make sure I wasn't murdered." I bite my lip and feel him twitch beneath me.

"Do you have to get back right away?" His tone is hopeful without being needy, the perfect blend to persuade me to take advantage of Nick's offer to take my time.

"Not exactly," I reply demurely.

"I had a lot of fun last night." He starts massaging the back of my hands, the sensation sending jolts through my entire nervous system, and all I can think about are those hands on other parts of my body.

"Yeah, I did, too."

"Are you up for some more fun this morning?" His lips curl suggestively, and I almost salivate.

"Well, I can see *you* are."

He laughs and pushes himself to sit up and catch me in a long, sensual morning kiss. His left hand releases mine and drifts to the hoodie's zipper, pulling down slowly and allowing him to reach in and caress my breast with one hand as the other grips the flesh of my butt, beginning to push himself further against me. He lowers his head, teasing my bare skin with feathery brushes of his lips, my body jerking in response to the occasional sharp nip, and I throw my head back and let my mind go blank as my body takes over.

"I should really head home," I sigh as I nestle my head on Milo's shoulder and he strokes my upper arm. Both of us have been unable to move from this spot for at least fifteen minutes, our previously acquainted bodies producing an even more powerful result in the morning light. My body resists the idea of breaking our physical connection, but my maternal instinct is starting to wake up with the day, thinking of all I need to do for the kids and around the house.

"Yeah, I need to get around early for our matinee." Milo seems to share the same motivational dilemma as he continues stroking my arm, but he makes no other move to get out of bed.

I look over at his right arm and reach to bring it closer. I lightly trace the white line of his scar, mumbling, "I'm really glad you weren't successful with this."

He places a kiss on the top of my head and speaks into the mess of my hair. "Me, too."

I splay my hand across his chest and feel the beat of his heart. As humans, I think we sometimes take for granted all the heart has to do in keeping a person functioning. It stops, and the whole person is gone. "I still can't imagine you being willing to end it all."

"People change. I'm lucky I did. Or else I wouldn't be here with you." I can feel him tip his head down, and I look up to meet his smile.

"Yeah," I breathe. What I don't say is people can change in bad ways, and if not for that, I wouldn't be here, either. Instead, I snuggle in closer, focusing my attention back on his chest and ask, "Did you blame anyone? You know, for making you want to go through with it?"

A big breath causes his chest to rise. "Well, I thought I was doing it for Reagan because I loved her. But I didn't blame her."

"But what about your dad? For not being around? Or even your mom for having to work so much? Was there anything you could attribute to that willingness to kill yourself?" The questions tumble out of my mouth before I can shut myself up, but I have to ask. I have to know.

He sits up, gently sliding me off his body, allowing us to talk face-to-face. His eyes narrow questioningly. "Like an itemized list of grievances?"

I rise and pull the sheet over my chest, worried I've ruined this moment of connection. "I'm sorry. I shouldn't have asked—"

"No, it's fine. I just never thought of it that way. Give me a second to think." He rests his long arms on bent knees and cocks his head, considering. I watch him, wanting to reach out and stroke his back but worried I'll interrupt his musings. Finally, he turns to me. "I think when someone has made the decision to go ahead with ending their life, they're beyond the point of even being able to itemize or quantify. By that point, it's beyond making a pro and con list. I think it's just a blanket feeling smothering any potential glimmer of hope. For me, at least I reached out to my mom; otherwise, I would have probably gone through with it along with Reagan."

"You didn't blame anyone specifically?" I look into his eyes and imagine those same deep brown eyes belonging to a troubled teen. Was his mother able to see his hurt, his anger? Is it always there, hiding within the doorways of one's soul when considering death?

His face is relaxed as he shakes his head. It gives me the courage to keep asking.

"Not even Reagan, after the fact?"

He looks away, a heavy acceptance visible in the slope of his shoulders. "No, I never blamed her. I just felt like I let her down, first for not being with her like I was supposed to be, then later, for not being able to stop her, like I should have."

I reach over and grab his hand, wanting to comfort him, but still needing answers to thoughts which have kept me awake for over a year. "Do you think *she* blamed anyone? Like her dad?"

He focuses on our intertwined hands, rubbing his fingers back and forth on the skin between my knuckles. "No, I don't think so. She wasn't like that."

"Sorry." I feel a stab of guilt at transferring my pain onto him, but when he looks at me, there's no suffering striking his features. Perhaps a nostalgic sadness touches the fine creases next to his eyes, but overall, he remains calm and composed. I'm inspired—and jealous.

"No, I'm just saying I think her sadness went beyond any one individual in her life. Otherwise, why wouldn't I have been able to convince her otherwise? I struggled quite a few years with that thought." The moment of reflection leaves him, and he flips back to the present, knitting his eyebrows in wonder. "What makes you ask all this?"

I turn my gaze to the floor, not wanting to reveal all my deep intentions. "I guess I just wonder how those left behind should feel about their part in it, you know? Like, how does one move on from that kind of guilt?"

"I think a person has to move on in any way possiblc, because if they hold onto that kind of guilt, it'll destroy them." He squeezes my hand, and we sit in silence.

"Yeah, I guess," I sigh and scan the room, searching as my mind analyzes his advice.

"Are you thinking about your husband?"

I nod slowly, still looking away.

"How did he die?"

A large intake of breath cuts through the comfort of our closeness. The question shouldn't surprise me. Of course, it was bound to come up, but even in this incredibly safe space of just the two of us, I don't feel ready. "I'm sorry…I can't…" I try to explain, the words of resistance even too difficult to utter.

He leans back and pulls me with him, curling me into his side. "It's okay. You don't have to." We lay there, wrapped up in the weight of our pasts, waiting for the heaviness to dissipate.

As we settle into one another, our heartbeats match up, pairing together as if finding solace in a kindred spirit. It makes me start thinking of the concept of "us," and while I'm nervous to ask, I've already done so much more these past few weeks than I thought possible. I might as well keep going. "So, what now?"

"What do you mean?"

"Well, we had a pretty incredible night—"

"And morning," he interjects with a smile, his hands caressing the length of my arms.

"And morning together. But I don't want you to think I expect anything; I mean, I'm not going to get all clingy and needy. I totally understand if this was a one-time thing." I look down at the bed sheet, at the light sneaking in through the egress, anything but Milo's face.

A light touch on my chin brings my face up to his. "I don't want it to be a one-time thing. In fact, I was planning on getting very clingy and needy." I roll my eyes in jesting disbelief, but he continues holding my gaze intently. "Annie, I don't want this to be a one-time thing. I like you."

I compress my lips to keep from smiling too readily and giving away all my emotional leverage. Butterflies burst in my stomach, and I'm caught off guard by the relieved unclenching within my chest. "Okay. I like you, too. But how is this supposed to work? There's the kids, an hour commute, your busy schedule…" My logical brain is starting to tick away the roadblocks, but he shushes me with a thumb to my lips.

"Hey, let's just go with it, okay? We'll just find time when we can. We have class on Tuesday—"

"Yeah, but I have to get home—"

"But Nick can watch Penny and Thatcher a bit longer, right?"

"I guess…"

"And we'll just figure it out from there. If we want to spend time with each other, we'll make time, okay? Can you trust me?"

"Yeah, I can try."

"Okay." He shifts to place a light kiss on my forehead.

"Just please don't hurt me," I whisper against his cheek, surprised by the smallness of my voice. He pulls me in closer, sealing a vow with skin and silence.

"Hey, how about we get dressed, get some coffee, and I'll take you to your car?"

"Really?"

"Of course. It wouldn't be very gentlemanly of me to just drop you on a train and go on my merry way. Plus, I have to be at the theater in a few hours anyway. I'm all about efficiency." I playfully slap at his arm, and he squeezes me tighter, binding me as he begins to tickle my bare ribcage. I squirm to get away, and he relents, but not before giving me a long kiss that leaves me weak in the knees and confident he'll live up to his end of the deal.

21

Spin

A turning action on the ball of one foot

The garage door announces my arrival home, and I am welcomed by a string of high-pitched excited shouts of "Mommy!" as my legs are attacked in loving tackles. Nick is in the kitchen washing the electric griddle while the smell of pancakes wafts in the air.

"There's the strumpet!" Nick shouts, lifting a sudsy arm from the sink in a salute, soap bubbles flying through the air. I give him a warning glare, but it's too late.

"What's a strumpet?" asks Penny.

"It's an instrument. It sounds like this," Thatcher replies, putting his hands together in fists against his mouth and making a sound somewhere between a dying goose and an obnoxious fart. Penny erupts in giggles at Thatcher's bubble-blown cheeks, and he continues, relishing her squeals of delight. She sings along, "Mommy's a strumpet!"

"That she is, Penny. That she is." Nick winks at me and returns to attending the sink while trying to carry on a conversation above

Thatcher's trumpeting. Penny follows him like he's the Pied Piper, their sounds thankfully gravitating to the living room. "So, you have a nice time?"

I kick off my heels, throw my purse on a nearby chair, and stand there in my rumpled dress with my arms spread out as if to say, Case in point. Nick looks over his shoulder and laughs. I plop down in a chair at the dining table and lay my head down.

Without another word, Nick dries his hands and brings over a plate of pancakes, a bottle of syrup, and a fork. My nose leads the rest of my body upward, and I dig in.

"My hero," I mumble from behind a mouthful of pancake.

"Good ole' Bisquick," Nick says as he takes the chair across from me. He tells me all about his and the kids' night as I scarf down my breakfast, and I nod at the appropriate spots, showing my appreciation for his perfect blend of fun and discipline (his words, not mine). "So tell me about your night," he finally says as I take my last gulp.

"Really?"

"Yeah, but without the explicit details." He wrinkles his nose in mock disgust.

I stick out my tongue but proceed to describe the show and the bar, ending with a quick, "And then we went to his place."

"And you're good?" he asks. His teasing tone is gone, which sets me in defense mode.

"What do you mean?"

He leans back, resting his socked feet on the table and balancing on the back two legs of his chair. I glare at him, hating when he does this, but he ignores me and says, "Shit, I remember the first time I was with someone after Jessica. It was nice, but it was weird. I still felt like I was cheating on her even though we'd been broken up for three months."

"Well, I've had a bit longer to acclimate. Jason's been dead over a year." I reach over and shove his feet off the table. He quickly catches himself from teetering backward, furrowing his brow at my sternness.

"I know. I just thought I'd check." He waits a moment to see if I will respond, then asks, "So, do you like him?"

"Yes…" I say, looking at him sideways, afraid to show too much too soon.

"Are you going to introduce him to the kids?" He taps the table, an irritating habit of his.

"He's met the kids." I reach over and place my hand on his to stop the tapping. He straightens up, pulling in his limbs away from my reach.

"Yeah, but not as your boyfriend."

"I didn't say he was my boyfriend."

"Oh. My bad." He holds his hands up in surrender, but his lips curl in amusement. Like any little brother, he can't help but take pleasure in irritating his big sister. He sets his hands flat on the table and eyes me seriously. "But you want him to be your boyfriend, right?"

I stand up abruptly, upsetting my wobbly chair. "Oh my God, Nick! I don't know what's going to happen. Can I just have some time to enjoy the fact I even survived my first date after Jason before having to sit through an official interrogation?"

Nick crosses his arms, assessing me coolly. I break beneath his gaze and sit back down. "I just don't want to upend their world too soon. I don't even know exactly what's happening; I don't want to drag them into something just to have them lose someone again." I start looking around the front room as if taking inventory of cleaning needs, but really I'm avoiding Nick. I don't want him to see how much I'm struggling with this fear. I know I've only spent one night with Milo, but I already know it would hurt to lose him, and that is terrifying.

"That's the spirit; go into it with low expectations." He sighs and starts heading toward the basement stairs, probably ready to be child-free and prepare for a day of single adulthood. I can't blame him; I had one night of it, and it's magical. My jealousy comes through as sassy defensiveness.

"It's not low expectations; it's just being cautiously realistic."

He stops and turns abruptly, frustration evident in the tightness of his stance. I've finally cracked his morning joviality. Regret seeps through the cracks and washes out any enjoyment from our sibling banter. "Okay, Annie, but you had fun, right?" I nod. He holds my gaze with raised eyebrows. "Then enjoy it. You deserve it. I can watch the kids once in a while. A little Uncle Nick rubbing off on them will do them some good. I got Thatcher burping the alphabet. But don't say anything. He's planning to surprise you." A smile eases his tense exterior, and I know he's back to his relaxed Sunday self. However, I am thrown when he tosses me a curveball of news. "Oh, by the way, Maggie called me."

"She called *you*?" I rack my brain, wondering why my mother-in-law would be calling my brother, why she would even have my brother's phone number. Maybe he gave it to her during the Applebee's fiasco?

"Yeah, she said you haven't been picking up her calls. She wanted to make sure you were okay." *Shit.* I *have* been missing (aka ignoring) Maggie's calls. However, she does tend to call at the most inconvenient times. Over the past two weeks, she's called twice while I've been working, once when I was at therapy, and then not too long after when I was at dance class. I probably should have called her back, but I've been so preoccupied, and honestly, I didn't want to talk to her. She has a way of making me feel inadequate, and I've had enough to deal with these past few weeks.

"What did you tell her?"

"I told her you were doing great. That you were on a date."

"Nick! No!" A sound similar to when the kids step on Marsh-mallow's tail rises from the depths of my chest, and we both look at each other, wide-eyed and shocked.

"What? I thought you two were still on speaking terms."

"Sort of. But not really?" He looks at me quizzically. I can't help him out. I've confused myself. Sure, she did what she had to do for her son and grandkids. We may all be better for it, but I still feel shame when I'm near her. Despite some curt calls to catch up with the kids and short text conversations, I would rather not talk to her if given a choice. There's just too much history between us and too much of Jason in her.

Nick waves at me as he heads downstairs. "Well, have fun. I've gotta go run some errands. You don't need me for the kids until Tuesday, right? No quick rendezvous in the city before then?"

"Just go." I wave him away, and he laughs good-naturedly. I suddenly remember all he's done for me the last twenty-four hours, so I shout my appreciation down the stairs. "Thanks for the pancakes. And for watching the kids. And for being so supportive."

"Sorry about Maggie," he hollers up, but I swear I can hear the smile on his face.

I start picking up toys, pillows, and blankets. As I dive back into my maternal duties, the magic of the previous hours is shoved aside by the dread of confronting a mother I disappointed.

~ ~ ~

My butt and back are cold, pressed up against the hard tile of the bathroom floor. When I look around, I can only see a small circumference of fish-lensed surroundings before the edges blur into a black tunnel. My brain is foggy, and my breathing is labored. The only vivid feeling is the clenching within my guts. I manage to maneuver my body around, embracing the toilet. My dizziness drowns me, and I proceed to puke up what feels like all of my internal organs. Instinct takes over, and I start hollering for Jason. He's always been the one to take care of me when I'm sick—it's our thing. I holler again when he doesn't immediately arrive.

"Annie, what are you—" Maggie stands in the doorway, her dressing robe closed tightly over a pair of pink pajamas. Her hair is flattened in the back and spikey in the front, as if she has just jumped out of bed. From my blurry peripheral, I see her jaw drop and her mouth round, as if she is making a sound, but I can't hear her. My ears roar with white noise hammering my head, leaving my body sore and shaking.

I feel hands on my back, rubbing vigorously, but the pressure pushes me over until I fall onto my side. I clumsily roll to my back and stare up at the circle of radiance emanating from the ceiling bulb. Maggie appears above me, but my eyes track to the side, continuing to stare at the light. My eyelids feel heavy, and a comforting numbness has begun to settle within my bones. As my eyes begin to close, I see the outline of Jason's head appear over me, hovering next to his mother. I try to say his name again, but my mouth is so dry and I'm so tired. All I can do is mouth his name silently. A tear slides down into my hairline as Maggie continues her pantomime of panic.

"Jason." The name finally slips past my lips as I pass out. The light is gone, and there is nothing but black.

22

Swing

A free movement around a fixed point

"So you and the dance instructor have become more serious?" Dr. Collins asks, his voice flat and colorless.

My appearance must have given it away. I'm probably trying too hard, but I haven't seen Milo since Sunday morning when he walked me to my car and kissed me against the door. I want to make sure I look as confident and attractive as I wish I felt, so I'm dressed up in a coral V-neck short-legged romper, my hair pulled up with messy tendrils framing my face and the application of shimmery eyeshadow and mascara to make my blue eyes pop.

"Is it that obvious?" A coquettish way to answer, but talking about Milo causes me to unfurl, my petals blossoming open toward the light of the sun.

Dr. Collins adjusts his chocolate-brown blazer and clasps his hands together. "And how serious is your relationship now?" And just like that, clouds darken my skies.

"Are you supposed to ask me that?" My annoyance is evident,

and he shifts uncomfortably in his seat.

"You're right. It's not my place to ask. And you don't need to answer. But, as your doctor, I am concerned about your ability to be in a relationship at this point in your recovery, as we have discussed several times now."

"I get that. But wasn't the whole purpose of joining dance class to meet new people and learn about myself? That's essentially what I would have done if I'd gone to the support group you kept harping about. I don't see the problem. Milo's a great guy. He's communicative, honest, kind. I think he's really good for me."

"I don't disagree with you about that. But do you think you are good for him?" *Ouch*. An arrow strikes me in the heart at his words. This whole time, I've been thinking of Milo's impact on me, on how he has allowed me to squash some of the grief and guilt that constantly infringe on my every thought and action, but I haven't given much thought to how I could be impacting him. Dr. Collins seems to read my mind. "You didn't think about that, did you?"

I go to rebut but find myself speechless. A few more seconds of mentally floundering, and I do manage to find a shred of dignity when I respond, "It's not like I'm some sort of train wreck. I am a functioning adult. Sure, I have my moments; but I manage to take care of my children, work full-time, and keep up a house."

"I'm not saying you don't have tons to celebrate, Annie. I'm just worried you are using this relationship as a way to validate yourself while not considering the needs of the gentleman involved. You don't want to bring this man into a situation which could be detrimental to him."

"I'm not *detrimental* to him…I would never hurt him…I don't understand where this is coming from," I stammer, trying to connect my thoughts. I feel betrayed, backstabbed by the professional who is supposed to be guiding me, not scolding me.

"I know, Annie. I don't mean to say you would intentionally hurt him. I just wonder if you have thought this all through." He pauses, waiting for a response, an affirmative I have carefully considered all consequences, but I just sit glowering. Leaning into my stubborn silence, he continues. "You say he is communicative. Are you?"

"Yeah," I answer dumbly.

"Have you told him about Jason?"

"Yes. He knows my husband died. Of course."

He removes his glasses to look at me without lenses separating our gaze. It somehow makes me feel more bared, more vulnerable when he asks, "Does he know the entire story? Does he know why you promised to see me every week?"

I look down at the bare skin on my thighs, my attention snagging on a few missed hairs from shaving. From my safety of shielded eye contact, I mumble an acquiescing "No."

"From what you have shared with me, it sounds like this man has a lot to offer in terms of insight and experience, and I think it's a beautiful thing when two people can connect on a deeper level. But I do believe in reciprocity, and if you are planning to continue this relationship, you will eventually need to not only come to terms with your own knowledge and understanding of the events surrounding your husband's death, but also share those same events with any potential partner, much of which you haven't even shared with me. Just something to think about."

I nod, then open my mouth with one more attempt to defend my actions. "He really makes me happy. Isn't that a good thing?"

Dr. Collins smiles sadly, replacing his glasses and settling back. "It is. But it would be even better if you could find a way to be happy by yourself and with all you already have."

It's like he's punched me in the gut, but I refuse to let him see how much that comment hurts me. I can be happy on my own; it wasn't like I was *unhappy* before taking the class and meeting Milo. I was fine being alone and in my little protected bubble. It was Dr. Collins who kept pushing me to get out there, who made me see all I had been missing. I was doing just fine hanging with my kids and brother, but now I see there's still a chance for a different kind of companionship, a kind that leaves me feeling vibrant and alive; I can't just give that up. My heart has bloomed at the idea that the hole Jason left within me can possibly close and mend. And that shouldn't take away from the love I have for my children. But now Dr. Collins has insinuated it does.

He has struck me in the soft underbelly of my maternal instinct, and I don't want him to know the power he has wielded over me. So when he asks me "What else is going on?" as if he hasn't just stolen and popped my positivity balloon, I coldly oblige by telling him about Maggie, and we spend the rest of the appointment rehashing old issues and discussing new strategies. But I hold my pride close and refuse to give any more of myself to therapy tonight.

As I walk toward my car post-session, Dr. Collins's gloomy observations hover over me like a pesky storm cloud. But Milo texted me last night, asking me to come over early, so I immediately drive over to Truitt Two-Step Studio, trying to clear the smog from my once-blue skies.

I pull open the door and see Milo leaning on the mirrored wall, his legs crossed elegantly at the ankles as he scrolls through his phone, probably picking out music for tonight's session. His face lifts with my entrance, and his smile instantly shines through the grayness of my mood, causing my heart to swell and my face to break into its own smile.

"Hey!" he exclaims, pushing off the wall and tucking his phone into his back pocket. He's wearing a black collared shirt open over a white tee with dark wash jeans. Simple and casual but still capable of making my knees weak. He seems to appreciate what he sees, as well; as his eyes scan me up and down, the corner of his lips twitch with what I can only hope are thoughts that mirror my own. He steps forward and holds his hand out. "Come with me," he says, and I meet him halfway, grabbing his hand before getting dragged toward the back of the studio. He pulls me into the back room, a small insular space illuminated by one singular covered lightbulb in the center of the ceiling, its three walls lined with open shelving containing an assortment of items: dismantled barres, rolled up mats, random shoes, storage bins of various colored props, old speakers, and even an ancient boom box. The only sliver of flat wall is right next to the door, with which I become acquainted when pushed up against it as Milo crushes his mouth to mine, his hands ravenously running over my body, outlining the curves, and grabbing greedily. I meet his enthusiasm with my own, my hands deep in his hair and my body pressed into his. This is what I had been hoping for: a greeting to prove he'd been thinking about me as much as I had about him. But even with this fervent welcome, Dr. Collins's admonishment still nags at the back of my mind.

Milo hooks his left arm under my kneecap and lifts my leg up around his hip. His hand begins to creep up under my romper and fiddles with the hem of my underwear, daring to tickle the cotton and heated flesh beneath, but I flinch, distracted not only by the doubts floating in my head, but also by the possibility of being caught by a classmate. Seriously, if someone comes in, how are we going to explain coming out of the back room together? Ever aware of my body's reactions, Milo freezes and pulls back slowly, gently dropping my leg to the ground. His face is flushed, his lips swollen, and his breathing labored. Part of me is pleased I can affect him so quickly, while another part of me is kicking myself for showing the slightest hesitance.

"What's wrong?" His voice is gravelly, still caught up in the act of seduction. His pupils are blown wide with want, but he keeps his hands safely at my shoulders, kneading them in reassurance. I throw my head back in frustration, causing it to thud against the wall, and sigh loudly.

"I'm sorry. I'm all in my head."

He leans in close and starts placing small kisses on the sensitive skin framing my hairline, asking, "What's going on in this head of yours?"

"My therapist doesn't think I should be getting involved with you."

"Your therapist?"

"Yeah. I just mentioned I was spending time with you…outside of class…and he's…well, he's the cautionary type. You know, classic shrink: reserved, doesn't talk about himself, a bit stuffy. He's worried I'm not in a good place, that I'm not good for you…" I'm rambling and Milo cuts me off by placing two fingertips on my lips, quieting me instantly.

"He thinks you're not good for me? Is that even his place to say?" A tightness within my chest unravels at that comment. By rambling off the bad news, I was preparing myself for Milo to suddenly realize Dr. Collins was right and hightail it out of this storage room— and my life. But the flash of indignation that crosses his rarely-stern face lets me know he's in this with me.

"That's what I said!" I mumble from behind his fingers. His frown softens back into a small smile; he obligingly removes his hand, his fingers moving to my neck, caressing below my ear. I try to continue with my original indignation, but his fingers on my skin derail my train of thought. "I just…I don't want to be a burden…I'm new to this and we don't even know what this is…"

Having heard enough, he finally shuts me up by sealing his mouth over mine. All thoughts evaporate, including the negative ones planted by Dr. Collins. When we finally part, he rests his forehead on mine and says, "Annie, I'm a grown man. I know what I want, and I can take care of myself. And what I want is you. So can you stop thinking about your therapist and just be with me?" I slowly nod, my forehead still plastered to his. I'm about to say something when Milo whips his head up, looking through the wall in the direction of the main entrance. I hold my breath, not wanting to interfere with his auditory investigation. We both hear it a moment later: the sounds of the front door opening and feet clicking across the floor.

"Shit," Milo mutters and pulls away from me, turning his attention to the boxes. Hands on his hips, he scans his options, finally pulling a clear tub with a tangle of multicolored ribbons visible inside. He hands the tub to me, then grabs two rolls of black fabric from a top shelf. "Follow my lead," he says.

"Always," I respond, a bit giddy from the excitement of sneaking around, and we share a quick smirk as he opens the door and ushers me through. Just my luck. It's Lorraine and Dave standing in the middle of the studio, gawking as Milo and I emerge from the back.

"So, do you think this will work for your kid's pageant?" Milo asks a little too loudly, signaling me to play along.

I take an extended pause before answering with a mildly convincing, "Oh yes, Thatcher's teacher is going to be so grateful. I'll be sure to have it back by next week."

Milo then directs his attention to our in-awe audience as if just now noticing their presence. "Oh! Hi, Lorraine! Hey Dave! Great to see you. You're a bit early. I was just helping Annie here with some fabric for her son's play at school. I'm going to run this out to her car and be right back."

Dave has a knowing smirk as he looks from me to Milo, but

Lorraine seems to come to her senses. She turns to her fiancé, placing her hand on his shoulder, trying to bring him back to polite ignorance; but he continues to leer, making me feel even more exposed than I normally would in a tasteful summer romper. He stares at me and I look away, but Milo refuses to drop the charade. Lorraine just tosses her hair back, rolls her eyes at her husband, and says, "Sure, no worries. We were just hoping we could chat with you about possibly choreographing a reception dance for us."

"Oh, that sounds great! Yeah, we'll be right back," Milo answers cheerfully, and we stride past the couple. I refuse to look them in the eyes as we head to the parking lot and drop the tub of ribbons and the rolls of fabric in the back of my car. We huddle behind the lifted trunk for a bit of privacy as we talk.

"Well, now that I have all this fabric…" I wave my hand over the collection of material.

Milo laughs. "It was a good plan though, right?"

"They totally know, Milo. You saw how Dave was looking at us, right? Like I was standing there devoid of clothing and you were the freakin' man." Milo chuckles internally, unable to form words. "Seriously, are we going to get in trouble?"

Having gotten his fill of amusement, he composes himself and perches on the ledge of my open trunk. "It's fine, Annie. I doubt they would say anything. And if they do, it's not like I signed paperwork or anything saying I couldn't fraternize with students."

"Oh, so you've done this before?"

He glares at me instead of answering. "As I was saying: if anything, I might get a warning, but I'm only part-time. It wouldn't get me fired. So don't worry about it. And do me a favor—stop worrying about everything else. Can you do that for me? Give yourself at least one hour of worry-free time?" He reaches out and grabs my hand. It's already familiar and comforting, and I wonder how Dr. Collins can possibly think this is wrong. I know he's trying to watch out for me and my mental health, and I know it can get hairy, attaching my self-worth and happiness to a man of romantic interest, especially since I'm still learning how to let go of my life with Jason. But it can't possibly be a bad thing to have someone around to calm me down, make me laugh, release me from my usual constant state of stress, can it? Dr. Collins might have my best interest in mind, but so does Milo, and right now, I'm more convinced by his methods than Dr. Collins's.

I answer, wanting to please him with my effort toward being carefree. "I can try. As long as we aren't too obvious when we're dancing together. No roaming hands!"

"A little roaming hands?" He reaches over as if to graze my breast, and I slap his hand away.

"No. None. Zero roaming hands."

Milo sighs with playful disappointment. "Okay, I'll try to keep it professional."

I attempt a stern composure, but a curious smile betrays me as I look over to him and ask, "So, what are you teaching us tonight?"

His hand squeezes mine before he looks up, a flash of mischief in his eye. "The tango," he states simply. My eyes widen at the news, and Milo nearly barks with laughter.

"Well, we're fucked." A blunt statement, but accurate in so many ways. How are we supposed to look like we aren't sleeping together when we're dancing one of the most iconic of sexy dances?

"One can only hope," Milo replies without a beat. Our eyes meet, and we both crack up, shaking with laughter. Milo leans over to give me a quick peck, then heads in to talk business with Dave and Lorraine. I hang out in my car until other students show up, not wanting to be under Dave's perverted scrutiny again. As I wait, I try to think of the most unsexy things possible as I prepare to dance one of the

sexiest dances with a sexy man with whom I have shared some
incredibly sexy time all in an effort to make people believe Milo and
I are not having sex. How drastically life can change in a week.

The tango has a slew of sexy moves, but we spend most of the
class mastering the basic eight count. Milo begins by showing the
slow, slow, quick, quick, slow rhythm with me. We probably should
have practiced beforehand, but I guess we've been busy with other
physical exertions when alone. I'm not terrible, but he definitely has
to nudge me in the right direction a few times. I try not to get distracted by the feel of his right leg nestled between both of mine, especially on the rock steps; but when he leans over me, my senses are
assaulted with the touch and smell of him, and I'm only human.

Throughout the instruction, I ascertain that Milo is a far more
talented performer than I will ever be. Not once does he seem distracted or rattled by our proximity. In fact, he is all business throughout the entire class. He easily flows between showing the moves with
me, guiding the leaders with directions, then modeling for the fol-
lowers, and finally coming back to me after checking everyone's
holds and steps while partnered up. Once we mostly master the basic
eight count, he shows us some of the fancier moves, the ones often
highlighted in movies. I'm as helpful as a mannequin for most of
these, my body stiff as Milo drags it around his; but I eventually manage to relax and let him maneuver and bend me to his will.

He models the *ocho*, which is easily applied to the basic walking
step we just learned. Then he attempts to teach us a few turns and
grapevine moves, with a variety of outcomes. I'm actually impressed
by the grace of Mary and Leo, whose flame-hot intensity almost
leaves me blushing more than when Milo breathes down my neck
while giving directions during a bend. Finally, he ends the experimen-
tal section with a dragging move called the *barrida* and pairs it with

a *calesita*, which requires him to slightly lift and walk around me.

When he puts on some instrumental tango music for open dance and walks around for more individual coaching, I take the chance to sit and drink some water. I am all sorts of riled up from essentially an hour of foreplay. My entire body is flushed visibly against my coral outfit, my brow is glistening with sweat, and my breathing is shallow. From my chair perch against the back wall, I watch Milo glide around the room, repositioning, partnering, and finally releasing students into a more elegant gait and hold. He's really good at what he does, and his confidence is intoxicating. It's easy to imagine him performing on a grand stage in New York, a thought that pulls at my chest more than it should. I just found him, and I'm already imagining how I am going to lose him.

I try to shake the thought as I watch him circulate through all the students and make small talk, completely relaxed and in his element. I eventually drown out my downtrodden thoughts by focusing on the different couples swirling around the room as they smile and joke with one another. Watching couples dance almost feels like spying on their most intimate moments, and I catch myself staring too long at times, wondering if they look this relaxed when alone, or if they ever let the pressure of life encroach upon their connection.

Milo's announcement about the end of class stirs me from my trance, and I linger near the back, smiling and waving goodbye at the other students as they leave. Dave and Lorraine share a look and bend their heads together as they pass by me, but I ignore their quiet snickers and anxiously await the moment it's just the two of us.

Finally alone, Milo puts on a song, saunters up to me, and raises an eyebrow, holding out one hand in front, the other bent behind his back in a formal bow. "Can I have this dance?" I grab his hand and take my position. "Very good," he says, complimenting my form. "You must have a great teacher." I laugh and he nuzzles the right side of my neck with his nose, his breath tickling the sensitive skin that sends sparks of pleasure down my spine and across my belly. He moves me forward with his left foot, and we start gliding across the dance floor. I let him direct me completely, my eyes closing at times, focusing on the pressure of his hand on my back and the heat brewing between us.

I perk up as I recognize the instrumental. "Why do I know this?"

He leans close to my ear, tickling my earlobe when he says, "'Por una Cabeza.' It's been in a ton of movies. *Scent of a Woman, Schindler's List*."

"*True Lies*!" I answer with excitement and blabber on, reminiscing about a beloved movie from my childhood. "Man, Jamie Lee Curtis is so foxy in that striptease scene. Wait, how was I allowed to watch it as a kid?" I feel his smile against my cheek.

"You're foxy." He kisses my cheek, a sweet gesture silencing my erratic memories. "'Por una Cabeza' is the quintessential tango song. I saved it for you," he whispers, then moves me into an attempt of the *calesita*. As we spin around, he pulls me in closer, all the professional restraint he exhibited during class gone as his hands begin to stray from proper positioning. He moves his head so our noses are nearly touching, his eyes so close I can see the thin lines of light and dark brown slicing through his iris. He halts our dancing, eyes staring deeply into mine and asks, "Would you like to put those ribbons back in the storage room before you have to leave?"

My eyes widen with realization and I nod slightly, enough for him to register my agreement, causing him to comically break our hold, pull me toward the rear of the studio, and lock us in the storage room, back to where we left off before class.

The ribbons and fabric never make it out of my car.

23

Tick

*A very light double-take motion
of the head, neck, and spine*

I'm awakened by agonized cries echoing from Thatcher's bedroom. I groggily make my way down the hall to find him thrashing and hollering, still deep asleep.

I'm no stranger to night terrors. Jason struggled with them increasingly through the years. Between deployment and emergency room horrors, he had a wealth of subject matter from which to pull. Thatcher's night terrors were developmental, common for many toddlers, but he had a resurgence after Jason's funeral, kicking and screaming in multiple episodes a night. Thus began a month-long stint of sleeping in bed with him unless I couldn't sleep, which was most nights, and I would get up and wander the house until his screams called me back. Quelling bad dreams became second nature to me unless they were my own bad dreams. Then there was no one to soothe me except the silent walls of a sleeping house.

Those nights pacing alone warped my mind into believing I was helpless and hopeless, haunting me with possibilities of escape from the heaviness of grief. They made me forget that I was still alive and not part of the darkness. It's the only thing I can blame besides myself for the unforgivable actions made that torturous summer after Jason's death.

But I'm stronger now, and I can handle my son's pain along with my own. I sit down next to his writhing body and begin rubbing his back in soothing circles, attempting to calm his nightmare with quiet murmurings and tender endearments. A few minutes of this and his eyes slowly flutter open.

"Hey, sweetheart," I coo softly, surprised by his waking. Usually, he just drifts back to a calm slumber, but now he sits up and nuzzles closer into me, pressing his face into my chest. "Did you have a bad dream, honey?" He nods against my body and I stroke his hair. "Do you remember what it was about?"

Thatcher looks up at me, his big blue eyes glassy. His voice comes out cracked and troubled between sniffles, piercing the stillness of the house with its anguish. "I had a dream you died. Please don't die, Mommy."

"Oh, buddy. I'm sorry." I curl myself around him, cradling his body until he falls asleep. Even then, I don't leave. I hold him the entire night, my eyes wide open as I stare at the ceiling.

I am beset with death: death of loved ones, death of relationships, and the death of my previous self. The night Maggie found me, I could have died—but I'm still here. Maybe I should start putting an end to the cycle of loss and start forgiving, beginning with my relationship with Maggie.

By the next evening, forgiveness is the furthest thing from my mind. I burst into the kitchen and slam the offending piece of cardstock onto the counter, surprising Nick as he's standing in front of the open refrigerator, searching for an evening snack. He turns around slowly, his eyes wide as a spooked cat's.

"Look at this shit! She sent me a fucking postcard!" I spit through my clenched jaw.

Nick closes the fridge and slowly approaches the evidence of Maggie's and my broken relationship, gingerly picking up the card. "Oh, that's a nice picture of her." He starts reading, and I interject, ripping the paper out of his hand.

"Margaret freakin' Bishop! She fucking got married! She got married and didn't even tell me or her grandchildren, Nick!" I thought she was calling to mend fences between us, but now that's a blown theory. I'm fuming with rage, and I search wildly for something non-breakable that I can throw. I see a stuffed Paw Patrol doll and chuck it into the other room. Not even the soft thud of it hitting the floor can ease my anger.

Nick quirks his brow, probably questioning my sanity, as he watches me let loose a string of curse words that would make a pirate blush. The kids are safely in bed for the night after having put me through the ringer with whining, fighting, and running all evening. I was so looking forward to a relaxing Wednesday night, maybe even soaking in a bath for the first time in forever, but no—I had to go and check the pile of mail next to the front door. And there was Maggie's smile, which happens to be Jason's smile, looking up at me. In the picture, her back leans against the chest of a silver fox whose arms wrap around her possessively. They both look at the photographer, a gleam of joy in their eyes.

So many things are wrong with this development. For one, who the hell is this guy? It certainly isn't Friedrich. I met Friedrich at Jason's funeral, and while I wasn't the most aware of my surroundings or the people in it, his shaggy dark hair, prominent nose, and dark eyes were very different from this tall, broad man with a gray buzz cut, smaller symmetrical features, and light blue eyes that match the surrounding seascape. Maggie's green eyes, sun-kissed skin, and fluttery green sundress radiate happiness. I continue ranting, unable to dam the stream of suspicions and complaints flowing through my mind.

"And they eloped! Oh, she knew she was in the wrong. I mean, how dare she marry someone she's never even told me about, change her name, and look all content and adjusted! Does she not even think about her grandchildren anymore? Did she forget she had a son? I mean, I know she couldn't care less about what happens to me, but what about the kids? They haven't even met this man! Is she just going to expect them to start calling him Grandpa, or Pop Pop, or whatever the hell grandkids call older men?"

"Hey, Annie. Do you need me here for this or can I make a sandwich and head downstairs?" Nick interrupts my raving, and I freeze, thrown by his bluntness. He continues, his voice steady in its effort to calm my crazy. "Seriously, Annie, she's been trying to call you for the past two weeks."

I interject with a sharp, "Probably to tell me she was already married!"

Nick pierces me with a warning gaze, trying to snap me back to attention. "Okay, and even if that's the case, she's a grown woman. It's not like she needs your permission. Did you ask for permission to date Milo?"

"That is not the same thing! I'm not getting married! I'm not abandoning my family!" My voice comes out choked at the end of this line, and I slump onto a kitchen stool, burying my head in my hands.

I hear Nick's feet shuffle around the island before feeling the gentle tug on my fingers as he tries to pry them from my face. "Annie, look at me."

I'm mortified by my outburst, but mostly, I'm ashamed by my weakness. I'm supposed to be stronger, not crumpling at the smallest thought of another family member leaving me behind. But as much as I want to disappear into the ether, Nick refuses to let me hide. He finally succeeds in pulling my hands down, and he leans in front of me, forcing me to meet him eye-to-eye.

"Annie, just because Maggie is married doesn't mean she's abandoning you and the kids. You are not alone. If anything, you'll always have me."

Tears and snot are starting to flow, and I sniff between staggered breaths, keeping my eyes on Nick's as he anchors me to the real world. I manage to gasp, "I know," between sobs.

"People can move on and still keep you in their life. I'm going to move on someday, get my own place like a big boy, but you'll still always have me. Maggie's been trying to talk to you for how long now? I'm sure she has no intention of wiping you and the kids from her life. And you will move on, too, but that doesn't mean you are abandoning anyone, especially the kids." His stern tone is keeping me at attention, and I nod along with his words. Beginning to feel more grounded, I manage to squeak out my main concern.

"What about Jason? Are we just abandoning his memory by going on with our lives?"

Nick stops short, almost pulling back from my honesty.

"You have to go on with your lives, Annie. If you don't, there's no point in even being here."

We both freeze, the truth of his words seeping into our bones like a cold chill. He continues to hold my gaze.

"You want to be here, right?"

I nod.

"Just making sure. I thought you were doing better, even acting happier; but you and I both know that people can hide what they are really—"

"No, Nick. I am. I'm better. Happier…I'm sorry…I just…there's so much going on in my head. What with Maggie and Milo—"

"You could just call her, hash this out, and tell her you're in a better place. Maybe the two of you can work on getting back to a better place together." I wince, imagining the unbearable awkwardness of that dreaded phone call. Nick is undeterred by my face as he says, "You could ask about her new guy. Tell her about yours."

"Absolutely not." I shake my head, unable to think of anything I would rather do less than gab about Milo to Jason's mom.

Nick sighs and turns back to the fridge. I watch him as he grabs a block of cheese, a tub of ham, a jar of pickles, a head of lettuce, and a container of mayonnaise. He cradles the ingredients as he pivots around and kicks the refrigerator door closed. When he dumps the food on the counter, he's ready to give me his verdict.

"Do whatever you think is best, Annie. But when you actually take my advice and it ends up working out, I am definitely going to rub it in your face and tell you 'I told you so.' Things to remember about me: I'm usually right, and I'm the opposite of humble when it comes to that fact." He grabs a loaf of bread from the counter and starts constructing his sandwich.

I feel dismissed, but before I leave, I reach out and grab his wrist, stopping him in his mayo-spreading tracks. "Thanks, Nick. It means a lot you're here."

He smiles and winks, and we say goodnight. I scroll through my phone at the list of missed calls over the past few weeks as I make my way upstairs. Maggie's tried to call me at least ten times. I should probably call her, but when I go to select her name, my body halts, and I find myself selecting the text message stream with Milo instead. I quickly tap out: **What are you doing tomorrow?**

I need to talk to Maggie and get this all sorted out, but I also really need to just get away: from work, from kids, even from Nick and his smug wisdom. I think it's time to play hooky.

Pivot

A turn on the ball of the standing foot

Even though I've filled out the appropriate information and my day of leave is legit, I still feel like a teen skipping class when I drop the kids off at school and daycare and head into the city instead of returning to my home office for a day of claim analysis and responses.

Milo was more than eager to spend the day with me, asking that I meet him in front of the Art Institute around 10 AM, which gives me a little over an hour–plenty of time for coffee, traffic, and a walk along Lake Michigan. I secure my car in a parking garage and prepare to take in the warm spring day.

I'm dressed for the weather in a mid-length flowy cream skirt paired with a bright yellow ribbed tank. I figured I would drape myself in what I wanted to be today: bold, optimistic, and carefree. Sure, I might be the opposite of these most of the time, but it's worth a try. My feigned boldness has not transferred over into my calling Maggie, something Nick was sure to question me about this morning.

But I want this day, no, I *need* this day for myself before I go traipsing through the passive-aggressive pastures of Maggie's and my conjoined past.

There are quite a few people out on the streets, even for a Thursday morning. Most people are working, but an early lunch crowd is already gathering. Bicyclists and runners are taking advantage of this beautiful day, and a few seasonably early tourists are easily identifiable by their constant taking of selfies and checking of Google Maps. The anticipation of summer break is an electric buzz of promise radiating from the new growth of green, the cloudless blue sky, and the hot edge to the breeze coming off Lake Michigan.

I spot the iconic lion statues that guard the Art Institute a block ahead; I can see the sidewalks are teeming with pedestrians, peddlers, and performers. Something registers in my mind: a buzzed conversation with an Elton John reference? As I cross the last intersection before reaching the museum, I see the pods of people surrounding various points of attraction. There's a juggling clown on stilts swaying haphazardly above a family, much to the delight of the three young children who throw dollars in an upside-down hat. A woman with pink-streaked blonde hair strums a guitar and sings a cover of a Tom Petty song. I walk by, searching for Milo, hoping his height will help me spot him amongst the crowd, but as my eyes catch a gleam just past the pink-haired singer, I realize a search was unnecessary.

Milo's working—he's one of the buskers. And though he warned me, the details must have gotten lost in that action-packed night, and I had totally forgotten up until this moment what his side gig entails. He's a shiny dancer. *The* shiny dancer. The sun bounces off of his silver painted skin, hair, jacket, jeans, and boots. Every inch of visible skin is covered in a metallic lacquer. He remains still as a statue until someone drops money into a box; then, he springs to life with jerky, robotic movements, moving his body in mesmerizing ways. He resembles a machine, a mechanical Pinocchio as his limbs jerk, pop, and shift in unhuman-like ways. And then, he slows and stills as if a power cord has been pulled, prompting the gathered viewers to clap and move on or offer more money for another quick round of awe-inspiring limb manipulation.

I watch from a distance, not ready to reveal my presence and almost nervous to approach. I'm feeling a weird mixture of giddiness and fear. I want to be near him, but then others will look at me. I've missed him since seeing him two days ago, but that hasn't stopped me from overanalyzing us, wondering about his intentions and worrying about my ability to connect. Despite the internal battle, I reassure myself that Milo invited me here; he wanted me to see him in his element, and that gives me the small burst of courage I need to approach my silver-slathered swain.

I register it in his eyes when he locates me: a sparkle of mischief reflecting off his outreached right arm, his left bent akimbo at his side. Even though no one has paid, his right wrist cranks clockwise so his palm faces up, and he beckons me over to him with quick staccato bends of his fingers. I wince and look around, almost hoping his coaxing is meant for someone else, but no, a quirk of his lips and another robotic gesture convinces my legs to move me forward in a jerky, but much less impressive flow of motion.

I bite back a smile as I stand four feet away. He beckons. I scoot a foot nearer. He waves me closer, still in character, but the lack of finesse gives away a bit of impatience. Finally, I'm less than one foot away from him, completely in reach, his arm stretched out past my shoulder. The smell of paint fills my nostrils, and my skin prickles with the knowledge of Milo's nearness.

I raise my chin and tilt my face up to meet his, still unmoving except for his eyes, which haven't left me this entire time. "Okay, you've lured me here. Now what?" I tease, figuring if no one pays him, he's stuck like this. I don't really think that's true since he's essentially his own director and boss, but if I know Milo, I know he does not mess around with his art, so my bets are on his not breaking character.

A few people have circled around to see what I'm doing, facing-off with a busker. We're in a silent stand-off; then, I see Milo's eyes flick to something behind me. I glimpse backward and see a little girl place a bill into his box, her braided pigtails bouncing with her retreat. I haven't even turned back to face Milo before I am whipped into a hold, his hands on my waist and shoulder. Suddenly, I am part of the show as he spins, twirls, and lifts me in a strange amalgamation of ballroom dance and street style. I don't dare fight his lead. That could cause us both to end up sprawled on the concrete; instead, I follow, I melt, I bend. I let instinct take over, curated over the last few weeks in class and through my connection with my dance partner. I stand when he moves behind me, his limbs encircling me in entrancing rhythms. Then just as fast, he's in front of me again, and as a finale, he directs me into a *calesita* where I pivot on one foot as he dances around me, and then dips me so I'm propped against his bent knee with his face bowed over mine. His silver lips curl into a silent smile, and I throw my head back in laughter.

I feel free. In this moment, I *am* free. Free of grief, free of responsibility, and free of shame. I continue laughing, enjoying the feel of my body as it shakes and stretches. But then, my moment of reprieve is broken by applause from the crowd, which has tripled in size during our frenetic dancing. In my moment of emotional ecstasy, I had forgotten we were essentially on a stage in a very public venue. A line of people drop money into the box. My body tenses with the weight of multiple eyes on me as Milo gently pulls me up to standing. As the people move on, I ask quietly, "Can we leave now?" To answer, he holds his index finger up to his lips, collects his money box, then grabs my hand and directs me down the block and away from the institute. At the first crosswalk, he pulls me off of the main Michigan Avenue drag into a side alley where he finally drops the silent act, his whole body relaxing into normal Milo mode.

He runs his silver hands down my bare arms as he offers an apology. "Sorry to just throw you into it, but it was fun, right? And you were so good! And you look so beautiful. It was difficult not to kiss you in front of everyone," he says and envelopes me in a hug, pressing his smooth lips to mine.

I speak against his mouth, "That was impressive. I didn't know you could move like that."

I feel his lips curl against mine in a mischievous grin, and his hands dip to cup my butt, pulling my hips up to his groin. "Really, because I thought we've established my physical capabilities pretty adequately…" I squeal—still aware of our very public stance—and pull away, my head still bent close for a private conversation.

"Okay, I know you can move in many talented ways, but I guess I didn't realize you had such a different style from what I've seen so far."

"If I didn't have any surprises, it wouldn't be any fun, would it?" A pinch placed dangerously low causes me to yelp with surprise.

"I guess…" I take a step back, if only to calm down his wandering hands. His eyes droop with disappointment, but he recovers with one of his quintessential charming smiles.

He reaches out and strokes a piece of hair before tucking it behind my ear. "Thanks for meeting me here. I wanted to get in a few hours of work before hanging out with you, which I am so looking forward to. Thanks for letting me be a part of your day off."

Any hesitations I may have harbored are razed by his genuine politeness, and I can do nothing but reach up and kiss him tenderly, my lips warm against his matted mouth. I end the kiss reluctantly and ask, "So what should we do today?"

He reaches up and cradles my face. "Well, it's your day, so it's up to you, but first, I need to change and get this off." His head dips to reference his shellacked body and outfit.

"Oh."

"Don't worry; it comes off easily in the shower."

The image sparks a pulse of desire within me, and I curl my lips in a closed smirk. I know what I want to do today.

"Well, I guess a shower is first on our itinerary."

Two hours later, a shower is the only item accomplished on our itinerary. I lay naked on top of Milo's bare chest, my ear pressed against his heartbeat, my body rising and falling in sync with his breaths.

After a subway ride heavy with sexual tension and prolonged stares from strangers (more likely directed toward Milo's attire rather than the sexual tension), we barely made it through Milo's apartment door before clothes started coming off. The shower, though small, proved capable of removing the silver body paint, and we proved capable of using all of the hot water. We then managed to dry off before moving our escapades to the bed. And now we lie here unable and unwilling to move or even peel our bodies off one another.

I remember when Jason and I were in this phase of our relationship, where our sexual appetites could not be satiated. Add in his stints away for military leave, and we would almost combust with primitive physical need upon reunion. Though we were always sexually compatible, what I missed most after he died was the physical closeness, the pressure of his body on mine, the feeling of having someone know me like no other. While Milo and I don't know everything about each other, I still find myself comforted by our contact and at home in his arms. And the sex…well, it's fantastic. When we are together, it's as if we've stepped into a vacuum of existence where nothing can interfere, where my brain is silenced by the sensations assaulting my body. But in the afterglow, guilt and apprehension have a nasty habit of creeping back into the spotlight, something Milo can sense in the tightness of my muscles as he strokes my back.

"Are you going to tell me what prompted this spontaneous day off?" His voice rumbles deep in his chest against my ear, and I lift my head, resting my chin against his sternum.

"Are you complaining?" I ask demurely, my hand dipping down and my fingers skimming the hair around his navel as if reminding him of our recent joint activities.

A light grunt of pleasure vibrates deep within his chest, and one of his hands rises to dig into my hair, mindlessly twirling and brushing with his fingers. "Absolutely not. But I can tell something is bothering you."

I remain silent, thinking about everything that runs through my mind at any given moment. This seems like a lot to unload on him, so I go with the most recent thing. "It's my mother-in-law. Or I guess my ex-mother-in-law…I'm not sure how that works. The kids' grandma. She's been trying to talk to me the last few weeks, and I've ignored her calls."

"Why?" He lifts his neck to try and coax me to elaborate, but I lay my head back down to avoid eye contact.

"We've gone through some tough times since Jason's death." I sigh against his skin, my hot breath filling the pocket of air between us.

"Like what?" He waits.

"Just stuff about the kids," I answer, and he continues to wait. His hand stops playing with my hair, and I can sense an edge of impatience, a desire for me to explain, but I can't. There's a blockade in my throat, halting any information that might give away too much.

"So that's all I get." Disappointment drips from his voice, and I feel guilty I can't give him what he wants.

"For now."

"Okay…" His fingers go back to weaving through my strands, but it seems less lazy, more anxious than before.

"Well, anyway, I got this postcard from her yesterday, and it turns out she got married."

"Okay?"

"Without telling us."

I wait for him to get angry at the injustice of it, to validate my own indignation, but instead he says, "But you weren't talking to her anyway."

"Well…I know…but still…" My hands, which have been softly pressed against his collarbone dig in a bit, hoping to ignite some fury for my plight.

"So how can you be mad at her?" This is not the fury I was hoping for.

I whip my head up and lift my body off his, pulling the sheet over my breasts as I sit up next to him. "Why are you siding with her?"

He sits up to match my stance, our sex-induced lethargy quickly evaporated by the turn in conversation. "I'm not. I don't even know her, but I'm just trying to make sense of what you're telling me, which is never a lot."

I'm taken aback by this sudden accusation. "That's not fair. I tell you things."

"Really? Because I feel like every time I try to learn something about you, you freeze me out. I'm an open book, but every time I ask you something personal, you avoid it or change the subject."

I search for words, trying to deny this, but I can't. He's right. I do freeze him out. He watches me expectantly, waiting for my rebuttal. The only thing that comes to mind is more self-justification. "You just…you wouldn't understand, Milo."

His face screws up with disbelief edging toward anger. I know I've insulted him, and I tense, ready to guard my stance. "Are you kidding? I've been through my own shit, which I've shared with you. Why don't you give me a chance before assuming what I can and can't understand?"

"It's just different. You're younger—"

He throws his hands up in the air before dropping them forcefully onto his sheet-covered lap. "Oh my God, Annie. Get over it. I'm eight years younger. It's not that big of a fucking deal." His eyes are on fire, his body primed for offense.

"But you don't have kids, you didn't lose a spouse—" I scramble for an excuse, but he is quick to refute any of my futile attempts at reasoning.

"Lots of people have lost spouses, Annie. It doesn't make you special." I flinch backward, away from the uncharacteristic coldness of his tone.

"That's uncalled for," I say, my voice small with hurt. His vexation seems to relax as his shoulders lose some of their tension, but his eyes still shine with irritation, his nostrils flared with provocation.

"Okay, you're right. I'm sorry. But I just wish you would trust me enough to let me in." He looks at me, waiting for a response, an end to this mismatched dance, this game of cat and mouse where Milo keeps trying to catch me in an honest moment and I keep scurrying into the nearest hole.

"I'm sorry. But I can't."

"Can't what? Trust me? Talk to me like an adult?"

"Milo, I don't know what you expect from me!" I cry out, my inflection rising as I shake my hands in the air, losing my cover with the motion. I quickly replace the cotton shield over my nakedness and continue fuming.

He turns his head, his body taut and his chest heaving with anger.

He pins me with his gaze, his words piercing me and the connection I thought we had. "I expect for you to at least treat me like a human worthy of your respect rather than just some fuck boy you picked up to make you feel a little better about yourself!"

We're both surprised by the volume of his voice, the echo of his personal attack seeping into every crevice of the room, poisoning the once carefree air with toxic resentment and bitterness. I stare at him, unable to move or blink. The wave of emotion surging through my body is a mixture of anger, sorrow, and shock. His words make me feel dirty and pitied, and I need to leave. Immediately. "Wow," is all I manage to make out, and I start picking up my clothes.

"Annie, stop. I'm sorry…" His tone changes as he, too, rises from the bed, searching for pants and awkwardly trying to dress and chase me at the same time.

"Let me remind you that *you* pursued *me*. You were the one who showed up at my house. Twice! You're the one who invited me out, took me back to your place," I exclaim as I pull on clothes and shoes, punishing them as I stretch the fabric and push my limbs and head through the openings. I intersperse my dressing with accusatory points in his direction, and when I discover a white T-shirt on the ground, I toss it at his face, hoping he'll cover up his stupid, gorgeous body.

"I know. I was wrong. I shouldn't have said that. I shouldn't have said any of it. I didn't mean it. I'm sorry." He pulls the shirt on and stands there, slumped with remorse.

I've managed to pull on my skirt and my tank top, but I clutch my bra to my chest as I spin toward him. "No, Milo. You did mean it, or else you wouldn't have said it. So that's what you think of me? As some sad widow just looking for a side piece?"

He puts his hands up in surrender, bent over as if to address me on my level and calm me down. "No, but I do know you're lonely—"

"What?" I blurt in outrage, but he continues his desperate ramble.

"And unhappy with your life—"

"You've got to be shitting me," I snort, not believing what I'm hearing.

"And if you would just open up, talk to me…"

"About what? About my dead husband? About his mom and how she has moved on while I can't? About how I'm stuck in a house with my two children and my brother, and I feel like I can't escape? About how I only feel at peace when I'm with you and how guilty that makes me feel? How shitty of a mother I must be, that they're not enough to make me feel better? Is that what you want to hear?"

"Annie, I'm sorry…" he tries to interrupt, but I am in full attack mode now. He wanted me to open up and now all my secrets are bursting out.

"Or how about the fact I'm the one who found my husband's body? That I have to relive that scene almost every night? How I rack my brain every day, every hour, every minute wondering what signs I missed, what cries for help I outright ignored, how I could have been so oblivious? How fucking stupid and ashamed I feel for how I fucked up his life and how I almost fucked up my own? How I am trying so hard to be okay because I'm supposed to be, but I just can't? Is that what you want to talk about, Milo?" I spit out his name and stand silent, chest heaving as I try to catch my breath.

He approaches cautiously. "Annie, I'm sorry. I didn't know…"

"Of course you didn't know. Because I didn't want to tell you."

"But if you talked about it, don't you think you'd feel better?"

"Now you're starting to sound like my shrink." I glare at him, daring him to say what he shouldn't.

"Well, maybe he's right," he says. And I'm done.

"I have to go." I search the floor for my purse, finding it next to the door, and reach out for the doorknob.

"Annie, wait—" He tries to intercept my exit, but I'm too quick, too purposeful in my intent to escape.

I rip open the door, step into the hallway, and holler back, "Thanks for the fuck. I feel so much better now." And I slam the door.

All I wanted to do was continue to hide what an awful person I truly am from him, and now I've put her on full display. I hate Milo for making me reveal that part of myself, but I still hate me more.

~ ~ ~

"Why can't you tell me what's wrong?" I plead. Jason is leaning over the sink in our bathroom, refusing to make eye contact. I stand in the doorway leading to our room, blocking his escape. His shift was supposed to end at seven, and he just arrived home shortly before midnight, this being the fourth night in a row he's come home late. I've asked him what's wrong almost every day this past month: when he snaps at the kids, when he seems to forget what chore he was going to complete, when he doesn't come to bed at night and I find him in the basement the next morning. Each time I ask, he gets more irritated, and tonight, as he burst into the room, grabbed his carry-on suitcase from the closet and started tossing clothes in it, I asked again in a disorienting mix of grogginess and panic. He answered with a harsh, "Can't you just shut the fuck up for once?" and retreated into the bathroom with a slam of the door.

My body winced with each slam of a cabinet door and slap of a hand on the counter or wall. I opened the door slowly and watched my husband bend over the sink and suck in ragged pulls of air, his eyes wild and unfocused. I asked the question, softer this time, and am waiting for his response, any sign of recognition.

"Where are you going, Jason? What's with the suitcase?"

He squeezes his eyes shut and turns away, but I can see every-thing in the mirror. Pain contorts his face and wrenches my heart. He had a plan, but now he's battling with that version of himself, fighting to stay in place. I step forward cautiously, my right hand stretched out to warn of my approach. Jason's never hit me before, but he's never started packing in the middle of the night, either. I'm in new territory here, and I opt to tiptoe through the minefield rather than trudge across with heavy steps.

My fingertips touch his back, and a sharp inhale expands his ribcage. I lay my hand flat, encouraged by his stillness, and move forward. "Jason?" I put my other hand on his back and rub up and down, my touch stretching from his shoulders to his waist. "Jason, can you talk to me?" I wrap my arms around him and bend my body over his, my head flush against the rough cotton of his scrubs, moving up and down with his quick inhalations. We stay like this for a few minutes as his breathing begins to deepen and slow, and I remain silent, afraid to rouse the belligerent beast that just burst into our bedroom.

Eventually, he stands up straight and turns in my arms, wrapping me in a hug and tucking my head into his chest. He rests his chin on the top of my head.

"I'm sorry, Annie. I know I haven't been a good husband to you lately."

I hug him tighter, afraid he will still try to leave. "You're always a good husband. I just don't know what's going on. You're scaring me, Jason."

"I'm scaring myself." His voice catches, and I feel a sob rattle inside his chest. I look up and see tears pooling in the corners of his eyes, wet trails beginning to snake down his rough cheeks. His knees buckle, and we sink to the floor, holding each other.

"Please, just let me in, Jason. Tell me what's wrong. What can I

do?" I continue to plead with him, but he doesn't speak, just cries, soaking the right sleeve of my shirt. I'm covered in his tears, his scent, and his fear.

We don't leave each other's arms all night, but I've never felt more alone.

25

Sway

An inclination of the body away from the moving foot

A major fight always leaves me feeling as if I'm floating in time, my mind still in the argument while my body is going through the motions. While I replay the altercation with Milo, I rage-clean the house to the soundtrack of my cussing and wishing I'd never wasted a day off on such an ungrateful member of the male species. I even go so far as ruing the day I went to Ballroom Basics in the first place. I'm pissed.

I make spaghetti for dinner, and the kids don't even negotiate or complain. They eat in silence, most likely sensing my edginess. I'm proud of them for being able to pick up on my bad mood cue but also disappointed in myself that they would even have to know how to do that. Again, a notch in the column for poor parenting by Annie Obless.

After dinner, we curl up on the couch, a kid on each side of me, and watch one of our favorites: *Up*. Of course, I am in tears after the first montage where the wife dies, and Penny and Thatcher take turns soothing me by petting my arms and back, repeating, "It's okay,

Mommy," and, "Mommy, don't cry. It's just a movie."

That night, we all snuggle in Thatcher's twin bed, the three of us crammed together, and fall asleep reading *The Boxcar Children*. I wake an hour later when I hear Nick rustling around downstairs, another late night at the library. A weariness has settled in my bones and brain, but I gather the energy to deposit Penny in her room before I collapse onto my own bed, ready to put an end to all things related to this day and Milo. I plan to turn my phone off and ignore him and his hourly messages, but I take one last look before I hit the power button:

Annie, I'm sorry.

That was shitty of me.

Can I please just explain myself?

Annie. Please call me.

I understand you're mad. How can I make it up to you?

I'm sorry.

I'm not even mad at him anymore. I get it. Our interactions have been a bit one-sided the entire time we've known each other. He's always been the one to initiate a conversation, to reveal himself through a story or confession, to lead both on the dance floor and in the bedroom. I've been fairly passive in our relationship, letting whatever happens happen and not trying to invest too deeply. So I can't really blame him for calling me out on it.

What I find hard to forget is how he accurately detected my loneliness. Is it so pervasive that he sensed it all along? Is that what he was initially attracted to, the challenge of a lonely widow? Maybe he spoke out in regret, having second thoughts about getting involved with a mess like me.

I don't answer him. To do so could validate my fears and warrant further wariness. And that would break me the most. Because, as much as I tried to safeguard my heart, these past few weeks have given me a glimmer of hope that I could get back to a place of happiness, a place of joy, a place of future possibilities. And if it was all a lie, then maybe that glimmer of hope is just my imagination, and there's no escape from the cage of my grief and guilt.

I go to sleep alone, yet escorted all night by thoughts of men who have abandoned me and let me down.

Friday is a monotonous repeat of my standard day: get the kids to school, work from my home office with little human interaction, pick up and feed the kids, clean up their endless messes as they entertain themselves, and go through the bedtime routine. Penny and Thatcher aren't as easygoing on me. I guess yesterday's night of parental pitying passed its expiration date. They fight over who gets to stand in front of the sink while brushing their teeth. Thatcher calls Penny a stinky buttcrack head, which apparently is the worst insult ever if Penny's reaction of sobbing, throwing herself on the ground, and kicking her feet is the gauge of injury. Penny refuses to listen to a book Thatcher picks, and I end up skipping bedtime songs and just closing their doors and letting them cry themselves to sleep. Yep, just another Friday.

Nick came home for an hour this evening before heading out for drinks with the renovation crew. He flashed me a toothy grin as he told me he was going to Applebee's. Not in the mood for his favorite game of Let's Rehash Annie's Most Embarrassing Moments, I rolled my eyes and continued urging the kids to eat the meatloaf I thought I would try on them, hoping increased skills in the kitchen could move me up the adequate mother meter.

The rest of the night has involved me getting lost in rosé and random crime documentaries. If anything, this helps me feel better about myself as a human being. At least I haven't stalked a family, murdered them in the middle of the night, and thrown their bodies off a bridge.

Maybe I am winning in this game of life.

A detective is stiffly narrating the details of the home invasion when my phone pings.

Can we talk?

This is the first I've heard from Milo today. When I powered my phone on this morning, a few more messages popped up, but he apparently gave up or went to sleep, and it's been radio silence since. I place my phone face down next to me, prepared to turn it off again if he plans a repeat of last night. I hear the ping of another message and roll my eyes. But as I read, my annoyance shifts into alarm.

I'm here at your house.

I nearly jump out of bed as I rush to my bedroom window and peer from behind the blinds. Nick's truck, having rumbled into the driveway an hour ago, is indeed blocked by a car I don't recognize. I consider ignoring Milo, pretending I'm asleep; if I do that though, he might start knocking or ringing the doorbell, which could wake up the kids, or even worse, get Nick's attention, and then I would have to deal with his snide comments.

I rush down the carpeted stairs and head to the front door, sticking my head out while keeping my pajama-clad body covered. Milo stands on the front porch, instantly perking up at my presence. He's wearing a gray T-shirt and gray sweatpants, and his hair sticks up in random tufts. As I crack open the door, my senses are assaulted with the scent of Ivory soap, his brand of choice, which causes me to think of yesterday's shower encounter. My body strains to welcome him, but my mind refuses to give in so easily.

"What are you doing?" I ask through clenched teeth.

His brows are furrowed together and the corners of his mouth are turned down, not a look I'm used to seeing on him. He leans even closer since I'm still restricting him to the porch, and I defensively pull back inside a bit, causing a look of shock to flash across his face.

He takes a step back, palms open, a white flag meant to assuage my fears.

"Annie, I need to talk to you."

"As you mentioned several times yesterday."

"I know. I'm sorry. That's usually not my style, but I just couldn't let you go thinking...I just couldn't let you go." He takes a big breath, and his shoulders drop with his exhale.

"It's late," I weakly offer as an excuse.

"I know. But I had the show tonight, and I wanted to shower before I came over." Realization dawns on me. Of course he had the show. He had a performance last night, too, since *Rent* runs for three weeks Thursday through Sunday, which means he was texting me all throughout the show last night. Shame fills me as I imagine him sneaking backstage in hopes of my replying, and the thought is enough to break my resolve and hear him out. I look back into the house, faint light coming from the basement suggesting the probability of Nick still being awake. I step inside and open the door more, signaling him in. His eyes instantly latch onto my pajamas, a top and shorts set made of soft thin cotton, covered in cartoon cats. Plus, I'm not wearing a bra, which is very apparent with the evening breeze that follows him inside.

I widen my eyes to scold him out of his distraction and direct him to follow me upstairs with a toss of my head. But before we walk on the carpet, I look at his shoes and wait for him to remove them at the entryway. I might have been a lousy mother tonight, but I still don't want my kids playing on dirty carpet.

I lead him to my bedroom, passing by Penny's and Thatcher's closed doors as quietly as possible. Sure, on most nights, they wouldn't even stir if I started blasting music, but kids have a way of knowing the worst time to break norms. That's the last thing I need right now.

I shut us inside my bedroom, and words start spilling out of Milo's mouth as if a dam has been released. "Annie, I'm so sorry. I should have never lashed out at you. I know you've been through a lot, and I understand if you're not ready to talk about things yet, if you're not at that place yet. But I want you to know I am. I'm ready. I'm there. I want us to be honest with each other; I want to tell you things I don't tell other people. Annie, I'm ready to be all in, but if you aren't, that's okay. I can wait."

It's a lot to take in, and I plop onto the foot of my bed, trying to collect my thoughts. Thankfully, Milo gives me the space and time I need, frozen in place, waiting patiently for my response. I make him wait, and even then, my answer is slow, my words tenuous and fragile. "It's just hard for me to let you in because if I do, it's going to be that much more painful when I have to let you go."

"You can't think like that, Annie." He steps over and kneels down in front of me.

I'm not angry with him anymore. How could I be as he looks at me with those soft brown eyes? The same ones I've stared into during our most intimate moments? But I have to be honest. He deserves at least that much. My voice is shaky as I say, "I have to think like that, Milo, because the last time I didn't, it almost killed me. It broke me. I'm still broken, and I'm worried I'm just going to destroy anyone else who gets too close to me."

He reaches forward and grabs my hand in both of his. His eyes glitter with intent, and I can't look away as he utters softly, "Then destroy me. Please."

"Stop—" I try to interrupt and pull away from him, but he refuses both actions, talking over my negations and anchoring me with his strong arms.

"No, I'm serious. I can handle it. Life already tried to beat me down, and I survived. I got a second shot, and now I make sure I live every day going for what I want, making the most of my time. And right now, I want you. I want to be with you, Annie, just as you are. So try your best, tear me to pieces, destroy me. But know I'm not going anywhere."

I know it's a false promise. No one can make that promise. Life is too unpredictable, too cruel, but I want to believe him. And right now, that's enough. He remains kneeling, head tilted up, waiting for my answer. His hands have drifted to the top of my thighs, clinging desperately. I place a hand on each of his, curling my palms around his fingers and pulling him up.

I could release him at this moment, tell him it will never work—that our lives are too different, and I don't want him. But I would be lying. To him and to myself. I want him more than anything I've wanted in a long time, and I don't even care if it goes against what others may think is proper or right. I loved Jason. I was a good wife. I love my children, and I try to be a good mother. But how much of myself do I need to sacrifice to prove those very things to everyone else? I'm done proving myself.

I reach up and run my hand down his cheekbone, his eyes closing with relief. I trace his jawline and grab his chin, tipping it down toward me. My hand continues its journey, tracing his neck, his collarbone, until it rests flat on his chest. My other hand wraps around his neck, my fingers sinking into the soft hair at the base of his skull as I pull him down and into a slow, lingering kiss. His arms wrap around my waist, his hands resting on the small of my back, pressing his body hard against mine. My lips part, inviting his tongue to dart in, stroking the length of mine. I groan with longing, and his hands suddenly grip me tighter and lift me up. My legs instinctually wrap around him, pulling him in as close as possible, and we continue kissing as he gently lowers me down onto the bed and covers the stretch of my body with his.

We continue kissing and touching as Milo mumbles against my skin how sorry he is, how special he thinks I am, and how beautiful I look in my cat pajamas. Our clothes come off in slow increments, allowing us to enjoy each new reveal. Even though we've already seen everything, this is different. We aren't rushing with frenzied passion; we are taking our time, enjoying the process, and reveling in each new baring of both body and soul.

When we are both finally naked and shivering with desire, Milo enters me slowly, my body clenching and melting at the same time. We move with languid arcs and rises, a radiating pleasure morphing from a small flame into an inferno threatening to burn through my entire body. I'm unable to stifle my cries of ecstasy, and Milo covers my mouth with his, continuing to move until he succumbs to his own conflagration.

Afterward, we fall asleep in each other's arms. I don't dream, I don't see Jason, and I don't make the fateful journey down our basement stairs for the first night in over a year.

26

Connection

A physical non-verbal communication between dancers to facilitate synchronized or coordinated dance movements

The persistent pressing of a cat hungry for food and attention wakes me up. I roll over, upsetting Marshmallow's balance on my legs, and burrow deeper under the covers. I flop my arm out and touch warm skin. Jason's name forms on my lips, but last night's images begin to scroll through my brain—a montage of touch, bodies, and pleasure—and I relax back into the pillow, closing my eyes tight against the bright sun seeping in through my window.

A sudden thought alarms me. I twist around to check the time on my clock. It reads 5:43 AM, and the pounding in my chest slows down an iota. I recently bought the kids each a special alarm clock that emits a red light during bed time, then turns green when they are allowed to leave their bedroom, bathroom breaks being the exception, of course. On weekends, the green light is set for seven, not that they always wake up that early. But it's prevented unreasonably early mornings, and I think the kids are grateful for the set standard. I know

I am. Especially today, since a naked man is still in my bed.

Guilt tugs at me for planning to wake him, but we need to get ahead of the situation and figure out if he is going to sneak out or make up a blatant lie. Milo lays on his stomach, his arms folded under his head like a pillow. His face is turned in my direction, one cheek squished and red, his eyelashes fluttering in contrast with his deep breaths. I scoot closer and start tickling his face, my fingers dancing across his temple, cheek, and gently flicking his nose. I mutter his name softly, and he groans and shifts further to his side. His eyes slowly squint open and a smile lights up his slack jaw.

Without a word, he reaches out and wraps me in his arms, pulling me in close and grunting in morning welcome.

"Milo, it's almost six."

"Okay?" he mumbles into my hair.

"My kids usually get up at seven."

"Good. That means we have another hour." He tightens his hold, and I protest with only partial seriousness, keeping my giggles at whisper-level, not wanting to wake the other humans in the house.

Safe against his warm body and secure in last night's intimate rawness, the need to finally reveal my secrets and take shelter in his shared knowing bubbles ferociously within my chest.

"Milo," I say again, attempting a firm tone amidst the choked laughter.

"Huh?" He bends his head to nuzzle into my bare chest, and I try to push him away.

"I really want to talk to you."

"Okay," he says, his voice muffled by my breasts, but he still makes no move to take me seriously.

"Milo! I'm ready to talk. About all of it." He finally catches on and lifts his head, hair sticking up comically, face flushed with heated playfulness.

"Really?"

I nod, my lips twitching in a hesitant smile. He adjusts his body, so he's still turned toward me but gives me space in which to breathe and talk. He props his head up on his hand and looks at me expectantly, ready to listen.

I'm also propped on my side, finding comfort in our mirrored positions. I sigh and begin: "I've never told anyone this. Not my brother, not my mother-in-law, not even Dr. Collins. I mean, they all know what happened, but I've never actually said it out loud. All they know is what was in the police and coroner's report." It dawns on me that I have denied my husband's story and an important part of my story for the past year by refusing to discuss it. The realization makes me sad but also makes me more resolved to finally set things right.

"I just haven't been able to go through the details, to live that night over again." I pause, and Milo reaches out to grab my hand, stroking my thumb in encouragement. I continue, "The truth is, I relive it over and over again, every night when I dream about it and sometimes in the day when I see Jason. The only night I haven't dreamt about him was last night. The first night in over fourteen months, so maybe it's a sign that I'm ready; that if I talk about it, I'll be closer to being better."

Milo interjects softly, "It's not about being better, Annie. You're perfect the way you are." He lifts my hand to his lips and kisses my thumb.

"I know. But I want to be better at talking about it. Someday the kids are going to want to know the full story, and I need to make sure I'm strong enough. I won't be if I keep running away from it."

I flip onto my back and look at the ceiling. Milo continues to hold my hand but makes no move to encroach on my position of safety. After a prolonged pause, he urges me on softly. "So what happened?"

"Jason and I met in college. We were together for almost fifteen years, and like in any relationship, we had our ups and downs.

"Jason, I can't keep doing this!" I scream, safe enough in the basement, so the kids won't hear us. I've discovered him hunkered down here, where he always seems to be these days. Far away from me and the kids.

"Doing what? Giving me the space I need? Not getting what you want every day of your life?" His words feel like a slap on my cheek, and I take a step back.

"Why are you being like this? What have I done?" I'm pleading, but this is bigger than him and me. This is our family, our home, our whole existence.

The vicious gleam in his eyes suddenly disintegrates, his gaze softening. "You haven't done anything, Annie. I'm sorry." He's always sorry now. We both are.

"The last year was by far the roughest. The kids were even needier than they are now, if you can imagine; his anxiety was hard to manage and his work was really stressful. He was an ER nurse at Lakeview United, and he started working longer and longer hours."

Jason stands at the kitchen sink, staring out the window as I come up behind him and touch his bicep. He startles, and my eyes dart to the soft, veiny-patch of his inner elbow as he swivels toward me. "Ouch, one of your students really got you bad." A cluster of angry red punctures and yellowing bruises stain his skin.

He goes to cover the injury with his other hand. "Oh, yeah. You know how nursing students are. Give them a primed vein, and they'll hit muscle." He raises his arms to lift them over me and pulls me in tight against his chest. I let him steer me and the conversation elsewhere.

"I didn't think anything of the track marks. But there were other signs, too. Constant night terrors, difficulty focusing, extreme mood swings. I attributed it all to some form of PTSD. He had been an

Army medic, spent two tours in the Middle East, and his dad died while he was on active duty. But it wasn't all the time.

"The night he died, he actually came home as planned. He played with the kids, he laughed, he flirted with me…I thought everything was back to normal…"

The bed feels cold and empty. It's almost three in the morning, and Jason's not here. I make my way down to the basement, lured forward by the soft glow of his desk lamp. The shadows distort my depth perception, and I run my hand along the wall to keep my balance. My bare feet finally slap against the new laminate landing. The cold seeps through my soles and sends chills to the base of my neck.

I look to the corner, where Jason is slumped over, asleep at his desk. His laptop is closed and his arm is spread across the jumble of papers, folders, pens, and knick-knacks. Several of the kids' drawings are scattered among the desk and floor where they seem to have fallen or been pushed.

I whisper Jason's name, wanting to wake him, but not jar him too quickly. I place a hand lightly on the back of his neck and gently shake. His neck is cold on my fingertips, and even colder on my palm as I lay it flat against his skin. Confused, I repeat his name louder, more insistently. I shake him aggressively. My gaze starts at his shoulder and trails down to where his arm is stretched out, the fleshy part of his inner elbow propped up awkwardly.

"I tried to wake him, but he wouldn't wake up. And then I saw the needle, glass container, and pill bottle underneath his outstretched arm. Otherwise, there weren't any other of the things you see in the movies: no tourniquet, no blown vein…I would have sworn he was asleep…"

I need a moment, so I sit up to catch my breath. I'm feeling too exposed, so I grab a baggy sweatshirt, underwear, and leggings from my dresser. Milo uses the time to find his own items of clothing, returning to sit on the bed and holding out his arms for me. I let him hold me close, my back to his chest as he leans against the headboard.

He places a soft kiss on my temple and asks quietly, "What was it?" I angle my head in question. "In the bottles."

I'm surrounded by the sterile white floors, sad gray walls, and stale air of a windowless hallway in Lakeview United. My eyes zero in on the stitched name above the pocket of the doctor's lab coat: Dr. Goldstein. It's all I can do as he drones on about the toxicology report.

"We found high levels of fentanyl, which matches what was found on his person. A mix of liquid and pill form. Did you have any idea he was using? Apparently, there were reported suspicions he was stealing from the med station, but he would have been purchasing off the street, as well. With such a high dose, he must have been using for a while; he could have built up a tolerance. Mrs. Obless, are you telling me there were no signs?"

I manage to croak out a weak reply, my eyes tracing the cursive etchings above his breast pocket. "But he was a really good nurse... he would have known..."

"I'm sorry, Annie."

"I just don't know why he would have started taking it. He knew what could happen, he knew what drug addiction could do to a person...But what I worry about the most is... what I sometimes think is...it was my fault."

"Annie—"

"My fault for putting pressure on him, for not controlling the kids better, for being too needy or erratic or just too much...And what I'll never know is whether or not that night...was he just trying to get high and overdosed on accident, or did he do it on purpose? Could he just not manage to be around me and the kids without a fix? Or did he just not want to be around us at all anymore?"

"You can't think that way."

"Well, I did, and sometimes I still do, but I'm starting to less and less."

"How much did the kids see?"

"When I realized he was dead, I called 911. Then, I woke the kids and took them next door to Mr. and Mrs. Montgomery's…I don't remember much after that…"

"That's a lot of trauma." He strokes my hair, soothing me as I relive the events of that night.

"That's not even the whole story. Remember my mother-in-law, Maggie? She came to help with the funeral, and she ended up staying for several weeks, waiting for me to get back on my feet, figure out how to navigate life on my own…Well, I couldn't do it. I couldn't do life and I couldn't sleep…"

The orange pill bottle sits on my nightstand, mocking me with its fake promises of sleep. Atarax was supposed to reduce my anxiety, help me fall asleep amidst the constant flashbacks and sightings of Jason. But it's only allowed me maybe an hour of uninterrupted sleep before a dream brings me back to my own living hell.

I open the top drawer and grab the unopened white bottle with bold black letters identifying the contents inside: Xanax. I unscrew the top, catch one of the white rectangular pills in my palm, and pop it in my mouth. I grab my half-filled wine glass and wash down the pill with a gulp of Chardonnay. I know I'm being careless, but I'm desperate to sleep. Is this how Jason felt? Desperate to stop the horror film in his brain, just needing a break where his mind could be blank and unbothered by bullying thoughts?

My sight gets fuzzy, and my head feels heavy as I finally start to drift off, destined to eventually wake up and live my nightmare all over again.

"One night, I took too much, and Maggie found me."

"Oh, Annie," Milo mumbles. I lean my head back into the hollow of his neck and stare at the ceiling.

"I threw up and passed out after some hefty hallucinations. I wasn't trying to die, I swear, and I wouldn't have…I don't think…I told the doctors it was an accident, but Maggie didn't believe me. She threatened to take me to court for custody of the kids if I didn't start seeing a therapist." I shift within Milo's hold and lean my shoulder into the crook of his arm, so I can see him. His face is attentive, but serene. Devoid of judgment or horror. He hasn't tried preaching to me, telling me how poorly I behaved, something I feared would happen after sharing the truth. He's just listening to me. Being able to talk this through feels like a rebirth, a chance to emerge anew into my current life.

"Maggie was never the most available grandmother. Hell, she wasn't the most available mother, yet here she was threatening to take my children away."

"It's not up to you, Maggie!" I cross my arms and plant my feet, staking a claim in my own kitchen.

"Annie, you are a threat to yourself and the children—" Maggie starts to say, but I cut her off.

"My children are not in danger." I glare across the room, ready to play my last pawn. "Maggie, I will go to therapy. But I will not leave my home nor my children. Nick is going to move in, and I would appreciate it if you'd give us some space."

She pauses, her green eyes glittering. "Is that what you really want?"

"Thank you for your help, but I think it's time you went back to Kalamazoo." I set my jaw, ready for a rebuttal, but it never comes. Maybe she's as ready to move on as I should be.

"That was the last time I saw her. She called weekly at first, but the calls turned to texts, and eventually she stopped… Maybe it was because I was so short with her, but I think it's hard for us to be around each other knowing all we had in common was Jason. And now...that's gone... He's gone."

I stop, having reached my limit of emotional revelations for one day. I'm mentally spent from this conversation, but leaning against Milo helps; I feel safe, heard, and optimistic.

"Can I say something?" He broaches the question with hesitance and respect for the heavy moment, making it easy for me to nod my permission. "And you won't get mad?" I glare with mock warning. "It's a good thing Maggie did that, isn't it? It was what you needed to get back on track, right?"

"I guess," I admit reluctantly, even though I've said this to myself many times.

"Well, have you told her? Maybe even thanked her? She probably feels guilty for what she did to you, but if you told her how much it helped you, maybe you could mend your relationship."

I stare at Milo, wishing a smart quip could salvage my side, but no words come to mind.

"You don't have to do it right now, but I think it would be good for you both, give you both some closure." I lean into him and rest my head back down. He tilts his head to touch his lips to mine. I wasn't expecting a kiss to be what I needed at this moment, but it is. I relax into it, my breath catching as he pulls away. He rests his forehead against mine and says, "Thank you."

"Thank you? For what?"

"For telling me. That means a lot."

"Well, thank you for listening."

"Always."

I can't help but kiss him again, rising so I'm sitting in his lap. I've been so resistant to talk about Jason and that night, but finally giving in and opening up has actually made me feel even more connected to Milo, less burdened by the past. As our kissing intensifies,

I place a leg on each side of his hips in a straddle, his groin already pressing with need against me. We start to move, our bodies eagerly picking up on the opening notes of this song, but just as his hands start to lift at the hem of my shirt, I hear a door click open and feet scamper down the hallway.

Milo and I break apart just as my bedroom door is thrown open, so we are perched on opposite sides of the bed when Thatcher appears in the doorway, rubbing his eyes.

"Hey, baby! Good morning!" My voice is a little too bright, a little too high-pitched, but he doesn't seem to notice as he lumbers over to my side of the bed and drops his head in my lap.

"Mommy, what is Milo doing here?" he asks, his voice sleepy and muffled. I rub my hands through his hair and turn to Milo with wide eyes. We narrowly escaped getting caught red-handed, but we still have to explain ourselves.

Milo stands up suddenly, a story at the ready. "Hey, buddy! I had so much fun with you on your birthday I thought I would come back and hang. Is that cool?"

Thatcher lifts his head and assesses Milo's proposal with somber consideration. "Did you bring donuts?"

"Donuts!" Penny bursts into the room, wearing nothing but My Little Pony underwear. The girl knows how to make an entrance.

"Penny! Where are your pajamas?"

"I got hot!" she gleefully hollers as she skips over to me, already competing with her brother for my attention. Only then does she seem to register Milo's presence, pointing and squealing with delight, "Hey, Milo's here!"

Milo takes the opportunity to break the news. "No, I didn't bring donuts..." The kids groan with disappointment. "But I can make pancakes. If that's okay with your mom, of course."

My cheeks hurt from trying to contain too big of a smile, and I nod as the kids start shouting.

"Pancakes! I love pancakes!" Penny is definitely a breakfast food enthusiast.

"Uncle Nick makes the best pancakes, though." Thatcher stares at Milo, sizing him up based on his reaction to this declaration.

Milo rises to the challenge with a smooth, "Well, I guess you've never tried my pancakes before. But first I have to ask, do you have bananas? And chocolate chips?"

The kids yell with excitement and rush downstairs to start collecting ingredients. I stop Milo at my bedroom door with a hand on his shoulder. "I'm sorry you got wrapped up in all of this."

"Don't apologize. This is exactly where I want to be." He gives me a quick peck on the lips and grabs my hand, leading us downstairs after the children. As we leave the bedroom, I feel as if I've left something in there, something I've been trying to shed for a long time; and I step into the bright possibility of a Saturday morning of stolen glances, secret messages, and fluffy pancakes.

"These are pretty good. I don't know if they're better than mine, but definitely a contender." Nick tucks into a pile of banana chocolate chip pancakes smothered in syrup as Milo and I sit across from him in awe at his ability to pack the stacks away. The kids helped Milo ransack the kitchen, ate two pancakes each, and then vacated the area just as Nick was lumbering up the stairs. We received a knowing look from my brother, but Milo immediately made up a plate and I shoved it at Nick, hoping to either distract him or occupy his mouth before he could say something stupid. As he takes his last bite of pancake, I realize that strategy was short-lived.

"So, I'm assuming you didn't pop over for an early morning visit, and this is what you were wearing last night, young man." He shakes a fork up and down in Milo's direction.

"Nick…" I warn.

At the same time, Milo scoffs, "Young man? Aren't we pretty close in age?"

A fork in Milo's direction. "I'm still your elder." Fork swings to point at me. "Sis, I'm just using the power of deduction. Plus, I was blocked in all night."

"How would you have known that?" I call his bluff.

"I left my phone in my truck and saw that little outfit." He gestures toward the driveway where a white Toyota Corolla sits.

"Oh man, I'm sorry. That's my mom's car. I didn't want to park it on the street."

"Nah, that's fine. Sure, I couldn't get out for the 5 AM kickboxing class I had on my calendar—"

"You did not, you liar—"

"But I'll forgive you due to the fact that you make a mean pancake. My regards, good sir." He tips an invisible hat in Milo's direction, and I roll my eyes before rising to clear the dishes.

Milo gets up to help me tackle the baking battlefield that is my kitchen while Nick remains seated, hands behind his head in full-belly relaxation. "Wait, that's your mom's car? Do you not have your own car then?" I think back to the silver Acura he's driven here the last few times.

"No, I just borrow from my mom or friends if I need to get out of the city. You saw how bad parking is at my place." He flashes a smile at me and starts filling the sink with water.

"Oh, did you now, sis?" Nick says from the peanut gallery.

"Whose car was it you drove here before?" I ask as I drop a stack of plates into the soapy water.

"Just a friend's," Milo answers nonchalantly.

"Still discovering new things about each other. What a fun phase."

"Nick! Don't you have something to do this morning? Isn't there another kickboxing class you could go to?"

"Oh God, no. That sounds awful." He rises and heads toward the basement, tossing back a quick, "Oh, hey Milo, could you move your mom's car? Thanks, bud."

Milo nods and looks around, realizing we're finally alone. He takes two steps to catch me in his arms and plant a long, sultry kiss on my lips. "What do you want to do today?" he mumbles against my mouth.

"Don't you have a show tonight?" I pull away, not wanting to be a burden.

"Yeah, but call-time isn't until six. I usually busk on Saturdays, but it'd be a late start…"

"I'm sorry," I blurt out.

"No, it's fine. I'd rather be here. Anyway, I told Thatcher I was here to hang. Let's hang." A silly grin crosses his face, so infectious a grin of my own slices through my worries. I lace my arms around his neck and pull his mouth back down to mine just as high-pitched screams break out from upstairs. Hollers of "Mommy!" and various accusations drift down the stairwell.

I sigh. "Well, we fed the little monsters and now they have boundless energy. You sure you're up for a day with this?"

"Of course. You forget, I have boundless energy, as well." He starts to lead me up the stairs, ready to tackle whatever chaos awaits.

"How could I ever forget?" I smile coyly. He delights in my innuendo with a toothy grin and one of his signature winks that flips my stomach.

"You want me to check on them? Let you hop in the shower?"

"Sure. I'll make sure they haven't murdered each other first, but yeah, I'd love a shower. It'd be better with you…" I reach out and slip my hand under his shirt to graze his abs, and a groan of desire echoes from his throat, but another chorus of battle cries interrupts our amorous approaches. I indicate upstairs with my eyes and we march into the skirmish.

A sense of déjà vu overwhelms me as Milo enters Penny's bedroom and tries to break up the fight. It feels good to have a partner in this again, but it also feels...wrong. I just shared the story of Jason's death. That doesn't mean I'm ready to replace him. I do my best to shake away any doubt. This is a good thing. This is going to be a good day. But for some reason, I can't believe things can be this perfect. And if they are, I certainly don't think I deserve it.

27

Lilt

A gentle rise and fall, an intonation or cadence with a rhythmic quality, suggesting a place of weightlessness or a carefree state of drifting

The following week ends up containing more joy, laughter, and spontaneity than the past two years of my life. Milo stays at our house all day Saturday until he has to leave for his show; this prompts a slew of questions from Thatcher and Penny, so now we're planning to go watch the last performance next Sunday. Sure, there's sex, drugs, and AIDS, but I think they will be too distracted by the dancing and music to really catch on—at least I hope so.

On Sunday, I get grocery shopping done, as well as collect summer day camp supplies for the kids: new lunch boxes, water gear, and snacks—lots of snacks.

On Monday is work and school as usual, with lots of texting back and forth with Milo. We decide we can wait until Tuesday before one of us makes the drive, but then Milo surprises me at nine. I'm certainly not disappointed about having to share my bed. He does leave before the kids and Nick wake up, but Nick seems a bit suspicious about my good mood, calling me out on it several times before he leaves for work.

On Tuesday, I arrive at Dr. Collins's, ready to share my tale with him. Milo and I agreed it would be helpful to my healing process to go through the story with Dr. Collins just as I had with Milo. Since it has already been recounted once, the second time proves easier, my brain well aware of places in the story where I might need a break or diversion to avoid a complete meltdown. Dr. Collins is overjoyed with my progress, saying, "I'm so glad you finally allowed yourself to open up and be vulnerable. This is just the beginning, but I think we're in a really good place." His positivity prevails even when I admit my relationship with Milo is becoming more serious. He can't help but lecture me about the undesired effects of codependency, but even that doesn't ruin my enthusiasm for my upcoming class with Milo.

Our second to last class is the mambo. A lot of the instruction involves having everyone face forward in a line just to get the basic foot moves and hip rolls. When it's time to partner up, I suggest that Milo dance with all the female students, as well as Ted and Nathan. While he does that, the rest of us mix up partners. The other women have been eyeing Milo more predatorily the last few weeks, all riled up from the Latin dancing, so they are more than willing to get their hands on him—literally. Wanda's the worst, blatantly gripping Milo's ass. He handles it like a pro, sliding away demurely and handing her back to her frowning husband. I just laugh while trying not to get stepped on by one of the other older gentlemen. Oddly enough, Lorraine doesn't take the bait, maybe because she and Dave are really set on making the mambo their own, their flight to Rio being less than two weeks away. But I do notice her regular glances my way, as if monitoring my reactions to Milo's being mauled by matriarchs. Her efforts are wasted because I am more than amused by their antics. However, I also know who will really get the last handful of Milo tonight.

After class, Milo locks the doors, turns on some random mambo playlist from Spotify, and we finally get our time to dance together. It's fun, liberating, and passionate, ending with another trip to the back storeroom before having to say goodbye in the parking lot.

Wednesday is Thatcher's last day of school. The afternoon is a field day where students compete in random games and contests. I didn't make it last year, still too overcome with my own issues to see to my son's needs, so I make sure to be there this year. I cheer him on as he competes in tug-of-war, plays noodle tag, and navigates an obstacle course. Afterward, I take him out for ice cream, a rare mommy-son date that leaves my heart so full I decide I need to make time for even more in the future.

With Thatcher's school year over and day camps not starting until next week, he stays home with me on Thursday while I try to work and keep him occupied at the same time with varying results. There are a couple hours where he complains of boredom and decides I need to entertain him. Apparently, coloring on misprinted reports is only fun for a limited amount of time in the eyes of a seven-year-old. I complain to Milo over text that evening, prompting an after-production pop in. He sleeps over, and the next morning acts as if he's just arrived to hang out with Thatcher while I work. Thatcher lights up with importance, thinking he's the sole reason Milo is visiting, or maybe he is the sole reason and I am the disillu-sioned one, thinking our late night capers are the main draw. Either way, all three of us end up being the winners.

Sunday finds me sitting in the dark auditorium with Penny and Thatcher, who keep standing because they are so excited to see Milo on stage. Even though she's never heard the songs before, Penny instantly starts singing along, her favorite being "Seasons of Love." She and Thatcher erupt in giggles when the character of Maureen starts mooing during "Over the Moon," but it's the song "Without

You" that surprises me. Sure, I saw the show two weeks ago, but I must have been too focused on Milo to be too responsive, or maybe my recent disclosures have opened me up and left me more emotionally impacted—or maybe a bit of both.

The kids are captivated with Mimi and Roger's duet; Milo and his co-star hit all the emotional gut punches and harmonizing notes that leave my chest feeling concave. The kids both start joining in, able to pick up on the "without you" repetition, but the last combined words release a well inside me as Mimi claims to die while life goes on.

I'm sobbing by the end of the song, and the kids spend the next scene trying to soothe me. I try to tell them they are appreciative tears because the voices are so pretty, but inside, all I can think about is how Jason must have felt that last year, living a double life between his family and his addiction. And how, when he finally gave up, I was the one who had to go on even after I had already died inside.

As I watch Milo kiss his Mimi co-star onstage, I try to convince myself I'm breathing again, inhaling fully and living life. I'm here because I didn't give up. And the two biggest reasons are currently having the best day ever, which makes this one of my favorite days, too.

The curtain call is met with a standing ovation, something that delights Penny and Thatcher almost more than the entire show itself. They clap, sing, and giggle, hollering Milo's name when they see him waving on stage. As the music ends and the cast and crew tearfully leave the stage after their last show, I usher the kids out to the lobby, ready to greet Milo.

I see him, his arm draped around a woman's shoulders as he animatedly talks to a small group. The woman is probably in her fifties, hair in a long dark braid, round cheeks and kind brown eyes radiating pride as she looks up at Milo. As I approach, the resemblance becomes even more apparent, and my stomach twists at the realization that I have been thrust into an impromptu meeting of his mother.

"Hey, guys!" Milo throws his arms up and rushes toward the kids, kneeling as they run up and wrap their arms around him. I can't help but stare fondly as he listens attentively to Penny's and Thatcher's unoriginal observations:

"We saw you on stage!"

"You were singing!"

"You kissed that lady!"

"Mommy cried!"

"Thatcher had to use the girl's bathroom!"

"A lady farted in there! It was really loud!"

"Okay, kids. That's enough. I'm sure Milo has lots of other people to talk to." He ruffles Thatcher's hair and softly boops Penny on the tip of her nose, making them both erupt in a fit of laughter before standing to greet me.

"Hey," he states as nonchalantly as possible as he leans over and kisses my cheek. We've agreed not to engage in much touch or affection around the kids; we're definitely not ready to have that conversation. I know he's playing it cool for our audience, but I still feel his mother's watchful eyes on us. He opens up to gesture toward her, and she steps forward as he introduces her. "Annie, I want you to meet my mom, Diane. Mom, this is Annie Obless and her kids, Thatcher and Penny."

Diane smiles and holds her hand out. "It's lovely to meet you, Annie." I take it and feel like I'm seventeen meeting my prom date's parents, nervous I'll do or say something wrong. But Diane is nothing but polite, turning her attention to the kids, bending over to ask them how they liked the show, how old they each are, and whether or not they like to sing and dance. It's apparent how Milo gained his ease with children. Penny and Thatcher are eating up the attention, and I'm happy to watch and stand next to Milo, sneaking in brief brushes of our hands and arms.

Milo turns to me, projecting enough to get the kids' attention. "Hey, I'm pretty hungry. I'd love to go for some ice cream, but Thatcher and Penny don't like ice cream, do they?"

An instant chorus of ice cream-loving affirmations fills the lobby, and many lingering patrons glance over at the little humans bouncing up and down while hooting joyously. Milo's face lights up, and he looks toward his mom and me. "Annie, does that work? Then, I have to get back in an hour for strike and the cast party."

"Yeah, that sounds great."

"Mom, do you want to join us?"

"Oh, thank you, honey, but I need to get home. Archie is going to be ready to go out for a potty break. Archie's my pug," she informs me.

"Okay, well, let's have lunch this week." He hugs his mom and kisses her cheek. I avert my gaze as she holds him, whispering praises in his ear. When he breaks away, she pats his cheek. He turns to me and says, "I need to go change and then we can go get ice cream. I'll be right back." He leans in to kiss his mom's cheek one more time and says goodbye.

Thatcher tugs on my shirt. "Mommy! Can we play over there?" He points to a raised ledge by the front window. It looks harmless and most of the crowd has cleared out, so I tell them to be careful and watch them bound off.

Diane clears her throat and steps up to stand next to me as I watch the kids. "They're adorable. Lots of energy. I bet they can be a lot, can't they?"

"Yeah, I suppose. Some days I feel like I'm losing my mind dealing with them, their fighting, the constant questions and negotiations... but when I actually get a moment to myself, I can't stop thinking about them, worrying, wondering what they're up to."

"So goes the predicament of motherhood." We stand in silent understanding, but then Diane decides to break the small talk. "You know, it never ends. The worrying about one's children. I still worry about Milo." In my peripheral vision, I see her turn her head to gauge my reaction. "You know what he went through, right?" I nod while still looking ahead, watching Penny and Thatcher play follow-the-leader around the lobby.

"Yeah, he told me. He told me how bad he felt for what he put you through, too."

She sighs and shifts, using the kids as her focal point, as well. They're an emotional buffer as we edge closer toward painful memories. "Well, that's what being a mother is all about, right? Putting your own well-being, happiness, everything aside to do what's best for your child. I almost failed at that; I missed the signs, or at least, I ignored the signs and convinced myself I was raising an independent child who could take care of himself." She takes a beat, turns to look at me again, demanding my attention. I turn to meet her watery eyes. When she speaks again, her voice is shaky with emotion. "But I was wrong. I almost lost him. Sometimes we overestimate what people can handle, including ourselves."

"I'm sorry you went through all of that, Diane. I really am."

"And I'm sorry you've gone through what you have. Milo told me you lost your husband last year."

"Uh, yes, that's true."

"He's also told me he cares about you a lot."

I blush with the weight of her stare. "Well, I care a lot about him, too. He's really helped me these past few months. Both with my dancing skills and…other stuff."

She smiles knowingly. "It's important to find people who can help us find our footing, but we still have to be able to stand on our own." She looks at Penny and Thatcher then back at me. "Especially when we're responsible for directing others along the path."

I swallow hard. "Uh, Diane, I appreciate your concern, but I can reassure you I am always thinking about what's best for my children."

"Of course you are. You're a mother. I just think back to when I was dealing with Milo and the aftermath of Reagan's death. He was so angry, so lost. I was trying my best to be there for him, but Tony helped me see I needed to guide him to the point where he could be there for himself."

"Who?" My ears trip on a name I should know.

"Tony. Reagan's father. He was dealing with his own grief but opened his heart to us. He could have been angry at Milo for his part in everything, but instead, he treated him with nothing but graciousness and eventually became a valued member of the family. He's like a father to Milo, for sure." I stare at her, eyes wide, praying for a coincidence rather than the outlandish suspicion that is settling within my mind. As I listen, her voice seems to be coming from inside a tunnel, her words quavering and running together. "Has Milo never mentioned him? Oh, I'm sure you two will meet soon. In fact, I asked him to come with me today; he usually sees multiple showings of Milo's performances, but he said he was busy with work. He's a very successful therapist. He helps a lot of people deal with loss and grief. He's been doing so ever since Reagan's death. Milo even helps him with a support group. As you know, he really has a talent for connecting with people." She pauses, her voice filled with motherly devotion, and says, "I'm so proud of him, and I hope you both treat each other well. I know he deserves it, and I have a feeling you do, too."

I can't move. I can't blink. I can't breathe. And I certainly can't talk.

"Annie, are you okay?" Diane asks for what must be the third time. I notice Thatcher pushing Penny as they play tag, and I use the excuse to run over and chastise him. It's then that Milo emerges from the backstage door. I stare at him, unable to put into words what is terrorizing my brain.

"Hey, Mom. Did you change your mind? Are you joining us?"

"Oh, no honey. I was just talking with Annie. I'd better head out. Call me about lunch and let me know if you need the car. And if I can't, Tony can probably help you out this week." I notice Milo's eyes dart in my direction at the mention of Tony, but just as quickly turn back to his mom with a strained smile. She waves at me while I struggle to hold onto each kid's arm and tells me how nice it was to meet me. I feel bad I can't do more than nod goodbye, but I'm still processing.

Milo comes up to us, leans close to kiss me on the temple, but I remain stiff and unresponsive. "Everything okay? Did my mom say something?"

I have to make a decision. Do I confront him here, in front of my children, possibly make a scene, and then deny my kids the ice cream they have somewhat patiently been waiting for? Or do I keep my mouth shut, pretend everything is okay, and think about all of this later when I am alone?

Diane said being a mother is putting everything aside to do what's best for your children.

"No, she seems great," I say. For now, it's ice cream for the win.

He slings an arm around me as we start corralling the kids out the door. "Yeah, she is great. And, you're great, too." I force a smile as we walk the block down to the ice cream shop. I do my best to enjoy an hour with my kids, Milo, and ice cream, but at some point, I will have to address the nagging voice inside my head. But there's too much in there right now: haunting lyrics from a musical about death, drugs, and love; Diane's parental preaching; and my own sense of self-flagellation, telling me I should have known better.

28

Counterbalance

*Each partner stretches to the left with
equal and opposite body weight*

On the way home, the kids end up falling asleep, their little necks bent over at painful-looking angles. I drive in silence, replaying the conversation with Diane in my head. What I should do is just ask Milo. He's the one that said he's all in, ready to be open and tell all. But if I confirm he's purposefully kept this hidden, I don't know if I could forgive him—which is probably why I didn't just come out and ask him. What if it's just a coincidence? A nearly impossible coincidence? If it is the same Tony, maybe it just didn't come up naturally in conversation, but surely I mentioned I was seeing a Dr. Collins, right? And I've mentioned the support group. For Milo to just breeze over such a large part of his life is more than concerning.

I turn onto my street and see a white Lexus sedan in my driveway. I've never seen it before, and Nick's truck is next to it, blocking my entrance to the garage. I groan with frustration, as I'll probably have to play nice when meeting Nick's guest. I park on the street in front of the house and gently try to cajole the kids awake. Thatcher wakes up, eyes unfocused and a deep frown drawn across his flushed face, but Penny is out, so I carry her into the house, her limp body slung halfway over my shoulder.

I manage to open the door with one hand, let Thatcher through, and almost drop Penny when Thatcher screams out excitedly, "Grandma!" Apparently, it is the day of mothers. *Motherfucker*.

Nick and Maggie are seated at the dining table, a mug in front of each of them. Maggie stands to greet the kids, and Nick looks at me apologetically. I glare at him and mouth, "What is she doing here?" only to be met with a shrug. Penny lifts her head groggily, eyes half open until she realizes what Thatcher's outburst was about, and she clumsily joins in the welcome. The kids shout out updates, chattering on top of each other, spilling hollered details about our day and our lives.

"We went to a play!"

"Mommy's friend was in it."

"Milo!"

"He kissed a girl on stage, but I saw him kiss mommy on the hair."

"We had ice cream!"

"I finished school. I'm going to be in second grade now. And Penny will be in kindergarten next year."

"Yay! Kindergarten!"

"Mommy has been going to dance class. She says it's her adult time. That's where she met Milo. He came over and spent the entire day with me on Friday while Mommy was working. He came for me, not for Mommy or Penny."

"I want Milo to come see meeeee!"

"Alright, let's give Grandma a break. Why don't you go find some of your favorite toys to show her in a bit?" They don't seem to hear me as Thatcher is now teasing his sister while she whines about not spending the day with Milo.

Nick, being the opportunistic hero he is, jumps up from the table, eager for an exit plan. "Yeah, I'll help. Come on, kiddos!" Finally managing to halt their arguing, they all clamber upstairs, leaving a vacuum of silence in their absence.

Maggie looks amazing. Her hair is long, currently pulled back into a sleek ponytail, and dyed platinum blonde. She wears a form fitting cream tank dress, and damn, her hourglass shape looks great. Her skin is smooth and hydrated, and her bright green eyes seem to be sparkling with youthful joy. Next to her, I'm sure I look like a drab, tired slab of a woman, or at least, that's what I feel like. All I wanted was to sulk and obsess about the possible Tony and Milo connection by myself, and now I have to entertain the woman who tried to take my kids away.

I decide to be cordial, approaching Maggie and leaning over for a rigid hug. "Maggie! What are you doing here?" I try not to sound accusatory, but really, she shows up without warning?

"I tried to tell you I would be in town." *Oh, shit.* She states this matter-of-factly, but I know she meant it as a burn. I've gotten used to Maggie's lingo tricks.

"Yeah, sorry. I've been busy." She gives me a look, letting me know she doesn't believe that. "I, uh, got your postcard. Congratulations." On her finger a large blue stone surrounded by small diamonds catches the light coming in from the window, sending rainbow prisms on the wall. *Damn, that is one big, clean ring there.*

"Oh, yes. Well, I wanted to tell you myself, but again, you never answered your phone, so I just went ahead with the announcements." There's just a hint of remorse in her tone, but not enough to make me drop the interrogation.

"When and where was it?"

"Well, we went out for a week in March to Jamaica and we held the ceremony, just me, Chuck, and the officiant, on the twenty-second."

"Uh, excuse me?" My body freezes, iced in both movement and temperature. The date of March 22 is not one to be celebrated in my book. In fact, I spent the whole day trying to forget the date, keeping busy with work, playing with the kids, and then cracking open a bottle of wine while watching reruns of *Modern Family*. Then I had another bottle, followed up by a late-night call to my therapist. Definitely not a day I'd want to attach to a new relationship.

Maggie launches into a prepared defense: "I know what you're thinking, but I wanted to take back the date. Instead of thinking about the death of my only son, now I can think about all I have to be thankful for."

"I know it's tough to think about his death, but he's your son…"

"Yes, Annie, I know. But I'm choosing happiness. I don't want to forever associate Jason with his death; I want to remember him for his life. And what better way to honor him than to go on with my life?"

I don't really know what to say, so I turn away and start picking up toys, shoes, and artwork that have been left in random places. As I move to the front room, Maggie gets up to follow me. "Now don't try to make me feel guilty, Annie. My therapist thought it was a lovely way to memorialize Jason."

"I'm not trying to make you feel guilty, Maggie."

"After losing both Roger and Jason, I decided I wasn't going to settle anymore. So I broke up with Friedrich—"

"I liked Friedrich. He was polite, and he had a neat accent."

"He was a lame duck in bed—"

"Maggie!" I stand up, clutching a stuffed Grogu doll as if to protect myself from my mother-in-law's salacious stories.

"But when I met Chuck, it was like lightning hit my body. I felt tingles from my fingers to my toes all the way to my—"

"Ew, Maggie. Why are we talking about this?" Maybe other in-laws talk about this, but Maggie and I have never discussed sex. I'm not a prude, but seeing her close her eyes and sink into her mental wanderings is a bit much for me, especially after the many shocks I've just endured.

"Because...I want you to know I don't blame you, that I'm not mad at you anymore," she says as she places a hand on my shoulder.

"You're not mad at me anymore? *You're* not mad at *me* any-more? Oh, how wonderful! Now I can finally sleep at night!" I say with a facetious lilt to my voice. I spin out of her grasp and march past her, trying to put distance between me and her ridiculous notions. I can't go upstairs because of Nick and the kids, so I head to the living room, tossing Grogu in a corner where I'm sure he'll stay until I pick him up a week later.

"Now, Annie, there's no reason to get snippy. We both know you were not at your best those few months after Jason died."

"Geez, I wonder why, Maggie!"

"But you're a mother of two young children, and I was just doing my part as a mother, the only mother you have, to make sure you would all be okay." She blocks the entrance from the living room to the kitchen. I have nowhere to go, but I can't just listen to her justify her betrayal. I take off in the direction of the only exit and find myself heading down the stairs. Maggie calls after me, following me in my retreat. "Annie, I'm trying to make amends. I'm entering a new chap-ter in my life and part of that is making sure we're on good terms. For Thatcher's and Penny's sakes. They've already lost so much. Can't we just agree to move forward? Chuck said it would be best for all of us if you and I could get along."

"Oh, well if Chuck says..." My flight suddenly ceases as I find myself standing in the middle of the basement's big gathering space. There are sections filled with toys, Nick's mostly-neglected exercise equipment, a large couch in front of a wall-mounted television, and a craft-covered desk. The same desk where I found Jason slumped over, his heart halted by the overwhelming effects of a self-injected narcotic. I feel as if the floor is rolling beneath my feet, making my stomach flip and bottom-out. I try to warn Maggie, but I can't catch my breath. Images of that night start swirling through my brain, interspersed with cameos from Milo, Dr. Collins, and Diane. Maggie's hollering of my name seems to be echoing deep from within a well as I fall down into a dark tunnel of my own.

~ ~ ~

"Annie. Open your eyes."

My eyelids are heavy, but I manage to slit them open enough to see a blurry figure above me. I feel a cool palm on my forehead, then a trail of cold as it moves down to my cheek.

"Annie, sweetheart. You have to wake up. They're waiting for you."

I strain to see the source of the voice softly lulling me, helping me pull through this thick fog of uncertainty. It's been two months since I've seen Jason alive, heard him speak, felt his touch, but my body responds instantly, yearning for the known, pulling toward a person who is no longer there.

His silhouette is all I can make out, backlit by an illuminating light. I want to block the light, see the lines and angles that make up his face, trace the ridges and terrain of his skin with my fingers. But I can't move. I try to lift my arms, but they're pinned to the floor beneath me as if sunken in concrete. My chest and head feel leaden, and my eyes are slow in their tracking.

I didn't mean for this to happen. I don't want to die here on this floor. I just wanted to stop hurting. I just wanted to get some sleep. I just wanted Jason.

I feel a hand spread across my chest, my heart pounding beneath its steady pressure. The form leans closer to my head, and I feel dry, cold lips touch my heated brow. My body mourns the absence of his touch instantaneously, and sore emptiness seeps through me. My eyes begin to roll back underneath fluttering eyelashes as a whisper echoes loudly in my ear.

"Annie. I love you."

I manage to utter one phrase before I am once again consumed by blackness. "Then why did you leave?"

~ ~ ~

"Annie. Open your eyes."

My eyes squint open, and I see the outline of my brother sitting on a dining chair pulled up next to the living room couch. He crouches down, his gaze calm but intense as he thrusts a glass in my direction.

"Here, drink some water."

With one eye open and the other still firmly squeezed shut, I push the top half of my body to a sitting position, grab the offered glass, and drain it greedily in one draw.

"What happened?" I croak after releasing a waterlogged burp.

"You fainted in the basement. Maggie said you two were in a heated discussion when it happened. You're lucky you didn't hit your head on anything more damaging than the floor. Between me and the kids, it's a minefield down there."

"Shit." I rub my left temple, a splitting pain stretching across the back of my head outward. "Where's Maggie now?"

"She's upstairs with the kids. They're showing her their bed-rooms. Didn't even realize you were incapacitated. Maggie and I handled it pretty stealthily when she came up to get me."

"You carried me upstairs?" I grimace as he nods. "Sorry."

"Oh stop. I'm a strong, young buck. Carrying you was nothing." He flexes his right arm, kissing his bicep for good measure. A small chuckle catches in my throat, but I'm not able to laugh out loud tonight.

"Okay, but it's still embarrassing." I look off to the side, lost in a mental inventory of all the embarrassing moments of my recent existence.

Nick scoots his chair forward. "You haven't gone down there since Jason died, huh?"

"Yep. A successful year of avoiding the basement all ruined by one panicked attempt to escape my mother-in-law." I look up at him with a small smile. It's taking all my effort not to cry.

"Annie, you've got to put this all behind you," Nick says, reaching out to touch my knee.

"What are you talking about?" There's too much going on right now to truly isolate what he means.

"Your disagreement with Maggie. I know what she did was hurtful, but I think she just sees it as tough love. And it did get you back on track, and it brought me here."

"I know. I get it. But it's not just that. She remarried on the anniversary of Jason's death. Who does that?"

"I'm sure she had a good reason. I doubt she would do something specifically to hurt you."

"I don't think she did it to hurt me. I don't think she's done anything intentionally to hurt me, but…it still hurts…." I drift off, lost in my thoughts.

"Annie?" Nick attempts to redirect me.

I look up into his face, and I see our father's coloring, my mother's nose, memories of other people in my life I have loved and lost. But Nick's here and Maggie's trying to be, so maybe I should start trying to meet everyone halfway.

"It hurts to think everyone is moving on, including me."

"That's a good thing though, right?"

"But I feel like we're leaving Jason behind, that he's becoming nothing more than a shadow in my memory. It used to be that his was the only face I'd see at night, and now…." I lose my words, my throat catching. "Nick, I think Milo might be lying to me," I blurt out, finally giving air to my theory. By saying it out loud, it becomes more real, and by saying it to Nick, there's someone to help share the burden.

"Is it a big lie or a little lie?"

"I'm not sure yet."

He raises his brow, grappling for direction. "Have you asked him? He seems like a fairly upfront guy." I shake my head. "Well, there's your next step."

"But what if he is? What am I supposed to do then?" I drop my head in my hands, wishing I could just run away from all that ails me at the moment.

"You do what you've been doing your whole life. You keep going. You get through it." Nick and I have definitely had our fair share of getting through unfortunate situations. If anything, at least we've learned to keep going, or maybe we've just become desensitized. Nick interrupts my inner debate about the benefits of trauma by asking, "Could you forgive him?"

"I'm not sure. And if I don't, then I'm right back where I was a few months ago, sad and alone."

"Annie, you've never been alone," he says with conviction, making me raise my head and look him in the eyes.

A throat clearing causes us both to turn and see Maggie standing in the entrance.

"Sorry to interrupt, but I need to get back to Chuck. We're staying at the Hampton Inn," she adds unnecessarily, pausing before asking, "Annie, are you doing okay?"

I nod slowly.

"Okay. Well…" She starts to back up awkwardly, as if hoping I will stop her but trying not to look too desperate. I will talk to her, but just not tonight. Tonight, I need to get my thoughts in order and figure out my next move. But, there's no need for her to suffer in the meantime.

"Maggie, thanks for coming over tonight, even if we really didn't get a chance to talk. Can you come back tomorrow?"

She nods and smiles. "Yes, of course. What time?"
"Well, I need to run into the city at some point. Can you be here by the time the kids are home at 3:30?"

"Sure. And I can stay with the kids while you run your errands. I'd love to spend time with them." Maggie has never been the one to offer to watch the kids without some masterful manipulation, so the fact she just did so unprovoked shows she may be serious about mending things between us.

"Yeah, they'd love that, Maggie. We'd all love that."

"They've grown so much since I last saw them." She has a wistful look about her as she goes on about the kids. "I really missed them. I've missed you, too, Annie." The heaviness of her gaze settles over me, a salve on the open wounds of our relationship.

I nod my head and smile. I can only have so many powerful heart-to-hearts in one night before I start getting woozy. It's a miracle I haven't completed my signature move of throwing up tonight. Staying stationary is my saving grace at the moment, and I wave as Maggie smiles, bids us goodbye, and almost floats out of the house.

Nick and I are left in stunned silence, watching the spot where she just stood. He settles back into his chair, whistles, and then asks, "Is it too soon to say, 'I told you so'?"

I drop my arm, groping around the ground next to the couch until I find a fallen pillow and chuck it at his face, which he easily catches. He sticks out his tongue, stands up, and starts pummeling me with the pillow despite my cries of dissent, reminding him I just fainted and could possibly puke at any moment. Our commotion causes the kids to scramble down the stairs to see what's happening, and they end up in a dogpile on top of me.

This is a good moment, and I wish it could last. But tomorrow will be here soon, and if my gut is telling me anything, this good moment will be short-lived.

29

Drag

Drawing the free leg toward the standing leg

I'm not expecting to light on fire the moment I step into the church, but it still doesn't make it easy to do so. Holy Trinity Church on Dickens Avenue is a beautiful monolith of pale concrete blocks with ornate Gothic pillars and intricate stained glass windows. I can see how many people would feel lucky to walk beneath these detailed stone overhangs and enter into a structure promising of peace and forgiveness. But as I stand on the front sidewalk, I only feel a promise of dread.

After battling with myself all day, I decided the only way to curb my conflicted turmoil was to follow up on my suspicion. With Maggie watching the kids, it's now 6:58 PM on Monday night, and that suspicion has led me to the Holy Trinity Church where I head down to the Mother Mary Meeting Room for Dr. Anthony Collins's weekly Survivors of Suicide support group, or SOS. The acronym makes me hate it even more. Sure, it's relevant and catchy, but it's also annoying that it's so relevant and catchy.

Dr. Collins has been trying to get me here for almost a year, and while he'll finally succeed tonight, it's not for the reason he desired.

I'm here to confirm whether Diane's Tony—the one that's like a father to Milo, the one Milo has failed to mention by name—is in fact the same as my Dr. Anthony Collins. And though I think I already know the answer, I still hope I am wrong.

My body is tense as I take a first stiff step forward. Walking up the stairs, through the tall wooden doors, and following the laminated signs pointing the way to SOS, I feel as if I'm actually floating above my body, watching it go through the motions while my mind is at a safe distance. I remember feeling this way when Jason was having one of his night terrors or even during those tumultuous months after his death. It became a way to protect myself, to ensure that while my body was going through something difficult, I could detach and come back when it was safe.

My stomach feels as if it is going to open up and devour the rest of me as I stand in the doorway of a nondescript meeting room–a large enough space for a wake, wedding reception, or presentation. Small rectangular windows line the top of the back wall, letting a glimpse of natural light blend in with the fluorescent lights lining the tiled ceiling. The beige walls are bare, except for a cross and a few informational flyers taped to the wall nearest the doorway. At the far corner of the room, chairs have been moved into a circle.

I quickly scan the people, still standing in small groups before the official meeting begins. I count seven, varying in age, gender, and dress. Dr. Collins is there, wearing a gray blazer over a light pink button-up paired with jeans. He approaches two women talking, turns his attention to the older lady with shocks of silver running through her thick black hair, and he opens his arms. She walks into them, and he embraces her, a sympathetic smile and closed eyes showing a connection of closeness and compassion. I've never seen this side of

Dr. Collins. He seems more relaxed, less professional, but in a good way. He releases the woman, claps her on the shoulder, and makes an announcement for everyone to take their seats. I'm still standing in the doorway, unsure of what to do, when Dr. Collins notices me.

His eyes widen with pleasant surprise, and he begins walking toward me. I could retreat now, but since I don't see Milo, my fight-or-flight instinct is dissipating and a weariness from stressing over apparently nothing begins to invade my limbs.

"Why hello, Annie! I'm surprised to see you here. I didn't know you had changed your mind about group." Dr. Collins stands with his hands in his pockets with a warm smile, as if attempting to put me at ease. I didn't think this far ahead. What do I say to him? That I was doubting the honesty of the new man in my life, proving my lack of trust and self-esteem? Do I have to stay now that I'm here? Or can I just duck out and say this is too much? He's waiting patiently, and I see a few people look back at us, trying to identify the hold up.

"I, uh…thought maybe there might be something here I needed to see for myself," I finally say. Sort of the truth, so at least I'm not lying in a church.

"Okay. Well, we are more than happy to have you." He gestures toward the group, all of whom are now staring at us silently. There's no judgment in their looks, only compassion as they probably have seen or been in this same situation before.

Dr. Collins turns around, and I cautiously follow him. My eyes skip from face to face. Each person here has lost someone to suicide, and now they know I may have, too. It's as if I have been marked with a scarlet letter, my chest blazing with the shame of not being able to keep a loved one alive. Instead of buckling with nerves, I try to focus on the fact that none of these faces are familiar, which allows my breathing to be a little less constricted. Dr. Collins escorts me to an open seat between the lady he was hugging and a middle-aged man with thinning blond hair. They both smile at me as I sit down, my body balancing on the edge of the chair, tense and prepared to flee at the first sign of danger.

"Good evening, everyone. I'd like to introduce you to Annie Obless. She's decided to give us a try. Annie, would you like to introduce yourself and state why you are here?"

Oh Lord, I am in no way ready for this. Even if I had come here under pure intentions, I would not be ready for this. Sure, I've told Milo and Dr. Collins my story, but that's different from telling a group of strangers. Strangers that are looking at me expectantly, believing they already know the basic plot points of my tale.

My face contorted in a grimace, I look from Dr. Collins to the others and stammer my way through an excuse. "I, uh, I don't know if I'm ready to talk. I guess I was just hoping to listen, maybe like an audit situation. I really don't think—"

"Hey, sorry I'm late, but I brought donuts." A voice that has curled around me like silk in the inky dark of night now rings out from the kitchen. My heart shatters. Milo appears behind the serving counter, holding a large cardboard donut box. He wears a short sleeve shirt and athletic shorts, unafraid to show his scars in this gathering of people with whom he is apparently so well acquainted. A welcoming grin is plastered on his face as he greets the group, but the moment his eyes meet mine, his smile freezes, his eyes widen, and his grin slowly drops, creating a comically ironic effect, if one were able to find this situation at all comical. The donut box slaps the counter at the same moment I pop up from my seat. I'm aware of eight pairs of eyes flitting between us, but I don't care. All I want to do is run.

"Excuse me," I say and squeeze between my chair and the man next to me, knocking into his shoulder. I apologize and start rushing back the way I came in. I hear both Milo and Dr. Collins call my name, but I don't stop. My fears have been realized. I've been played, duped, betrayed—again.

I take the stairs with cartoonishly fast steps, almost tripping on my ascent, and I burst outside, continuing my mad dash down the stairs and along the sidewalk to my parallel-parked car. Milo catches up with me easily and intercepts me, his body blocking my driver-side door.

"Get out of my way, Milo," I warn through clenched teeth. Tears are stinging the corners of my eyes, but I don't want to cry in front of him and show him how much he's hurt me.

He raises his hands, palms up, and says, "Annie, please, just hear me out."

"Why? So you can explain why you've lied to me this whole time?"

"Annie, it's not like that."

"Then what is it like?"

"Annie, if you would just let me—"

"Stop saying my name like that!" I yell, making him jerk back in surprise. I bring my voice down but keep the intensity as I say, "Stop saying my name like we're in some sort of goddamn therapy session." My voice cracks, and I find it hard to see through my blurry vision, which I almost prefer, because looking at Milo sends prickles of pain through my extremities, all collecting in the seemingly hol-lowed-out cavity of my chest.

He drops his hands, a look of defeat dulling his dark eyes. When he talks, his voice is bland, as if trying to placate a tantrum-stricken child. "I'm sorry. I just want to talk to you. Explain the situation—"

"Oh my God! Fuck the 'situation'! You sound just like him!" I sense eyes on us as passersby cross the street to avoid getting too close to the crazy woman yelling on the sidewalk. I don't care. I'm hurt and mad, and I want everyone to know how I feel. "How could

I have not known you two were fucking besties, that you were in cahoots to try and fix me?!"

"It wasn't like that—"

I advance on him quickly, sticking an accusatory finger in his face. "No! You don't get to talk right now. I get to talk." He recoils from me, freeing up the car door, eyes filled with remorse. Now that I have his attention, I don't know what I want to say. But I know how I feel, so I let that direct my next words. "I knew it. I knew it was too good to be true." I pause, and we just stare at each other. Both of our chests rapidly rising and falling with the exertion of emotion. My body is a dichotomous blend of exhausted and stimulated, saddened and angered. It's a sickening combination, and I wait for him to interrupt again, but he just looks down at me, his hands dropped to his sides in defeat. "I asked you not to hurt me. Why did you have to lie? You, Dr. Collins, Jason…you all lied."

Milo makes one more attempt with a lackluster, "Annie, I didn't lie. For the last time, please just—"

"Get out of my way." My voice is cold and emotionless. It stops Milo mid-sentence. I bring my gaze up and look him in the eyes. "Get. Out. Of. My. Way!" I repeat, punching each word to hit home my point, and he backs up to the middle of the sidewalk. I hit the unlock button on my car, rip the door open, throw myself into the driver's seat, and jam the key into the ignition. I can feel Milo's stare through the window, but I refuse to give him the satisfaction of a backward glance. I don't even look in the rearview mirror as I drive away. I focus on the road in front of me and blink, tears suddenly streaming freely now I'm alone.

I knew it. I knew it couldn't last. Nothing good ever does.

~ ~ ~

"Ma'am. Can you tell me what happened? Mrs. Obless, I need your statement before we move the body." A uniformed officer stands in front of me as I sit at my neighbor's dining table, staring at their red-and-black checked wallpaper. The center of the wall is adorned with a mahogany grandfather wall clock, its golden pendulum keeping perfect time, refusing to let me backtrack to the past or speed forward out of my nightmarish reality. The ticking affirms that life goes on as normal, but I've just found my husband's body. My kids are sitting in the living room, watching some cartoon on PBS, maybe Clifford *or* Daniel Tiger. *I don't know. All I know is their dad is dead, and I'm going to have to tell them.*

"Ma'am, I know you've had a shock—"

I mumble, incoherent, and the officer leans forward. I smell coffee on his breath, and the burnt earthy smell nauseates me. If I had anything left in my stomach, I'd probably vomit again, but apparently the other two times have emptied it out. The antique clock refuses to be silenced even by tragedy.

Tick. *"What was that, ma'am?"*

Tock. *"I found my husband dead,"* I manage to say a bit louder.

Tick. *"Yes, I know. That's why I want your statement."*

Tock. *"I found my husband dead! That is my statement!"* I say loudly, causing the cop to recoil. I remember the kids are in the other room, and I close my eyes and purse my lips, praying they didn't hear.

The officer mumbles something under his breath and leaves the room. I'm starting to see spots of black. As I look at the plaid-patterned walls, darkened spots seem to eat away at them, tearing them apart from within. I scrunch my face shut, trying to clear my vision, but now all I see is a mix of white and black orbs.

My breathing comes fast again. I try to focus on slowing it, but I can feel my heartbeat picking up. It's pounding in my head, seeping into the back of my eyes and making everything in my sight vibrate *like a speaker with the bass turned up. A pattern of thought begins to match the vibration within my brain, a pendulum swinging between the mundane and my new reality matching the rhythm of the wall clock. I focus on the even sound, hoping it can anchor me to this world even as part of me wants nothing more than to escape it.*

Tick. The front door clicks closed. Mr. and Mrs. Montgomery speak in tense whispers.

Tock. Jason was regularly using drugs, had been for almost a year.

Tick. Thatcher and Penny are singing along to the cartoon, a song about sharing.

Tock. Jason must have been stealing from the hospital.

Tick. A toilet flushes somewhere in the house, the pipes rushing with water.

Tock. Jason was going to leave me at one point.

Tick. The flashing of lights in the driveway signals to all the emergency inside.

Tock. Jason's body was so still, so cold.

Tick. Gail Montgomery comes into the room, kneels before me, and asks what I need.

Tock. Jason lied to me about so many things. He lied, and now he's gone.

Tick. A tear pools in the corner of my eye, falling and trailing down my cheek.

Tock. I am now a widow.

The clock strikes the hour with four deep metal chimes, signaling the start of a new morning, a new day, a new chapter of my life. And it is then I am struck by a new undeniable truth: Life is never going to be the same. I am never going to be the same.

30

Swivel

A foot turn with weight, feet turning faster

One minute my car is squealing away from Milo on Dickens Avenue, and the next I am pulling into my garage. Emotions are powerful in that way. They have the ability to distort time, break through reality, and completely change perception. I'm reeling from this change of perception as I turn the engine off and sit in my car. I focus on my breathing, trying to calm myself down before I go inside and greet Maggie and the kids. The last thing I want is for her to see me upset about a man who is not her son.

A couple minutes of listening to my own breathing, and my heightened anger is starting to morph into a cavity of emptiness. At least I can function with emptiness. Emptiness is familiar; emptiness is doable. With anger, I can't see anything but red. It's messy, inconvenient, and difficult to hide. Thankfully, I feel myself settling into survival mode as I step out of my car and shut the door.

I'm about to reach for the doorknob when a silver Acura pulls into my driveway right behind my stall. Milo steps out and starts walking toward me, his movements strained, his face full of determined resolve, causing my dormant anger to quickly wake from its light dozing. I whip around and close the distance, cursing through my teeth as my palms flatten against his chest and I try to shove him back. He has much more core strength than I do, however, and easily holds his ground, eventually wrapping his arms around my wrists to stop my assault.

"Why are you here?" I finally manage to articulate, still struggling to get out of his hold. His grip is soft, yet firm. It infuriates me that he can manage to be both considerate and overpowering at the same time.

"I want you to hear me out. Let me explain everything."

I crane my neck around his shoulder, zero in on the car he has driven here, and remember the relationship which has caused this whole ordeal. "That's his car, isn't it? So he knew the whole time you were coming out to see me? Did he offer his car? Tell you to chase me down, seduce me, get me to reveal all my sordid secrets?" My voice rises in volume and pitch with my intensity. I can see how everything could have unfolded this way these past few months, how I could have been nothing more than a target, a project, a pathetic patient in need of pity.

Milo's eyebrows furrow and his lips form a thin line, telltale signs of his quickly evaporating patience. He lets go of my wrists, taking a cautionary step backward, and runs his hands through his hair before gesturing sharply, emphasizing his points. "Of course not, Annie. This is ridiculous. Yes, I borrowed his car a few times to come here, but he didn't know why. I borrow his car a lot. And yes, he suggested my dance class once he knew what your interests were, but only because he knew I could be a friend if you wanted one. It wasn't anything more than that."

"So you had no idea about my *situation*?" I spit out the detested word, making him flinch as if I have slung mud at him.

He swallows hard, taking a beat, then answers solemnly, "I knew your husband had died and Tony had tried to get you to come to group, but that was all, I swear. I didn't know any of the details."

I want to listen to him, try to understand, but my heart is cowering in the corner, crying while my temper has taken over the wheel. It's telling my mind that if he lied about one thing, he could easily have lied about more. My head shakes, denying his testimony, as I choke out, "So what? You figured you'd do some digging, get in my pants, and earn a pat on the back from your dead girlfriend's father?" I know Milo wants to be liked, and I play into his need for affirmation in the worst way. It seems to work, his face screwing up, pinched with building irritation.

"Of course not. Come on, Annie. You know me better than that," he pleads, and I want to believe him, but I don't believe anyone right now, especially not myself. I repeat the facts to him while reaffirming why I should not trust him.

"Really? Because you never even mentioned Reagan's father practically adopted you into the family. Must have forgotten to add that detail when you were relaying your life story."

"He asked me not to mention him. Just in case it would upset you." His voice trails off, the irony not lost on him. He looks down at his feet to shield the shameful shine in his eyes. I attack his weakness, wanting to fuel my own need for vindication.

"Gee, I wonder why?" My voice is loud, flippant, and obnoxious.

His eyes shift back up to mine. "He was just trying to help you." When he speaks, it's with a quiet timbre that only sets me off in the opposite direction.

"By manipulating me? By listening to me go on and on about my feelings for my new dance instructor while he knew it was you the whole time? He even discouraged me from seeing you! Was that all part of the game, to make me want you more?"

"You're way off base." He takes a step toward me, his arms still held out between us, ready to defend himself if needed. My ensuing reaction is proof of his accurate instinct.

"Off base? Of course, I'm off base! I'm off base about you! You've lied to me the last two months! You made me feel like you were genuinely interested in me, my life story…my kids…but instead you were just doing Tony's dirty work." I lean forward, yelling in his face, taking pleasure in the fact I have the power in this moment; I have the upper hand, the truth on my side. "So, do you do this with other patients? Go all undercover and try to get them to break?"

"Annie, just stop and think—"

I'm rolling faster and faster down this hill of accusation and righteousness, so I continue on, concocting a theory I know will sting.

"Tell me, do you think helping him with sad, lonely patients will somehow make up for your part in Reagan's death?"

He pauses, almost paralyzed with disbelief at my ruthlessness. "That's uncalled for. I worked for years to get over my guilt about Reagan, and Tony never made me feel like it was my fault. He was actually the one who helped me get over it. And he could help you, too, if you would just stop being so closed off and stubborn." He tries to reach forward and grab my hand, but I swat him away.

"So that *is* what this was all about, huh? To get me to open up? Did you figure if you slept with me, got me to fall for you, I would finally open up? Is that some kind of saying: open legs, open heart?"

I can tell he's had enough when his face contorts with confused anger and he stands up tall, taking up space to try and regain a position of control. His voice rises in volume as he says, "I never lied to you about my feelings for you! The only thing I kept from you was my relationship with Tony, and I was going to tell you. After… after I realized how much I was falling in love with you… I was going to tell you, but…" His voice loses steam, fizzling on the last word.

"But what, Milo?" I ask, devoid of compassion for his sudden paralysis.

"But I didn't want to lose you."

His voice is quiet and sad, and I continue to balance his calmness with chaos. "You called *me* out for not talking to you about important things. You made *me* feel like I was at fault for my trust issues when all along you were keeping this, a pretty goddamn important thing, hidden from me."

He reaches forward, catching my wrist this time, trying to pull me toward him. I resist, and to his credit, he doesn't overpower me even though he could. We stand there in a tug-of-war of our own making. "You're not even going to acknowledge the fact I just said I'm in love with you?"

"No, I'm not! Because how am I supposed to know that isn't a lie, too?" It's a pathetic answer, revealing the weakness that I really do want to acknowledge his declaration. I want to curl up in those words and let them protect me from all the bad things in life. But I can't. I know how harsh and violent life can be, and I have to go through it—bare and alone.

He grabs my other wrist and pulls me in, his head tilted down toward mine. I try to look away, but even though I'm mad at him, my body still longs for him. I settle for a flaming glare, trying to focus all of my fury at him but find it burning out fast, leaving my body exhausted, yearning to collapse into his arms.

"Come on, Annie! Will you please stop fighting dirty and just think about this logically? I love you. From the first time I met you, I couldn't stop thinking about you. And I already knew what you had gone through, and yet, I still wanted more. Most men wouldn't be able to handle all that, but I can! I want to. I want you, including all the mess from your past. I want to help you through it, and I want you to help me. Because Lord knows I still need it. I need help, Annie, and I need you. So can you please forgive me and figure out a way to move on from this?"

I want to walk into his arms, press my body against his, and forget everything else. I want to believe he really loves me, that it was just an error of judgment on both his and Dr. Collins's parts, but now I can't see him and not see Jason. When Jason's lies began, it was close to the end. Milo and I are only at the beginning and already doused with dishonesty. How would we ever move on from this? I open my mouth to speak, but nothing comes out. Milo takes it as an invitation, an acquiescence, and he starts to move his mouth towards mine. However, his advance is interrupted by the front door opening, light from inside spilling into the darkening driveway. Maggie sticks her head out, calling out urgently, "Annie, is everything okay?"

I look up at him one last time, lose myself in the dark brown embers of his eyes, the ones I have let myself fall into while shedding the protective shield of my past. I want to dip back in, soak in the softness of his gaze and his hold, pretend none of this matters—but it does. A home destroyed by lies cannot be rebuilt on a foundation of deceit. Therefore, I must replace my guard, broken in pieces at my feet to be picked up. I spin out of his hold and back up slowly, still looking at him when I say, "I'm fine, Maggie. We were just saying goodbye."

"Annie, please—" Milo lurches forward, eyes and body pleading. Oh, how I wish I could soothe them, give them what they want, but I need to give myself what I need. It's over. It has to be.

"Goodbye, Milo."

I take one more beat, knowing this is how I'll remember Milo when I see him in my memories. A defeated understanding pulling his shoulders down as his eyes trace my body, trying desperately to find the soft underbelly of my resolve, a last-ditch effort to get through my thickened skin. *Sorry, Milo.* I am completely calloused and resolute. I pivot quickly and make a beeline to where Maggie holds open the door. Thankfully, Milo doesn't follow me this time, and Maggie shuts the door firmly. She turns to me and asks, "What was that all about?"

I start sobbing, my body heaving with the effort. Maggie holds open her arms and I walk into them, letting her wrap me in them as she strokes my hair and back. She whispers that everything is going to be okay, and her voice is so assured, I almost believe her.

I wrap my hands around the warm mug of tea Maggie has fixed for me, letting it radiate through my nerve endings and soothe the aching hole in my chest. After Maggie put the kids to bed, I told her about everything: dance class, Milo's story about his scars, our growing flirtation, the night we slept together for the first time, our big fight and reconciliation, the blissful few weeks together before I found out it had all been a lie. She listened without interruption, getting up only to make some chamomile tea, then sat back down at the kitchen table. I've finished filling her in, my face streaked with dried tracks of tears, my nose sniffling annoyingly in the silence. We are two women marked by loss, our scars etched violently on the inside, as we placidly stare at each other, taking in the other's pain.

Missing my mother is a constant feeling, but only the biggest moments in life have left me overwhelmed with her absence: my wedding day, Thatcher's birth, Penny's birth, and Jason's death. They all managed to surge the tide of grief within me to heights as high as the day my mother took her last rattling, cancer-ridden breath. This moment, this heartbreak, is now another one of those times where my entire being mourns for her.

Maggie could never step into that role for me. She and I were amicable from our first meeting, but at that time, my mom was still battling cancer and I was stubbornly against any other woman taking her place. Maggie was still fresh from the loss of her husband. Ever since we've known each other, we've been stained by grief, unable to comfort the other or cross the chasm between us. After Jason died, instead of coming together, we drifted further apart, but now I need an anchor, I need a mother, and I'm ready to open up.

After spilling all the details of my life post-Jason, I don't know whether to keep talking or to wait for her to respond. I bite my tongue in an effort to go against my nature of filling the awkward silence. Finally, Maggie cuts through the quiet of the kitchen with her words.

"I'm sorry I haven't been more of a mother to you since Jason died."

My jaw visibly drops. I was expecting a chastisement, perhaps a flippant comment directed at my dramatic silliness; an apology was nowhere near a reality in my mind. I stammer, not knowing what to say, but she holds her hand up gently, as if asking for the floor.

"For so long I held it against you that you couldn't handle it when Jason died. That I needed to step in. I somehow equated your experience with my loss of Roger, and I couldn't understand how tough of a time you were having. We had both lost husbands, yet you seemed much more grief-stricken than I ever was. And even with Jason, I couldn't quite reconcile the idea you were mourning my son more than me." Her eyes drift down to her hands, wrapped around her own mug.

"Maggie, I don't think you can—" I start to defend her, but she waves me off.

"I know, it's not comparable. We're different people. You'd lost both your parents in different ways, and you have much younger children than I did when I lost Roger. But it's not just that." She lifts her head and pins me with her gaze, ready to deliver a diagnosis. "You love more deeply than I ever have. Not that I didn't love Roger, and definitely not that I didn't love Jason. I'm just different with my love. Or at least I was. I was more shielded, more protective. It's probably because I was a military wife and then a military mom. Or maybe it's just who I am. But Chuck's brought out a different side of me. He's shown me what it is like to love big, feel big, live big. When I'm with him, I'm filled with a pleasure so all-consuming…."

I clear my throat, a polite reminder to stay on subject.

"Yes, sorry. But as I was saying, you, you've never been that way. You've always been big with your love, with your emotions."

I think back to the past year, how I've been so quick to anger, so slow to open up, and so scared of getting hurt again—which, I remind myself, I did. "I don't know if that's me anymore, Maggie."

"Of course it is. I remember Jason talking about you when you first started dating. He went on and on about how full of life you were. I could hear his smile whenever we talked on the phone. No one ever made Jason laugh like you…." Her voice wanders off, lost in the memory of past joy. "I could never make Jason laugh like that. He and I actually argued more than anything. It was such a tug-of-war with him. And I think that's why he fell for you, so different from me, so expressive and quirky." She pauses as I sit awkwardly with the compliment until she manages to articulate her own complicated feelings. "Sometimes I worry he didn't think I wanted to be around him. I should have visited more. I should have taken more of an interest in you and the kids, but I just felt replaced—"

"Maggie, you're his mother. You could never be replaced." I need to be an active participant in the conversation, and I strive to reassure her.

She smiles up at me, fully aware of my efforts, and she reaches over to encircle my wrist. "I should have never even entertained the idea. Those fears probably made me even more distant, and I'm sure you both doubted me as a mother and grandmother."

I can't let her take all the blame. I step up to the plate, ready to reveal my own guilt. "I never doubted you, Maggie. If anything, I doubted myself. If I had been a better wife, I would have noticed the signs. I should have—"

"That's not your fault. None of what happened to Jason was your fault. He was a medical professional; he knew better." Maggie brings her hand back to settle in her lap, and the heaviness of that idea stops us both: he knew better. Doesn't everyone know better when it comes to drugs? Hardly anyone can argue drugs aren't addictive, drugs aren't bad for one's health; yet there are still millions who try it, and many who participate regularly. Yet, everyone acts so surprised when someone dies. No one thinks it's going to be them. Maybe Jason thought he could regulate it—or maybe he didn't care.

"I hate that I couldn't help him. I knew he was in pain, but I never would have thought…He lied to me." My voice cracks as I give life to my confession. This is my burden, the pain with which I still can't make peace.

"He lied to everyone, Annie. Including himself."

I've thought it before, but I've never said it, and I never imagined his mother saying it. Jason is at fault here, and while it seems useless to blame the dead, there's also a satisfying release to it. I wasn't the only one tricked in the end.

"When I think about Jason, it's sometimes difficult not to focus on the end, to forget all the times we were happy. Because all I can think about is how he lied and that's what hurts the most, you know? The fact we had been together for so many years, agreed to tell each other everything, yet in the end, one year of lies ended us. Ended him…And that's why I'm afraid I can't forgive Milo."

Maggie takes a moment to consider this, her eyes trailing around the room as she sighs and says, "It sounds like he really cares about you. He came all this way to explain himself. And he makes you happy, right?"

"He makes me feel alive." It's a reflexive answer, and I inhale sharply at the realization. But along with it, a deep ache throbs within my chest.

"Well, that's definitely something."

"But how could I ever trust him again?" My heart is so raw and my life so in need of stability for my children that I can't fathom a future built on a cracked foundation.

"Not every relationship is meant to last. Sometimes people are meant to come into our lives and stay; others are meant to rush in with authority, carve an indelible mark, and leave us with the lessons." In her eyes, I see the past relationships and people informing her advice, allowing her to speak from a place of experience and acceptance. But I still need to offer a modicum of cynicism, or else I wouldn't feel like myself.

"And what lesson would Milo have taught me? That men lie?" I reply with an acidic smirk.

"How about the fact you can still *feel* alive?" Her words hit me with their accuracy.

If these past few months have shown me anything, it's that I am still the woman who named the dead cat, puked on Jason's shoes (twice), laughed at her own mistakes, spent countless hours making love in a twin-sized dorm bed, survived the loss of her mother, the abandonment of her father, and has still lived a life full of laughter and joy. These past few months, I have connected more with my children, my brother, my therapist, my mother-in-law, and myself, all because I allowed myself to connect with Milo. I let my body feel pleasure through dance, sex, and play. And I allowed myself to move forward, forgive, and forge new memories. I can *feel* alive because I *am* alive, and I shouldn't feel guilty about it.

The many conversations of the past few months swirl through

my mind, and I remember those featuring my uncouth behavior surrounding my mother-in-law, who is patiently letting me sift through my thoughts without intrusion. I suddenly shoot my hand across the table and hold hers. I need her to understand that I *want* to be alive.

"Maggie, I'm sorry. I shouldn't have pushed you away after... well, after that night. I did mix sleep meds and alcohol, but I promise you, it wasn't an attempt. I was just drunk, sad, and confused... I should have thanked you for doing what you did. If you didn't give me an ultimatum, I don't know if I would have gotten my act together."

She takes her other hand and places it over the back of mine. Her eyes shine with tears, a small smile dancing on the edge of her lips. "Thank you for saying that. You really did scare me, though."

"I know. I'm sorry." This could be enough, the end to a powerful conversation, but I need to ask her a question that has haunted me ever since finding Jason's body in the basement. I need to share this burden in hopes of crumbling it completely and walking away whole.

"Maggie, do you think Jason did it on purpose? Do you think he wanted to die that night, or do you think he just got carried away?" The silence after my question seems to hang like a dense fog, pressing in and clouding my vision.

Maggie finally answers. "I don't know. And I don't know which would be worse. And maybe it's a blessing that we don't really know. So at least we can choose to believe whichever one makes us feel the least shitty."

With that answer, I feel a weight evaporate from my chest. Hearing this from his mother, being given the permission to live in uncertainty, allows me to break free from my long-clinging self-doubt and hatred. I'm not sure which option I'm ready to label as my truth, but I feel optimistic that I will someday.

I smile, ready for our new start. "So, when do I get to meet

Chuck?"

Maggie's grin grows wide, her eyes crinkled with the happy knowledge we are beginning again. She pats my hand and whispers, "You tell me, and we'll be there."

31

Syncopation

To deviate from the basic timing of a dance

The unassuming brownstone looms in front of me, a fortress I must enter only by agreeing to drop my own walls. I've entered this building numerous times, but this time is different because I know it will be the last time. I'm here to break up with my therapist. I could have just called and canceled indefinitely, but he deserves to hear it from me: the good and the bad.

While I'm done with my therapist, I'm not done with therapy. I'm self-aware enough to know I'm not quite ready for that. If anything, I'm prepared to work on myself more, a fact Dr. Collins would be overjoyed to hear me admit, but I don't think I'm evolved enough yet to tell him.

I've been standing on this sidewalk for far too long to seem socially acceptable. As I struggle to lift my foot onto the first step of the steep staircase leading up to his three-story home, I can imagine his daughter standing in one of the top floor windows, staring down at me, judging the woman who is unable to take one step.

I'm sad for Dr. Collins. I always imagined he was a bachelor by choice, never guessing he had a family once and that they departed his life in tragic succession. Logically, I now understand his intense concern for helping others, why he pushed the support group on me, and why he inserted Milo into my life. He wants to help others deal with the same sort of grief he has experienced himself, as well as prevent others from making the same mistakes. I've done some research in the past twenty-four hours, learning that those who lose a loved one by suicide are much more likely to attempt their own. It's easy to understand why; losing Jason, whether his death was intentional or not, completely collapsed my foundation. Losing the person I had planned on spending the rest of my life with made me careless and rash. It made me take my own life for granted.

But I never wanted to kill myself. I know that as much as I know I love my children with every ounce of my being. But to anyone on the outside, that would be the surest conclusion. Of course she wanted to die, they would think. She lost the love of her life. Of course she would try to be with him. But the thing is, Jason wasn't the love of my life. The loves of my life are currently at home eating bologna sandwiches and arm wrestling their uncle. Jason was meant for me, but that doesn't mean he was meant for me forever. He gave me many happy years, and together we had Thatcher and Penny, and for that, I do owe him. I plan to repay him by being a present, patient, and proactive mother. At least, that's my goal for every day. I'm sure I'll make mistakes.

I made a mistake by being careless with the sedatives, by letting my loved ones think I would ever purposefully abandon them. Not that I think Jason purposefully abandoned us; Jason was dealing with demons no one else could see or battle for him. His struggle was more than he could bear, and he made a mistake. I forgive him, and I forgive myself. I have to if I ever want to move on.

I don't know how much of this I'm going to tell Dr. Collins. But as the click of the doorknob grabs my attention, I know I've lost my time to contemplate anymore. The door opens, and I tilt my gaze up to see Dr. Collins standing in the gaping entryway. His hands are in the pockets of his light gray trousers, and he's casually adorned in a white collared shirt with the top two buttons undone and no jacket. I had thought maybe he'd given up on me. It's more than twenty minutes past our start time. But he doesn't look angry or even disappointed. A small smile rests on his lips, and he greets me from his peak position. "Good evening, Annie. I'm so glad to see you."

I take a deep breath and start a slow ascent up the stairs. At the top, I wait until I'm standing immediately in front of him before saying stiffly, "Hello, Dr. Collins. Sorry I'm late."

He chuckles lightly and removes a hand from his pocket to gesture for me to come inside. "Honestly, I'm surprised you even showed up. Pleasantly surprised, of course, but after last night, I didn't know if I would ever see you again. Come on in."

He holds the door open for me as I walk through, but instead of turning right toward his office, he points to the stairs. "Please, follow me."

He leads me up the dark-finished wooden staircase that winds up into another gathering space consisting of a cozy sitting area connected to a modest open kitchen. A small table serves as the boundary line between the two spaces, but the whole effect is one of comfort and relaxation. Unlike his office area, this space is filled with pictures, books, and piles of papers, pillows, and throws. The wall opposite the couch is a custom-built bookshelf with a small television nestled in the middle. The contents of this bookshelf are what hold my attention as I see the story of Dr. Collins's life unveiled within the images.

I take a step forward, then look to him for permission. He gives a small nod but continues standing in the middle of the room, his hands in his pockets. He's giving me access to his past, and I can't help but greedily absorb what I can.

I start on the left side of the bookcase, examining the framed pictures interspersed between volumes of books, both professional and classic. There's a picture of a young Anthony Collins holding a baby wrapped in pink, her little face screwed up in the middle of an annoyed cry. His face is tilted down, focusing on his new daughter, unaware of the camera. Another picture shows a little cherub of a girl with curly black pigtails. Her eyes crinkle with the effort of her toothy smile, and her face is illuminated by her bright pink shirt.

I keep drifting in my perusal. One family picture exists of Dr. Collins, a woman who I assume is his wife, and a happy little sprite all standing outside in front of a massive oak tree. Their arms are all wrapped around each other, their connection as a family complemented by the rooting of the tree. His wife has a mass of curly black hair framing her sharp cheekbones, wide smile, and sparkling dark eyes. The rest of the pictures tell a tragic story of love and loss. A wedding portrait of the young couple in love, their foreheads tilted toward one another as they smile at the camera. Progressive pictures of a little girl growing into an awkward preteen with braces and pimples. A stunning young woman with dark hair and wide brown eyes the exact replica of her mother's. She smiles, but her eyes lack the same lift, as if unable to lie to the camera.

This was Reagan. A striking, lonely girl who couldn't grasp love from others enough to be saved from the sinking depression that would end her life. What a cruel end to a bright light.

"She's beautiful," I mutter, filling the quiet room with my humble observation.

"Yes, she was," Dr. Collins responds softly.

My eyes continue scanning up and across the shelves, the subject of the pictures changing abruptly. Now a young man, tall and lanky with a wide smile, disheveled dark hair, and brown eyes is featured in images from school plays, outdoor adventures, and graduations. In some of the pictures, Dr. Collins drapes an arm around the boy's shoulders, a proud father-figure present for his accomplishments. In the graduation pictures, Dr. Collins and Diane bookend the boy, all of their faces bursting with celebration.

Milo has become the focus of the mantel piece, smoothly sliding into the vacancy left after the death of Reagan. I stare at an image of Dr. Collins and Milo posing on a rocky forest trail, hiking backpacks secured around their shoulders. Each one of them places a victorious leg on a higher rock, as if claiming the terrain for their own, both looking ready to crack up with laughter. Milo radiates happiness and life, making me ache for him as I gawk at the picture, almost forgetting I'm not alone until Dr. Collins steps up to stand beside me.

"When I lost Leah, I didn't know what I was going to do, or how I was going to raise a four-year-old girl all on my own. But I tried my best, and these pictures capture the good times." His voice sounds out of place, as if speaking too loud in a library or church service. I listen attentively while still lost in the printed images. "But they don't show the inner struggles Reagan battled every day just to create this happy facade. I was so busy with work I didn't see it. I didn't see my little girl slipping away, fighting the struggle of being pulled under by the weight of her own cognitive white caps. And then one day, she just sank."

His pause fills the room, our shared grief enough to speak in the moment. I turn to look at him as he continues to stare at the wall. "There were moments when I challenged my own mortality, questioned the value of my own life. I was angry. At myself, at the world, at the young man I thought had led my daughter down such a dark path." He turns his head now, eyes teary with the memory. "Of course, I never lashed out at Diane or Milo, but I felt it every day: a resentful undercurrent of blame and indignation. I wanted justification for why Milo could go on living, why Diane could go on watching her child grow up while my own was buried in the ground next to her mother."

I inhale sharply at the image but do not dare interrupt. I don't think I've ever heard Dr. Collins speak this long without turning the conversation toward me. It's fascinating and eye-opening to hear about the man who has been sitting opposite me for the past year.

"When Diane reached out about Milo's continuing struggles, I was conflicted. For one, I had never formally met the kid. To me, he was a thief, the boy who stole my daughter and my reason for living. But then, I realized he was the closest connection I had to Reagan, so I waded through my ill will and started meeting with him. As I helped him work through his grief and regret, I felt myself becoming less burdened. And eventually, we both healed and formed a strong bond. I consider Milo the last gift Reagan ever gave me. I lost my daughter, but I gained a son."

At the mention of Milo, I turn my head away as if to casually look around the room, but Dr. Collins is no rookie. He knows avoidance when he sees it. I hear him shuffle his feet presumably to angle toward me. I try to focus on a piece of artwork featuring the Chicago skyline painted in a mix of abstract shapes and authentic recreation, but below the picture is a buffet table adorned with three more framed pictures. One features a soft-lensed headshot of Milo, probably a senior photo. I'm reminded of our first meeting and how stricken I was with his kindness, expertise, and attractiveness. Another is a cast picture from one of Milo's productions, the subjects of the photo colorful and animated in their costumes, stage makeup, and enthusiasm. The last picture shows his body posed robotically, the concrete of the city contrasting starkly with the silver matte of his busking persona. This image ignites the memory of our day of meeting in front of the Art Institute, causing my body not only to long for his embrace, but for the feeling of freedom following our public performance. However, that was also the day of our first fight, his begging for me to open up and eventually breaking the lock on my heart's secrets. The reminder stings, and I worry if I have been led into a trap, unable to escape the handsome face of the man I already cannot stop seeing in my mind.

"Are you going to see him tonight?" Dr. Collins's question stirs me from my mental sojourn, and I shrug without looking, unprepared to answer or decide just yet. "It's the last scheduled class for your session, correct?"

I take a deep breath and let it out loudly. "Yes," I say, giving up the silent treatment. I suddenly spin, noticeably catching him off guard, his body jerking at the surprise of my quick movement. "Why did you bring me up here?"

He holds my gaze, never one to back away from a tough conversation. He's back to being the calm, confident therapist unafraid of the truth, no matter how awkward or painful. "I thought I owed you my side of the story after what I put you through the past twenty-four hours. I can imagine it has been difficult."

"Why just the past twenty-four hours? Why aren't you sorry for all of it?" I question, unsure of the direction of this apology.

He shifts, crossing his arms in front of him, his professional shield beginning to show after a brief respite. "Well, until you knew about our connection, you were enjoying your time with him, weren't you? Wouldn't you say meeting him was a good thing, that you gained more good from the experience than bad?"

"I, uh…"

"I want you to think about yourself and your life before you met Milo, and I want you to compare that to you and your life in this very moment. Would you rather go back to the you before, or be the you in this moment?" He pins me with his gaze, demanding a thoughtful answer. Instinct tells me to reply with a snarky comment as I have so often done in the past, but the me in this moment decides to be an adult.

"I guess when you put it that way, yes, I'd rather be who I am now," I admit, but I'm not done yet. I take a step forward. "But who's to say it wouldn't have worked out the same way if you had just been honest? If you had told me your nearly-adopted son was the dance instructor?"

"Would you still have gone to the class if I had told you?" He waits, his brows raised in a question to which he already knows the answer.

I throw my hands in the air. "No, probably not," I say in defeat as I cross my arms over my chest, an opponent bested in a debate of wills. Actually, I know for sure I wouldn't have gone. Knowing the dance instructor was a convert to the Book of Collins would have caused me to dig in my heels and refuse entrance, cutting off any possible interference from my therapist and, thus, any possible benefits. I'm not proud of my stubbornness, but I know that's how it would have unfolded. Without a doubt.

"And that's what I have never understood about you, Annie— why you have resisted any help I've offered. In all actuality, I figured you were going to stop seeing me a month into our meetings. You've never been enthusiastic about therapy, and I came to believe you somehow enjoyed the combative back and forth. Tell me the truth, has seeing me even helped you this past year?"

"I think so," I say, but a halfhearted shrug fails to sell the sentiment. I mean, of course, being able to talk through my feelings and fears concerning my children helped me, but I never told him much about Jason until recently; so, in terms of that, no, I guess he wasn't the instigator of my well-being.

"And what has helped you the most, Annie?"

We both know the answer, and I want to look away so badly; I want to brush past Dr. Collins, rush down the stairs, and escape to the sidewalk and out of this cage of honesty. I should have run when he opened the door. But, no, I had to be a decent human being and treat him with respect. I blame my Midwestern manners.

He repeats the question, and I know I'm not going to let myself run out like a child. I'm going to be an adult about this.

"Milo. Milo's helped me the most." My voice is clipped, as if annoyed I have to admit this.

"You know you would have met him if you had just come to the support group in the first place." I don't appreciate this dose of logic, and I feel myself retreating.

"I guess," I answer sharply.

"But you're still going to punish him and yourself by being angry about his keeping a secret? A secret I asked him to keep?"

This accusation, this doubt of my ability to think rationally sets me off, and I feel myself burst, the aftershocks coming through in my verbal explosion. "I'm not punishing him! I'm letting him go. I'm setting him free. A person like Milo doesn't need to be saddled with a project like me. He's got his whole life ahead of him, and my whole life is here and it belongs to Thatcher and Penny. I want to make sure I'm a strong enough mother for them before I try being anything else to anyone else. And maybe someday I will be strong enough to be more. I hope so. But who knows how long that will be—maybe a few months, maybe a few years. But Milo doesn't deserve that. He deserves to be someone's everything, to start from a clean slate, to begin a life together with someone without baggage."

"As I've told you before, Annie, we all have baggage. The unpacking of that baggage is what makes a relationship strong, authentic."

"Yeah, but I think I need a bit more time to get used to the weight of this on my own before I burden another person with it. I want to carry it on my own; I want to prove to myself I can carry it on my own."

"Well, I can't argue with such a noble quest." His mouth lifts at the corner in a sad smile of acceptance, and I shift, feeling the end edging closer. "You know, for what it's worth, Milo is an extraordinary man, one I think would be more than capable of meeting or even exceeding those expectations. If you asked, I'm sure he would do whatever you needed. He cares a lot about you."

"I know."

"And while I didn't plan for your relationship to progress as much as it did, or particularly support it at first, I'm still adamant your meeting him was a good thing, for both of you."

"Of course. I agree."

"I'm not sorry you were able to take what you needed from the experience. But I am sorry for my part in any of the added emotional turmoil."

I shrug nonchalantly, despite my racing heart rate. "Well, I guess it's just more emotional turmoil to add to my character, right?" I start to move toward the stairway. "I think I need to get going."

He opens up his angle to let me pass by. "Yes, of course." I get to the landing before he stops me with another question. "So, am I going to be seeing you again? Or will you be seeking out another therapist?"

I wince, wishing this part could have just gone unsaid. "This will be our last official meeting, Dr. Collins. Thank you for the past year, but I think it's time to move on."

He nods, and I turn to head down the stairs, but he says one last thing. I listen without turning around. "I did it for you, you know. But more than that, I did it for your children. They'd already lost one parent. I knew if you didn't come to terms with your husband's death, find some peace, some sense of understanding, they could lose you, too. And that could just perpetuate the cycle. I've seen the cycle, Annie, and it's taken too many. Just please know it all came from a place of wanting to help your family."

His breath catches while discussing my children, the pain of his life seeping into the cracks of his normally steady voice, and I no longer see him as an untouchable professional; no, he's just as damaged as me, but with the years and practice of focusing his damage into self-improvement. His pain became his motivation to do better and help others. And that is the greatest lesson I will take from my time with him.

"Thank you, Dr. Collins," I say quietly, and I take my leave down the stairs, bidding goodbye to this shrine of loss and memories, my first and last glimpse of the real Dr. Collins.

32

Blending

*Making a smooth and seamless transition
from one figure to the next*

My classmates are smiling and laughing, dancing with celebration and joy during the last class, but I am witnessing it from a distance. I've been parked in front of Truitt Two-Step Studio for the last half-hour, watching the dance jubilee of the last session. Milo had told the class he was going to make it more of a dance party where everyone could be featured. Each couple was to pick a dance and a song. Milo and I had even prepared one. We talked about it while curled up in my bed, basking in the afterglow of lovemaking, chuckling at completely absurd and inappropriate suggestions before settling on the final choice.

It was meant to be a celebration of how far I've come, but now I am only aware of how far apart Milo and I currently are.

I had over an hour to think about my conversation with Dr. Collins before finally parking in the studio lot. Dancing has been good for me. It brought back a sense of fluidity to my life after feeling stagnant for so long. It opened the door for possibility: the possibility of failure, of betterment, of connection. But it wasn't dance alone that did it; much was aided by the addition of Milo to my life. He carried laughter, encouragement, and confidence back into my life, and for that I will always be grateful.

I meant it when I said goodbye last night. At that moment, I was done. The truth was revealed, and I was ready to slam the door on our relationship. But after all he has done for me, such an abrupt parting would be a gross injustice.

I quickly glance at the display, and the time of 6:58 signals the end of class. Back in the studio, I see everyone has stopped dancing, their heads turned toward Milo as he closes up the class with words of inspiration and recognition. I can't see him, but I can imagine how the others watch him, their faces shining with pride and energy. It's hard not to smile when looking at Milo. I imagine all the crowds of people that will do exactly that throughout his life.

The front door opens, and couples begin to leave. I see George hold the door open for Wanda, let a few others through, then grab her hand as they walk to their car. Mary and Leo leave with smiles and flirtatious glances thrown each other's way. Nathan and Ted head out together wearing immaculate outfits of pressed trousers, crisp white shirts, suspenders, and bowties. I wish I could have seen their rendition of the swing.

A few more couples leave sporadically, a line of people probably having waited their turn to thank the instructor individually. I mourn the lost opportunity to see how everyone blossomed under Milo's attention as they left class for the final time, but I've chosen my path tonight, and that path doesn't intersect with any of my classmates'. He's influenced each of them with his joyful spirit and patient tutelage, but they will never know how much he has influenced me, changed me.

Lorraine and Dave are the last to leave. I remember how they were planning to hire Milo to choreograph their reception dance. I wonder if he will get to be there, if he will somehow get roped into showing his moves on the dance floor, if he will catch the eye of some woman and end up letting the night go in a new direction. My heart clinches painfully at the possibility, but I chastise myself. It's not my place to worry about his nights and who stars in them.

I stare at the closed door, my heart pounding in my chest with the anticipation of seeing Milo. Will he open the door and look for me, sensing I am here? Or will he waste no time in leaving and rush out before I have my chance to see him? Fear suddenly floods my body, and I have to fight the stiff stubbornness of not wanting to move with the real possibility of not accomplishing what I came here to do.

My legs feel like phantom limbs, gliding without thought, as I open the door and step out of the car. As I approach the windowed front of the studio, my hand wavers before grasping the metal handle and pulling the door open.

The studio stands empty in front of me. The air is thick with the recent activity, a musky smell evident of sweat and festivity. The mirror-covered wall serves to double the emptiness, the polished wood floors stretching out into a reflected abyss. I stand by the door, my eyes frantically searching. My jaw begins to quiver, whether in disappointment or relief at Milo's apparent absence, but before I completely lose my nerve or composure, the storage room door opens, and Milo appears, calling out a breezy, "Did someone forget something?" His welcoming smile instantly fades into a grim line as he realizes it's me who has entered the studio.

He has a white hand towel slung over his right shoulder, and while he isn't drenched with sweat, a sheen mists his brow and dampens his hairline. True to his habit of running his hands through his hair, it curls upward in an unruly wave. He wears black slacks and a white undershirt. He was wearing a white dress shirt during class, so I can guess he took it off as soon as everyone left, only able to reveal his scarred past once alone. I don't pity him for it, but I certainly ache for him as he shuffles toward me with his head down. He stands across from me, and we stare at each other, close enough to feel the pulsing heat between us, but too distant for us to touch.

I'm filled with an intense longing to rush to him, to hold him, to stroke the side of his face as I stare at him and see awareness tauten his shoulders, back, and jaw. He looks both older and younger in this moment as he stares at me blankly, his eyes a swirl of disbelief, confusion, and irritation. His arms are crossed over his chest, guarding his heart as I shift uncomfortably under his gaze. It's my move. I've intruded upon his territory, so now I must take the first step.

"How was the last class?" I ask, just hoping to break the ice with a question of goodwill.

"Really?" he scoffs, throwing his head to the side and looking at a far corner. He whips the towel off his shoulder and wipes his forehead before tossing it to the side. He looks back at me and, with a clipped tone, answers, "It was good. Everyone had a great time." His voice gets quieter, and his gaze dips to the floor as he says, "We missed you, though. Everyone asked about you."

My heart swells with the knowledge my absence was noticed, then drops with the loss of sharing in one last celebration with strangers who have become friends. "I'm sorry. I just thought it was for the best if I wasn't here. So you could lead class without distraction."

"Thanks for your sacrifice," he says, a tenuous blend of sarcasm and truth edging his voice. He places his hands on his hips as if waiting for more.

I feel the pressure to direct our conversation and blurt out, "I saw Dr. Collins this evening. He brought me to his living room, showed me all the pictures from his life including Reagan, his wife, you...."

Milo's shoulders drop, a softening evident in his hard veneer. "He's so proud of you," I say, my voice a strained whisper.

He nods silently while searching the room with his eyes, landing on anything but my face. This is a topic that is emotional for both of us; the lie that could break us apart is also a relationship responsible for keeping two men whole. Talk about an impossible compromise.

"I could never fault you for honoring a relationship so crucial to the both of you. I mean, I'd have to be some evil witch to demand your allegiance to me over him," I say.

"Annie, that has nothing to do with it."

"I know. I'm just saying I get it. I understand why you didn't tell me."

His body instantly relaxes, and his eyes search mine. He takes a step forward, reaching for me as he asks, "You do? So that's it? We're okay now?" Hope seeps into his voice with an upward inflection.

I take a wary step backward, my shoulder blades close enough to feel the cold metal and glass of the door, as I admit, "I don't know."

Milo's head draws back, and he stalks forward, frantic energy combusting with his bewilderment. "Why don't you know? You just said you understand why I kept that from you. Annie, I never meant to hurt you. That's the absolute last thing I wanted." His words spill out quickly, a last-ditch effort to plead his case and win me over. "And now, all I want to do is to keep you from hurting—"

"But you can't do that, Milo," I interrupt, my words deceptively calm while my head and heart wage war within me. "You can't protect me from everything, and I wouldn't want you to. That's not your responsibility. *I'm* not your responsibility."

"You could be—"

"Milo, no."

His expression goes slack. "So why are you here?"

I almost regret coming tonight, putting him through this. But it wouldn't be right if I didn't. I have to get him to see how important he's been to me while still understanding why this is where it has to end.

"I know I said goodbye last night, but that wasn't enough. You deserve a better goodbye."

His eyes shimmer with the realization I haven't changed my mind, but they sharpen with focus as I move, locking the front door, pulling out my phone, and bringing up a song–the song we had discussed, the song we had planned for tonight, the song for our last dance together. I hit play, set my phone down on the ground, and take my place in front of Milo.

The G-flat piano chord from OneRepublic's "Lose Somebody" sends vibrations down my spine, the melodic notes of hopeful longing filling the empty studio. I hold my hands out in front of me, gulp, and tilt my head up, preparing myself to be turned away, rejected; instead Milo straightens his posture and reaches for me. Relief courses through my veins as our palms fold against each other and our bodies pull together like magnets. My right hand holds his left tightly, wanting to remember the security in his grasp; my left hand clings to the back of his shoulder, his right hand burning through my dress as it presses against my middle back, his fingers tickling my vertebrae.

He nudges me backward with the slow, slow, quick, quick, slow movement of the tango as Ryan Tedder begins crooning out a ballad of love, loss, and the resulting lessons. Our feet glide between each other's legs with the rhythm, the circular motions replicating the waves of emotion carried by the song's lyrics.

We chose this song as an anthem to our similar pasts, the losses we've suffered and the strength we've gained through those events and from each other. Only a few nights ago, we were giggling with the flood of oxytocin accompanying our physical intimacy.

Milo and I had gone back and forth, jokingly suggesting songs such as "Bohemian Rhapsody," "A Hunk of Burning Love," and even "Barbie Girl." Touches and tickles threatened to give us away as Penny and Thatcher slept down the hall. But my body had stilled, a feeling of rightness spreading through me as I thought of "Lose Somebody." OneRepublic had been Jason's and my band, but now, I was ready to name it as my own, to share it with another while honoring a past love.

We spent the next few hours blocking out the dance as best as we could in my carpeted bedroom–Milo, bare chested in a pair of black boxer briefs, and me, wearing only a bra and pajama bottoms. We matched the tango to our song of choice, the words becoming even more resonant with the sharp movements, holds, and lifts of our favorite dance.

Now, as Milo holds me and leads me through those same movements, I can't help but revisit that night.

~ ~ ~

"Okay, so for this position, you want to straddle my leg and hook your right over—"

"Why, Milo, are you trying to seduce me...again?" I waggle my eyebrows and look at him suggestively, causing him to stumble against me with laughter. We are standing in my bedroom, partially dressed, as Milo tries to block out our final dance. We've chosen the tango, the first dance we performed after sleeping together. While it was this dance that really ignited our passion and solidified our connection in a fairly memorable evening, I don't actually remember all the specifics of the footwork. Milo has been patiently taking me through the steps while I have been consistently trying to distract him with innuendos, touches, and bare skin. I can't help it. I'm high

on sensual dancing, good sex, and the sight of a tightly muscled man in a snug pair of boxer briefs. Okay, so maybe I'm the distracted one.

"Now, now. You have a dance to learn," he chides playfully, his hands finding their position again, though letting them drag across my bare back languidly to sweeten the journey.

"We have a dance to learn," I correct him as I squeeze his leg between my own, causing both of our bodies to shiver with desire. He shakes his head, bringing his forehead down to mine and touching the tips of our noses.

His dark eyes glimmer with mischief as he says, "You have a dance to learn. I already know the dance. Or did you forget you were sleeping with the teacher?" His hands drop down to cup my butt, and he squeezes, almost lifting me up in his arms. I squeal while pretending to squirm out of his hold, but it's all for show. I don't plan on escaping anytime soon.

Feigning seriousness, I lean away from him while still wrapped in his arms, purse my lips and squint my eyes in an attempt to stifle my giddiness. "Okay, Teach, show me what to do. My body is yours. Do with it as you please." I accentuate this with a sly smile, and the reaction is instantaneous.

A hungry growl rumbles in his throat, and he drops all pretense of trying to dance, dipping his mouth to the hollow of my neck, kissing and nibbling. I throw my head back, pulses of pleasure shooting through my core, a strangled mix of gasp and giggle pushed out of me as he lifts me up and wraps my legs around his waist. He starts backing me up toward the bed, bending to lay me down, and I try to stop him by shaking my head and gripping both of his shoulders, digging in with my fingernails. My body ultimately resists my weak attempt at interjection and refuses to be pulled away from its desire.

"Stop, stop, stop," I repeat with ragged breaths. "We have to focus. We have to do our homework."

Milo pulls his head up from my chest, his face flushed after being buried in my breasts. He's short of breath as he struggles to say, "How 'bout I give you a pass this week? Or we can work out some extra credit or something. I have some ideas." He drops me onto the bed and settles himself firmly over me. His mouth covers mine, and I nip at his lips with frenzied want, interjecting with lackluster exclamations of opposition.

"No, you're right, I need to learn this dance. I really do want to make a good impression for our last class."

"Oh, you're making an impression, alright," he says, his hips thrusting forward, driving all cohesive thoughts out of my brain.

"Milo, this is my fault. Now I've distracted you and we're not going to master the dance and I'll have ruined our last class together—"

He suddenly stops his dutiful ministrations toward my recently liberated right nipple and lifts his gaze to meet mine. His pupils are blown with arousal, his eyes a dizzying void of longing and need. My eyes drift to his lips, plump and red from use, and I watch them round and stretch to say, "Annie, I will teach you this dance, and it will be beautiful. But first I am going to ravish you because you are beautiful and I would much rather be distracted by your naked body than worry about correct foot placement." His words wrap around me like cashmere, caressing my skin and lighting a fire within my belly, begging for release.

I fake gasp in alarm. "Milo Warner, speaking ill of foot placement? What's gotten into you? You could lose your dance cred!"

"Why, you've gotten into me, Annie Obless. I'd do anything for you." He smiles and I want to lose myself in his smile, in his kiss. I reach up and run my hands through his hair and pull his face down. His long lean body presses into the entirety of mine, our bare skin sensitive to every clinch, shift, and slide. Our lips meet, and we move

against each other, our lips parting to enjoy every suck, nip, and stroke of the tongue. It is a long, deep kiss that threatens to swallow us and the rest of the night whole, leaving us satiated while still wanting more. This moment is perfect. But we have a dance to learn, I remind myself, though my body is already occupied with its own dance. And I don't want this moment to end.

~ ~ ~

The moment did end, and we finally learned the dance only after having lost ourselves in each other multiple times. And now, in this moment, our final moment, we can only lose ourselves in the dance, in the very thing which brought us together.

I have to believe things were meant to happen this way. That I was meant to meet Milo at a certain point, and if we had met differently or even honestly, either we wouldn't have fallen for each other or we may have found a way to stay together. But if that were to happen, then what would I have really learned?

There's so much I want to say, need to say, but we remain speechless, letting our bodies have this moment together before we break them apart forever. To know this is an ending is a curse and a blessing. While I'm dreading the final note, I'm soaking in every sight, smell, and touch, branding my brain with the perfect final memory of us together.

With Jason, his death was thrust upon me so suddenly I couldn't prepare, couldn't protect myself from a future haunted by unanswered questions. Did he know how much I loved him? Did we share enough moments of laughter and affection to set him at peace? Or were those final moments what drove him to do what he did, whatever exactly that happened to be? As I dance with Milo, visions of Jason snap into my head like a strobe light, transporting me between worlds of different men, emotions, and senses of self.

Jason stands next to me, holding my hand even though the nurses warned him not to for fear of my breaking it with my contraction-induced strength. "Come on, baby, you're doing so good. Just keep pushing." His eyes are glistening with excitement at meeting our baby boy but creased with concern as I bear down and push, a guttural moan of pain and exhaustion filling the delivery room. Moments later, he's holding up a screaming newborn, Thatcher's limbs flailing with anger, his high-pitched squeals only quieted as he is fit into my arms. Jason and I are both weeping as he leans in to brush his lips against my temple just as I kiss the soft scalp of our son.

Milo guides me backward through the studio, our feet quickly weaving in and out of each other's stances, our hips turning and brushing past each other with a slight breeze, our gazes intent and unbroken as we trust our bodies in the same space of rhythm and movement.

Jason shows up at my dorm door wearing a cornflower blue thermal and dark-washed jeans. He fills the doorway with his broad body, and I smile up at him coyly, leaning against the door jamb. "Hey, beautiful," he says as he takes in my official first date outfit of tight jeans, a red tank, and a denim jacket. "You look like you feel a lot better." My cheeks blush at the memory of puking on Jason for the second time last night, but my hopeful anticipation of our date outweighs any embarrassment. "Come here," he beckons and he leans forward, wrapping his arm around my waist and pulling me into him as he bends his head down for a welcoming kiss.

Milo spreads his hand, nestling it in the space between my shoulders, holding me steady as I sweep a pointed foot across the floor in a graceful arc before falling into a traveling grapevine. Both of his hands then slide down my back and sides to my waist, squeeze, and lift me onto his hip as he spins us around, my breath caught by the movement as much as by his touch.

Jason is lying on his stomach on the living room floor, head to head with Penny as she contorts her squishy infant face with disgust, upset by the whole concept of tummy-time. Her arms reach out in front of her, grasping the air as if pleading for her daddy to save her from this horrible fate. Jason mocks her own cries, which pisses her off even more, her irritated whines evolving into tortured screams. Two-year-old Thatcher gets up from his blocks and jumps on Jason's back in an attempt to save his distressed sister. They end up rolling and wrestling, as I holler warnings to be careful while preparing a bottle in the kitchen. "Okay, sweetheart, that's enough," Jason relents and pulls Penny into his lap. Thatcher can't miss out and plops himself onto the pile that is now my whole world.

Milo raises his arm and leads me into a turn, and I lean away from him, our limbs stretched across the distance, our hands linked together, anchoring me to him. He tugs at my hand and I obey, spinning toward him until I am caged within his arms, my back against his chest. I feel his lips graze my neck, and my eyes flutter shut as I take a deep breath, bottling the longing inside. And then I feel his hand slide down to my inner thigh, where he then pulls upward, swinging me up into an elongated lift and spinning me around, my top leg straight while my bottom leg bends in support, his other hand secured at my waist, bolstering my position with his own strength.

Jason opens his arms wide, a self-satisfied smile spreading across his face as he reveals our dining table covered in all of my favorite take-out foods: deep-dish pizza, chili-covered French fries, pierogies, fried chicken, and cheesecake. The gesture is so sweet I don't even voice my concerns about the inevitable bloating and heartburn. "I know you've been pretty frazzled with the kids lately, and I wanted to do something special for you, to let you know how much we all appreciate you." My face breaks into a huge grin as tears sting the corners of my eyes. I've been so exhausted for so long this act of affection completely unravels me. I hurry over to Jason, place a kiss on his lips, then reach down for a fry, stuffing it in my mouth before returning my smiling lips to his.

Milo gracefully drops me back down to the earth as our spin slows, my shoulder pressed firmly into his chest, his face bent low so his breath tickles my ear. I snake my arm up to wrap around his neck, and I bend backward as he leans over me, his leg angled out to brace my weight. My eyes trace the details of his face, trying to etch them in my memory, a moment in time when I feel adored and healed.

Jason stands in front of me, a handsome soldier in his military dress blues, reciting our wedding vows. Wind from Lake Michigan whips the ends of my hair, escaped from my pinned updo, and Jason reaches over to tame my wild strands, tucking them behind my ear as he recites, "To have and to hold from this day forward, for better or for worse, for richer or poorer, in sickness and in health, to love and to cherish..." A gust of wind blows through the space between our bodies, twisting my lifted veil and ballooning the skirt of my dress. Jason grips both of my shoulders, bringing me closer, and we laugh as the officiant announces us as husband and wife. We close the space with our first kiss as a married couple, the sound of the roaring breeze softening the applause of our friends and family. Jason cradles my head in both hands, and we smile giddily at one another, knowing this is the beginning of our new life.

Milo leans over me and brings his forehead to mine as the song's final notes fade out, our chests heaving with our deep breaths. I search his eyes with mine, hoping I'll always be able to recall the way his lashes sweep, how the intensity of the lines at the edge of his eyes deepen with his smile, the swirl of dark brown and black in his irises that give so much depth and soul to his stare.

I should move away, spin out of his hold, but I selfishly desire one final taste to last me a lifetime. He seems to know my intention, his grip unrelenting, and he finally releases any restraint, dropping his lips to mine in a kiss bursting with notes of longing, regret, and acceptance. Milo lifts me up out of our bend, our mouths still pressed together, and we stand, clinging to each other tightly in the middle of the empty studio. His hands hold me desperately by my shoulder blades, his fingertips digging into my skin as if trying to bond himself to me. My hands linger at his neck and jawline, tracing the angles and curves with my fingers, a picture I will recreate in my mind when overcome with feelings of loneliness and want.

We finally pull away, breathless, and I lay my head against the rise and fall of his chest, listening to his heart pound with desire and adrenaline.

"Annie, do we really have to do this?" Milo's voice echoes through his chest, and I lift my head to look up at him. His hair sticks up at various angles, framing his face with a desperate wildness. His eyes search mine, glittering with hope, and his body trembles with the vulnerability of his ask. I anchor my hands on his upper arms and begin to rub his biceps up and down soothingly as I prepare to break his heart.

"We have to," I say, my voice fracturing the heady thickness in the air. "I have to. I need to be by myself, be strong by myself."

"But you can be strong with me." He dips his head to touch mine, his eyes turned down as he pleads. "I'll stand by you. I want to be with you, with the kids. I want you so much, Annie." His voice cracks, mirroring the fracture I feel within my chest.

"I want you, too. I really do," I choke out amongst a sob.

"Then why? Why can't we be together?" His grip on me tightens around my waist, and I know I need to release him completely.

"Because…this was our time, this was our moment. And now,

it's done. I feel it, and I know you do, too. We were meant to have this, but now it's over, and we both need to move on." I frame his face with my hands, forcing him to look me in the eyes. They are dark and deep with grief, but I try my best to calm his turmoil, to settle his unease. "But we can't think of this as a tragic ending; it's been a gift, a beautiful unexpected gift to know you, Milo, and I will never look back on us with any regrets. But I can't move forward with you. I'm sorry. I just think we've both suffered so much, and now we can go on, leave that suffering behind, and become even stronger versions of ourselves after this. You have so much to look forward to, Milo. And I do, too."

He pushes his face against my hand, nuzzling the pad of my palm with his mouth. The warmth of his breath heats my wrist as he whispers, "You know I love you, right?"

I nod my head.

"Do you love me?"

I nod my head again.

"But that's still not enough? We still have to say goodbye?"

"At least we get to say goodbye, Milo." He knows as well as I do this isn't always the case, how a parting without a goodbye can eat away at a person's thoughts, devour confidence, and break one's soul. But with this goodbye, this opportunity to tell him what he has done for me and how much I will cherish our time together for always, this goodbye will keep me at peace for years to come. I gently push his head up from my palm, stretch my hand over his cheek, and kiss him one last time. The firm pressure of our lips carries the rest of our words in their touch: I'm sorry. I love you. I'll never forget you. Thank you.

We part and I pull myself away, my body stiff with stubbornness. I grab my belongings from the floor and stride purposefully to the door, unlocking it before turning around to look at him one last time.

Milo Warner, my hero in so many ways—helping me to open up, realize my worth, take responsibility, and accept that I can love and be loved again—is staring longingly at me. Although his shoulders slump and his arms hang loosely at his sides, his eyes are bright with the knowledge we are leaving this the best way possible. In the mirror, I can see the reflection of his back, the tension in his frame, and the red lines where I have held his neck and shoulders in my last chance to touch and hold him to me.

He suddenly takes a step forward, a final request before we part. "Will you say goodbye to the kids for me? Tell them I'll miss them?"

I can easily grant this request. "Of course. They'll miss you, too."

We share one last smile before I whisper across the quiet of the studio, my words bouncing off the tiled floor, mouthed in the mirrored wall. "Goodbye, Milo."

"Goodbye, Annie," he answers, raising a hand with a small wave, and I turn and exit the dance studio. I've said my piece, I've released him and myself, but there is still more to do.

33

Body Flight

The natural release of body weight

Going home while the kids are awake seems like too harsh of an entrance back to reality; the calm, aching resolve in my chest is unable to handle the chaotic energy of my children just yet. I text Nick, tell him not to wait up, and drive aimlessly around the Chicago suburbs. I pass by rows of brick apartment buildings looming intimidatingly with their uniformity. I drive through brightly lit commercial districts advertising low interest rates and prices while beckoning customers with their glowing signs. And I steer within dimmer neighborhoods of varying two-stories which, while different in color and design, all hold similar promises of security and family.

So many different worlds within such a small proximity of space. So many different experiences, struggles, and dynamics. It makes me wonder what others passing by my house would conclude about my life. Would they know two babies were brought home, filling the space with their needy cries, calmed down by the soothing caresses of their sleep-deprived parents? Would they be able to feel the love and laughter that attempted to blanket any pain and argument? Or would they ever fathom a man had died in the basement while his family slept two stories above?

Real life stories are far from predictable, and they rarely end like a fairy tale. There may be fantasy-like moments that keep us satisfied and motivated as we trudge through the murky hardships of human existence, but we still need to realize a successful life is not one free from tragedy; rather, a successful life is one in which a person is able to surmount tragedy, move forward, and become better. I want that life.

I need to stop beating myself up over Jason's death. In the end, he was the maker of his own destiny, the one who made a choice, causing a powerful aftershock to crack the foundation of his family. But our life together allowed us to build deep enough so the kids and I can rebuild and continue living, surviving, even enjoying life.

And I don't regret the past few months with Milo. I've learned more about myself in this short amount of time than I have the previous thirty-five years. I learned I could transform from a widow shrouded with grief and anger to a woman imbued with the knowledge she can take pleasure in her body, engage in vulnerable intimacy, and even love again. And I can be a strong individual, caring sister, and good mom, the last being my top priority.

But to truly move forward, to bid adieu to the former shell of myself from the past year, I still have one more goodbye I need to say.

I pull into my driveway a little after ten. The kids should be deep asleep, and I'm hoping even Nick has retired for the night. The outside sconces illuminate the front of the house, which is currently darkened with slumber.

The garage door closes and I enter the house, silent save for the ambient sounds of the refrigerator. Instead of turning on lights, I tread through the darkness, not wanting to disturb the peaceful settling of the night. I sneak up the stairs and peer into Thatcher's bedroom. Nick lays in the center, snoring, as both kids are sprawled against him. The sight sends a rush of warmth through my chest, knowing my children are safe and loved, which allows me to feel safe and loved. It gives me the strength to tread back downstairs, through the front room, the kitchen, into the living room and then stand in the center of the room, watching the moonlight shining in from the window slant across the floor. It points back toward where I entered the house, and I know now this is it. This is what I must do.

I walk to the door leading to the garage but turn to face the gaping blackness of the basement stairs. I hold out my hand, blindly guiding myself down the stairs as I trail my fingertips across the walls. I've made this trek downward many times before, and even though I haven't purposefully stepped down here since Jason's death, muscle memory carries me forward despite the lack of light.

I get to the foot of the stairs, and I gaze out over the large room. Moonlight sneaks in through the egress window, and I see shadows stretching from Nick's weight set, an elliptical, and the comfy old furniture placed in front of a wall-hung television. Most of the toys have been picked up and line the sides of the room, nestled in primary-colored organizers, but a couple of Barbies lay abandoned on the floor, and a few markers and art supplies are scattered about; my own foot kicks a Sharpie across the floor.

Jason's desk is no longer against the back wall; instead, it is transformed into a craft area featuring a myriad of art supplies. Nick did this shortly after he moved in as an attempt to free this place of some of the dark memories, but I never made the trip down to see the fruits of his labor. I walk to the now empty space next to the far wall, and I bend my knees until I am crouching down, finally releasing myself to lie flat on the rug-covered floor and look up at the ceiling.

I focus on my breathing, my chest and stomach rising with my deep inhales, then caving in with each exhale. My arms are stretched out perpendicular to my torso, my body creating a cross in the space which will act as my confessional. I close my eyes and start saying what I came here to say.

"Jason, I miss you," I say to the empty room. It feels awkward at first. I've only ever spoken to him in my dreams since his passing, never seeking him out while awake, as I was too filled with shame or fear. But I am full of resolve now, and I keep speaking. "I do. I miss you so much. I promise I still think about you every day. But you see, I've been angry with you. I don't know why you did what you did, why you felt you couldn't tell me the truth. I would have helped you. I could have tried to save you." I pause and open my eyes, looking up at the spattering of texture on the ceiling, my brain forming the random patterns into recognizable images of faces, animals, and shapes.

"That's not fair. I don't know if anyone could have saved you but yourself. That's what I need to come to terms with—that I'll never know why. But I'm ready." Looking up, I feel the smooth caress of someone's gaze on me, and I turn my head to the left, my sight traveling down my outstretched arm. And there, lying on the floor, mirroring my position, looking back at me with startling green eyes, soft lips, and chiseled features is Jason. His hair is dark in contrast to his smooth, pale skin, and his lips are set in a solemn smile. My heart lurches at the vision. Surely, it's not him, probably just my mind concocting his presence as I pour my heart out, allowing my feelings to spill onto the easel of a real person. But even if it is just my mind, I react as viscerally as if he were standing in front of me, living and breathing and being.

"Jason." His name escapes from me as an exhale, and I stretch my arm further as if trying to touch him. He remains still but unmoving, a beautiful apparition continuing to look at me with an overwhelming sense of love and understanding. Tears begin to fall down my face, wetting the rug with each drop, but I refuse to move, refuse to break the connection I have so longed for since losing my husband.

"Ever since you left, I've been trying to blame someone. Trying to figure out who was at fault, who can pay for your death. But there's no one. Because to blame someone means someone meant to hurt me, meant to hurt the kids, and I don't think anyone wanted that. You didn't want that. But we did hurt, Jason. We've been hurting for a long time. But I need to stop. I need to say goodbye."

He continues with his stoic stare, and I speak again, knowing this is my moment and not his. "Goodbye, Jason. I love you. Thatcher and Penny love you. And we forgive you." I squeeze my eyes shut, and when I reopen them, I am staring at nothing but the blank space shadowed by the back of the couch. Jason is gone, and with him goes the pit of pain in my heart that has weighed me down for so long. I roll my head back up and stare into the span of the ceiling, imagining the clouds and stars that exist beyond, wondering if that is where Jason is now. Wherever he is, I hope he is at peace. Like me. I'm at peace. Finally.

I drift off to sleep, a sleep of softened blackness and dreamless rest, but before I lose consciousness, while floating in the blurred line between wakefulness and slumber, a phrase caresses my ear and settles within my soul: "Goodbye, beautiful."

I hear my name and lie with my eyes closed, assessing the stiffness in my back and neck, as well as the coldness of my limbs. A pair of giggles causes a smile to lift my lips, and I slowly peer through heavy lids, shielding my sensitive pupils from the streak of light shining from the ceiling.

I'm lying flat-backed on the basement floor as Nick, Thatcher, and Penny stand over me, their heads turned down with wide-eyed wonderment as the kids each cling to random stuffies. Nick's look is one of concern, but the kids are visibly amused, their legs bouncing and their hands coming up to stifle their rising laughter. I open my eyes wider as they dart from face to face.

"Did you sleep here all night, sis?" Nick asks, scratching his beard, his bewildered squint assessing the scene.

My throat is dry and my voice raspy as I say, "Uh, yeah, I guess so." Nick lowers an arm, and I grab his proffered hand. He pulls me up, both of us groaning with the effort, and I bounce on the balls of my feet as I try to catch my balance.

"Mommy! You're not supposed to sleep on the floor! You're supposed to sleep in your bed!" Penny scolds me with a little index finger pointed my way.

"I know. Mommy didn't mean to fall asleep on the floor. I just did."

"Mommy, why were you on the floor? Are you okay?" Thatcher asks, his big blue eyes thoughtful as he tries to solve the puzzle of my displaced waking.

"Yeah, Annie, is everything alright?" Nick asks, hands on hips, steeling himself for news of heartbreak or breakdown. The man's seen it all, and he's emotionally prepared. Which makes me a lucky big sister.

I bite my lip as I try to think of how to answer this. Am I alright? Sort of. Am I better than I've been? Of course. Am I a bit sad? For sure, but I know I will be alright again. And that's a certainty I haven't always had, so I hold it close, a treasure in my emotional toolbox.

"Annie?" Nick asks again as he brings his arms across his chest, and I reach out and grab his forearm.

"I'm good. I'm here. And I know I'm going to be even better…

someday. Someday soon." I flash him a smile and he creases his brow before tossing an uneasy smile my way. Oops, I've confused him, and I throw my head back and laugh out loud. It feels good to laugh so heartily, and I continue, ruffling Penny's and Thatcher's hair until they both tackle my legs and drag me to the ground. We continue wrestling, Nick watching us with bemusement until the kids squeal for help, caught under my overpowering weight and determination. He shrugs and suddenly squats and flexes his biceps, emitting a gladiator-like roar as he grips each kid and rips them off of me, spinning them until their giggles are a mass of cacophonous swirls of sound. I turn my attention to him, pulling at his jeans until he falls to his knees, the kids pummeling him with their tiny fists, and he crashes dramatically to the floor, a fallen titan. The kids and I jump up in celebration, and I pull their wriggling bodies into mine, burying my face in their necks.

This is my home. This is my life. This is my purpose.

I'm back.

EPILOGUE

Balance

Correct distribution and maintenance

~ Six Months Later ~

"If Santa hears you talking like that, he's going to put you on the naughty list," I warn as a stream of very adult language escapes my seven-year-old's mouth.

"It's not my fault! My tablet isn't working. It's making me lose the game." Thatcher tosses his tablet to the floor in frustration over a generic football game.

"Thatcher Obless, you do not throw your tablet! Now pick it up and get washed up for dinner." I ready myself for a hollered retort, but to my surprise, he gets up, grabs the tablet, and plugs it into the charger on the wall with only one groan of dissent before retreating upstairs. Huh, I guess I can put a tally on the nice column today. There's only one more week until Christmas, and the kids are officially on winter break. I'm bracing myself for a few knock-down fights with the kids spending so much time together, but so far, it hasn't been too bad.

That's not necessarily the case concerning the cat, I think, as Penny tears around the corner, chasing after Marshmallow whose claws scrape across the floor, undoubtedly leaving a gash in the wooden slats.

"Penny! Stop terrorizing the cat!" I yell, but she only continues on her quest of torture up the stairs where she'll corner the cat under my bed and circle like a shark until Marshmallow breaks out and runs down the stairs to continue the cycle yet again. *Dumb cat.*

My phone rings and Nick's picture lights up the screen. It's a selfie he took and put as his contact image–a very close close-up angled too far upward, centering on the inside of his overlarge nostril. *Classic Nick.* I touch the answer icon just as Thatcher screams at Penny from his bedroom. I guess the cat tried to hide under his bed this time. Great, now there will be a territory dispute.

"Wow, those screams really make me miss living there," Nick teases instead of answering with a traditional greeting.

"Well, hey, they are free for a sleepover anytime you're feeling nostalgic," I offer, a note of warning in my voice. Nick laughs on the other side of the call and I hear another voice warbled by the distance.

"Is that Celeste?" I ask eagerly. Nick and Celeste, a preschool teacher at Penny's old daycare, have been dating for three months. She's there pretty much anytime Nick calls me from his apartment, which he's been at since August. It's amazing how fast he secured a girlfriend once he moved out of my house, although I don't think Celeste would have minded his living situation with me. She adores the kids, and she and I have had some hilarious conversations over wine and reality television. Selfishly, I hope she is The One, because while Nick finally has a great girlfriend, I've gained a pretty great friend for myself.

"Yep, she says 'hi,'" Nick dutifully answers. "She wants to know if you're still up for the New Year's party at my place." I hear more garbled words, but Nick covers the phone, limiting me to muffled sounds and voices.

I'm sure they're talking about her college friend, Paul, with whom she is determined to set me up. I keep telling her I'm not quite ready, but she and Nick have been calling bullshit on my excuses, so I figure I'll get a babysitter, put on a pretty dress, go to the party, and make nice. If anything, I'll get to enjoy some bubbly drinks and get the two of them off my back. She has shown me a few pictures on his Instagram, and the guy is handsome in a Bradley-Cooper-as-an-investment-banker way. He just moved back to Chicago after working in Seattle for five years. She claims he needs to meet new people, but I know what she's really up to. Tell a girl one secret fantasy inspired by *Bachelor in Paradise*, and she makes it her mission to set me up.

"Yes, yes. I'll be there. We'll be back in town by the twenty-ninth, which will give me a few days to get the kids reacclimated after a week of breaking rules at Grandma's house."

I hear a delighted squeal and guess I just made Celeste very happy. "Hey, so I'm just checking on the time you need me to pick you all up tomorrow," Nick says. The kids and I are catching a plane to Florida in the morning. Chuck has a condo in Key Largo, so he and Maggie have officially become snowbirds, spending their winter in the warmth, away from the cold winds of Kalamazoo. Luckily for me, they were super excited to have me and the kids visit for the holidays, even paying for our plane tickets. I like Chuck, and I *really* like free travel, and I especially like the ability to escape the frigid Windy City in December and spend more than a week on a tropical island.

"Our flight leaves at nine, so we need to be there by seven. Can you pick us up at six?" I recite the itinerary details as I rummage through the refrigerator. I'm trying to figure out what to make for dinner, but due to our impending trip, I neglected to restock groceries. Looks like peanut butter saltine sandwiches and applesauce. As I close the refrigerator, a school-made magnet wiggles, freeing up the postcard it's been securing and sending it sailing to the floor. Nick proceeds to tell me about which food kiosks to avoid at the airport as I bend down to retrieve the postcard.

It's a picture of Times Square at night, complete with pedestrian-filled sidewalks, cab-frequented streets, and neon marquees advertising Broadway musicals and popular products. I flip it over to read the scrawled note on the back. I have it memorized, but seeing the slanted print brings a feeling of comfort and pride.

Annie,

I did it! I'm dancing on Broadway! Your honesty and bravery gave me the push I needed. So thank you. For everything. I hope you and the kids can come watch me someday. And maybe you'd give me the honor of another dance? I'll always want another dance with you.

Love, Milo

"Annie? Are you still there?" Nick's insistence wakes me from my daydream, and I stick the postcard back on the fridge before moving to the cabinets for our meager dinner ingredients.

"Yep, sorry. Just got distracted." I grab a plate and start spreading peanut butter on square crackers, hoping the kids will find this to be fun and novel. If anything, I'll distract them with packing, which is still very much on our to-do list.

Nick dramatically groans and says, "Okay, well I'll see you at six. You're lucky I'm such a good brother."

"I know. You're the best brother I could have ever asked for," I say, disguising sincerity with extra gooeyness. Nick chuckles, but I can tell he's touched by the way he gulps before he says goodbye.

I set my phone down and continue making cracker sandwiches. Peanut butter ends up on my wrist and forearm, and I lick it away. As I set the table, I holler up the stairs, "Kids, it's time for dinner!"

Dissent carries down the stairs as they protest having to stop their play. Apparently now they're getting along. I stand at the bottom of the stairs and project my negotiation. "Okay, but we have to eat before we pack. Remember, we're getting on a plane and going to Grandma's tomorrow! If you're good, I'll give you each one of your Christmas presents." It's a moot point; their Christmas presents are new suitcases and they'll get them no matter how well-behaved they are. But they don't know that, so I'll use it to my advantage if it means coaxing them downstairs to eat our pitiful dinner.

I'm met with the expected reaction: the kids screaming with joy and scrambling down the stairs with exaggerated speed, until they land in a tangle of limbs and laughter, tripping over each other as they clamber toward the table.

When I hear them scream, I still think about Jason. I think about how he would love to see their excitement, how he would be celebrating right along with them, and how lucky we are to have happy memories of him being our kids' biggest fan. When I hear my kids scream, no matter if it's from laughter, anger, fear, or hurt, I think of how grateful I am to be their mother, to have this life with them, and to have this chance to see them change and grow each and every day. There will undoubtedly be countless more screams in the coming years. More fights, more tears, more pain. But there will also be more laughter, affection, and discovery of all this world has to offer. As a mother, a sister, a woman, I have so much more I will go through in this life. No longer do I retreat to darker places; instead, I look ahead into the light. And I smile at all there is to come.

Acknowledgements

Thank you to Dr. Anthony Paustian and the people at Bookpress Publishing for taking a chance on me and guiding me through this process, making it enjoyable and exciting.

Thank you to Ann Hanigan Kotz for our meetings and readings at Mickey's. Your belief in me gave me the validation and push I needed. I am so grateful to have found a writing friend in you!

Thank you to my English department friends and the "Lunch Bunch" who have listened to me bemoan, provided me with advice, supported me unconditionally, and celebrated with me. You all make me a better, more confident, and more joyful person at work and at home.

Thank you to Sarah Ehlers, Tara Rechkemmer, and Marissa Kuiken, my beta readers and dear friends. You've been there throughout the process, and I am grateful for your conversation, ideas, support, and championship.

As always, thank you to my mother, Dixie Carder, who always worked her hardest to provide me with all I needed so I could pursue my dreams. You have always believed in me, while keeping me grounded. As the first reader of this novel, you made me believe in myself and the story. That was one time I was glad to make you cry!

Thank you to my sister, Gina Sedore, the most badass nurse I know, for your help with my medical questions (along with my life questions, though you've been helping with those for nearly forty years).

Thank you to all my family and friends who have willingly (or unwillingly) listened to me talk about the writing and publishing process.

Thank you to my children for giving me the creative inspiration, real experience, and constant motivation to better myself. Also, thanks for those days where you would play in the basement and let me write. That was awesome.

And, finally, thank you to my partner in life, Jeremy Youngers. While you were struggling with anxiety and depression, writing was my outlet and lifeline. It gave me purpose, control, and strength while you fought to be there for our family. And as you continue to heal, you have shown nothing but support for my dreams and willingness to be honest and open. Marriage is a marathon, and I'm so glad to be running it with you. Thank you for our life.

And thank you to all that have helped to show me that it is perfectly acceptable to invest in myself. This has been a joy, and I can't wait to see all there is to come.